"A brilliant mix of adventure, romance, and Oscar Wildesque absurdity—one of the wittiest, most original rom-coms I have read all year."

—Evie Dunmore, *USA Today* bestselling author of
Bringing Down the Duke

"There's no literary experience quite like reading an India Holton book. *The League of Gentlewomen Witches* is a wild, rollicking, delicious carnival ride of a story, filled with rakish pirates, chaotic witches, flying houses (and bicycles, and pumpkins), delightful banter, and some serious steam. You've never read Victorian romance like this before . . . and it'll ruin you for everything else."

—Lana Harper, *New York Times* bestselling author of
Payback's a Witch

"Fantastical, romantic fun! Sparkling with witty allusions to Shakespeare and Austen, whimsical adventure, and tenderhearted romance, *The League of Gentlewomen Witches* is a book lover's dream come true." —Chloe Liese, author of the Bergman Brothers series

"Sexy, funny, and utterly charming, *The League of Gentlewomen Witches* is like a deliciously over-caffeinated historical romance novel. Not only does Holton treat us to a fiery feminist witch as our heroine and a dashing pirate as our leading man, but she also gives us lyrical prose and crackling banter to enjoy on the side. Buckle up, readers, because this is a ride you won't want to miss."

—Lynn Painter, author of *Mr. Wrong Number*

"What happens when a prim and proper witch crosses paths with a dashing pirate? Flaming chaos and delicious debauchery, of course. *The League of Gentlewomen Witches* is another wickedly funny romp through this glorious world created by India Holton."

—Harper St. George, author of *The Devil and the Heiress*

"When a prickly witch meets her match in a dangerously endearing pirate . . . the match bursts into flames! India Holton's joyous, swoony, genre-exploding novel is a marvel, bristling with wit (and weaponry!) and brimming with love. *The League of Gentlewomen Witches* will steal your heart, fly it to the moon, and return it to your chest, sparking with magic and just in time for tea."

—Joanna Lowell, author of *The Runaway Duchess*

"Filled with wit and an intriguing enemy-to-lovers romance. For fans of Jane Austen and Evie Dunmore."   —*LibraryReads*

"Holton takes readers on a wild ride through a fun, limitless world, where frivolity and whimsy reign supreme and skilled swordwork and grand displays of magic abound."   —*Bookpage*

"Clever wordplay, delightful double entendres, and adventurous high jinks will delight fans of smart, witchy romances, including the first in Holton's Dangerous Damsels series, *The Wisteria Society of Lady Scoundrels* (2021)."   —*Booklist*

PRAISE FOR
THE WISTERIA SOCIETY OF LADY SCOUNDRELS

"Holton is having as much fun as the English language will permit— the prose shifts constantly from silly to sublime and back, sometimes in the course of a single sentence. And somehow in all the melodrama and jokes and hilariously mangled literary references, there are moments of emotion that cut to the quick—the way a profound traumatic experience can overcome you years later."

—*New York Times Book Review*

"This melds the Victorian wit of Sherlock Holmes with the brash adventuring of Indiana Jones. . . . A sprightly feminist tale that offers everything from an atmospheric Gothic abbey to secret societies."

—*Entertainment Weekly*

"*The Wisteria Society of Lady Scoundrels* is easily the most delightfully bonkers historical fantasy romance of 2021! Featuring lady pirates in flying houses and gentleman assassins with far too many names, I enjoyed every absorbing moment."

Jen DeLuca, author of *Well Played*

"The most charming, clever, and laugh-out-loud funny book I've read all year—it is impossible to read *The Wisteria Society of Lady Scoundrels* and not fall in love with its lady pirates, flying houses, and swoonworthy romance. India Holton's utterly delightful debut is pure joy from start to finish." —Martha Waters, author of *To Have and to Hoax*

"India's debut is charming, clever, action-packed, with masterful bantering-while-dueling choreography: it reminds me of *The Princess Bride*, except swoonier and more fantastical. It's an instant beloved favorite." —Sarah Hogle, author of *You Deserve Each Other*

"With a piratical heroine who would rather be reading and a hero whose many disguises hide a (slightly tarnished) heart of gold, *The*

Wisteria Society of Lady Scoundrels is the perfect diversion for a rainy afternoon with a cup of tea. What fun!"
—Manda Collins, author of *A Lady's Guide to Mischief and Mayhem*

"Holton's writing is gorgeous and lyrical, her dialogue clever and witty, and her characters loveable and unforgettable. The story contains so many enthralling elements—lady scoundrels and spells, pirates and explosions, romance and flying-house thievery!"
—Raquel Vasquez Gilliland, author of *Sia Martinez and the Moonlit Beginning of Everything*

"With secret identities, secret doors, and secret histories to spare, this high-octane layer-cake of escapism hits the spot." —*Publishers Weekly*

"In this joyride of a debut, Holton draws us into a madcap world of courtly corsairs, murderous matrons, and pity-inspiring henchmen. . . . As if the Parasol Protectorate series met *The Princess Bride* and a corseted *Lara Croft: Tomb Raider.*" —*Kirkus Reviews*

"A tongue-in-cheek swashbuckling adventure." —*Library Journal*

TITLES BY INDIA HOLTON

The Wisteria Society of Lady Scoundrels
The League of Gentlewomen Witches
The Secret Service of Tea and Treason

THE
SECRET SERVICE
OF
TEA AND TREASON

INDIA HOLTON

BERKLEY ROMANCE

New York

BERKLEY ROMANCE
Published by Berkley
An imprint of Penguin Random House LLC
penguinrandomhouse.com

Copyright © 2023 by India Holton
Excerpt from *The Ornithologist's Field Guide to Love* copyright © 2023 by India Holton

Library of Congress Cataloging-in-Publication Data

Names: Holton, India, author.
Title: The secret service of tea and treason / India Holton.
Description: First Edition. | New York: Berkley Romance, 2023. |
Series: Dangerous damsels
Identifiers: LCCN 2022038765 (print) | LCCN 2022038766 (ebook) |
ISBN 9780593547267 (trade paperback) | ISBN 9780593547274 (ebook)
Subjects: LCGFT: Novels.
Classification: LCC PR9639.4.H66 S43 2023 (print) |
LCC PR9639.4.H66 (ebook) | DDC 823/.92—dc23/eng/20220829
LC record available at https://lccn.loc.gov/2022038765
LC ebook record available at https://lccn.loc.gov/2022038766

First Edition: April 2023

Printed in the United States of America
2nd Printing

Book design by Laura Corless

For Taylor, Kristine, Bridget, and Stephanie.
And for the team behind the curtain, making magic happen.

TABLE OF SIGNIFICANT CHARACTERS

- In Order of Appearance -

Alice Dearlove . . . a professional woman

Primula Tewkes . . . a lady of *le ton* and a pain in *la croupe*

Daniel Bixby . . . a bibliomaniacal assassin

Dahlia Weekle . . . pretty in pink

Mrs. Kew . . . aunt-in-chief

Cornelius Snodgrass . . . a genius, allegedly

Competence . . . just as the name suggests

Miss Darlington . . . a pirate lady of some magnificence

Jake Jacobsen . . . her husband

Mrs. Rotunder . . . a pirate lady of some other magnificence

Mr. Rotunder . . . her husband

Jane Fairweather . . . a wannabe villainess

Frederick Bassingthwaite . . . tedium incarnate

Veronica Vale . . . an ardent fan

Assorted pirates

Various household servants and spies

Alexander O'Riley . . . an old ~~friend~~ assignment

Charlotte Pettifer . . . a wicked witch

Mia Thalassi . . . an agent of deliverance

Cecilia Bassingthwaite . . . the beloved heroine

TABLE OF SIGNIFICANT CHARACTERS

Ned Lightbourne . . . charm on two tightly trousered legs

The Baby . . . an object of all affections

Pleasance . . . an enthusiast

Hazel Coombley . . . therapeutically curious

Agapantha Ketlew . . . a return to ignorance

THE
SECRET SERVICE
OF
TEA AND TREASON

1

It was the best of dress shops, it was the worst of dress shops. It sold the most beautiful garments, it sold the ugliest scraps, and Miss Primula Tewkes fell in love and despair as she walked amongst its displays. Her maid, Alice Dearlove, followed like a shadow, black-garbed and silent, arms full of hatboxes. Primula declared herself to be in Heaven, but Alice privately wished the lady would go direct the other way.

"I cannot attend Lady Hessop's soiree in anything but the most exquisite ensemble," Primula averred. "The most exquisite!"

"Yes miss," Alice said.

"You wouldn't want me to be ridiculed for wearing something outmoded, would you, Dearlove? Would you? Well?"

The lady's eyes widened. Alice guessed from this that alarm was required at the prospect of the Honorable Miss Tewkes drinking mimosas and making nice conversation while garbed in anything less than a fashion masterpiece. Unfortunately, she felt such little alarm that she did not even blink as she looked at her mistress from behind the load of hatboxes. Her own eyes, dark, cool, remained their normal size. Her countenance was so deadpan it ought to have been given the Last Rites.

"No miss," she said, glancing at the glass-paneled door, which offered the only escape from the shop.

"You are tedious, Dearlove. Tedious! Surely even a lady's maid has enough imagination to appreciate my dire circumstance?!"

Alice hesitated, unsure which of *yes miss* and *no miss* was required here. *No* would have been accurate, for although she possessed a sterling imagination for such things as secret libraries, lost libraries, and indeed any type of library possible, she could not imagine what was so dire about not being able to choose a dress.

On the other hand, *yes* was also accurate, for even Alice felt obliged to describe herself as tedious. For example, at this very moment all she wanted was to put down the hatboxes, take off her shoes, and lose herself in a really good dictionary.

"Yes miss?" she hazarded.

Primula huffed, turning to flip her hand through a rack of frothing pastel dresses. "I am wasting my time here! Wasting it! I don't know why you even suggested this boutique. We should have gone to Harrods."

"Yes miss," Alice said, blowing a loose strand of fine brown hair from her face. The hatboxes swayed and she swayed with them, only just managing to keep them balanced. She glanced at a clock on the wall, then again at the door, before turning back to Primula. "Perhaps that purple lace dress would—"

A delicate chime interrupted her as someone entered the shop. Looking around at once, Alice saw only a servant, his expression bored as he held the door ajar despite carrying half a dozen bags. He appeared nondescript—brown-haired, clean-shaven, wearing spectacles and the general masculine uniform of dark suit and bowler hat. Nevertheless, Alice's heart fluttered inexplicably. Realizing she was staring at him, she began to turn away, but just then he glanced over and their eyes happened to meet. Alice's face remained impassive; her heart, however, went from fluttering to perfect stillness in, well, a heartbeat.

Nonsense, she thought. If her cardiac organ had stopped, she would not be standing, nor breathing (to be fair, she did not currently seem to be breathing, but that was beside the point), nor indeed blushing like a schoolgirl just because a handsome man looked in her direction. Alice felt unclear exactly how he had transformed from nondescript to handsome within the space of seconds, but no doubt an encyclopedia could explain it. She'd visit the library this evening and—

Suddenly masses of frothing pink and yellow swamped her vision. Alice blinked frantically. Either the patisserie across the street had exploded or a fashionable woman was walking in through the doorway.

"Really, Bixby? This is what you consider a suitable dress shop? We should have just gone to Harrods."

"Yes miss," the man replied without inflection.

Alice's vision recovered enough from its shock to recognize the Honorable Miss Dahlia Weekle, Primula's exact social equal and therefore most bitter rival. At that moment, a cake explosion would have been more welcome.

"You were right, miss," she murmured to Primula, nudging her eastward as Miss Weekle veered west toward a glove display. "We should indeed leave this very moment."

"Steady on, Dearlove. I am not a sheep to be herded. Why the hurry?"

"*Primula! Darling!*"

Alice winced.

"Dahlia!" Primula's dismay was so fleeting, Alice barely saw it. "How unexpected to meet you here! So unexpected!"

The ladies gripped each others' shoulders and kissed the air, their lips making a sound like rapiers tapping at the start of a duel.

"That color is *remarkable* on you, dear," Dahlia said.

"Such a *unique* hat!" Primula countered.

The door chimed once more. Alice caught Primula's arm, the hatboxes swaying perilously, and attempted to tug her away. But it was too late.

Two men burst into the shop, brandishing pistols. "This is a robbery!" one shouted.

Primula and Dahlia squealed. The shopkeeper squealed. Alice sighed.

"Hands in the air!"

Immediately the ladies obeyed. Alice, pleased for an excuse to set down the hatboxes, placed them on a small table then raised her own hands. Hopefully this business would be over soon and she could go home for a cup of tea and a biscuit.

"You!" The thief turned to Dahlia's manservant. "Hands up!"

"Do as he says, Bixby!" Dahlia wailed.

Bixby carefully lowered the carry bags. But instead of raising his arms, he folded them together across his chest. "This is highly inconvenient," he said in a reproving tone. "Miss Weekle has an appointment with her hairdresser in fifteen minutes' time and it cannot be postponed. Kindly find another store to burgle."

The thieves glanced at each other and laughed.

"Just shoot him, Merv," one said. "Make sure *he* never needs no hairdresser again."

"A hairdresser," Bixby corrected.

Silence slammed down upon the scene, broken only by a sharp click as Merv cocked his pistol.

Alice frowned. Clearly matters were about to become even more time-consuming. "For heaven's sake," she began—

But it was no use. Without further discussion, Merv shot Bixby.

A loud *twang* followed, and across the shop a gilt-framed mirror shattered under the impact of Merv's bullet. Blinking confusedly, Alice realized that Bixby had removed his bowler hat at remarkable speed and utilized it as an apparently bulletproof shield. The resultant ricochet had cast seven years' bad luck upon the shop but saved the manservant's life.

"Bloody—" was all Merv had the opportunity to say before Bixby threw the hat at him. It struck his face with more force than brushed felt regularly offered. Merv screamed, dropping his gun. From there it was a simple matter of one kick from the manservant, one punch with a black-gloved hand, two swift and efficient jabs to the throat, and the thief ended up senseless on the ground, his last word having proved prophetic as blood dripped from his nose. Bixby stepped back, calmly straightening his cuffs.

The other thief snatched wildly for Dahlia's purse. Alice pushed the young woman aside, so the thief grabbed Primula's purse instead, yanked it from her hand, and was out the door before anyone could react.

"Help!" Primula screamed. "Help!"

"Oh dear, miss," Alice said with an attempt at comfort that fell so flat a dozen steamrollers could not have crushed it more. "I'm afraid he's long gone. We should get you home." She picked up the hatboxes and was turning to the door when suddenly Bixby stepped forth, offering a crisp, shallow bow.

"Ma'am, allow me to recover your purse."

"Oh!" Primula flushed in singular delight.

"No," Alice answered, shaking her head. "We cannot ask—"

But apparently a request was not required, for Bixby immediately took off after the thief.

"How exciting!" Primula cried, flapping a hand before her face.

"Goodness me!" Dahlia added, clutching at her bosom.

"Fiddlesticks," Alice muttered under her breath. And tossing the hatboxes aside, disregarding how they emptied across the floor, she jumped over Merv's unconscious body and followed after Bixby while Primula wailed about crumpled bonnets (crumpled!) behind her.

"Don't! Stop! Thief!" she shouted, and gave chase in a most unexpected manner indeed.

Three years Daniel Bixby had worked as a butler for the rogue pirate Rotten O'Riley. Three years flying a rickety, ensorcelled house at speeds one could only describe as improper, smuggling pennyroyal tea into Ireland, and washing O'Riley's laundry. Yet after just one week in Dahlia Weekle's service he was exhausted. Criminal life had nothing on the rigors of shopping with an aristocratic lady.

This purse-snatching offered the best entertainment he'd had since his return to London (or, to be fair, second best, since nothing could surpass yesterday's discovery of a *Utopia* edition in the original Latin). Indeed, he might have stopped the hoodlum at once by using a phrase from the magical incantation that pirates employed to fly their battle-houses and witches to move small objects—O'Riley's witch wife had taught him how to bring down a man with just one enchanted word— but it was invigorating to give chase (not to mention that witchcraft was highly secret, highly illegal—and, according to pirates, highly, er, low behavior).

About three hundred feet along the street, he caught the thief. After a struggle, he twisted the man's arm behind his back, relieved him of the purse, and held it out of reach.

"Thank you," said a woman's voice behind him.

Daniel felt the purse removed efficiently from his grip. Glancing around, he was astonished to see the lady's maid. Time seemed oddly suspended as he stared, arrested by the sight of her. *You,* said something inside of him, like a memory or a dream. It had whispered to him in the dress shop but spoke louder now, as if she'd removed a mask and he could see her more clearly. Her delicate face was framed by a coiffure so severe it made him think of backboards and plain, starched undergarments—

At which point, time dropped into the pit of his stomach with a crash that sent reverberations through his entire nervous system.

"Ma'am," he said, taking refuge in politeness even while his nerves clamored and the thief swore and kicked in an effort to get free. "It was a pleasure to be of assistance."

"You are too kind," she replied, her voice civil but her expression making it clear she was speaking literally. She turned and handed the purse to the thief.

Daniel blinked, trying to comprehend the evidence before his eyes. He had not been so confused since hearing Wordsworth described as a poetic genius. And confusion was dangerous in his line of work (i.e., when he felt it, other people became endangered). He twisted the thief's arm further, causing the man to holler, and took the purse from him once more.

"I beg your pardon," he reproved the lady's maid.

At his somber tone she cringed, her big dark eyes filling with tears, her lashes trembling. Daniel felt like an utter cad. "Please don't cry," he said, holding out his hand in apology.

And she grabbed the purse in it, tugged hard, and jabbed the fingers of her free hand up into his armpit.

Daniel gasped at the sudden pain. His grip weakened, and the purse disappeared once more from his possession. The woman returned it to the thief, who took it with an attitude of bemused uncertainty.

"For goodness' sake," Daniel muttered. Although years of piracy had presented little opportunity for heroics, he felt certain they did not usually involve the victim attacking her rescuer. Wrenching the thief about, he snatched the purse from him and—

The woman grasped his wrist with both hands. Daniel attempted to shake her off, and she attempted to emasculate him with an upthrust of her knee, and he saved himself (and his future children) by quickly blocking her with his own knee, leading to her stomping down on his foot, and him twisting her arm, and both of them stopping abruptly to watch the thief escape along the street.

"Is that your pearl necklace he's carrying?" Daniel asked mildly.

"Yes," she replied.

"Oh dear."

She shrugged. "Hopefully he won't bite the pearls to see if they're real. They are in fact cyanide capsules."

As the thief turned a corner and disappeared from the narrative, Daniel released the woman. She took a careful breath, her fingers twitching at her skirt, and he frowned with concern. "Are you hurt?"

The look she gave him was such that Daniel immediately wanted to find a chalkboard and write *I will not ask stupid questions* one hundred times upon it.

"Yes," she said in a quiet, terrifyingly precise voice. "I have a headache, my feet ache, and it has been six hours since my last cup of tea. Six hours! And now I even sound like her. Do you realize how much work went in to shepherding that woman into position so her purse could be stolen? How many boutiques I have endured this week? Do you realize how many conversations about penny-dreadful novels I have been forced to endure?"

"I—"

"One such conversation would be too many, but there in fact have been dozens, all mixing together into a ghastly, giggling blur. And yet there goes Putrid Pete back to his gang's headquarters *without* the tracking device in Miss Tewkes's purse, thanks to your dratted chivalry."

"I—"

"Furthermore, what were you thinking, bringing Miss Weekle

shopping on Bond Street today? Her servants coordinate with Miss Tewkes's servants so as to ensure the ladies never meet. The last time they did, there was a fracas over a parasol, and Miss Weekle's footman ended up with his nose broken. You have disrupted everything. Therefore I say good afternoon, sir. This ends our acquaintance."

And grabbing the purse from him, she turned and marched away.

Daniel stared dazedly after her. His memory was shouting for attention . . . His body, however, drowned it out with a hot, uncomfortable throbbing. Perhaps he had strained something in his fight with the thief. He would have to consult a medical encyclopedia this evening.

The woman took an unrelenting course along the footpath, obliging more genteel ladies to leap out of her way. She moved with the dangerous grace of someone entirely aware of her surroundings and entirely unafraid. He watched her, knowing she would know that he did.

And for the first time in living memory, Daniel Bixby grinned.

"Fiddlesticks," Alice muttered, smacking the purse in a one-two beat against her thigh as she strode back toward the dress shop. Frustration and indignation dueled for possession of her mood, but annoyance already had it tied up in knots at the thought of all the undisciplined things she'd just done. Running in the street! Wrestling! Using the word "dratted" like some—some *hooligan*!

She counted her breath in, counted it out again. She imagined smacking the purse not against her thigh but in the face of the manservant. He might have been handsome and fit, with a masterful style and eyes the alluring colour of gunmetal behind those dark-rimmed spectacles, not to mention the hard—

Which is to say, he might have been somewhat good-looking, but he had ruined a careful operation and seriously disturbed her inner tranquility. Also her outer tranquility. And several tranquil layers in between. Her hands still tingled from having touched him. Her nerves were a wreck. If she never set eyes on him again it would be too soon.

"Clacton-on-Sea," he said.

Alice sighed. He had caught up to her, and now kept pace with ease.

"I remember where I've seen you before," he said in a pleasant tone. "It was when you mugged me last year in Clacton-on-Sea. You *are* Miss Dearlove, aren't you? Erstwhile lady's maid to Mrs. Chuke. You stole my wallet and cufflinks."

"Nonsense," Alice retorted.

"I assure you, madam, my memory of events is as clear as a daguerreotype."

"Oh, I agree it happened. But it is nonsense to say they were cufflinks. They were miniature communication devices."

"Well, yes, such things are a necessity when one is butler to a pirate. Captain O'Riley was forever wandering away from my supervision." His eyes seemed to lighten as he regarded her. "If you know that, then I assume you are a member of the secret service. Is that why you attacked me in Clacton?"

"I am not aware of anything about a secret service," Alice replied promptly.

"Of course you aren't. Neither am I. Never heard of its existence. Never drawn a paycheck from its coffers."

Alice cast him an austere glance. "I might have guessed, considering your bulletproof hat. Very well. I was observing a clandestine ladies' league—"

"The Wicken League of gentlewomen witches?"

"You know them?"

"A petty amount. They enjoy a generational feud with the Wisteria Society of lady pirates. Both groups possess the same magical incantation, inherited from the adventurer Beryl Black, but they disagree on its proper use. Witches have a greater concern about being caught, since employing magic to manipulate people without their knowledge is generally considered more wicked than employing it just to fly houses—unless you are an urban planner, I suppose. But if you asked me to name any other difference between them, I could not. They are equally lawless and shameful."

"Villainous," Alice agreed.

"Dangerous."

"Terrible taste in hats."

He smiled at her fleetingly, sending a flurry of confusion through her body. Had she said something amusing? Should she smile in return? Her training had not included how to undertake polite conversation on the street with a man of brief acquaintance. Falling back on instinct, she frowned, crossing her arms tightly.

"While observing the League I was also managing the rogue pirate Lady Armitage and keeping an eye on the Wisteria Society."

"Busy, busy."

"One tends to be when one is the best agent of a secret government organization."

"The best?" His eyebrows slanted eloquently.

She raised her own eyebrows in response. It was like the clash of swords, only with barely noticeable facial expressions.

"I am stating mere fact, sir. While there exist several committees and squads dedicated to fighting the pirate scourge—or at least sitting back and complaining about the pirate scourge, since there's not much that can be done against people who fly weaponized houses—not many have been able to infiltrate the Wicken League of witches. Those who have tend to meet a dreadful end, choking on tea cakes or tripping and hitting their head on the ceiling. It is fair to say I may have overreacted toward you in Clacton-on-Sea, but I was in a tight spot. And I was disinclined to trust the butler of a pirate whom even the Wisteria Society considers a loose cannon."

"Excuse me, but Captain O'Riley's cannon is bolted in securely. I supervised the work myself."

"Is that meant to be a joke?"

"Good God, no. One does not joke on a public street."

She nodded in reluctant approval. "That day I had planned to question you about O'Riley's intentions. But . . ." When the moment had come to ask if he'd like to join her for an ice cream and stroll along the beach so they could discuss matters, she'd taken one look at his handsome face and calm eyes and decided bashing him on the head was the less stressful option.

"But?" he prompted.

"Oh look, we are back at the shop." She hurried forward the several dozen steps necessary to make that statement true. Taking a deep breath, she settled her countenance into the quiet docility of a lady's maid. Bixby, reflected in the door's glass panels, straightened his tie. Their eyes met briefly via that reflection; something dark and intense flashed between them. Then Alice opened the door.

"*—and people of good sense don't wear so much pink!*"

Crash!

Alice stared into the shop. Its owner knelt weeping over a tangled heap of dresses and broken racks. The thief Merv moaned, half-hidden beneath a pile of hatboxes. A mannequin lay broken across the counter, a coat hanger impaled in its back; another protruded headfirst from a wall. In the center of this, Primula and Dahlia wrangled over a ballgown. It seemed the ladies' tête-à-tête had escalated into a full-blown tit-for-tat.

"I had it first!" Dahlia shouted.

"I was just robbed, therefore I deserve it more!" Primula countered. "More!"

"Ahem."

As Alice cleared her throat, both women turned to stare at her. Not one speck of reproach showed upon her countenance, yet they blanched guiltily. Primula dropped the dress and smoothed her disheveled hair.

"You may have the rag," she said haughtily to Dahlia. And clambering over the mess, she moved to the door, where she snatched her purse from Alice's hand. "Come along, Dearlove. We are going to Harrods."

"Yes miss." Alice turned to follow her. "Good afternoon," she murmured to Bixby.

"Good afternoon," he replied, bowing

And she walked away, no doubt never to see him again.

✤ 2 ✤

ALICE VISITS HER AUNT—TEA AND APOLOGIES—
AN ALPHABETIC SURPRISE—THE UNUSUAL SUSPECTS—
ALICE IS NOT WHO SHE SEEMS—AN ENGAGEMENT

Alice walked in beauty like the afternoon of cloudy climes over Westminster, where all that was the best of dark and bright met in a sky about to rain. She entered a rather dingy building whose bronze doorplate advised that the tenants were Bover & Sons, Brushmakers, est. 1785. Within could be found a small manufactory of brooms, dusters, and specialist brushes, which oddly enough had not been applied to the cluttered and dusty premises. An old man whittling a broomstick looked up and nodded as Alice entered.

A lady like her, dressed in a smart, dark blue walking suit with the merest hint of a bustle, and bearing a hat so discreet it could have been safely employed as an ambassador to France, did not usually patronize such an establishment. But this was no real manufactory. And Alice was not in fact a lady like her. She nodded to the old man, then strode across the room, her bootheels tapping smartly against its wooden floorboards.

Alice loved that sound. It made her feel like a capable woman. An intelligent woman. A woman who had this morning made an omelet without it turning into scrambled eggs!

Certainly not a woman who had tossed and turned all night, trying to ignore visions of a bespectacled butler straightening his cuffs after having bashed a man senseless.

She paused, looking around the manufactory. "You need a fan in here," she informed the old man. "The air is decidedly hot."

He nodded, since he was deaf and would have nodded even if she'd told him the place was burning down. Continuing on, Alice wondered what brand of starch Mr. Bixby used to get his cuffs looking so precise. The slide of crisp linen against his skin must be soothing indeed—although oddly enough her own clothes felt suddenly scratchy and constrictive. She would have to reconsider the ingredients of her laundry soap.

Arriving at a closet, she slipped inside, angling herself amongst its collection of mops. Shifting one to reveal a faded calendar picture of a woman in a bathing costume leaning against a horse-drawn carriage, she pushed against it. A panel swung aside to reveal another closet, this one empty. Entering, Alice closed the door and tugged on a clothes hanger suspended from the ceiling. The closet began to descend. Instantly bored, Alice took a small dictionary from her dress pocket to read.

Sensual . . . sensualism . . . sensualist . . . sensuality . . .

Well, that did not provide as helpful a distraction from thoughts of Mr. Bixby as she had hoped. Snapping the book shut, she returned it to her pocket just as the ground reacquainted itself with the spirit of its name. Before her stood another door. An abacus was set into its center panel, and Alice adjusted the beads along their horizontal tracks until the door clicked and swung open.

She stepped through to the headquarters of the Agency of Undercover Note Takers.

A.U.N.T. was England's most secret intelligence agency, fortunately better at espionage than at naming itself. It had been established in the reign of Henry VIII, when his queens' troubles led household servants to realize the tremendous power of gossip. Since then, the covert web of chambermaids and butlers, housekeepers and footmen, grooms and sweeps, had grown so extensive it had become in effect a downstairs government. With an information-rich net of service providers spread across the realm, A.U.N.T. ensured, amongst other things, that every scheme of the Wicken League was known, that pirates did not make too much trouble, and that spoiled rich girls were kept from killing one another on shopping sprees.

"It's like one big family," the man who recruited Alice had explained when he'd removed her from the orphanage where she'd lived for the first six years of her life. He'd given her lollies and set her inside a carriage with blacked-out windows, and Alice had thought she was going to meet her hitherto unknown aunty. She'd asked nothing, since she barely spoke in those days; she'd just hugged her battered volume of *Alphabets and Pictures for Children* (and hidden the lollies beneath the carriage seat cushion, since they were bad for one's teeth). Only after arriving at the Academy of Household Management and being assigned her first broom had she finally realized the truth.

Mind you, considering her sole understanding of "family" up until then had come from fairy tales, she was just grateful the teachers and other students did not throw her down a well or cut off her head. Ten years of service training passed before she even met Chief Servant Mrs. Kew, and another two before she graduated as a lady's maid and spy.

Now her friends (which is to say, people to whom she said a polite hello when passing, and watched laughing together at the agency

Christmas party) knew her as A—ranked first, equal with the mysterious B, whose identity was kept secret even from her. Sometimes she almost forgot her Christian name, so seldom did she hear it. But that did not matter. Only service mattered. Well, that and returning library books before they accrued a late fee, of course.

"Don't you ever wish for real friends?" Hazel Coombley had asked her once, soft-voiced and gentle-eyed, as they sat drinking tea.

"No," Alice had responded. And she would have given the same response even if Hazel hadn't been the agency clinician undertaking a psychological evaluation of her.

The only person in whom Alice felt any genuine interest was B, whose reputation had developed over the years into something close to mythology. For example, it was said B had saved Princess Louise from assassination, thanks to being in bed with her at the time. From this, Alice, an exceptional intelligence officer, deduced that B must be a woman. After all, who else would have a pajama party with the princess?

She herself rather wished to attend such a party with B. Whispering together under blankets, sharing intimate secrets . . . she imagined this would be entertaining indeed. In a way, she felt closer to B than to anyone else in the world, for surely no other could understand better what it was like to be essentially unknown.

That thought veered close to an emotion, and Alice stopped, halfway across the A.U.N.T. lobby, beneath the rose painted on its ceiling and just past the statue of Queen Victoria's butler. The threat of melancholia rattled around inside her, disrupting her tranquility and sending her pulse into free fall. Suddenly the whole world felt like it might break apart. Fiddlesticks!

Slipping one hand into a skirt pocket, she tapped her fingers against her thigh with a steady one-two beat. This calmed her, and she was soon able to continue on. In an office at the far side of the lobby, she found Mrs. Kew awaiting her.

"Come in," the woman called as Alice knocked on the door. "You're right on time."

Alice entered the office and felt her calm instantly turn to the same color as Mrs. Kew's walls—i.e., custard. Everywhere was white lace, cream lace, frothing pink lace, as if a maniacal bride had run amok with decorator tools. It framed the map of England on one wall. It wrapped around flower bouquets set on lace-clothed shelves. Even Mrs. Kew's fluffy white cat wore a lace bow. Alice suspected one more delicate, finely spun ribbon set anywhere in the room would cause the whole place to collapse in a suffocating heap.

Tap tap went her fingers in her pocket.

"Sit down, dear, have some tea," Mrs. Kew urged from a plump lace-trimmed armchair at one end of the room. Alice turned to offer the Chief Servant a curtsy—

And froze.

Mr. Bixby sat on a sofa opposite Mrs. Kew, holding a teacup.

Tap-tap-tap-tap.

He looked back at her with a stare so void of emotion, Alice struggled not to dreamily sigh. A woman could never drown in eyes like that! She could stand on safely dry ground while other women flailed about in swooning, adoring gazes. His posture within his dark suit and black overcoat was rigid. He wore no hat, and Alice observed that, although his hair was cut to regulation in a short, precise style, near the back of his neck a tattoo could be seen rising an inch above his collar, suggesting some uncouth mystery seared into the naked skin below . . .

Goodness, but the air in this room was even hotter than that in the broom factory.

Belatedly performing the curtsy, Alice crossed the room, her bootheels smacking hard against the floor. As she sat beside Bixby on the plump, embroidered sofa, he blinked, and her heart blinked in response. *Guard your tranquil layers*, she chided herself.

"Remind me, dear," Mrs. Kew said, leaning forward over an array of tea things, cakes, and roses on the low table before her. "Do you take sugar?"

Alice smiled politely at the Chief Servant—although not quite looking at her from sheer self-defense. Mrs. Kew was as decorative as her office, with lace and jewelry set upon every available surface of her soft, middle-aged person. But Alice had watched this same woman kill a man at ten paces with a Royal Jubilee commemoration plate and was not fooled.

"No, thank you, ma'am. Just milk. And please allow me to apologize for the disturbance on Bond Street yesterday—"

"I have already apologized for it," Mr. Bixby interjected coolly. "It was entirely my fault."

Alice bristled. "I beg your pardon, sir, but it was my fault. And furthermore—"

"Now, now," Mrs. Kew said soothingly. "I'm sure everyone was to blame. I heard all about it from Lady Hassan's butler. A fight in the street! Histrionic aristocrats! And a missed appointment with London's most exclusive hairdresser! It sounds very dramatic. Really no sugar, dear?"

"None, thank you. I must insist on apologizing."

"Oh good. After all, sugar makes one's teeth sparkle."

"I meant I am sorry about the Bond Street debacle."

"Never mind, I was going to take you off that case anyway. Something more important has come up that requires your special skills."

"Oh?"

"Yes, it's— *Goodness me, what is that?!*"

Mrs. Kew gasped, staring wide-eyed over Alice's shoulder. Alice turned, reaching instinctively for the petite gun in her waistband, but saw nothing untoward. (Well, a statuette of Queen Victoria swathed in golden lace, but nothing else untoward.) As she turned back, she noticed a tiny, fleeting smile on Mr. Bixby's mouth.

"Must have been just a shadow," Mrs. Kew said, and handed Alice a delicate pink teacup.

"Thank you." Alice took the cup and, lifting it from its saucer, sipped discreetly. Only years of training prevented her from spitting out the liquid.

"I went ahead and put just a speck of sugar in," Mrs. Kew confessed. "For the sake of your health."

"I see." Clearly, her notion of a speck and Mrs. Kew's diverged by several teaspoons' worth.

"Now, regarding your new assignment," Mrs. Kew said, easing back in her chair and smiling merrily at the agents. "A, I need you to—"

"Excuse me." Mr. Bixby's teacup went down in its saucer with a disapproving *clank*. "Did you just address Miss Dearlove as A?"

Mrs. Kew's smile widened. "Of course I did. A for Alice, since our dear Mr. Digglesby-God-rest-his-soul will forever be Agent D. I thought that you knew this, B. When you—"

"Excuse me." Alice tapped a fingernail against her teacup with an unhappy *clink-clink*. "Did you call Mr. Bixby by the name B? *Mr.* Bixby?"

"Yes, dear. Daniel Bixby, who has just come out of deep undercover as butler to the pirate Alexander O'Riley. He is our most reliable investigator. Daniel old chap, allow me to properly introduce Miss Alice Dearlove, our best fixer."

Alice and Daniel glanced sidelong at each other, eyes not quite meeting, and gave a brisk nod.

"Don't be shy," Mrs. Kew urged. "Shake hands!"

Alice extended her hand reluctantly. Daniel hesitated the merest moment before taking it in his own with a firm grip. Just then an earthquake occurred in Whitehall, located directly beneath the sofa in Mrs. Kew's office, and both snatched their hands back. Daniel drank tea; Alice rubbed at a crease in the lace cushion beside her.

"I'm glad to see you getting along so wonderfully," Mrs. Kew said, showing a level of astuteness at odds with her position as chief of an intelligence agency. "This bodes well for your assignment together."

Teacups rattled.

"I work alone," Alice said.

"I work alone," Daniel said at the same time.

Mrs. Kew smiled. "Of course. I appreciate how you feel, and it's entirely fair. Just now I'd like to try unhooking you from that custom, and although you're *absolutely* my star agents, nevertheless lifting you even higher, to a new level of professional—"

She stopped, her smile becoming stiff, as she registered their frowns. "Let me rephrase that. I need you to do as you're told. We received warning this week that someone is planning to assassinate Queen Victoria."

"Again?" Daniel said.

"I'm afraid so. Fifteen warnings, to be precise, but the one which concerns us most involves the pirate Frederick Bassingthwaite."

Daniel stirred his tea in a manner that suggested he was laughing behind his inscrutable countenance. "I would not worry. Frederick Bassingthwaite is even greater a moron than Mr. Collins."

"Who?" Mrs. Kew inquired.

"From *Pride and Prejudice*," Alice and Daniel replied in unison. They very carefully did not glance at each other.

Mrs. Kew's gentle confusion failed to lift. "Is that a crime-fighting duo?"

"No, ma'am," Daniel told her. "It is a book."

"I see. Well, where were we? Ah yes, murdering the Queen. Perhaps it is better to say that the danger is from Frederick's wife, Jane Fair-weather, a dastardly creature if ever there was one. Our intelligence network reports that she has come into possession of a new kind of weapon, which she plans to use on Her Majesty. Jane's motive is, and I quote, 'to prove once and for all she is as much a scoundrel as that revolting Cecilia Bassingthwaite.' What this weapon is, we do not know. Where Jane obtained it, we do not know. Where she is keep-ing it—"

"Let me guess," Daniel said. "We do not know."

"Actually, this one we do. Inside Starkthorn Castle, ancestral bat-tlehouse of the Bassingthwaites."

"Where inside Starkthorn Castle?" Alice asked. "It is an immense building."

"Ah. Well. That, we do not know. Frederick is holding a house party this coming week, and several Wisteria Society members will be attending. We do not know—but we strongly suspect!—that they too have learned of this weapon and intend to steal it. Your mission is to steal it first."

"Why would Frederick and Jane risk inviting the Wisteria Society to their house when they are keeping a secret weapon there?" Alice asked.

Mrs. Kew winced slightly. "I am going to say again that we do not know, but you cannot blame me this time. No one understands why pirates do anything." Leaning forward, she took up a porcelain sugar canister and lifted its lid to her ear before speaking into the bowl. "You can come in now."

Four clerks carrying large, gilt-framed paintings entered the room, lining up against a wall. Mrs. Kew waved a finger, and one of the men closed the gas tap for the overhead light. As darkness filled the room, Mrs. Kew angled a lamp on the tea table so its light shone directly at the paintings.

"The Bassingthwaite fortune has diminished in recent times," she said, "but Frederick and Jane still have high regard for themselves." She waved forth one of the clerks, who held a portrait up to the light. In it, a bony young man with sleek black hair and mustache sat primly on a golden chair; standing beside him, one hand clamped to his shoulder, was a bespectacled woman whose posture suggested she stored a number of officious opinions up her proverbial.

"Neither Frederick nor Jane can be trusted, but we do not believe they are the greatest danger. It is the other Wisteria Society members with whom we are most concerned."

The clerk stepped back and another advanced. "Elizabeth Boffle," Mrs. Kew said, frowning at the new portrait. "A wicked villain and odious blight on England's fair shore."

Alice regarded the plump, smiling face and puffed white coiffure of an elderly lady dressed in so many pink flounces Dahlia Weekle would have swooned at the sight. Every instinct of her orphan heart suggested this was a woman to whom one could go for baked goods and cozy bedtime stories.

"Also known as Bloodhound Bess," Mrs. Kew said. "Both of her husbands were found floating in the Thames with pillowcases over their heads."

"That doesn't seem like a very safe way to swim," Alice remarked.

Daniel choked on a mouthful of tea. Mrs. Kew raised one eyebrow. "They were less swimming and more sleeping with the fishes, dear," the Chief Servant said.

Alice frowned. "How—"

"Dead," Daniel told her. "They were dead."

"Oh."

"This portrait is somewhat outdated," Mrs. Kew continued. She waved her finger again, and the man holding the painting took out a pen knife and slashed Bess's face. "That's better. She was scarred during a vicious skirmish with the chairwoman of the East Anglia Potted Flower Club. Very passionate about her oleanders, is Bess. Next, we have Verisimilitude Jones."

"Millie the Monster," Alice and Daniel said in dire tones as a third portrait was brought forth.

"You know of her?" Mrs. Kew inquired.

Alice looked at the painting of the tiny, eye-patched woman. "Only one pirate lady has a more alarming reputation than Millie."

"Funny you should say that," Mrs. Kew murmured. The fourth clerk stepped up with a portrait that trembled slightly in his hands as he lifted it for view. Represented there in oils was an elegant older woman wearing a fur coat, scarf, and gloves and holding a sun parasol. In her free hand she aimed a pistol at a thin, red-gowned lady whose hair stood erect like a fan and whose actual fan bristled with iron spikes.

"Miss Darlington," Daniel said, his voice so dire this time it ought to have been surrounded by yellow tape and skull-and-crossbones signs.

"Indeed," Mrs. Kew confirmed. "Seen here in conversation with her old chum, Lady Armitage, whose recent fall from grace made quite the splash."

Alice frowned again. "Lady Armitage toppled out of her house into the harbor and drowned."

"Yes, dear, that's what I said. With Armitage out of the picture—"

"She is right there," Alice pointed out. "In the picture."

"I mean, with Armitage dead—"

"Presumed dead," Daniel corrected.

"Yes, dear," Mrs. Kew said through gritted teeth. "With Armitage presumed dead from drowning and therefore being out of the picture, *so to speak*, Darlington is the most significant piratic threat. She is also

Frederick Bassingthwaite's great-aunt, and therefore has been invited to his house party."

"Will Cecilia Bassingthwaite be attending too?" Daniel asked. At his question, one of the clerks set down his portrait and rummaged through a sheaf of unframed images before presenting a rather blurry watercolor of a young, red-haired woman that had been re-created at larger size from a locket portrait.

"That's her," Daniel said. "I know she's not a Wisteria Society member, but she is an infamous pirate and the rightful owner of Starkthorn Castle."

Mrs. Kew chuckled. "I don't believe I've ever before heard the term 'rightful owner' used when referring to pirates. No, apparently Miss Bassingthwaite's response upon receiving the invitation was, 'Over Jane Fairweather's dead body.' I'm afraid her housemaid took this rather seriously, and we only just caught up to her half a mile from Starkthorn Castle with a crate of gunpowder. But Miss Bassingthwaite would not attend anyway, considering she has a new baby. The worst you'll have to contend with is Miss Darlington."

"Sounds simple," Alice said.

"Not really," Daniel argued. "Even Rotten O'Riley fears Jemima Darlington. If she doesn't assassinate you directly, she will do you in with terror stories about scrofula and rabies."

"Nevertheless," Mrs. Kew said, "contend with her you must. You and Alice will be attending the party at Starkthorn Castle. We have several underservants already assigned, but for an assassination plot this serious we require our best agents on-site. Naturally I thought of you."

Daniel leaned back, crossing one leg over the other and resting his arm against the rim of the sofa behind Alice in a pose that plainly said, "A.U.N.T.'s best agent, at your service." Alice went taut—but since she was already so taut one could have safely balanced a full teapot on her head, nobody noticed.

"I will need a new set of correct butler attire," Daniel informed Mrs. Kew. "A goat ate mine."

"A goat?" Mrs. Kew's eyes widened with astonishment.

"O'Riley's household was an interesting place. On another occasion a woman ate my—actually, never mind."

Alice was fascinated to see a blush stain Mrs. Kew's face. Why would a culinary anecdote embarrass the Chief Servant?

"Leave us," Mrs. Kew said to the clerks, all of whom were smirking. As they departed, they turned the light back on, and Alice winced at the sudden brightness. When she could see again, Mrs. Kew had recovered her composure and was cutting slices in a large cream cake. "I will have you meet with Snodgrass after this to be fully outfitted," the Chief Servant said. "But you won't be needing a butler's getup. Cake?"

"No, thank you," Daniel said. "Why not? I hope you aren't suggesting I pose as a footman." Disapprobation shadowed his face.

"Cake?" Mrs. Kew offered Alice.

"No, thank you. If Mr. Bixby has associated with pirates, won't there be a danger of him being recognized? Should he not be withdrawn from the case on that basis, and I do the mission solo?"

"That is unnecessary," Daniel answered as Mrs. Kew busied herself plating two plump wedges of cream sponge. "O'Riley strove to avoid the Wisteria Society as much as possible; consequentially, I never met any of them. On the other hand, your work last year brought you in extensive contact with pirates, Miss Dearlove. I fear you'll be in danger, and therefore the mission should be mine alone."

"They will not remember me. I am a master of disguise."

"You look exactly as you did last year in Clacton-on-Sea."

She turned to him. Focusing on where his hair angled neatly at the edge of his face, she softened her expression, relaxing its mouth and half lowering its eyelashes to cast a softness over the eyes. She hunched a shoulder slightly and tipped her head toward it in a gesture of obsequiousness so repellent, one's gaze naturally wanted to turn away from it, forgetting what one had seen. The brisk, competent woman who had been sitting a moment before on the sofa was replaced with a girl whose self-effacement rendered her practically faceless.

"Fascinating," Daniel said.

Shrugging, Alice allowed her regular countenance to settle once more upon her. "God has given me one face, and I make myself several others."

Daniel's eyes narrowed. "You are paraphrasing Shakespeare," he said in a tone that teetered between disapproval and respect.

"How clever of you to notice," Alice retorted in a tone that did not so much teeter as ricochet between disdain and sarcasm.

"So we're all set, then!" Mrs. Kew beamed as she held out the plates. "Now, are you sure you won't have cake? I made it specially for this meeting."

Alice eyed the frothy confection. For the first time, she noticed two tiny gold bells set atop the icing. "Do you mean for me to be a chambermaid?" she asked with horror.

"I am too old to be a footman," Daniel argued.

"You are only twenty-seven, dear," Mrs. Kew said. "But fear not. And Alice, you won't be a chambermaid. You two will attend the party as a married couple."

Alice and Daniel stared at her.

"See, you're the perfect choice! Just keep looking like that and people will absolutely believe you're married. Oh, don't be so glum. After all, you're about to join a pirate's house party—most likely you'll be dead within a week." She grinned. "More tea, my dears?"

✷ 3 ✷

All that glisters is not necessarily gold. Daniel regarded his new wedding ring with dislike, guessing that within a week the skin beneath would be green. Beside him in the slowly descending linen closet, Alice had already taken to fiddling unconsciously with hers. It looked too heavy for her delicate hand, and Daniel wondered if the etchings on the inside irritated her as much as they did him.

He would have preferred to have slipped the ring on her himself, for no other reason than that it would have been proper to do so, even if their marriage was a pretense. Certainly not so he could hold her hand, slide a band slowly along the fine-boned length of her finger, listen to her breathe as his thumb stroked her palm. After all, he had not been imagining her for the past year since their encounter in Clacton, nor hunting everywhere for the rosewater scent of her hair, nor remembering the gentle, tremulous way she had fluttered her eyelashes as she'd begged his pardon for threatening to shoot him. It just so happened he *liked* taking cold baths.

The woman displayed no gentleness or tremulousness now. She was as stiff as—

Well, probably best not to finish that thought. Alice Dearlove was Agent A, his greatest rival. If Daniel failed to keep distant from her, he'd be risking emotions—disturbance—disorder—the complete and absolutely catastrophic upheaval of the world. It was vital therefore that he focus on work, and not on the graceful curve of her jaw above that pale, kissable throat.

"Atrocious," she said, and Daniel's heart leaped, wondering madly if he'd spoken his musings aloud. But Alice was staring at the shelves of linen that stood opposite them.

"Hm?" he said.

She flicked a finger toward the shelves. "Look at those fitted sheets, just rolled up however you may please."

"Hm," Daniel agreed.

"And where is that dreadful music coming from?" She frowned around the closet. Daniel attempted to reply, but at that moment their descent halted and the door swung open. Daniel indicated to Alice that she precede him, after which he followed her into the A.U.N.T. laboratory.

There before them lay a large room styled as a kitchen. People in white coats bustled about, attending to tasks at benches and cluttered tables. A wall of clocks displayed countdowns for different tea times in the major households of London. Several large sinks contained dishes, plants, and incomprehensible devices made of extruded metal; a hand-written sign above one begged people to wash their own detonation triggers after use.

"Over here!" called a thin-haired man with a bristling mustache, waving from where he stood beside a collection of teapots. Daniel felt his skin crawl. He disliked Cornelius Snodgrass for no better reason than instinct, which was not a good reason at all, but he could not seem to argue himself out of it. There existed no doubt, however, that the man represented the best in scientific invention. He was an acclaimed genius—or at least would have been acclaimed were he not working for a highly secret organization—and much of A.U.N.T.'s success belonged to his laboratory and the remarkable tools it developed to assist agents.

As Daniel walked behind Alice, he heard two people debating the velocity factor of a silver plate versus one made of china; a woman chanting Latin while waving a pink-feathered duster; and a trio of men clapping excitedly as a kettle boiled (and then cheering as it exploded). Something burned in a sink; the smell of it made Daniel frown.

"Good afternoon," Snodgrass enthused as Alice and Daniel joined him. His scrawny limbs seemed to skirmish with each other as he stepped forward to offer Alice a handshake. She pretended not to see it. Blinking marsh-colored eyes, he instead began to move the hand in Daniel's direction but, noting the stony look Daniel gave him, withdrew it hastily. "I say, Mrs. Kew told me all about your assignment. Terrifying business, what?"

"I would call marriage more aggravating than terrifying," Alice replied coolly.

The man's mouth wavered. "Er, I meant about the house filled with pirates."

Alice stared at him, uncomprehending.

"Never mind." He tossed out a trembly little laugh; no one caught it. "Jolly good stuff. Speaking of which, ha ha, I have a few gadgets here that you might find helpful."

"Teapots?" Daniel asked repressively.

"No, these are just a few clandestine telephones that are being sent out to butlers tomorrow morning. *This* collection is for you."

Turning to a small table, he gestured with a flourish at its clutter of ordinary objects. Daniel and Alice regarded him in unimpressed silence.

"Er, yes, well . . . I say, here is just the thing for a beautiful new bride!" He presented Alice with a gold-and-enamel brooch. "Press your thumb over the rose design and you will be able to hear people's conversation even from a distance. I call it the *super rosa* device, ha ha."

Alice just looked at the brooch. Snodgrass, rocking excitedly on the balls of his feet, grew abruptly impatient and took it from her, turning it over before placing it once more on her palm.

"See, this etched text is a phrase of the incantation, which we adjusted to—"

"Incantation," Alice said.

"Why yes, you did know that we use elements of the pirates' magical flight incantation to create our special devices?" (He paused while something exploded in the laboratory behind them; "*Sorry!*" a man sang out.) "Although I should not call it the pirates' incantation, ha ha, since really Beryl Black was a scientist at heart, even if she did use magic to fly houses, what? She and her husband were undertaking a geographical survey when they shipwrecked on that island where she found the incantation. The pirates may have grabbed it for themselves, but after A.U.N.T. infiltrated their households and stole it from them, we began applying it to its *true* purpose, the noble pursuit of—"

"Yes, I know all that," Alice said. "I meant, I do not need the incantation to help me hear distant conversations. My hearing is good; perhaps too good. For example, those two women some twenty feet behind us are talking about uses for a teaspoon that I would rather not repeat."

"I say." Snodgrass's face sagged. He took back the brooch, laid it softly on the table.

Alice bit her lip with what looked to Daniel surprisingly like pity. "But if you have one of your parachute hats . . ."

"I do!" Snodgrass perked up as he reached into a box beneath the table and brought forth a bonnet so hideous, Daniel actually took a step back. Lined with puce velvet, wrapped by more lace than even Mrs. Kew would abide, and athwart with beads, baubles, and what appeared to be fragments of bone, it was indeed the sort of hat one tossed out a window to make it fly—only not with oneself attached to it.

"On second thought," Alice said, "if I need to jump off a roof I will just risk the broken leg."

This time it was Snodgrass's shoulders that sagged. "I have something for the gentleman," he said, trying to keep his tone chipper as he replaced the bonnet.

But Daniel already had a razor that doubled as a lighter, and a lighter than could cut through wire; and the onyx ring containing a pistol proved too large for either of their hands. When Alice removed the backing of the hairbrush/voice recorder, it caught fire, and when Daniel tried to put out the flames using a fire extinguisher disguised as a perfume bottle, they roared even higher and then the brush outright exploded. By this time so many parts of Snodgrass were sagging, he had to lean against the table to keep upright.

"I will take the umbrella, though," Alice said.

"I say! You will?" Snodgrass drew himself upright with such excitement he practically reverberated. He handed the umbrella to Alice as if offering his sword in fealty to a queen. "The spokes all contain darts, and if you press this button—"

"Actually, I just want an umbrella because it's raining outside."

"Oh." The scientist looked like he might cry.

"I'll have that silver fob watch," Daniel said. If Miss Dearlove could show pity, he could show it *even more.* "What amazing thing does it do?"

"Er." Snodgrass blushed as he took up the watch. "That's mine. I just took it off when I was working in the sink. But you can have it if you like—"

He held out the watch, and Daniel blinked hastily. "No. No, thank you. I think we have everything we need. Shall we be going, Miss Dearlove?"

"But you didn't take anything," Snodgrass said as the agents turned to leave. "You'll be facing a crowd of pirates with no more than your wits and experience."

Daniel gave Alice a dry look. She rolled her eyes.

"I think we shall manage, Dr. Snodgrass," she said.

"But my technical expertise is imperative to the success—"

The rest of his sentence was lost in a loud clap of noise as another explosion occurred, sending pink feathers through the air.

"Thank you all the same," Daniel said.

They walked back through the laboratory, weaving carefully away from small fires and shuddering mechanical devices, Snodgrass *but*-ing and *I-say*-ing behind them all the way. Daniel was glad to shut him out of the closet.

"I like to consider myself an accepting kind of fellow," he said as the closet slowly rose, "but that is one man I cannot abide."

"I detest him," Alice said, although her mild tone suggested she was less interested in Snodgrass than in surpassing Daniel at even this. Propping the umbrella against a wall, she took a fitted sheet from the shelf and began to fold it.

"Other corner first," Daniel instructed.

She speared him with a quelling look. Undeterred, he stepped forward, reaching for the sheet. "No, really—"

"I beg your pardon." She pulled it closer to herself. "I know what I am doing."

"Clearly not, since that is the wrong corner." He took another step.

"Touch this sheet and you die," she advised calmly.

He stared at her for a moment, then shot out his arm sideways and slammed the heel of his hand against the emergency button. The closet shuddered to a halt.

Alice raised one eyebrow.

And Daniel loosened his collar for the battle ahead.

On the floor above, several people stood waiting for the closet. And waiting. And still waiting, so that a number of them drew watches from pockets restively. Others tapped repeatedly on the button as if that might hasten the closet's arrival.

Suddenly, a crash echoed up the shaft. The group exchanged alarmed glances. Then the floor began to shudder, and a series of rapid bangs vibrated through the wall. Everyone stepped back from the closet door, murmuring worriedly.

Ping! The button lit, and the group moved back even farther. The door swung open.

Daniel Bixby stepped out, brushing an invisible speck from the lapel of his long black overcoat. He appeared to not even see the group—for which they were grateful, since even those who didn't know he'd spent three years working with a pirate could sense he possessed an energy about as unbending as a sword and equally dangerous. Behind him came Alice Dearlove, who was reputed to have informed the Queen to her royal face that it was *try to*, not *try and*. She was carrying a furled umbrella under her arm and the group cringed, half expecting her to jab them with it. But without a word the two agents strode off along the corridor, allowing the group to breathe again. They cautiously approached the closet and peered in.

Several people gasped.

Never before had the little room been so clean. Every item on its shelves was not only folded to perfection but organized according to color and purpose. Spiderwebs were gone from corners; scuffmarks on the floor had vanished. The group looked at one another nervously, then turned away and took the stairs.

Alice was bemused to find Mr. Bixby following her out of A.U.N.T. headquarters, into the gloom between rain showers. She felt all-peopled-out after the morning and wanted to go home, close the curtains, and hug a book until her nerves settled. She certainly wanted some distance from this particular man. Agent B attracted her in a way that was (1) entirely unprofessional, (2) physically daunting, and (3) holding one edge of her tranquility and smiling with a suggestion that any moment now it might tug.

"Forgive me, sir," she said, glancing at him. "But you do understand we are not in fact married?"

"I do," he said, ironically enough. "However, I thought I might escort you home and along the way we could develop our cover story—share about our hobbies, for example, our favorite foods, our family histories."

Alice huffed a small, dry laugh at that last suggestion. Surely the man was joking. A.U.N.T. never promoted anyone with family to their elite force. The risk of emotional conflict, blackmail threats, or people wanting to take Christmas holidays was simply too great.

"I do not think my orphanage childhood is an appropriate subject for decent conversation," she said. "Perhaps, if needed, I could invent jolly, red-cheeked parents who live in the countryside and send me knitted goods on my birthday."

Daniel frowned. "I doubt that would work."

"Why not?"

"Well, granted I was raised in an orphanage too, so have little knowledge of families outside of novels, but jolly parents who acknowledge one's birthday sounds dubious to me."

Alice considered this, then nodded. "True. I shall do research and provide a written sheet of information when we report back for duty."

Daniel looked up from the black gloves he was donning, and while his face remained impassive, Alice saw a glint of a smile in his eyes. Either that or a reflection of street lighting. Although it was not raining at the moment, dark clouds so clogged the sky that the lamps had been lit. In the feral shadows between them, with his black clothes, and his hair slightly breeze stirred, Daniel Bixby looked a lot like a man who had consorted with pirates and knew exactly how to make a woman walk the plank.

She paled at the thought.

"What?" he said, noticing her altered expression.

"Nothing."

"Tell me."

She shrugged uncomfortably. "I was just thinking about how one would escape being thrust onto a piece of wood that is jutting out . . ."

"You mean like a pirate's plank? It helps to have either training in acrobatics or else a parachute." He gave her a long, penetrating look. "Do you have acrobatic experience, Miss Dearlove?"

"Not yet," she admitted.

"What, not even a handstand?"

"I'm waiting for the right trainer. I suppose *you* have experience, Mr. Bixby."

"Some." He went on looking at her, and she felt her stomach curl as if his gaze had reached right in and was stroking it. "I could teach you a few moves," he said. "A backward somersault maybe, or a cartwheel, so that when you find yourself walking a plank you know what to do."

Alice yanked herself away from that unblinking gaze and frowned in the general vicinity of nothing at all. The air had become so muggy she felt sure any moment there would be a great rush of rain, wetting her right through.

"I can manage myself, thank you," she said. "A woman is entirely capable of cartwheeling on her own."

"I agree," Daniel said. "But it is more enjoyable when you have someone else to flip you."

Alice opened her mouth to retort but could not think of anything suitably repressive. The fact was, mutual acrobatics sounded rather fun. But, Alice reminded herself, she did not do fun. She was sensible right through to her lumbar vertebrae and sternum. So they walked in silence until she stopped at the entrance to a narrow alley.

"I go this way. Therefore good day, Mr. Bixby."

Daniel eyed the grotty darkness of the alley. "I go that way too."

Alice bristled. "You do not. You believe I need protection and are being *gallant*."

"I am being reasonable."

"Hm. Interesting word choice. Allow me to offer a synonym." And she smacked him with the umbrella, turned sharply on a heel, and marched away down the alley.

A moment later, footsteps synchronized with hers.

"Knitting?" he asked.

She glanced at him briefly, irritably. "What?"

"Or embroidery? Or perhaps you paint watercolors?"

"I have no hobbies, Mr. Bixby." *Click-click* went her shoes against the cobblestones, and as she listened to the emphatic sound, Alice reminded herself she was a successful, professional woman, and Daniel Bixby was altogether allur—that is to say, *annoying*.

"Not even reading?" he asked, easily matching her stride.

"Reading is not a hobby," she said. "It is a way of life."

He was silent a moment as he considered this, then he nodded in agreement.

"I suppose you play guitar or put ships into bottles," she said in a tone so wry it sounded like it had performed several acrobatic moves and was now lying back smoking a cigarette.

"No. Just reading, same as you. By the way, you do realize there are a couple of suspicious figures lurking behind those bins farther along the street?"

"Of course. I am not worried."

"Perhaps you should be."

She arched an eyebrow. "Why, sir? Because I am a woman?"

"No, because you are dressed inconveniently for self-defense. Your bustle is too small to suffocate a man, your dress lacks enough layers to tangle someone up, and you do not have even one ribbon to employ as a garrote."

"Nevertheless, I am entirely capable of handling an attack."

"Hm" was all he said—but it proved more than enough to conflagrate Alice's temper, which had grown tinder dry since the linen closet. She stopped abruptly in the middle of the alley.

"You!" She pointed her furled umbrella at the suspiciously loitering men.

They leaped, startled. "Us?" one of them said warily.

"Yes. Come here, please. I require you to rob me."

The two ruffians glanced bemusedly at each other. "Er, no, thank you," one said. "Kind of you to offer, miss, but we ain't thieves."

"I'm sure you will do your best. Step quickly, if you please. I haven't all day."

The men now turned wide, rather pleading eyes to Daniel, who stood with his hands in his coat pockets and a mildly amused expression on his face. "Don't ask me," he said, shrugging. "I'm just her husband."

"You are not," Alice said disdainfully.

"No? Why don't you show the men your pretty wedding ring?"

Her eyes flashed. "Good idea." Yanking off her glove, she held the bare hand up to the ruffians and pointed to its ring. "You can steal this. It must be worth—" She turned her hand, considered the ring, then shrugged. "Well, probably not a lot, to be honest, but it will surely buy you a nice supper. Hurry up, now."

The men shuffled out of the shadows as if they were mice drawn irresistibly to a cat. "See here, lady," one said. "We're just minding our own business, and you've no call to barge in insisting we rob you. It's indecent, it is."

"I have three children at home," said the other. "Won't you think of them?"

Alice turned to roll her eyes at Daniel. He looked back with an expression somewhere between challenging her and wondering what on earth she would do next. Turning back to the ruffians, hoisting her umbrella, she motioned for them to get a move on.

They edged into the center of the alley. Most likely this was so they could run away, but immediately Alice launched into self-defense. With a leap—a kick—a swivel and punch—she had one man on the ground and the other scrambling to flee. Calmly aiming the umbrella at him, she squinted along its length, and then, satisfied she had her target lined up with precision, she pushed the button to activate the incantation.

Thwomp.

The umbrella burst open. The world exploded in light and squealing noise.

Oh dear, Alice thought in the fraction of a second remaining to her before she was flung violently backward. She crashed into Daniel and they went down together in a tangle of limbs.

Immediately he rolled her over, shielding her with his body from any further possible calamity. The hard weight of him pressed her against the cobblestones, but he tucked a hand beneath her head, lifting it gently. She felt the pulse in his neck beat against her lips. She tasted salt, smelled the cool vanilla scent of soap—and suspected that the umbrella had been electrified, because sparks were flaring all through her blood.

"Are you all right?" he asked. The words were muted, but she felt them vibrating through his throat, against her mouth. Several hitherto unknown instincts urged her to stroke her tongue against them in reply, even while more familiar ones were setting up barricades and unrolling barbed wire.

"I will be once I can breathe," she said.

He climbed off her, but she remained lying there, trying to adjust to his sudden absence. Fiddlesticks. The air was so much thinner, fretful, with him gone. He held out a hand to assist her; ignoring it, she clambered awkwardly to her feet.

"I'm fine," she said, despite the bruises she was likely to have tomorrow, not to mention the fact that her hat was on fire—thankfully farther along the alley, not on her head. "You?"

Daniel winced as he rubbed a hip. "Less inclined to say 'I told you so' than I thought I would be."

"Drat Snodgrass," Alice muttered, glaring at the umbrella, which lay several feet away. Smoke rose from its twisted, shredded wreckage. The ruffians were long since departed.

"It could be worse," Daniel said. "Imagine if you'd taken the brooch instead."

Alice brushed loose strands of hair away from her face. "At least this has shown beyond doubt that I am able to take care of myself. Aside from the explosion. And the being flung some distance. And the burning hat. Other than these minor issues, I have proved myself entirely in control. Therefore, I shall be going home alone from here."

"It would probably be safest," Daniel agreed. "Thank you for the brief and exciting honeymoon."

She gave him a bewildered frown, then shrugged. "I will see you later this week."

She turned to leave.

"Don't forget your umbrella," he said. "Littering is an offense."

He turned in the other direction.

And as they went their separate ways, the clouds burst open, emptying a storm over them.

✻ 4 ✻

RATTLESHACK—DANIEL ATTEMPTS HUMOR,
WITH FORESEEABLE RESULTS—HARDER—
CREEPING DAMP—SPIT, FIRE! SPOUT, RAIN!—
ALICE IS MORE SINNED AGAINST THAN SINNING

The better part of valor is deception. Alice, standing beside Daniel
in the A.U.N.T. stable yard, looking at the tiny, decrepit cottage
that was to fly them to Hampshire, convinced herself she felt not in the
least nervous. She also convinced Daniel of this, thanks to the tranquility of her countenance. She convinced the steward who kept handing her insurance disclaimers to sign. And she even convinced herself
that she really had convinced them, despite her pallor and the way her
pocket fluttered from the tapping fingers inside.

"Just keep all the windows shut and don't go above thirty miles an
hour, and you should—er, you *will* be fine," the steward said, handing
Daniel the key. Behind him, the cottage's window shutters clattered in
the mild breeze and a roof tile fell off. A false flag of piratic nature
flapped mournfully, more gray than black.

"What happened to the chimney?" Alice asked, eyeing the cracked
brickwork uncertainly.

The steward muttered something about an agent, an opossum, and a stick of dynamite.

"I thought this was a top-priority mission," Daniel said.

"It is," the steward replied. "Agent J over there is on a less important mission."

They looked behind them to where a young man wearing a black tuxedo and desperate expression was trying to kick-start a chicken coop.

"Now," the steward said, flicking through the papers on his clipboard. "I think we have everything in order. I just need to check your luggage."

"Why?"

Daniel's tone would have daunted most men, but the steward was not much more than half a heart and a stack of checklists, and the only thing that daunted him was running behind schedule. "I need to ensure you're not carrying items that might jeopardize the mission. Unauthorized weaponry and so forth." He waved his pen in peremptory fashion. "Open your suitcase, please."

Daniel shrugged. Crouching down, he laid his suitcase flat on the ground and opened it. The steward gasped.

"You cannot be serious!"

Alice peered into the case and almost smiled to see its contents. There must have been two dozen books crammed in.

"What about clothing? Personal accessories?" the steward asked.

Daniel indicated the duffel bag hanging from his shoulder.

"Surely that's inadequate?"

"I agree," Daniel said, "but I couldn't fit in any more books. Hopefully Starkthorn Castle has a decent library."

The steward shook his head with disapproval, then turned to Alice, flicking his pen at her. "You now."

She laid down her suitcase and opened it.

The steward rattled the pen against his clipboard.

"Hm," Daniel said, looking over. "Pocket editions. Wise choice. And is that a first edition of *Crime and Punishment* I see?"

"Yes," Alice answered. "I brought it along for a little light entertainment. After I've finished, you may borrow it if you wish."

He flashed her a warm smile. Stunned, Alice was trying to decide how she ought to respond when the steward's officious voice, tapping like his pen, demanded attention.

"So did *you* bring any clothes, Miss Dearlove?"

She lifted the duffel bag at her feet.

The steward regarded it incredulously. "My wife needs three times that space just for her unmentionables."

"I'm good at folding things," Alice said. She heard a snort of disagreement from Daniel but dared not look at him again lest he completely overwhelm her with another facial expression.

"I will just do a final check of your disguise," the steward said, "then you can go." He surveyed her critically. "That hat is not big enough."

Alice set a hand against the yellow structure balanced at a pert angle upon her intricately curled pompadour. "It has three feathers and a *papier-mâché* butterfly," she argued.

The steward sniffed again, unconvinced. He jabbed his pen at her dress. "Pink! It was supposed to be fuchsia. And do you call that a bustle?" Tucking the clipboard under his arm, he snapped his fingers and a young assistant dashed forward with a tape measure. The steward set it against the protruding rear of Alice's skirt. "Six inches. Entirely unsuitable for a pirate—you couldn't even fit a pistol in there. And you!"

Daniel stared stonily at the steward, but it was to no avail. "You

look far too good, Agent B. Your suit is impeccable, your posture un-
bowed by years of trying to manage a histrionic wife."

Daniel glanced at Alice. "She does not look particularly histrionic
to me, hat notwithstanding. And this suit was made by a tailor from
Panama, charming fellow, much in demand with pirate gentlemen.
Besides, I'll have you note my earring."

He turned his head to better display the small silver ring in his left
ear. Seeing it, Alice felt a surge of something indeed like histrionics in
her blood. The steward muttered again but reluctantly signed them
off, and without further ado, they entered the cottage.

Inside they found a single room furnished with one rather grimy
sofa and a crate serving as a table. A bench held tea supplies and the
kind of biscuits found in offices everywhere—plain, dusty, and inevi
tably soft when you bite into them. A wooden chair stood in front of
the steering array. The wheel itself was missing two spokes and had
been attached to the floor with a rusted bolt and strips of old adhesive
tape. The window in front of it lacked curtains, latches, or any indica-
tion of ever having been cleaned.

"How are we supposed to live in this for a week?" Alice asked,
already scratching in anticipation of fleas. "There's not even only
one bed."

"We'll stay in the castle," Daniel said as he inspected the naviga-
tional tools. "Most of the attendees will do the same, although they'll
park their own houses nearby in case of trouble."

"What kind of trouble?" Alice lifted the kettle, noting the incantation etched into its copper surface, which enabled it to boil water without the aid of a stove. That was a relief. She might contract tetanus over
the next few hours in this shack, but at least there would be tea.

"Any kind of trouble they can think up," Daniel said. "And pirates
have good imaginations." He opened a door, then regarded with some

bemusement the handle, which had come off in his grip. Reattaching it without much success, he looked warily into the room.

"Water closet," he reported, grimacing. "Considering its state, let's just say we're fortunate to have only a short journey."

"Fire extinguisher," Alice added, lifting the lid of the crate and peering inside. "Although it looks too heavy to lift, and"—she jiggled a loose switch on the side, causing a clatter inside the scratched and dented metal body—"I think it's broken."

"Even O'Riley's battlehouse wasn't so dilapidated," Daniel said. Seeing her expression, he smiled gently. "Don't worry. I can fly most things, and if it comes to the worst, we'll ditch the cottage and get some bicycles instead."

"Our suitcases won't fit on bicycles."

His smile tilted. "It was a joke, Miss Dearlove. A tactic to ease your nerves."

"I don't have nerves."

"That's all right, I don't have a sense of humor. Well, I'd better get us up."

He moved toward the wheel, and Alice shifted out of his way. But the space was more limited than either of them appreciated, and as he passed by, Daniel inadvertently brushed his hand against hers.

Three seconds later he realized this had been unfortunate, mainly due to the fact he was lying on his back with her booted foot on his chest. He blinked dazedly up at her, and she winced.

"I do beg your pardon," she said. "I am averse to being lightly touched."

"Yes, I noticed."

"May I help you up?"

"Perhaps that would be unwise, since it would require touching."

"A strong grip is fine," she said, holding out her hand. "Indeed, the stronger the better. I imagine it is a by-product of combat training. Do let me help."

He took the offered hand and she helped him to rise, although he was significantly more athletic than her, and whatever assistance she provided was by way of appearance only. Once he was on his feet, she expected him to release her hand, but he went on holding it, harder and harder, his face entirely quiet as he watched hers for a reaction.

She swallowed dryly as her fingers turned scarlet.

"You are remarkably tough for such a delicate woman, Miss Dearlove," he said.

"Fiddlesticks," she whispered. The bones in her hand began to burn in a most thrilling manner.

"Pardon me?"

"I may seem delicate, but most people are overly careful because of it. They are *gentle*." She shuddered.

"So," Daniel said musingly. "No light touches. No jokes. No sugar in the tea." He regarded her a moment longer, then took a step closer, twisting her arm so their clutched hands pressed against her heartbeat. His eyes had become almost silver. His expression was classified. "Shall we have an agreement, Miss Dearlove? I will not be gentle with you. Does that sound good?"

Licking her lips, but knowing it was futile—knowing all her words were ash—Alice nodded. Something creaked behind him, and they blinked at each other. Alice's stomach tingled as she recognized her own secret, silent language in Daniel's eyes. She nodded again in response, and he took half a step back, lifting her hand in his. She hauled up her skirt, set a foot against his thigh, and in one seamless movement he pulled her off the ground and spun them both around.

She kicked with her free leg, smashing the square heel of her boot into the man who had been creeping toward them. With a cry, he stumbled, then collapsed to the ground. Daniel released her, and Alice leaped over the body to land easily on the dusty wooden floor. But even before she had turned with her gun in hand, Daniel had his own drawn and was aiming it at the man beneath them, who cowered behind spindly arms.

"I say! Don't shoot!"

Sighing in annoyed unison, Alice and Daniel uncocked their guns.

"A word of advice, Dr. Snodgrass," Daniel said. "Do not approach A.U.N.T. field agents without announcing yourself first."

"Yes," Snodgrass said meekly, clambering up and rubbing his chest where Alice had kicked him. "I see that now. Jolly good. My apologies."

"Why are you here, Doctor?" Alice asked as she slipped her gun back into a secret pocket of her skirt.

Snodgrass held out a folded piece of paper. It trembled in his hand while Alice and Daniel regarded it expressionlessly. Realizing neither was going to take it, Snodgrass attended to the unfolding himself. "My assignment notice. See, here is Mrs. Kew's signature. I have been included on the mission as technical adviser, posing as your valet. I brought along several clothing brushes and a specially designed shaving set for the purpose."

"I'm going to die from my jaw catching fire, aren't I?" Daniel said to Alice.

"I'm afraid so," she agreed.

"How droll! Hahahaha," Snodgrass trilled—and only survived doing so because there were agency regulations against assassinating a colleague for the crime of being damned annoying.

"Very well," Daniel said in a tone that made clear it was, in fact, not very well at all. "There are sixty-five miles to Hampshire and it looks like a storm is coming in. I hope you don't get airsick, Doctor."

"I say. Not at all, what."

Alice sat rigidly on the sofa, gripping her mission briefing notes with white-knuckled hands and trying not to listen to Snodgrass vomiting in the water closet. She was not new to flying. She had even survived going up in Lady Armitage's battlehouse. They say a pirate's house is an embodiment of their soul; in Lady Armitage's case, this meant unstable, untrustworthy, and inclined to bunny hop wherever it pleased. But flying with her had been a gentle cruise compared to this journey. Rain battered against the little cottage. Turbulent air caused it to shudder and drop, taking Alice's stomach along with it. Kitchen utensils clattered, navigation tools slid back and forth across their shelf, and something beneath the floorboards moaned as if a resident ghost wished he was even deader.

"Uughgghhh," Snodgrass cried out. Alice found herself agreeing with him.

At the window, Daniel sat with one booted foot propped on the wheel, calmly reading Dickens and every now and then looking up to murmur a phrase of the flight incantation as his foot tipped the wheel slightly one way or another. His casual air of competency would have set Alice's nerves afire with ardor were they not trembling so much that any flame would have been immediately extinguished.

She had asked him earlier, out of concern for the long flight time, why he was not using the *momentum automatica* phrase to keep the cottage moving on its own. Standing beside him at the wheel, arms crossed, she'd been seeking something to criticize and this had been the best she could manage. The man flew like a pirate, albeit with a complete lack of swagger or hat feathers.

"Although the wheel is only a conduit for the incantation's magic," he'd said, "this one is so decrepit I doubt it could manage the *momentum automatica*. But there's actually no need for the pilot to incantate

49

without pause. One phrase can carry a house quite a distance." He'd given her a glancing smile. "Would you like to take the helm for a while, Miss Dearlove?"

"No, thank you."

"Fair enough. It is difficult weather."

She had bristled at the insinuation. What exactly he'd been insinuating, she hadn't known, but bristling had certainly seemed called for. "I could fly. If I wanted to. But I am disinclined to judge speed or distance."

"Disinclined."

She had paused a moment as dignity wrestled with pedantry. "Unable."

"It is simply a matter of mathematics."

"'Simply mathematics' is an oxymoron."

Daniel had stared into the middle distance with a mildly perplexed frown, as if trying to calculate how someone might not enjoy maths. "But you do know the incantation?"

"Of course." Alice's reply had been so defensive, she'd managed to fit a whole rampart, catapult, and cauldron of boiling oil into two words. "I wrote my third-year essay on Beryl Black. My analysis of her error in sharing the incantation with her book club, and the schism that followed when they split into pirates and witches, won me an award."

"Hm. Did you include Jemming's theory of Willful Contradiction?"

"Naturally."

"My dismantling of that theory, and the *real* forces behind the pirates choosing to use the magic for flight and the witches for telekinesis, won me an award for my third-year essay."

They'd stared at each other without blinking. Anyone walking between them at that moment would have suffered third-degree burns.

"We're about to hit a flock of birds," Alice had commented mildly.

Daniel had reached out and turned the wheel without looking.

"I graduated with honors," he'd said.

"I graduated with honors and my portrait hung in the student hall."

"Would I recognize it, or were you in disguise?"

At that, the strangest sensation had rippled through her throat. For one wild, disturbing moment, Alice had thought she might actually laugh. Lifting her chin disdainfully, she'd turned to glare out the window.

"I do know the incantation," she'd said, returning to their previous point of conversation, "but I cannot seem to get it from my brain into action. There is just too much—" Too much *feeling* involved. Too much energy infused with air, ocean, and feral power. She could barely breathe contemplating it; actually performing it left her a jittering wreck within minutes. Even when she applied the most basic *aereo* incantation to a mere teaspoon, she ended up dizzy, nauseated, and struggling to assure herself she was not a small piece of tableware. Making a house go *aereo* might just crush her mind.

But how could one explain that, especially to one's prime rival, without sounding peculiar? So she'd walked away, made tea instead.

Tea she now wished she had not drunk as the house lurched again, wind screaming through a gap in the window frame, tiles clattering overhead as they broke away and tumbled down the roof. From the water closet, Snodgrass wept. Daniel turned a page in his book.

Alice supposed she ought to study the mission dossier. She'd already memorized its essential elements: her name was to be Alice Blakeney, also known as Atrocious Alice. Daniel was hereafter Blakeney the Bad. (The steward's assistant had tried calling him Dreadful Dan, and Daniel had just *looked* at him until the poor boy nearly dropped his clipboard.) They'd received their party invitation from Frederick Bassingthwaite's butler, an undercover A.U.N.T. agent, on the premise of having recently returned from Amsterdam and being in need of new friends to visit, entertain, and hopefully one day assassinate. Married three years, they enjoyed such hobbies as—

Alice winced. Under no circumstances was she going to say her hobby was tilting at windmills. Once the storm had passed, she would have to discuss a more literate backstory with Daniel.

Suddenly the cottage dropped what felt like a thousand feet in one second. Snodgrass wailed. Alice clutched the edge of the sofa in a manner that was not at all due to fear—her hand simply felt most comfortable gripping the upholstery until turning (hopefully not appropriately) ghost white.

"It's fine," Daniel said from the wheel.

"I know, turbulence," Alice managed to answer through clenched teeth.

"Actually, that was a pirate flying past a little too close." He stood with the kind of casual, unhurried movement that sets off alarm bells in an observant watcher's mind; laying his book on the chair, he set both hands to the wheel.

"Miss Dearlove," he said lightly. "Would you be so kind as to brace for—"

Crash!

The house shook violently. Suitcases tumbled across the floor; the kettle fell. From the water closet came a splashing sound, and Snodgrass screamed.

"—impact," Daniel concluded.

Alice clambered from the sofa, and while the house tipped from side to side like a seesaw being operated by viciously competitive toddlers, she stumbled across to the flight window. Daniel glanced at her as she lurched against the wall.

"I recommend you return to your seat," he said in a calmly conversational tone. "You will be more comfortable there while I deal with—"

The sky flashed. Not lightning, Alice realized, seeing a large, ornate conservatory looming outside. *Cannon fire.*

"—this spot of bother," Daniel said.

"People in glass houses should not throw cannonballs!"

"True," Daniel agreed. "Unfortunately, pirates aren't very keen on shoulds. Hold on."

Alice assumed he meant to take a moment of silence to regather his thoughts, but in fact he meant *literally* hold on. Swinging the wheel starboard, he intoned several phrases of the flight incantation, and the cottage veered sharply. Something shattered. The sofa tipped upside down and skidded across the room to smash against a wall.

"Perhaps you would not have been comfortable there after all," Daniel remarked.

Alice, clutching the windowsill for dear life (and Dearlove, for that matter, since she feared if she let go she would suffer the same fate as the sofa), stared amazedly at the man. His face was entirely serene as he wedged a bootheel against one of the wheel spokes so as to force the wheel around even as it strained against the pressure of magic. The wheel groaned. The air seemed to twist and heat. Snodgrass crawled out of the water closet, soaking wet and with blood streaking his forehead.

"What is happening?" he wailed.

"Just having a small disagreement with a pirate," Daniel explained. "Nothing to worry about."

Crash!

Chimney bricks clattered over the roof and rained past the window. A cloud of black ash and dust billowed from the fireplace. Peering over the windowsill, Alice saw the conservatory's cannon smoking.

"If this is a small disagreement," she said, "what would happen in a large one?"

"We'd die," Daniel said. He removed his foot from the wheel, and spokes seemed to blur as the wheel spun back. A string of Latin words urged it faster, faster; Alice could have sworn she saw the wood sparking. A rumble shook the house—

"That was thunder," Daniel assured her.

He had barely finished speaking when another rumble sent shutters slamming across the window, then back again, leaving cracked panes in their wake.

"That one was gunfire."

"Bother," Alice said. She drew the pistol from her dress pocket, but Daniel shook his head.

"That won't have the necessary range. Dr. Snodgrass, did you pack any weapons in your suitcase?"

"Unnghghugh," Snodgrass replied.

Daniel and Alice exchanged a dry look.

"I'll go," Alice said. She reeled across the room, pushing herself from chair to bench to upturned sofa until finally reaching Snodgrass's suitcase. She wrestled with the latches, wincing as the lid suddenly flung open. A clutter of metal objects and underclothes tumbled out. Alice immediately snatched what appeared to be a rotary egg beater.

"Is this what I think it is?" she asked Snodgrass.

He peered up from where he had coiled himself against the kitchen bench. "You can't use that while in flight!" he cried. "It will be disastrous!"

Taking that for a positive reply, Alice clambered to her feet once more and staggered back to the window.

"Don't try it!" Snodgrass shouted desperately. "I say, don't try it!"

"Before you do," Daniel said, "show me your petticoat."

Alice rolled her eyes. "For heaven's sake," she murmured. "Men!" Nevertheless, she lifted her skirt to reveal the heavy, lace-trimmed petticoat beneath.

Daniel's mouth twitched with what might have been a smile or merely a consequence of speaking wild piratic magic.

"Satisfied?" Alice asked.

"Absolutely," he said.

Flinging her hem down again, Alice turned and unlatched the window, then pushed it ajar. Cold rain pelted her; the wind howled. Grimacing at the force of it, she leaned against the side of the window and took aim with the egg beater.

The pirate's conservatory hung above the cottage, silent and steady despite the storm. Alice found she could not line up the egg beater effectively at this angle, so she hoisted herself onto the windowsill and leaned out. The sky was a tumult of darkness. The ground was so far below as to be but a dream.

Propping her feet against the far edge of the window, wedging herself as securely as possible, Alice took a deep breath. Then she let go of the windowsill and turned the beater's rotary handle.

A stream of tiny missiles shot from the end of the beater, flaring with storm light as they flew. Hitting the conservatory, they triggered a series of explosions with unexpected force. Flames burst through the gloom; glass shattered. The conservatory lurched and began to topple sideways. Daniel steered the cottage away, but the beater's incantation jostled with the flight incantation, causing an imbalance. The cottage veered right into the conservatory.

As a fierce jolt went through her, Alice dropped the egg beater, sending it plummeting hundreds of feet to earth. Instinctively she reached for it. Daniel shouted something, but she did not hear him, for her balance went the same way as the egg beater and then she herself followed, tipping headfirst out the window into the storm.

✷ 5 ✷

The two most important days in your life are the day you are born and the day you choose to wear an enchanted petticoat just in case you fall from a flying cottage. As she plunged through icy, howling rain, Alice unbuttoned her skirt and let it fall away from her. With it went a pearl-handled revolver and an illustrated edition of Euripides's plays, which had been tucked into a secret pocket—but there was no time for mourning this loss. Alice yanked on a ribbon and with a gentle *thwomp* the petticoat blossomed into a parachute.

Peering down toward the ground, she sighed. It looked terribly far away. She could have done with a little light reading of Euripides to help her pass the time. Looking up, she saw the A.U.N.T. cottage ducking and diving around the glasshouse. Its chimney had disintegrated and the roof would need to be retiled. But the egg beater had significantly damaged the glasshouse, and Alice felt certain Daniel and Snodgrass would be safe from further attack. Now they simply needed to maintain the fragile stability of the cottage, fly safely through the storm despite having lost the chimney, and land without crashing, flipping, or for that matter outright plummeting—all of which they would do in considerably warmer conditions than hers, given that one corner of the cottage was aflame.

Thus reassured, Alice turned to contemplating her own future. With no map or compass, she would be doomed to asking directions from strangers. "Fiddlesticks," she muttered. Could this day get any worse?

At that very moment, a house glided into view below her. Tall and pale, with one round window in its attic like a baleful eye and smoke arising sedately from its chimney, it seemed to sally forth on a wind of its own self-importance. A black flag flapped jauntily above the roof.

Such a flag indicated a pirate's premises—although unnecessarily so, considering only pirates (and secret agents pretending to be pirates) flew buildings. Witches would not lower themselves (er, metaphorically speaking) to use the magical incantation in such an obvious manner. And although pirates trained their servants to pilot, should any run away and use the incantation for themselves, they would either succeed—and thus be pirates—or die trying.

Alice knew that Her Majesty's government had managed to secretly get hold of the incantation once, and had set up a committee to study it. Twenty years later, Parliament had tired of waiting and demanded results—only to discover that the committee had lost the incantation eighteen years ago and had spent the rest of the time discussing cricket over tea and scones. A.U.N.T. was aware of this because their agents had been the tea ladies.

Still pirates flew the black flag, although they did not need to. To them it was a matter of pride—much in the same way ferocious, man-eating lions had pride.

Alice supposed the house was headed for the Starkthorn Castle house party. "F-f-fabulous," she said aloud, her teeth chattering from cold. Angling down toward the warm golden light shining through its windows, she landed atop a white wrought-iron fence surrounding a balcony. Her petticoat deflated, and, before she could unbalance, she jumped down to the balcony floor.

Doing her best to smooth her sodden, wrinkled petticoat, she then straightened the sleeves of her velveteen bodice and tried without success to squeeze all the water from her sagging hat feathers. Her pompadour, which had taken an hour to establish, drooped in an as-yet-unfashionable manner, but without a looking glass, she dared not even touch it. Finally, as presentable as she was likely to get after falling hundreds of feet through a storm, she stepped forward to knock on the balcony's door.

Through a delicate lace curtain she could see shadowed figures clustered around a hearth fire. One approached and opened the door. It proved to be a stout, middle-aged woman in the mobcap and plain black dress of a housemaid. An enormous fluffy yellow feather swooped out from the top of the mobcap.

"Yes?" she said. "How may I help you?"

"I happened to be passing," Alice said, "and wondered if I m-m-might presume upon your hospitality? It is d-d-dreadfully cold out here."

The housemaid glanced back over her shoulder. "There's a girl as wants to come in," she informed the room's occupants. A murmuring came from over by the hearth fire. Turning once more to Alice, the housemaid nodded. "You may enter. Wipe your feet."

She stepped aside, opening the door wider and blinking against the damp chill of the wind. Alice brushed her shoes against the sodden doormat to no effect, then squelched in.

She found herself facing a bewildering cram of knickknacks and furniture, somewhere amongst which were theoretically four walls and a floor. Beside the hearth fire sat a finely dressed couple drinking tea and reading. The gentleman, gray-haired and with a face like a hatchet that has been struck repeatedly by another hatchet, looked up vaguely, but the woman continued perusing her novel. In one glance Alice added together precise ringlets, onyx earrings, and two shawls draped around a black bombazine dress, reaching a dire conclusion.

"Miss Darlington," she said.

"Hm?" The woman raised her head as if only now noticing Alice's arrival. "Oh, hello there. Competence, close the door, we are about to perish from eczema."

Competence did as ordered, and Alice blinked as the latch clicked into place with the same sound a bone makes when it snaps. Her teeth began to chatter even more violently. Of all the flying houses in England, she had fallen into the worst. Miss Darlington and her husband, Jake Jacobsen, scrutinized her in a silence that felt honed and polished on account of having pierced countless people before encountering her. Only by dint of two decades' ruthless training did she manage to neither blush nor lower her chin nor run screaming out the balcony door.

"What is your name?" Miss Darlington asked.

"M-M-Mrs. Alice B-Blakeney, ma'am." She considered curtsying but did not think her frozen knees would support the endeavor.

"Do you like black tea or green, Mrs. Blakeney?"

This had to be a trick question. No reasonable person would consider there to be any real choice, and the only dilemma was exactly how unreasonable a pirate was expected to be. "Black," she said and held her breath, waiting to see if Miss Darlington would throw her back out the door because of it. (Mind you, plummeting to earth was preferable to drinking green tea.)

But Miss Darlington nodded with approval. "Competence, a fresh teapot, if you please. And some digestive biscuits." She flicked a glance at the floor beneath Alice's feet. "And towels."

As Competence bustled from the room, feather swaying, Miss

Darlington returned to her inspection of Alice's shivering form. "I do declare, the fashions of young ladies today leave much to be desired. Why aren't you wearing gloves? Or a scarf and shawl? This late in autumn one must be on guard against sudden breezes."

Alice glanced out the window, where the breezes were currently not so much sudden as squalling furiously. Yet Darlington House slid through them without the merest tremble.

"I was indoors until a moment ago," she explained. The warmth of the room was beginning to seep into her body and she felt less in danger of breaking her teeth from clattering them together—although more in danger of various other body parts being broken by pirates. Miss Darlington's mouth was tightening; Jake Jacobsen had closed his book without even marking the page. Alice nervously advanced a placating compliment: "May I congratulate your pilot on their skill?"

"Pilot?" Miss Darlington's eyebrows swooped up like cutlasses. "Who says we have a pilot, as if we are pirates? Why would you make such an accusation, young lady?"

"Er, because we are currently several hundred feet above the ground? And because a black pirate flag flies from your roof? And furthermore I recognize that Gainsborough portrait over your mantel, which I last saw when visiting the London Art Gallery."

"They gifted it to me," Miss Darlington said. Her husband cleared his throat, and she shot him a look so supercilious it should have been outfitted with a crown and scepter. "They *would have* gifted it to me had they known I admired it," she amended. "Therefore I saved them the effort. Besides, Fanny Andrews, therein portrayed, was a pirate, so the painting is rightfully mine."

Alice did not even try to unravel this logic. "I myself am a pirate," she said, shaking back her hat feathers. "Newly returned to England after an unfortunate sojourn in Amsterdam. Unfortunate, that is, for the people I robbed, ha ha."

There came a decided lack of ha ha–ing from her audience. Alice's insides spun. Twenty-four years, most of them spent in espionage training, and she'd still not learned how dialogue worked. Really, Mrs. Kew should have assigned her to be a maid so she need not speak with anyone.

She hastily reviewed the Three Primary Rules for Normal Conversation as drilled into her by long-suffering tutors at the Academy. Hold eye contact for five seconds, blink, glance away, repeat. . . . Do not speak until the other person has finished talking. . . . Do not fidget or climb on the furniture while listening. Thus mentally refreshed, she tried again.

"My husband and I are traveling to a house party in Hampshire."

"Starkthorn Castle?" Jake asked.

"Yes."

"We are attending the same party," he said, giving her a smile that was clearly intended to be disarming, but which just made him look like a murderer planning to literally remove her arms. "Miss Darlington is the host's great-aunt."

"Indeed?" Alice inquired—although in fact she could have recited Miss Darlington's family connections back six generations. The lady was related to several villains, each of whose A.U.N.T. dossiers could have filled a bathtub, should someone inexplicably wish to store them there. Her former ward, Cecilia Bassingthwaite, tried to assassinate the Queen, stole an invaluable amulet from the British Museum, and was seen flying a bicycle over London. Cecilia's husband, Ned, was infamous for his meltingly gorgeous smile, one glance at which would persuade even the most sensible lady to remove her drawers (her cabinet drawers that is, to submit the valuables stored therein; Ned had surrendered his libertine ways upon marriage). And Darlington's niece, Cecilia's mother, had been known as the Queen of Pirates. They were a wicked lot, and Jemima Darlington the wickedest of all.

"Pudding!" the lady declared.

Her husband and Alice stared at her blankly.

"Pudding," she repeated, as if this made all clear. "I forgot to have Competence bring some chocolate cream pudding. Bother."

At that moment, Competence entered, bearing a tray of tea, biscuits, and pudding. Alice eyed her with interest. With perspicacity like that, could she be an A.U.N.T. agent? Or did Miss Darlington often desire pudding at midmorning?

Setting down the tray, Competence brought out several thick white towels that had been tucked under her arm and handed them to Alice.

"Thank you, I am glad for any server in a port," Alice murmured, which was code for *Are you a representative of the agency that is the true effective (albeit highly secret) government of England and has licensed me to kill you if these towels are not what they seem, or are you just a regular housemaid?*

"Hm," said Competence in a brusque tone before turning on a heel and marching away—which either answered that or completely did not.

While tea was poured and biscuits dunked into pudding, Alice dried herself as best she could. At last, Miss Darlington motioned for her to take a seat by the fire.

"Where is your husband, Mrs. Blakeney?" she asked as Alice laid a towel on an armchair and lowered herself gingerly, wincing a little as her wet clothes clung to her skin. "Not loitering on the balcony, I hope?"

"N—"

"Not *unwell?*"

"N—"

"Good God, Jake, she's brought illness into the house!"

"Dear, I'm sure that's not the case," Jake murmured soothingly. "She seems perfectly healthy to me."

Alice tried to quell the remnants of her shivering, lest Miss Darlington conclude she had malaria. "The last I saw Mr. Blakeney, he was flying west with a glasshouse in pursuit," she explained. "I imagine we'll catch up at Starkthorn Castle."

"That's very bold of you!" Miss Darlington said.

Alice blinked. She was starting to realize no one had taught this woman the Three Primary Rules for Normal Conversation, let alone the several dozen secondary ones. For the first time in her life she seemed to be playing on an even discussion field—that is, a field full of potholes, prickles, and discarded rakes just waiting to be stepped on so they could fly up and smash someone in the face.

"Your house might have been shot down, after all," Miss Darlington continued. "Struck by lightning. Exploded. Your husband's body might have been flung into treetops, every bone shattered—or perhaps a bottomless lake, from whence he will never be recovered."

Alice considered this. "True. The bottomless lake would be most convenient—no funeral costs."

Miss Darlington regarded her for a long, cool moment, then smiled and passed her a dainty, wisteria-painted teacup. "I have not added any sugar. Terrible stuff, quite rots one's gluteus maximus."

"I think you mean teeth, dear," Jake murmured.

Miss Darlington lifted her chin in much the same way another person might lift their battle-axe. "I have no teeth in my gluteus maximus," she declared, and it was all Alice could do to retain her mouthful of tea. Miss Darlington gave her a sharp look.

"I can plainly see who you are, young lady!"

Alice swallowed the tea and set the cup onto its saucer without the slightest tremble. *Eight steps to the balcony door*, she thought calmly. *It will be locked, so kick it open and climb onto the fencing, and then up to the roof if you can. Or jump, and hope the petticoat's incantation will work a second time.* "Oh yes?" she said in a neutral voice.

"If I asked you about ravens and writing desks, what would you answer?"

"I would say a raven should not be allowed anywhere near a writing desk. Think of the mess it would make. Not to mention the germs."

She returned Miss Darlington's bright gaze without blinking.

Jake held his breath. Competence, standing by the hallway door, held her breath. Even the sky outside seemed to hold its breath, the storm winds suddenly dying away. Alice watched firelight and shadow writhe over the pirate lady's face. *I'll never make it to the balcony*, she realized. *I'll be dead before I even get out of the chair.*

Abruptly, Miss Darlington laughed. "Clever girl." She waggled a crooked, bejeweled finger at Alice. "I was right, you are a scoundrel, no doubt about it. I wager you could talk the Queen herself into letting you steal her necklace."

"The Queen, you say?" Alice's instincts perked up.

"Yes, she is a close personal nemesis of mine, and I happen to know her neck—that is, her necklace—is ripe for the plucking if a girl has the moxie to try it. You certainly display moxie."

Alice had no idea what moxie was. (Some kind of hairstyle perhaps? She excitedly anticipated consulting a dictionary later.) Nevertheless, she shifted her mouth into a mild smile, even while her mind hastily took out its list of suspects and circled Miss Darlington's name, then drew stars and arrows around it. "How kind," she said.

"In fact, you remind me a little of my niece, Cecilia. Such a dear young lass. Sweet temperament, beautiful manners, can kill a man with one swipe of a butter knife. You would like her, I'm sure. I tried to convince her to join us at the Bassingthwaite party, but she is currently—"

The lady paused to reach over and retrieve a piece of paper on the tea table. Raising a lorgnette that had been hanging on a gold chain about her neck, she read from the sheet.

"—in Windsor, making preparations to steal Princess Beatrice's diamond tiara . . . had luncheon at the Singing Wattlebird teahouse on Tuesday, wore a suitably warm jacket, ordered tea and cream cake . . . was seen pushing an infant's perambulator through the park on Wednesday with her husband at her side but no regard for the twenty-five percent chance of rain showers . . ."

"Dear," Jake murmured, easing the paper from his wife's hand. "I am sure Mrs. Blakeney has no interest in the minute particulars of Cecilia's life. And nor should you, really."

"Well I never!" Miss Darlington huffed. "Is an aunty not allowed to care?"

"Care, yes," Jake said, smiling. "Employ a private detective to stalk her niece's every movement and report back to you, not so much."

"But I haven't seen her or the baby for ages!"

"Cecilia brought Evangeline to visit us five days ago. And we met Ned in the street after that bank heist last Friday."

"Ned," she spat in such a mother-in-law tone that Alice rather feared for said gentleman's well-being. It seemed evident Jemima Darlington was the one woman Ned Lightbourne could not charm with his smile.

Suddenly the house shuddered as if expressing Miss Darlington's antipathy toward the man who had stolen her niece for the nefarious purpose of a happy married life. Teacups rattled; the hearth fire sparked.

"We're here, ma'am," Competence announced.

Glancing out the window, Alice saw that they had indeed landed. The world outside was green and gold, shimmering with a lingering residue of rain.

Miss Darlington sighed. "I suppose this means we have to go say hello to that pompous Bassingthwaite boy. How tedious. And Gertrude Rotunder is bound to be there—insufferable woman, I will never forgive her for stealing back her diamond bracelet. It took me three weeks to set up that theft, and she just waltzes in and takes it back overnight! Some people have no shame. Just whose idea was it to attend this party anyway?"

"Yours, dear," Jake said.

"What on earth was I thinking?"

"About the twenty-four-carat-gold vase from the Ming dynasty that stands in the Bassingthwaite library."

The lady's expression cleared. "Ah yes. It's going to fill that gap in the corner just perfectly." She indicated an area of the room Alice could not see due to the clutter of at least half a dozen golden vases. "Bring my coat and hat, Competence."

"Yes, ma'am." The maid turned to leave.

"And Mr. Jacobsen's coat and hat."

"Yes, ma'am." She took a step.

"And gloves, scarves, galoshes, muffs, and an umbrella in case the rain returns."

"Yes, ma'am." Pausing, one foot tilted slightly off the ground, she waited.

"Also bring a coat for our guest. One of those I keep for when Cecilia visits."

"Yes, ma'am." She hurried off.

"I'm sure you're anxious to catch up with your husband," Jake said pleasantly to Alice as they finished their tea.

"Not at all, sir," Alice replied. "I am happily married, and my husband is very kind to me."

"Er . . . I mean, anxious about being separated from him."

"Oh no, he is Catholic and does not believe in divorce. I must say, this tea is excellent quality. May I inquire as to the brand?"

Jake frowned slightly in bemusement. "Earl Grey. But do you not fear—?"

"Leave her alone," Miss Darlington intervened. "The poor girl is no doubt in shock at the thought her husband may have crashed their house and even now may be dying as all around him the walls burn."

"I hope that is not the case," Alice said fervently. "I have several rare books inside that house."

She closed her eyes as she savored another mouthful of tea, thereby missing the fact that she became the first person ever to truly shock Jemima Darlington.

✸ 6 ✸

CRASH LANDINGS—IN THE PARKING LOT—AN ALARMING INVENTION—
MR. AND MRS. BLAKENEY ARE ROMANTIC—
DANIEL FACES TEMPTATION—AN EFFLUSIVE WELCOME—
BADLY DONE INDEED

Whatever pirates' souls are made out of, theirs and their houses' are the same. This notion explained why the Bassingthwaite clan, generally considered to be piratic royalty (i.e., pompous, boring, and good candidates for beheading), possessed a premises so grand, so unwieldy, that it took four people incantating in chorus just to get it off the ground. In other words, their souls were, in their opinion, "the most exalted object we are capable of conceiving"—and in everyone else's, just bloody difficult to manage. In any case, Starkthorn Castle was the greatest man-o'-war in England.

Although its pink frilly curtains did rather ruin the effect.

The castle stood astride a leafy Hampshire meadow like a warrior-king who had decided this would be the perfect spot for a picnic. Its granite body, crenelated along the upper edge, bristling with chimneys and cannons, seemed to have been dropped into the lush countryside without aforethought or aesthetic consideration. Partly this impression was due to its bleak appearance, and partly because it had crushed two trees and a fence on landing.

Alice felt claustrophobic just looking at it. She tapped her fingers together in the pocket of the green velvet coat Miss Darlington had insisted she wear. The building itself was not the problem, but the thought of having to exchange polite, cheerful greetings with its owner. She'd rather wrestle an alligator.

Although considering she was about to join a pirates' party, she might ultimately have to do both.

Miss Darlington's house had landed about five hundred feet from the castle in order that the lady and her husband could enjoy a holiday away from home and still be within running distance of that home if there was a problem (such as being caught with the Ming vase in their hands). Several other houses were already parked there, including the conservatory that had attacked them. Slightly to one side stood the A.U.N.T. cottage—although to use the word *stood* was rather excessive. In fact, the cottage hunched. It drooped. It had all the structural integrity of a free verse poem in a popular magazine. No doubt Daniel would face hours of insurance paperwork upon his return to headquarters.

Alice would have pitied him were it not for the fact that doing so might lead to suggestions of her helping with said paperwork.

Daniel himself was leaning against the doorframe, arms and ankles crossed, as he watched Dr. Snodgrass screw something into the wall of the cottage. Everything about him seemed just as it should be: shirt neatly buttoned up; tie straight; hair tidy; body unbroken and strong, so strong, he could probably lift her with no effort, pinning her against—

Which is to say, Alice thought, throwing a stern frown at her imagination, he was thankfully unharmed. Not that she had worried for his safety. She'd merely disliked being unable to confirm his status, for the sake of the mission. And that was why, seeing him now, her heart danced (a mazurka—at double tempo—with her nerves shouting *hey!* at every beat). Because of the mission.

He looked up as she approached. "Ah, there you are," he said mildly.

"What is Dr. Snodgrass doing?" Alice asked in a wary voice. "And do I really want to know?"

"This is an anti-theft device!" Snodgrass himself answered, turning to gesture excitedly with his screwdriver. Alice took a step back in case it exploded. "The small black box has been embedded with anchoring phrases from the incantation. All I have to do is press this button and—"

Eeeeee-ooooooo-eeeeee-ooooooo!

Alice and Daniel clasped hands over their ears at the sudden high-pitched scream emanating from the device. Frantic, Snodgrass smacked the button repeatedly, without success. Smoke began to gush from the box. The cottage shook. In the houses all around, faces appeared at windows, presumably shouting, although it was impossible to hear beyond the alarm.

At last, Snodgrass managed to restore silence. As the smoke dissipated and the air seemed to hold its breath, waiting for the cottage to collapse entirely from shock, Alice dared to lower her hands.

"Fiddlesticks," she said, the word hissing at its end much like the fuse of a bomb hisses when lit. "Fiddlesticks. F-f-f—"

Daniel took hold of her, firmly clamping her arms, his expression impeccably sober. "Miss Dearlove," he said in a voice as firm as his grip. "Willows whiten, aspens quiver."

The shuddering of Alice's senses was immediately diverted, easing into the course of Tennyson's rhyme. "Willows whiten, aspens quiver," she said.

"Little breezes dusk and shiver," Daniel continued.

"Thro' the wave that runs for ever."

His expression softened; he released his grip. "By the island in the river."

Alice resisted the urge to rub the tingling warmth in her arms where he had grasped her. "Flowing down to Camelot."

Breath calmed, tossing back its metaphorical hair and brushing the wrinkles from its surface as if the momentary panic had been intentional, thank you—merely a test of the system. Her constitution reasserted itself without even one tap of a finger.

Behind them, Snodgrass tittered. "I say, say what?"

The agents ignored him. Daniel reached out to touch Alice's hat. "Your butterfly is wingless," he said softly.

And just like that her pulse shook again. She swallowed, and Daniel withdrew his hand. They both looked away into the middle distance.

"All right?" he asked.

"All right," Alice confirmed, and he smiled briefly, efficiently. As his expression shut down again like a library catalog card slotting back into place, Alice felt her heart give a dreamy sigh . . .

But her brain strode forth to stop that nonsense at once. It snapped out a ruler and pointed to the fact that not only had Daniel recognized her sensory crisis, he'd known the exact Tennyson poem guaranteed to settle her—the one Academy tutors had used for that same purpose when she was growing up. This suggested only one conclusion.

He had gathered a data file on her.

Alice's heart gasped. The nerve of the man! She would have to punish him for such a breach of privacy! No doubt there was something in the data file she had gathered on him that would suggest a suitable penalty.

She narrowed her eyes to stare at him as if she might be able to discern the truth from his eyelashes and cheekbones and the perfect curve of his lips that must fit just right against a woman's mouth—but even as she hastily looked away again, blushing, he himself turned with flashing eyes to glare at Snodgrass.

The scientist flinched. "Sorry. That was rather unexpected, what? But I say, no one will want to steal the house now."

"No one would want to steal it in the first place!" Daniel countered with uncharacteristic anger. "It's a wreck. We'll be taking the train back to London."

"Oh, jolly good! I love a train ride."

The anger in Daniel's mood cooled abruptly, hardening to ice. "Doctor, no. When I said 'we,' I meant the lady and I. Perhaps you can—I don't know—invent a wheeled plank of wood to transport you back, or some such."

Snodgrass caught his breath—but not in offense, Alice realized. He reached into his jacket pocket for a notepad and pencil and began writing furiously. She heard him murmur, "A board to skate across the ground . . ."

Daniel's hand clenched. Turning away from the scientist, he caught Alice's gaze unintentionally, and she blinked at the cold wrath in his eyes. But almost instantly expression faded from his countenance, leaving him inscrutable once more. She sensed Snodgrass had narrowly averted assassination for the third time that day.

"Do not worry, Miss Dearlove," Daniel said, leaning a little closer so only she could hear him. "I am but mad north-northwest."

Her heart swooned at the line from Shakespeare. "That's fine," she replied in the same conversational tone. "I'm sure there is method in it."

He grinned, dazzling her with sudden beauty, and her heart promptly fell back in a swoon. Alice tried to haul it up again. This simply would not do! Feeling attracted to one's husband was entirely—

"Scandalous!" supplied an appalled voice. Alice turned, instinctively reaching for a gun that was no longer in her skirt—or that in fact was, albeit several miles away.

Miss Darlington approached. She was applying a walking cane to the ground with one hand while her other rested on the arm of a woman wearing a dress more ruffled than the feelings of a Romantic poet. Two steps behind them came their husbands, laden with suitcases. The ladies critiqued each house as they walked.

"What was Olivia thinking, painting her door that color?"

"Good heavens, look at those hideous curtains in Miss Dole's windows!"

"Does she call those spikes? Why, they are not even bloodstained."

"And here is Mrs. Blakeney from Amsterdam," Miss Darlington said upon arriving at the A.U.N.T. cottage. She gestured as though Alice were a vaguely interesting specimen in a zoo. "Charming girl, rather odd sense of fashion. Mrs. Blakeney, have you met my dear friend Gertrude Rotunder?"

The insufferable woman with no shame? Alice wanted to reply, but worried this might be somewhat inappropriate. Besides, she had indeed met Mrs. Rotunder while on assignment in Clacton-on-Sea last year, and was now keen to make the most commonplace impression possible.

"How do you do?" she said, nodding.

"I know you!" Mrs. Rotunder snapped her fingers and pointed at Alice, who very carefully raised her eyebrows in mild inquiry. From the corner of her eye she saw Daniel shift his hand toward the pocket inside his coat where he kept his gun.

"I noticed you fall out of your cottage during our playful skirmish. Such fun! We should do it again soon."

"Er, yes," Alice said.

"You took some good shots. Luckily I didn't bring my actual house with me, or else imagine the state of my carpets right now!"

(*"Our* house," Mr. Rotunder murmured, but no one paid him any attention.)

"Is this your husband?" Miss Darlington asked, perusing Daniel with a cool eye. "He appears to be free of disease, at least. How ecstatic he must have been to see you safe and sound."

"Indeed," Daniel said, reaching out awkwardly to pat Alice's arm. She tried not to flinch at the light touch. "I'm glad she survived her fall."

"Petticoat," Alice told him, and he nodded.

"Petticoat?" Miss Darlington repeated confusedly.

"It is a term of endearment," Alice said, thinking fast. "In Amsterdam a wife will commonly refer to her husband as 'my petticoat.'"

"Oh?" the pirates inquired politely.

"He in turn calls me his jockstrap."

Daniel choked on his breath. The pirates' husbands glanced wide-eyed at each other. Even Dr. Snodgrass covered his face with his hands.

"I see," Mrs. Darlington replied.

"How long have you been married?" Mrs. Rotunder asked.

"Three years," Alice replied.

"Three months," Daniel said at the same time.

They frowned with bemusement at each other.

"Are you sure?" Daniel said.

"Of course I'm sure," Alice told him, affronted. "It is written clearly in the—" She stopped, recollecting their audience, who were watching with fascination. "Er, in the wedding album. Three years this coming January."

"Oh yes. It only feels like three months due to the profusion of romance."

"A veritable excess of romance," Alice agreed. Daniel reached out to pat her arm again and she sidestepped before he could do so.

Miss Darlington's mouth twitched. "Well, goodness. I suspect this will be an intriguing week after all. No doubt we will spy some charming interludes and uncover many secrets of our hearts. Coming, Gertrude?"

With a parting nod, the pirate ladies proceeded together across the grass toward Starkthorn Manor, trailed by their husbands.

Alice shook back her ruined hat feathers. "Well," she declared, "that was a success."

"Hm," Daniel said, frowning.

"You doubt it?"

"I doubt we will be alive by the end of the day."

"Nonsense. I survived chatting with Miss Darlington in her sitting room. You kept Mrs. Rotunder from completely destroying our house. And it took no effort whatsoever to convince them we are a happily married pirate couple. I am entirely confident all shall be just fine."

Never had things been worse.

Daniel stood in the grand entrance hall of Starkthorn Castle, surrounded by pirates, and drew upon all his training as a secret agent in order to remain calm. His spectacles fogged with the effort of breathing regularly. Every instinct in him ached to retrieve both guns from inside his coat and fire until all their bullets were spent—a move that would see him dead within seconds.

Mind you, death might be preferable to spending one moment more listening to Frederick Bassingthwaite speak.

". . . And so with all my warm, palpitating heart I welcome you, Aunt Darlington, Mrs. Rotunder, Mrs. Blakeney, and associated gentlemen. Long have I yearned to see your dear and handsome visages, and I beg you find comfort in this my most humble and unworthy abode, from which the scions of Bassingthwaite have . . ."

At Daniel's side, Alice leaned close to whisper, "Do you think we can just blow the whole place up and be done with it?"

Daniel considered this suggestion. A few sticks of dynamite beneath the Corinthian columns and—

Wait. She was probably not serious.

Thud!

He jolted out of his thoughts to see a dagger reverberating in a portrait of Black Beryl that hung on the wall directly behind Frederick.

"Sorry," Mrs. Rotunder sang out. "My hand slipped."

Frederick's face had turned as white as the pearl handle of the dagger, but he nevertheless managed to trill a laugh. "Dear lady, allow me to declare there is no—"

"No need to apologize," interjected his wife. She smiled with such determination Daniel feared she would do an injury to her facial muscles. Marriage to Frederick would strain anyone, but Jane Fairweather seemed so tense she probably needed no weapon to assassinate the Queen—one curtsy and she might just explode. "The rest of the party are partaking of tea in the Orange Drawing Room," she said. "You are welcome to join us, or the servants will escort you to your rooms for a rest first. I know travel can be wearisome for the agèd."

Silence sharper than any dagger followed this statement. Daniel and Alice glanced nervously at each other.

But Miss Darlington only laughed. "I see marriage has improved you, Jane. That was almost nasty. Well done, dear!"

Jane nodded in receipt of the compliment. "But is dear Cecilia not with you, Miss Darlington? I am looking forward to seeing my darling chum!"

"She sends her regrets," Miss Darlington said.

"How disappointing," Jane murmured. Daniel regarded her thoughtfully, for her facial expression did not seem to quite match the words. He tried to compare its various microfeatures to those on his internal checklist of A Disappointed Countenance Type One: Female, but before he could begin, Jane was already smiling. "Well, I am glad you at least are here."

Miss Darlington frowned as she scanned this for insult. "I feel quite parched," she replied, as if the state of her throat was Jane's personal fault. "Come along, Mr. Darlington."

Behind her, Jake Jacobsen rolled his eyes fondly. Miss Darlington laid her hand in a queenly manner upon his offered arm, and they began to cross the hall toward a distant sound of laughter. Mrs. Rotunder and her husband hurried after them before Frederick could speak again, and Daniel began to follow.

"*Ahem.*"

Glancing back at the pointed sound, he realized he had forgotten his wife. She looked at him with a placid expression, but her eyes conveyed an urgent speech, complete with diagrams and flowcharts.

"I was thinking, Mr. Blakeney, that we might visit our room before meeting the company," she said aloud.

"But, Mrs. Blakeney," he replied, "we do not want to appear unfriendly."

"We also don't want to make a poor first impression, Mr. Blakeney," Alice countered. "And I would like to point out that I am not exactly dressed for tea."

"Oh?" As far as Daniel could see, she was thoroughly covered— although he did vaguely recollect that her skirt had been a different color before she exited the cottage. "Well then, you go off and get changed while I join the rest of the company."

This sensible suggestion was met with audible inhalations from Frederick, Jane, Snodgrass, and whoever was spying on the company behind a portrait of Sir Francis Drake.

Alice herself merely blinked at him.

Daniel winced. "I beg your pardon. Allow me to escort you upstairs."

(No one could ever fault him for being a slow learner.)

Alice smiled nicely. The witnesses exhaled. Daniel offered her his arm, she refused it, and they ascended the stairs, trailed by suitcase-lugging servants.

"That was badly done, Mr. Blakeney," Alice whispered as they followed a housemaid along a lamplit corridor. She did not look at him, but he felt her attention poking his heart. "It is not pleasant for you to hear, I'm sure, although it is pleasant for me that I must tell you: *badly done.*"

"Oh?" he said, his own eyes focused straight ahead.

"You argued with me. It was inappropriate. Married couples never argue."

"Are you sure about that?"

"Of course I am sure," Alice retorted. "The wife is always right."

She marched ahead of him down the corridor, and suddenly Daniel began to feel very married indeed.

❋ 7 ❋

THE USUAL NUMBER OF BEDS—TERRIBLE TOILETRIES—
THE PLAN COMES TOGETHER—THINGS HEAT UP—THE RULES OF
LOVE—FUN AND GAMES—THEY ARE PUT TO THE TEST

It is a truth universally acknowledged that a man and woman in possession of a false marriage license must be in want of separate beds. Unfortunately, when Daniel and Alice entered their suite in Starkthorn Manor, they found only one—which quite frankly would not have come as a surprise had they read more exciting literature than was their habit. They eyed it disconcertedly as the housemaid went about lighting lamps and prodding the hearth fire.

"I will take the sofa," Daniel said, removing his coat as if he was about to go to sleep that very moment.

"I would not ask you to do so," Alice said.

"I don't mind."

"No, I mean it's a bad idea. What if someone came in and saw you? It would not lend an impression of our being happily married."

"Miss Dearlove is right, sir," the maid interjected. Her name was Veronica Vale, and after sending away the footmen she had explained her designation was V-2: an A.U.N.T. agent fresh out of training and excited to work with her two greatest role models oh my goodness such luck at this early stage of her career and would they be so very kind as to autograph her duster?! Even when they had just stared in cool, wordless reply, her eyes never ceased shining with admiration. "I'm afraid, sir, that any chambermaid could walk in willy-nilly. Servants in a fine house like this never knock."

"Hm," Daniel said, unconvinced.

"We are professionals," Alice reminded him. "It will be fine. Just wear clothing and keep to your side—the left side, if you please—and don't eat biscuits in bed or take possession of all the pillows, and sleep on your stomach so as to prevent snoring, also kindly refrain from wearing cologne, and—"

"You certainly sound married, Miss Dearlove," Veronica remarked with a chuckle.

"Mrs. Blakeney," Daniel corrected her sternly.

Veronica flushed. "I beg your pardon, sir. It slipped my mind, what with you both being such stars. A and B, I still can't believe it!" She clutched her hands together against her heart. "Did you really shoot each other in Clacton last year?"

"No," they said.

"Oh. But did you kill three robbers this week in St. James using nothing but your hats?"

"No."

"I see." Her shoulders sagged.

"Well, that's done," Snodgrass said, emerging from the washroom. Although he looked as distracted as he had when flying through the storm, Alice was beginning to realize this was his resting scientist face. "I've installed an emergency toothbrush."

"Thank you," Alice said, "but there was no need, I brought my own spares."

"As did I," Daniel said.

"I meant in case you need to shoot someone with poisoned darts, what? Just be careful not to actually use it as a toothbrush, or you'll have a jolly nasty toothache. I say, ha ha!"

"Ha ha!" Veronica echoed.

"Hm," Daniel said. With a frown, he brought forth a map from his suitcase and unfolded it across the bed.

"This is the layout of Starkthorn Castle," he said as the others gathered around. "We are here." He indicated a small square that represented their bedroom. "We'll mark the likely places for a weapon to be secured, then organize a grid-based plan for searching. Dr. Snodgrass, do you have a pen?"

"You wish to blow something up?" the scientist asked.

Daniel stared blankly at him for a moment, then turned to Alice. "Miss Dearlove, do you happen to have a pen?"

Alice produced the required implement, and from there rooms and passageways were marked, arrows drawn, and numbers allocated to various squares, in consultation with Veronica, who had spent the past week scouting out the castle (and dusting it). A plan was devised and memorized.

"We will begin with the obvious," Daniel said. "Jane Fairweather's private sitting room." He tapped the pen briskly against a square numbered "one."

"Caref—" was all Snodgrass had time to say before the paper burst alight with blue flame. Veronica screamed, Alice sighed, and Daniel grabbed a pillow, pressing it over the fire while Snodgrass explained that the map had been incantated to self-destruct upon being tapped.

"It's really quite fascinating," he said, flipping back one corner of the paper. "If you just look here you will see the Latin written onto the—"

"Get out," Daniel said in a voice so cold it would have extinguished the fire had the pillow not already done so.

"Say what?"

Daniel pointed at the door. "Get. Out. Both of you, please. If you need to report—"

"We can telephone you," the scientist said. "Agent A has been equipped with a portable receiver in her shoe for just such an occasion."

"You mean this shoe?" Alice lifted her right foot and the sodden slipper thereon. It sparked slightly, and a rather forlorn buzzing sound stuttered from the heel. "Well, that explains it. I thought I had pins and needles in my foot."

"Oh, I say." Snodgrass drooped.

"You can just come find us," Daniel said, folding the map with disconcerting precision.

"But I have another device which—"

"Best to leave now," Alice said before Daniel grew so calm someone got injured. She hustled Snodgrass and Veronica from the room and shut the door behind them. Behind her, Daniel made no sound, but she could feel his anger clench the atmosphere.

"There have been far too many people for one day," she said.

"Hm," he agreed. He turned to unpacking, and Alice walked over to the fireplace to dry herself. She stood vaguely staring at the pale blue-and-white chintz wallpaper as her clothing warmed. The flames' crackling made her tap her fingers now and again, but she felt gradually soothed by rain pattering against the ~~escape route~~ window, and small noises Daniel made as he transferred clothes from his bag into the ~~potential barricade~~ chest of drawers. The morning's disturbances faded, and for a moment she remembered falling through the storm, unrestrained and truly peaceful for the first time in months.

If only she could tumble from a flying house every day, life would be much improved. She sighed at the thought of it.

Suddenly a shadow shifted over her face. Alice blinked out of reverie to find Daniel standing before her. She gazed up at him, still half-lost in the sense of falling, and he took hold of her upper arms as if to catch her. The pale murmur became a roar.

"You're so hot," he said, his eyes shadowy behind the firelit surfaces of his spectacles, his voice dark with a lingering residue of piratic magic.

"Um," she replied dazedly.

"You're smoking."

"Er . . ."

"Literally, Miss Dearlove. Your petticoat is catching alight."

"Oh!" Glancing down, Alice saw steam arising from her damp petticoat. The hem, embroidered with *descendeo lente* from the flight incantation, was beginning to spark.

"You're standing too close to the fire," Daniel said, drawing her away. He began divesting her of her velveteen coat as Alice fumbled urgently with the ties of her petticoat. Their hands tangled; their breath mingled; Alice almost felt like her heart was beating with his energy. Within seconds, she was stripped of all but chemise, drawers, corset, bustle pad, stockings, shoes, and hat. Strands of hair tumbled down her neck. Daniel's breath tumbled out of him. Although the threat of combustion had been thwarted, Alice almost thought she heard the air between them crackle and spark. She crossed her arms defensively over the thin lawn of her chemise. Daniel turned away, shoving a hand through his hair.

"I'll just—er, that is, you—I'll—you get dressed and I'll be over here checking for bugs," he said.

"Very well," Alice agreed, sidling over to her duffel bag. "Excellent plan. I'll—you—er, don't turn around."

"I won't," he said most assuredly.

She withdrew a small handful of purple and green silk from the bag and shook it so that voluminous layers of beribboned, braid-trimmed, and lace-bristling skirts unfurled with a *thwomp*. Alice grimaced at the sight of them. In such a gown she was going to look hideous enough to be piratically fashionable, but she might need a headache tonic to bear it. With eyes half-closed, she removed her hat, shook out her still-damp hair, and dressed as fast as all the requisite layers allowed. Retrieving her spare gun from the bag, she checked its ammunition load, then tucked it into a secret pocket. At last, she turned back to the room . . .

And her eyes opened so wide she strained a facial muscle.

Daniel was leaning over the vanity table in a manner that had salacious consequences for the trouser fabric across his posterior. Alice could not help but stare. The memory of Miss Darlington declaring there were no teeth in her gluteus maximus arose piratically, accompanied by a vision in which Alice applied her own teeth to the firm globe of Mr. Bixby's similar muscle. She immediately shut her mouth—and then realized it had been hanging open, and that she had been perilously close to drooling.

Drooling. Like a *hooligan*.

Fiddlesticks! Much more time spent in the company of this man and she'd end up casting off her tranquil layers to run amok, breaking windows and tearing out the pages of books. Agent B did things to her nerves that she could not comprehend. Clearly, he was dangerous—an assassin with a highly trained body, a mind like a loaded gun, a smile capable of destroying any common sense, and did she mention his body? Alice began to suspect his pajama party with Princess Louise involved more interesting activities than drinking cocoa and telling ghost stories.

"*Ahem. Ahem.*" She cleared her throat urgently, and Daniel straightened, glancing over his shoulder.

"All dressed, then?" he asked with complete ignorance of the wickedness rampaging behind her serene expression.

"All dressed," she managed to say.

"I'll just finish here, then we should go downstairs."

He turned to inspect a clock. Firelight caught on his earring, making it flash like a flirtatious wink.

"*Ahem! Ahem!*" Alice rubbed her throat, the interior of which had now been so thoroughly cleared it was beginning to ache. "Indeed. Yes. Good. Downstairs. Indeed."

Daniel frowned a little as he regarded her. "Are you quite well, Miss Dearlove?"

"Entirely well!" She gathered up her hair and began winding it into a tight knot. Daniel watched. He seemed tired, Alice thought—his eyes dark, his jaw twitching, as he followed her movements like one mesmerized. She brushed a hand along the side of her bare neck to catch a loose strand, and he jolted. "*Ahem,*" he said, and turned away to inspect the clock again.

"You really think the room will be bugged?" Alice asked.

"One can never be too careful." He lifted a lamp to look under it, then twitched aside a velvet drape. "These old houses are often riddled with cockroaches or spiders."

Alice shuddered. Thus far today she had been shot at by a pirate's battle-conservatory, fallen through a thunderstorm, lost her favorite copy of Euripides, faced the dreaded scoundrel Miss Darlington, been aurally assaulted by both an anti-theft siren and Frederick Bassingthwaite, and almost caught on fire in more ways than one. And now there was a possibility of insects. Just how much more perilous could this mission get?

Crash!

The chaise lounge toppled back, thudding against the floor. A reverberation went through the Orange Drawing Room, causing chandeliers to rattle and vases to rock perilously on tables. Alice winced.

But the three elderly ladies who had been standing on the chaise, and who skipped easily off its curved back to the polished wood floor, only laughed and clanked their wineglasses together in merry triumph. As crimson liquid splashed over their hands, Alice winced again, thinking of how sticky their fingers would be hereafter, and of all the floor mopping some poor chambermaid would be doing tonight.

"What's next?" came a call from somewhere amongst the mass of silk bustles, gaudy skirts, and terrifyingly fulsome hats crowding the room.

The question sparked fear through Alice's blood. She was a courageous woman. She had walked through the Whitechapel slum at midnight, spied on wicked witches who would have killed her had they realized her identity, and read William Blake's poetry. But nothing was more nerve-racking than pirates entertaining themselves with a few innocent parlor games.

Innocent, at least, until Miss Dole and Muriel Fairweather both tried to take the same seat during musical chairs. The resultant dispute had brought an end to that game, primarily due to the fact every chair had been smashed.

"Oops," Mrs. Rotunder had said when the literal dust settled. "It seems we got a little overenthusiastic." She'd dropped the chair leg she had been whacking over Bloodhound Bess's head and had smiled sheepishly at Jane and Frederick. "Terribly sorry."

"It is of no concern," Jane had said, although her smile had been so sharp she was in danger of putting her own eye out. "We had far too many priceless Chippendale giltwood chairs anyway, and could certainly afford to lose them. As you know, the Bassingthwaite family are tremendously, fabulously rich." This last word had come out like the crack of a whip, and Alice, from the corner of her eye, had seen Frederick flinch. "Having said that," Jane continued, "perhaps we should try a quieter game now? Pass the Slipper?"

"Jolly good!" the ladies had agreed with a worrying enthusiasm that was explained with explosive clarity when the slipper turned out to contain a bomb.

Now Alice stood on a pouf at the edge of the still-somewhat-smoky room, trying to calculate how long the afternoon had gone on thus far. Two, three years? All perception of time had long since fled for its life, taking with it a large proportion of her sanity. She was forced to concede herself bamboozled.

Although she had experienced pirates before, it had never been in such quantity. One Lady Armitage was a drain on the senses; fifteen Wisteria Society ladies together were a sinkhole—in a typhoon—during a tsunami. All the hours she'd spent learning parlor game rules in preparation for this mission had gone up in smoke—literally. Every muscle in her body was clenched, and the resultant tension sent a constant *twang* through her.

She'd always believed Wisteria Society ladies were dignified, elegant, and exquisitely well mannered (when not robbing banks and blowing things up). But this afternoon proved that they certainly liked to party. Alice had hoped an energetic game of The Floor Is Lava would tire them out. However, despite much leaping, clambering, and breaking of sofas, the trepidation on their husbands' faces suggested further mayhem remained likely.

Indeed, with the very next word spoken, Alice discovered the depths to which the Wisteria Society would sink.

"Charades!"

Several cheers arose at this suggestion. Alice stared wide-eyed and white-faced in horror across the room at Daniel. He just happened to be looking her way (as he had been each time she'd glanced at him, which was a convenient coincidence), and he grimaced in reply.

Suddenly, one pirate lady standing atop an armchair began tapping her wineglass with a dagger. "Not charades!" she shouted. "I have a better idea!"

"Mrs. Ogden! Mrs. Ogden!" the group chanted. Miss Darlington, thus far silently dignified in a corner, drummed the floor with her cane.

Alice warily eyed the plump, froth-haired woman. Her embroidered cardigan and plaid skirts suggested more of a granny than a grim reprobate, but Alice knew from A.U.N.T.'s database that, in the past year since being inducted into piratic ranks, Ogden the 'Orrible had catapulted herself to the heights of infamy, primarily by catapulting bombs into the depths of rich viscounts' houses. Most pirates did not attack civilian buildings, but Mrs. Ogden's motto was "robbers can't be choosers," and no one had the courage to explain that she'd heard it wrong.

"I shall spin around and point to someone," she declared, "and they must complete the dare I set them!"

"It's rude to point," Bloodhound Bess called out from a corner, where she was slipping a gold statuette of a Bassingthwaite ancestor into her skirt pocket.

Mrs. Ogden only laughed and began rotating herself unsteadily upon the chair.

Alice felt a sudden chill of doom. She was tensing even before Mrs. Ogden pointed directly at her.

"Mrs. Blakeney!" the old lady shouted.

Such a cacophony of applause, whoops, and whistles followed that Alice nearly burst into overwrought tears at the sound of it. But she was a professional, and ostensibly a pirate, and neither of those cried in public. So she took a deep breath, tapped her fingers against her thighs, and stepped down off the pouf.

"What is your dare?" she asked calmly.

"Goodness, how temperate," Mrs. Ogden remarked, shrugging her mouth with admiration and nodding around at the crowd, who smirked in reply. "You have a remarkably cool character, Mrs. Blakeney. But I know just the dare to heat you up."

"Yes?" She was ice, she was midwinter snow, nothing could trouble her.

"I dare you to kiss your husband."

And just like that she became a bonfire.

❊ 8 ❊

Nothing is so painful to the human mind as a great and sudden requirement to kiss. The sun might shine or the clouds might lower, but nothing could appear to Alice as it had the moment before Mrs. Ogden's dare. No creature had ever been so miserable as she.

With the possible exception of Daniel Bixby.

As she watched him being gently jostled and outright shoved across the room by pirates, his face calm but lamplight flashing wildly against his spectacles, Alice recalled a memory from her early days in the Academy. Forced into the center of a classroom with a dozen other children staring at her, she had been asked to demonstrate the basic first position for sweeping. Her small pale hands had clutched the birch broom at random. Her gaze had ranged unseeing around the room. She'd not spoken anything more than echoes of other people's words since being taken from the orphanage, and still screamed and flailed when anyone touched her without warning—so the concept of holding a broom correctly while a small crowd observed had overwhelmed her mental processing capacity and rendered her almost catatonic.

The instructor, exasperated, had demanded again—*first position!*—but had not dared to approach. The year before, a student had been pushed too far in the same situation and used the broom to damage every piece of furniture in the classroom. The teachers, if no one else, had learned their lesson well that day.

Standing in the Bassingthwaite parlor with pirates watching her avidly as they clapped their hands and chanted *Kiss! Kiss!*, Alice felt her gaze loosen in the same way it had all those years ago. Her heart began to thud. The only thing that kept her from hysterics was the knowledge that the student who had so drastically failed the sweeping exercise had been Agent B.

Daniel Bixby.

Who currently stood in front of her with his hands in his trouser pockets and such tension in his body she feared he might use himself as a birch broom and destroy them all.

Kissing was not the problem. Being stared at by a score of people was. It went against every instinct a spy possessed.

And, well, perhaps kissing was part of the problem. Alice had never experienced it. Her heart beat so forcefully, she wondered if she was feeling Daniel's pulse also.

He blinked down at her. She gazed up at him. The air roared with voices and bright, jagged feeling.

"So here is our first olive," he whispered.

Oh! gasped her heart, leaping up to wave a volume of *North and South* as it recognized the Elizabeth Gaskell reference. Her countenance, however, remained cool. "We should not make a face when we swallow it," she whispered in reply, and Daniel smiled. Seeing this, her heart clutched the book to its, er, heart with happiness.

Disturbed by such an unprofessional emotion, Alice tipped her face up toward duty. And Daniel set his lips against her cheek.

Immediately she was relieved. This need not count for her first kiss; this was nothing.

And then sensation flashed through her body. She felt not only his kiss but the whole Daniel-ness of him, from his physical presence to every memory she possessed of his warm, fleeting smile and the way his hand had felt holding hers until it pleasantly hurt.

He did not touch her now, besides where his mouth lay briefly upon her skin. She did not touch him. Merely one second later, they stepped apart. And yet, Alice feared she might swoon.

Professional woman, she reminded herself firmly. *Pirate.*

Daniel set one finger to the bridge of his spectacles, pushing them back up his nose, then turned away, patting her shoulder in a companionable manner as he did so.

The roomful of pirates stared gobsmacked.

"Er, right then," Mrs. Ogden said.

"I do believe I am going to overheat from the profusion of romance," Miss Darlington remarked.

"How long did you say you had been married?" Mrs. Rotunder asked in a hesitant voice.

"Three years," Daniel replied.

"Uh huh." She turned to look blankly at Miss Darlington, who shrugged her mouth with bewilderment.

"Ah, love!" Frederick's voice swelled through the awkward quiet. "That beacon for all dreaming hearts. Bestowed upon the most fortunate, and blessing them with the mellifluent—"

"Is it dinnertime yet?" Bloodhound Bess asked.

Alas, it was not, but this did not prevent the pirates from trooping to the vast, gilded dining room. Alice and Daniel found themselves carried inexorably along, propelled by chattering voices, bustled by bustles, and nudged by a few mild skirmishes as ladies literally battled to take precedence. The table settings were already laid, and the company had a moment's entertainment flicking embossed name cards at each other before sitting wherever they pleased. Two younger ladies appropriated Daniel, tucking their arms around his, practically hauling him to a seat between theirs. Alice was left to find a seat on her own. Every trained inclination in her wanted to stand back against the wall in proper servant fashion, but she was a pirate now, a rotten scoundrel, and so she slipped into a chair, murmuring apologies to her neighbors on either side as she did so. They smiled back in a manner that threatened polite conversation.

Looking down at her fingers tapping together in her lap, Alice silently counted her breath in and out. She would have been far more comfortable storming Starkthorn Castle solo to fight the pirates than *chatting* with them.

It was going to be a long two hours' wait before the scheduled dinnertime.

Five minutes later, food began arriving. Servants in a pirate household are always prepared for the unexpected.

Alice stared at the plate before her with disquiet. She'd felt obliged to take a little of whatever the footmen presented, and now was faced with a bewildering selection of foods, half of which she could not identify and the other half of which was tumbled together in a most distressing fashion. The roasted mushrooms looked delicious but were rendered inedible by their proximity to the honey-glazed carrots. And the cow's brain had been spoiled by—well, by being cow's brain, quite frankly, even had lobster sauce not dripped on it.

As she rummaged delicately with her fork, eating whatever was salvageable, she tried to arm herself for conversation. To her left sat

Mrs. Essie Smith, a young lady infamous for having stolen the Russian empress's favorite teapot; to her right, Mrs. Olivia Etterly, several decades older, with a swirling froth of lilac hair. Eventually, Alice turned to the latter and attempted some benign small talk.

"Tell me, madam, what do you think of the Queen?"

Mrs. Etterly paused in lifting an asparagus-laden fork to her open mouth. "What an arresting question," she said. "I have never spoken with Her Majesty, but she seems nice enough, for a queen."

"If you could assassinate her, how would you do it?"

The asparagus on Mrs. Etterly's fork flopped to the plate. "I—er—goodness me. Shoot her, probably?"

"I see."

"Er. Um." Mrs. Etterly made an effort to rally. "I hear you are newly back from the Continent, Mrs. Blakeney. How do you find England these days?"

"Oh, I have an excellent map."

The pirate lady appeared to choke, although she was not at that moment eating anything. "Well, that is certainly a helpful thing to have. If I may say so"—she leaned closer, whispering—"you also have an excellent-looking husband."

"I do," Alice agreed, and touched her cheek without thinking. She could still feel the little ache where he had kissed her. "According to science, Mr. Blakeney's face has the kind of symmetry that is universally considered handsome."

"Oh well, if you are going to speak *scientifically*," Mrs. Etterly said with a smile, "I'm sure there are many chemistry terms that would be quite suitable."

Alice considered this. "True. Mr. Blakeney is after all comprised of organic matter."

"I meant the *bond* between you two."

"Oh." Alice glanced across the table to where Daniel appeared to be demonstrating a stabbing technique, much to the amusement of the lady beside him. In a flash, Alice remembered the way he'd felled the thief Merv, all smooth competence, not even breaking a sweat. And then she began wondering what he would look like if he *had* broken a sweat—if he'd pulled off his coat, jacket, and shirt, and thus bare-chested had wrestled with Merv, perspiration glinting on his swelling pectoral muscles, hair—

She felt a peculiar rushing through her body, and thought with alarm that perhaps the mushrooms had disagreed with her.

Essie Smith leaned over to join the conversation. "Were he my husband, I'd be applying bonds quite tightly, if you know what I mean."

Her eyebrows bounced, and Mrs. Etterly responded with a laugh Alice realized there was a silent conversation occurring alongside their words, one for which she possessed no dictionary.

"There, there." Mrs. Etterly patted Alice's shoulder (and stole her earring). "We've made poor Mrs. Blakeney blush. Alias! Er, I mean *alas*. I hope we didn't spook you too much, dear."

"Of course we didn't," Essie said with a grin. "Mrs. Blakeney may look young and sweet, but I suspect she has a secret wealth of intelligence behind those private eyes of hers, and is no doubt tapped in to our intentions. Aren't you, dear?"

"I—" Alice began. She had no idea what the rest of her sentence might contain, but that did not matter, for Mrs. Etterly interrupted her before she needed to produce another word.

"Maybe, Essie, maybe. But *I* suspect she's not as wicked as she could be. Talk to your handsome young husband about bedsteads and bonds, Mrs. Blakeney. Investigate it thoroughly with him. I'm sure together you will uncover interesting results."

"Thank you for that advice," Alice murmured, and hastily proceeded to eat an artichoke heart despite it having touched the creamed corn—anything to escape the torture of small talk.

Over her head, Mrs. Etterly and Essie smirked at each other.

The company separated after dinner, ladies returning to the drawing room to drink tea and discuss such feminine concerns as fashion (what exactly should a lady wear when robbing a bank?) and lip rouge (which shade was best for writing ransom notes?) and recipes (could one substitute belladonna for digitalis in poisoned wine?). The gentlemen remained at the table to trade risqué jokes and ideas for scrapbook layouts.

But Daniel waylaid Alice as she was heading for the drawing room. As he stepped up beside her, she smelled his now-familiar scent of quality soap, and inexplicably blushed. Perhaps the warm gas lighting in the hallway was to blame for this, or perhaps her sudden vision of Agent B seated in a bath, rubbing soap against his bare skin.

"Madam," he said, "I perceive you are rather tired. It has been a long day; shall we retire early?"

Alice recognized the code for *Shall we go upstairs and snoop around rooms in search of the secret hidden weapon?*

"I am tired," she agreed. "Thank you for the suggestion."

"I spy our pretty young couple sneaking off," Mrs. Etterly said as they went.

"Good luck achieving molecular combustion!" Essie called after them.

Arm in arm they walked upstairs until reaching the first floor, whereupon they immediately stepped away from each other, brushing nonexistent lint from their clothing.

"Jane's sitting room is in the west wing," Daniel said. "This way."

They strode along the corridor. Anyone seeing them would have been impressed by their cool, authoritative aura, the sort that suggests guns are hidden in secret pockets and arrest warrants can be immediately produced if required. All that was missing was a slow-motion effect, rousing soundtrack, and recollection on their part that they were supposed to act like swaggering pirates. Coming to Jane's sitting room, they found the door locked.

"I have one of Snodgrass's lockpicks," Daniel said, removing his tie pin. He inserted it into the lock, but immediately sparks began to ignite. As Daniel pulled back his scorched fingers, the pin shot out, exploding in midair before dropping to the floor, where it proceeded to burn a hole in the carpet.

Alice shook her head with displeasure. "Let's hope that's the only thing that is blown tonight."

"Hm," Daniel answered.

The noise of the explosion drew a chambermaid from a nearby room. "Is everything all right?" she asked.

"Just fine," Daniel replied, placing his foot over the smoking lockpick.

"The eagle has eaten the frog," Alice told her in code—i.e., *The door won't open, damn it, do you have a spare lockpick on you?*

"Um," said the maid, her eyes widening.

"I don't think she knows your aunt," Daniel murmured. He smiled at the maid. "All is well, my wife merely has had too much wine. I told you this was the wrong door, dear."

"Thank you for that correction, dear," Alice said in a voice so wifely, A.U.N.T. really needn't have spent any money on the fake marriage certificate.

The maid, being used to piratic marriages, fled before swords were drawn. Alice and Daniel turned to frown at the locked door. "We could try the room upstairs," Alice suggested. "If it is accessible, we could climb down from its window to that of the sitting room."

"Good plan," Daniel said. He stared into the middle distance for a moment, his eyes flickering as if reading something Alice could not see. "That room has been allocated to Olivia Etterly and her husband," he said.

"You've memorized the castle map?" Alice was astonished.

He looked at her, and she suspected he was seeing angles against her skin, patterns, a network of bones. "A man does like to be adequate at his job, Miss Dearlove."

Hastening upstairs, they found Mrs. Etterly's door unlocked. "Hm," Daniel murmured as it opened.

"Perhaps she thought locking it would be useless in a house full of thieves," Alice said. Peering around the doorframe, she scanned the interior. "Clear."

They entered, Daniel shutting the door behind them before crossing to open the window. Alice stood unmoving, her attention riveted on the wrought-iron bedstead and tangled sheets of the bed, which dominated the room. Instinctively she wanted to launder those sheets, remake the bed, lay a mint chocolate on the pillow. Her imagination, however, remembering Mrs. Etterly's advice—*"talk to your handsome young husband about bedsteads and bonds"*—began to have other ideas.

"Dare . . . love . . ." The suggestion drifted through her awareness, and her imagination nodded in enthusiastic agreement.

"Dearlove. Miss Dearlove!"

"Huh?" Blinking, she yanked her attention away from the bed and found Daniel staring at her blankly.

"All clear outside," he reported. "And the sitting room window below is ajar."

"Right," she said in a brisk voice that fairly shouted *I am a professional woman.*

Focusing sternly, she unhooked the fine braided cord that decorated her dress, looping it from elbow to hand several times. Then removing a clip from her coiffure, she unfolded its metal arms so they extended into a three-pronged anchor. To this she tied the end of the cord.

"Hopefully it's long enough," she said, attaching the anchor to the windowsill and letting the cord unfurl down the castle wall. It reached to just above the sitting room window.

"I'll go first," Daniel said. Without further discussion, he was up and out, proceeding easily via the cord down the wall.

"Typical man," Alice muttered as she watched him go. "Always has to take the lead."

"Hff," came a sardonic comment from behind her.

Drawing her gun, she turned on a heel but saw nothing in the room. Clearly her nerves were still on edge after the long day spent in piratic company.

Really, Mrs. Kew ought not have assigned her to this mission. She may have mastered the Three Primary Rules for Normal Conversation and the Seven Standard Facial Expressions, but piratic behavior was a whole other kettle of fish. (Not that anyone had ever presented her with a kettle of fish—thankfully—but Alice had heard the phrase used before and suspected it was a lesser subclause of Normal Conversation that had been taught at the Academy one day when she'd been off sick.)

The Wisteria Society ladies had perfect manners—to assist them in committing perfect crimes. For instance, it was easy enough to understand a lady must always wear kid gloves in public, but it took a whole other angle of comprehension to see this was necessary so as to not leave fingerprints at a burglary scene. Alice knew she was entirely ill-equipped to learn the pirates' backward kind of etiquette.

But if she did not do so, and quickly, the Queen would die. And

Alice herself would likely die too. She was disinclined for that to happen.

"Drat it all," she muttered.

"Hff," came a whispered reply.

It must be a breeze through the open window, she thought. Looking out, she saw Daniel swing in through the window below. The line went slack. Returning her gun to its secret pocket, Alice began gathering up her skirts in preparation for rappelling.

"Grrr," the mysterious voice rumbled behind her.

Turning again with a confused frown, she went abruptly still. Her pulse, on the other hand, began to race around her body in hysterics.

Well, this explained why Mrs. Etterly did not bother locking her door.

As if it knew what she was thinking, the tiger emerging from under the bed grinned.

✹ 9 ✹

Tiger, tiger, burning bright, in the bedroom of the pirate. Although not literally burning, Alice thought sourly—a burning tiger would at least be less inclined to stalk her. It had a fearful symmetry indeed about its lithe body, but Alice found herself focusing instead on its even more fearful fangs. Although a pretty pink bow had been set about its neck at a charmingly cocky angle, this somehow did not ameliorate her terror.

"Fiddlesticks," she whispered. The open window beside her offered an escape, but as she reached with agonizing care for the sill, her hand fumbled against the rappel hook and inadvertently dislodged it. She tried to catch it but was too late: with a mocking clatter against the stone wall, her means of escape slipped away.

The tiger's eyes flashed as if appreciating Alice's worsening dilemma. It swayed in what she imagined was preparation for leaping, biting, tearing, and other gruesome activities.

With a wild flare of desperation, she waved a hand. *"Aereo,"* she gasped, trying to summon the ancient magic of the incantation.

A vase of flowers rocked gently on the bedside table.

The tiger's tail flicked.

"Fuck," Alice said—not strictly speaking a phrase of magic, but certainly piratical. Reaching blindly behind her, she caught hold of a large porcelain lamp and threw it as far as she could across the room.

In other words, three feet.

Thunk.

The tiger watched the lamp roll across the carpet, then turned back to Alice. Hunching down, its massive shoulders rippling with muscle, it began to creep toward her.

All the books she had read in her life flashed before her eyes. Unfortunately, none of them happened to be manuals on escaping deadly wild beasts. The tiger paused, its jaws closing. The disappearance of the enormous fangs proved less reassuring than Alice would have supposed. She watched everything about the creature grow tight and still, and realized she had seconds to live.

Sorrow rose from her heart, but her mind ruthlessly stomped it down again. Taking one last breath, she placed a hand on the windowsill and vaulted up, over—and out into the darkness.

Meanwhile, one floor down, Daniel was experiencing problems of his own.

"So interesting to see you here, Bixby," said the man aiming a gun at his heart.

"You too, Captain O'Riley," Daniel replied, his own gun not stirring an inch from the pirate's heart.

"I thought you were going to Edinburgh to open a bookstore."

"People can change their mind."

"Not you."

Daniel stared at the dark-haired pirate, silently calculating angles for attack, odds of getting pulverized if he attacked, and sudden painful nostalgia. For three years he'd used Alex O'Riley as a source of information and experience, cleaned his house, participated in his adventures, and come perilously close to loving the man with a depth of friendship he'd never before experienced. But the assignment had ended and the file closed, shutting away all such uncomfortable sentiments.

"Don't be so ridiculous," came a woman's voice from the edge of the room. Without moving, Daniel flicked his gaze toward it. His heart followed.

Charlotte Pettifer stepped forward. Dressed in black shirt, black trousers, and tall studded black boots, her strawberry blonde hair tied back to fall in a rippling stream almost to her waist, she looked like a wicked witch—exactly what she was. She gave him a look that suggested far more danger than any her brawny pirate husband with his passel of deadly weapons could supply. Daniel knew that, with one murmured word, she could have him out the window and broken on the ground far below.

"Hello, miss," he said with a smile.

"Don't hello me," she replied in that tetchy way she had, the one that warned you she was about to take your heart and shake it up, straighten it properly, then give it back to you like a gift. Before he met her, Daniel had never known it was possible to be so badgered you came to adore someone out of sheer self-defense. He'd kill for Charlotte Pettifer, not the least because she'd made Alex happy.

"Idiot," she said. Then she turned to her husband. "You too." She flicked a peremptory finger back and forth between the men. "Put those guns down and hug each other."

Daniel and Alex shared an appalled glance. "I'm not hugging him," Alex muttered, holstering the gun alongside another on his belt.

"I do not hug," Daniel said as he returned his own gun to an inner pocket. "Besides, I saw you only two weeks ago. An effusive reunion is unnecessary."

"It may have been two weeks for you," Charlotte said, "but it has been fourteen long days of washing our own dishes for us." She smiled at him then. Alex, muttering under his breath, offered a hand, and Daniel automatically shook it. All the while, his brain ran around shouting urgent orders and waving red flags, trying to forestall an eruption of emotion he absolutely could not afford. Alex and Lottie represented an old assignment, nothing more.

And his heart, sighing in defeat, packed up all its wild and hungry longings and went to hide under a blanket.

"Why are you here?" he asked. "I mean, obviously you have come for the weapon. But the captain should have done this job alone, Miss Pettifer. The castle is full of pirates. If they catch a witch—"

Charlotte shrugged. "I am not afraid."

Daniel glanced at Alex, who was rolling his eyes.

"You should be," Daniel said sternly. "The feud between the Wisteria Society and the Wicken League is no laughing matter."

"Actually," Alex said, "I found myself in hysterics last week when I saw Bloodhound Bess and the witch Mrs. Chuke fighting over the only ripe pomegranate in a greengrocer's stall. Mrs. Chuke sent all the fruit flying, then Bess sent the stall itself flying, and—"

"*Nevertheless,*" Daniel interjected. "If the pirates discover Miss Pettifer's presence, she may be in danger." He looked solemnly at Charlotte. "Your marriage to the captain notwithstanding, miss, the ladies are in a rambunctious mood, and might use the feud as an excuse to have fun at your cost."

"The auguries predict otherwise," Charlotte said offhandedly—an assurance that failed to impress Daniel, since not only did he not believe in auguries, but he suspected Charlotte didn't either. "Besides," she continued, "we are keeping out of sight. Attics, all the usual secret passageways, et cetera. We could not overlook the opportunity this weapon affords."

"I hear it has the firepower of two dozen cannons," Alex said, grinning like an excited boy.

"We could blow up half of Parliament," Charlotte added in a more businesslike manner, "and use the rubble to build schools for impoverished children." Her expression shadowed suddenly; stepping forward, she reached out and would have touched Daniel's ear had he not flinched back. "You're wearing an earring. And a wedding ring. What exactly have you been doing this past fortnight, Bixby?"

At that fortuitous moment, a voice called from the night beyond.

"Let me in! Let me in!"

Turning, Daniel was astonished to see Alice's pallid face floating behind the window's lace curtain like a wild and lonely specter roaming the darkness in search of her soul's master. He strode across and, pulling aside the curtain, discovered her bobbing awkwardly in the air.

"Mrs. Blakeney!" he said with stern disapproval. "What are you doing?"

"Trying not to die," she replied. "This is an old petticoat; its incantation is faded. I can't seem to maneuver. Would you do me a small favor, if you have a moment, and save me from plummeting to my doom far below?"

Taking her arm, Daniel hauled her through the open window. They stumbled against each other, and as Alice clutched his arms to stay upright, Daniel felt a tightening within him. The intensity of it almost caused him to push her out the window in a trained reflex he only just restrained. Instead, he stepped back abruptly in the same moment she did also, snatching her hands away from him.

"What happened?" he asked.

"A severe operational deficiency, that is what happened," she retorted. "Why did the dossier not include mention of a tiger? Hm? Answer me that, sir. One would assume something as significant as a tiger would be mentioned, even if only in a footnote. I will most certainly be adding this to my—"

She stopped, staring past him to where Alex and Charlotte were watching the scene with amusement. "Egads, it's the mad people!" she exclaimed in recognition—and then flushed as she realized she'd just broken her cover.

But it was too late in any case. As Daniel turned, he saw an answering recognition in Charlotte's eyes. Trust a witch to recognize a woman she last saw a year ago, when Alice had been working undercover with the Wicken League. No doubt Alice could have disguised herself as a scantily dressed, gold-haired opera singer (he paused to envision it) and Charlotte would still know her. The witch might have made a good A.U.N.T. agent were she not an unrepentant enemy of the state whom one day Daniel might be ordered to assassinate.

"Miss Dearlove," she said languidly, her voice rich with the promise of magic. "The last time we met you were clambering through a window too."

"I was not," Alice said, affronted.

"I beg to insist that I remember the occasion quite clearly."

"There was indeed a window," Alice agreed. "But I did not clamber through it. I never clamber. It is entirely indecorous. Except, that is, when a tiger is about to consume me." She glared at Daniel as if near ingestion by wild cat was his fault. He stared back at her implacably, never mind the tumult of his pulse as he met her dark, glimmering gaze. (Really, as soon as this mission was over he ought to get a medical checkup.)

Alex made a noise that would have been a laugh had he been a reckless man. Daniel turned to frown at him, and the pirate bit his smile in an effort to appear innocent. But Alex O'Riley could not look innocent even if all his weapons were removed and a pink ribbon tied in his hair.

"I see you finally said hello to the pretty girl," he remarked.

"I—I—" For the first time in years, Daniel found himself without words.

"What does he mean?" Alice asked.

"In Clacton," Alex said cheerfully, oblivious to Daniel's glare, "he saw you in a tavern but was too shy—"

"Too concerned with the brawl about to happen," Daniel amended sternly.

Alex shrugged, his smile tilting with a comment he did not make aloud, perhaps out of respect for Daniel, or more likely noticing how Daniel's hand was reaching again for a gun.

"Pretty girl," Alice echoed with disapproval. But Daniel saw her fingers *tap-tap*-ing.

Charlotte saw it also. Her eyebrow went up again. "I notice, Miss Dearlove, that you are wearing a wedding ring to match Bixby's."

A whole gang of Wisteria Society ladies with swords drawn would not have been as terrifying as Lottie making a politely quiet comment. "I—I—" Alice answered.

Daniel instinctively came to the rescue. "She is my wife."

Alex and Charlotte exchanged an astonished glance. And then they laughed.

Daniel bristled with disapproval. "Excuse me."

"I am so sorry, Bixby dear," Charlotte said, attempting to sober her countenance. "It is merely that I find it so unlikely you would be married in—"

"Sh!" Alex hissed suddenly. "Someone is at the door."

Charlotte snatched his hand. *"Aereo rapido,"* she said, and the two of them levitated at speed toward the ceiling, where a gap in the wooden paneling revealed how they had entered the locked room. They climbed through it, then Charlotte's head appeared again at the opening.

"This conversation is not finished," she warned before sliding the panel back in place, restoring the ceiling to its normal state.

Daniel and Alice looked at each other dumbly. Then the door rattled. At once, Daniel vaulted over a sofa to crouch behind it. Alice, walking sedately around that same sofa, joined him there in the dusty shadows.

"Ooh," she said excitedly, picking up a small book that had seemingly been tossed to the ground, its pages bent. Glancing at the cover, she wrinkled her nose and set it down once more. Daniel looked a question; "Wordsworth," she explained.

Just then, the door creaked open.

"Empty," came a whispered voice. "Quick, Mr. Rotunder, and lock the door behind you."

"Yes, Gertrude dear."

"I'm sure it will be in here somewhere. Jane Fairweather has no imagination. You search beneath that clothed table. I'll check in the writing desk."

"What exactly does it look like, dear?"

"Heaven knows. Dangerous. Maybe some kind of gun?"

Daniel and Alice exchanged a speaking glance.

"There's a box of chocolates under here. Could that—"

"Sh!" Mrs. Rotunder hissed suddenly. "Someone's trying to unlock the door. Hide!"

The sofa began to shudder. Daniel and Alice looked up in time to see Mr. Rotunder climbing over it. His wooden leg whacked Daniel in the head; his other foot stepped on Alice's back.

"Sorry," he whispered. "Pardon me. My apologies. Could you make a little space?" The agents shuffled aside and Mr. Rotunder crouched between them. "Thank goodness for hinges," he whispered, patting his knee, as Daniel and Alice stared at him.

The door creaked open.

"We'll have to be quick," came a hushed voice. "You look under that cloth-covered table, and be sure to put your gloves on first. Jane is so careless, this room is no doubt swarming with germs."

"Yes, Jem dear."

"And just look at the shambles on this writing desk! It is as though someone has pulled everything out of the drawers. I do declare, if the weapon is in this room, it has probably been rendered useless by dust."

"What—"

"Hush! Is that someone at the door? Hide!"

Daniel pressed his forehead wearily against the back of the sofa and thus escaped being kicked in the face as the great hulking body of Jake Jacobsen catapulted over to squat awkwardly in the crowded shadows.

"Good evening," he said to the men. He nodded to Alice. "Ma'am."

"Well I never!" came Miss Darlington's voice. "What are you doing, Gertrude, hiding behind the drapes *I* was intending to use as concealment?"

Suddenly the door opened, and feminine gasps arose.

"Miss Fairweather!" cried Miss Darlington.

"Never fear, Jem! I will save you!" Jake rose like a troll whose bridge had just been overrun by goats. The sofa rocked violently as his shoulder knocked against it, bashing into Mr. Rotunder, who tipped over with a cry, taking Jake down again with him. The man's head smacked into Alice and she lurched instinctively away. Daniel reached out to steady her before she crashed against a lamp-bearing cabinet, but his own elbow hit a vase-bearing cabinet, causing it to topple. Catching the vase before it reached the floor, he tripped against Mr. Rotunder, who fell backward, knocking Alice off her knees. Within seconds, the entire company behind the sofa was a tangle of limbs.

"*Ahem,*" Miss Darlington said. Her cane tapped against the floor. Like chastened children, the agents, Jake, and Mr. Rotunder clambered to their feet. They looked out across the sofa at Jane Fairweather.

Who had either aged five decades at the sight of so many people secreted in her sitting room or was in fact Miss *Muriel* Fairweather, Jane's grandmother.

"What is going on?" the lady demanded, hands on hips, hair feathers flapping.

"What do you think?" Miss Darlington replied, leaning nonchalantly on her cane.

"Something nefarious!"

"Nonsense," Mrs. Rotunder scoffed. "Just a spot of light after-dinner burglary."

Miss Fairweather's eyes narrowed as she considered this response. Daniel held his breath. He noticed Alice slip a hand into the pocket where she kept her gun.

Then Miss Fairweather shrugged. "Sounds reasonable. Has anyone looked inside that rosewood box yet?"

"*Aaaaggghhh!*"

At the sudden scream arising from the corridor, Daniel just about leaped out of his skin. He and Alice immediately drew their guns. The pirates glanced mildly at the door.

"My word!" Mr. Rotunder exclaimed. "Is that a Webley Mark I revolver you're holding, Mrs. Blakeney? Those are cracker guns, from what I've heard. Can I try it for a minute? Say yes."

"*Aaaaggghhh—huh—aaaaggghhh!!*"

As Alice wrestled with Mr. Rotunder for possession of her gun, Daniel strode to the door. He found it locked.

Crash! "*Aaaaggghhh!*"

Stepping back, Daniel kicked the door, causing it to splinter (and the key to fall from its lock to the floor).

The pirates exchanged a bemused look.

"Oh dear," Miss Fairweather said. "Jane is going to be so cross, and you don't want to see—"

Ignoring her, Daniel pulled open the door, and raising his gun in both hands, he entered the corridor.

And nearly got run down by a conga line of dancing pirates.

THE MISERY OF JOY—A DANGEROUS CONVERSATION—
ONE BED TOO MANY—PRIVATE EYES—RUDE AWAKENINGS

There is an order of mortal on the earth who do become youthful in their old age, and around whom everyone else is at risk of dying before middle age from sheer exhaustion. The Wisteria Society ladies were such an order—or, more accurately, *disorder.*

Alice had never met people so dedicated to the pursuit of happiness. She could not approve of this, nor of their determination to drag her along—literally, in the case of the conga. Oh sure, when off duty she enjoyed such pleasurable activities as giving the bedroom a good sweep and rubbing the entire body of her silverware collection until it shone. But wanton cheerfulness was like reading a book without first checking how it ended. The risk of surprise was simply too great.

Therefore, she was relieved when the pirates' conga line finally ran out of steam and she could sneak away with Daniel. Being alone in a bedroom with him would secure against any form of pleasure.

They were almost to their door when a pair of housemaids, laden with folded sheets, noticed them. Gasping excitedly, the young women hurried over.

"Is it true?" one asked in a loud whisper.

Alice and Daniel frowned with automatic disapproval. "Is what true?" Alice asked.

"Are you them?"

"A and B," the other maid clarified. She was surveying Daniel with such heated interest it could only be considered a miracle that her stack of laundry didn't combust.

"A.U.N.T.'s greatest agents!" the first added, bouncing on her heels.

Alice glanced around to ensure they were alone in the corridor. "You are being indiscreet," she chided.

But neither woman listened. Indeed, she'd barely finished speaking when the first said, "We heard you hijacked Miss Darlington's house on the way here."

"No—" Alice began.

"We heard you shot six thieves in St. James," said the other.

"No—"

Suddenly, Daniel reached out and removed the topmost sheet from the laundry of the woman nearest him. As everyone watched nervously, he unfolded it by half, realigned the corners, and refolded it with such precision its edges could probably be used to slice bread. He set it on the stack once more.

Pallid and trembling, the maids hastened away without another word.

"It seems they are giving any twit a license to kill these days," Daniel murmured irritably as he turned back toward the bedroom door.

"I should have shaken better sense into them," Alice said, "but frankly felt too tired to stir myself."

Entering the bedroom at last, Alice locked the door and stood just soaking in the dimly lit quiet. As she inhaled on a slow count to three, she heard Daniel do the same. Together at four, they exhaled. Then Daniel checked behind curtains while Alice inspected under the bed, looking for thieves, tigers, or dust balls.

Eventually Daniel turned and, pressing the heel of his hand against his brow, looked at Alice in a way that suggested he was still seeing Mrs. Ogden's bustle jiggling as the elderly pirate conga'd in front of him.

"Are you hurt?" he asked.

"Hurt?" No one had ever asked Alice such a thing before, and she struggled to process it.

"From before, when we were upstairs."

"Oh. Not at all. Captain O'Riley and Miss Pettifer laughing at the idea of you marrying me in no way wounded my feelings, or—"

"I meant physically. Did the tiger hurt you?"

"No, I managed to escape without harm. However, Frederick Bassingthwaite's hair oil splashed in my eye several times while doing the conga. Frankly, I knew this mission would involve danger, and a tiger in a bedroom was apropos, but *dancing*—?!"

They both shuddered.

"The things people are willing to do with their bodies," murmured Daniel, a man who had come close to breaking bones multiple times by somersaulting backward off walls, leaping between rooftops, and crashing through windows in order to catch criminals (or just get to his destination more quickly).

"The captain and Miss Pettifer," he said—then paused. He rubbed his forehead again. "They were laughing at me, not you. No one could be surprised at any man wanting to marry y—" He paused again, frowning so darkly at something across the room that Alice turned to see what it was. But unless some threat resided in a painting of an oak tree, she could not understand his concern. Perhaps he was angry at the pirate and witch.

"Would you like me to assassinate them?" she asked.

He looked back at her with an astonishment she had not thought him capable of. "What? No. Thank you, but I am familiar with their style of wit."

"You were undercover a long time in O'Riley's house. I imagine you formed a significant connection to each other."

His expression shut down, shoved a series of deadbolts into place, and set a stone atop itself. "It's late. We should go to sleep in preparation for . . . God only knows what tomorrow."

Alice could not argue against that. Taking her duffel bag into the washroom, she performed the usual ablutions and changed into a nightgown. She then paused for a series of deep, calming breaths.

Forget tigers and terrifying pirates—in a moment she would have to get into bed with Daniel Bixby. While she had earlier felt entirely untroubled by this, the stresses of the day—not to mention Daniel having kissed her, a kiss she could still feel, as if it had seared right through her tranquil layers to the very core of her being—made the prospect of sleeping next to him rather daunting.

She breathed in, breathed out. *I am a professional woman,* she reminded herself. *Besides, lying next to a man in bed is the same as standing next to him in a public room, only horizontal.*

And alone.

And significantly less dressed.

Finally, becoming dizzy from all the calm breathing, she re-entered the bedroom.

And halted so fast, her heart reverberated.

Daniel stood with his back to her, folding clothes. He appeared to be wearing some species of undervest that clung to his body and left his arms exposed to view. Not that Alice was viewing him. As a lady, she did not do such things. As a lady, she stared determinedly into the middle distance. The tiny brown specks in her vision must have been dust motes and not the freckles on his shapely bicep. Fiddlesticks!

Then he turned toward her, and the bold contour of his groin beneath long, tight underwear took her fiddlesticks, snapped them into pieces, and made of them a roaring bonfire.

Daniel had sensed Alice enter the room and had taken longer than usual folding his shirt, so as to ensure the aforementioned contour did not develop too steep an angle. Never mind her prettiness—the very *aura* of her, so determinedly tranquil, lured him out of cool professionalism and into the fires of lust. He'd been struggling ever since kissing her in the parlor, a kiss that had left his lips feeling bereft and his body murderous. To be alone with her now was proving harder than he'd expected—in more ways than one.

There was really no point in him wanting the woman. A.U.N.T. would never let him have her. They would see him almost self-destruct rather than allow him to fulfill any personal desires that might intrude upon his effectiveness as their agent. And although lust had always before been about scratching an itch, nothing more, in this case he feared it might take him somewhere deeper, somewhere painfully impossible. So he would just—not—want. Simple as that.

Getting his body to understand proved less simple.

Finally, by dint of careful breathing, ruthless self-control, and envisioning Mrs. Kew in a fluffy pink bed jacket, he was able to turn and look at Alice.

And hastily allowed the shirt in his hands to unfold, its length falling like a protective shield, since his body considered the idea of self-control for all of two seconds before rejecting it utterly.

Alice was dressed in a voluminous white nightgown even the most censorious observer would deem puritanical. But it was Daniel's job to be highly observant, and he needed only one glance to appreciate that the nightgown was not so much puritanical as *oh damn, sinfully tempting*. White roses embroidered on the bodice seemed to flutter and sway against the gentle swell of her breasts as she breathed. And the heavy drape of linen did not prevent him from being all too aware of what lay beneath, or how easily it might be accessed, one hand reaching under the loose garment while his other plucked the roses . . .

"Ahem," he said, urgently breaking his train of thought.

"Ahem," Alice happened to say at the same moment.

Their eyes met, then looked away, leaving Daniel feeling blistered.

"I—um—I think I will sleep on the sofa tonight," he said, staring at that item of furniture as if it was a holy statue of the Virgin Mary. With Baby Jesus in her arms. And the pope frowning solemnly over her shoulder. "Just to be safe."

"Perhaps that is wise," Alice conceded. "However, I will be the one to sleep on the sofa. I am shorter, smaller, less muscular—" She stopped abruptly.

Daniel glanced at her. She had plaited her hair, and he wanted to untie the ribbon holding it together and slip his fingers between the twisted strands, feeling the braid come apart for him . . .

Hastily, silently, he recited several mathematical theories until his blood cooled. Then he ran a weary hand over his head and down to the nape of his neck, massaging the taut muscles there.

Alice, staring at his bicep, reiterated firmly, "I will sleep on the sofa."

"I am the gentleman," he reminded her.

"Yes, I'm decidedly aware of that."

"Therefore, I will take the sofa. You will sleep in the bed."

She frowned. "I will not. Gender has no role here. The senior officer makes the sacrifice."

"Gender *absolutely* has the starring role here, Miss Dearlove. Besides, we are equal in rank."

"I am alphabetically superior."

"I am older."

"Very well," she conceded. "We will have to compromise."

Daniel had never heard anything more ominous.

The bedroom's sofa was an elegant Georgian creation, mahogany framed with scrolled ends, stiff cushioning, and such richly embroidered upholstery that it made a person scratchy just looking at it. Alice and Daniel arranged themselves upon it as comfortably as possible—which is to say, not at all—wedged at either end.

"I wish to go on record as disapproving of there being only one sofa," Daniel said as he tugged on the quilt they shared.

"Noted," Alice said, tugging back.

"And how is it that a quilt sufficient for a double-size bed is not enough now? Might I have at least enough to properly cover my legs?"

"Don't speak of your gross anatomy," Alice chided.

He raised an eyebrow (and tugged the quilt once more). "Are you calling my legs gross?"

"No." She sighed, rolling her eyes. "Gross anatomy as opposed to microscopic anatomy. Have you never read a dictionary, sir?"

"I have been too occupied reading literature. It offers more meaningful explanations. For example, 'Our bodies are our gardens—'"

"Nonsense."

"Shakespeare."

"Uncontextualized. Besides, if your body were a garden, it would be all vines, considering how it is monopolizing the sofa."

"Yours would be budding flowers," he shot back.

And an abrupt silence stunned them both. They stared at each other with a kind of primitive shock that slowly, inexorably, became electric.

"The mission," Alice said vaguely.

"Yes," Daniel answered in the same tone. Then he blinked, yanking his gaze away from her. "Yes," he repeated more firmly. "And for the mission to be successful, we need to sleep."

Alice hated to agree with him, but in fact she felt exhausted. Determined, however, to maintain at least one point of superiority, she claimed the final word: "Good night." And she reached for the nearby table lamp to extinguish its light.

"Good night," Daniel answered.

Her hand paused, mid-reach. "Sleep well," she said emphatically. After a moment's silence, she took hold of the lamp's valve.

"You too."

Alice frowned. *"Pleasant dreams,"* she snapped, and plunged them into darkness before Agent B could say one more thing.

For a long while thereafter, the quiet swayed with their rhythmic breathing. Rain against the window whispered gently; the fire was no more than a heap of smoldering coals. Finally, Alice sensed Daniel had drifted into sleep, and she exhaled with relief. (Internal relief, that is. Externally, her hip ached, her shoulder was angled uncomfortably, and there was no easing the hot ache between her legs.) Now at last she might rest.

"Aaahh! Take that, you varmint!!"

She almost fell off the sofa. Good grief, what on earth were the pirates doing out there?!

Hhshhh.

Now her heart was the one to fall. The soft noise at the other end of the sofa alarmed her more than the scream in the corridor. Was Daniel awake again? What was he doing? Adjusting his pillow, or turning so he faced her?

Fiddlesticks. She was never going to sleep tonight.

Dawn eased into the rooms of Starkthorn Castle like a witch come to tidy away the darkness and, while she was at it, steal a few dreams. Daniel woke abruptly, completely. His mind recollected the locations of his weapons even before it emerged from its usual vague nightmares. It straightened the files of his existence, bookmarked a few bodily needs, then opened his eyes.

And pieces of cognition flew everywhere.

He was crammed into the very end of the sofa, his torso tilted awkwardly back, his feet on the floor where the quilt had fallen, and Alice curled up with her head resting in his lap. Daniel could feel her slow, warm breath through the linen of his underwear. Instantly, the pillow she had made for herself became rock-hard.

Damn. He needed to get distant from the woman, and fast. Attempting to slide a hand beneath her head, he froze as she cuddled one of his legs with the endearing warmth of a woman and the strength of a well-trained assassin. He tried to count, but *what the hell were numbers again?* Alice murmured in her sleep, nestling closer, and he groaned.

At the sound, Alice jolted suddenly. She was upright on the floor before Daniel even processed that she was moving. A bare, rose-scented foot set itself against his throat, and only the fact that she was English, and therefore sporting, saved Daniel from the disagreeable effects of her applying a fatal pressure at once.

"Wake up, Agent A," he said calmly.

She blinked dark, heavy eyes, her vision coming into focus . . .

"Yoo-hoo! Blakeneys!"

This sudden cheerful call was followed by a violent hammering upon the bedroom door. Daniel and Alice stared at each other for one frozen moment. Then a mutual realization of what they must do blossomed wordlessly between them. Daniel clutched both hands around Alice's ankle and twisted.

She collapsed facedown on the quilt. As she began turning over, Daniel dropped from the sofa to join her, and instinctively, briefly, they wrestled. Within short order, Daniel found himself lying atop her, gripping her wrists over her head.

He frowned. This situation was as opposite to "getting distant from the woman" as possible without him actually being inside her—and *that* was a thought he did not want to be indulging right now.

Alice's face reddened as she looked up at him. Daniel watched her expression flash bright for one moment with caution—then shyness—then stark, desperate yearning. The pulse in her wrists began shuddering against his palms. The swelling between his legs throbbed. He lowered his head toward her, and she rose to meet him.

In aching silence, their lips touched—

The bedroom door slammed open.

"*Yoo-hoo!*" Mrs. Ogden sang out as she barged into the room, followed closely by Mrs. Rotunder. Both women stopped, staring wide-eyed, when they saw Daniel and Alice together on the floor. Daniel lifted his head calmly. Beneath him, Alice exhaled with relief that they had achieved a properly marital pose just in the nick of time.

"Goodness me!" Mrs. Ogden exclaimed, her face illuminated with a Disapproving Countenance Type Five: Secretly Titillated.

"You *have* noticed that you've got a bed?" Mrs. Rotunder asked slyly.

Daniel forced a piratic smile on his lips, although they were tingling so much from their brief touch upon Alice's, he struggled to control them. But he must have been successful, for the two ladies began backing toward the door.

"We just wanted to let you know," Mrs. Rotunder said, "that you should come—er—"

"Everyone's up," Mrs. Ogden explained. "You're missing all the fun!"

Mrs. Rotunder muttered something under her breath as she pushed Mrs. Ogden out the door and closed it behind them. Laughter could be heard trilling in the corridor.

"Fun," Alice echoed grimly.

"I have a feeling this does not bode well," Daniel said, and climbed off her before desire drove him madder than a houseful of pirates.

※ 11 ※

A DISCOURSE ON DEVILRY—A DEVOTIONAL IMAGE—
BAROQUE VERSUS ROMANTICISM—CAUGHT IN THE ACT—
DANGEROUS TROUSERS—A CONFUSION OF AGENCY

The road to hell is paved with piratic entertainments. They began before breakfast in the form of an impromptu game of tag initiated when Bloodhound Bess was caught stealing a pearl necklace from Mrs. Ogden's dressing table. Then came Capture the Flag with a pair of Mrs. Ogden's knickers. By the time the butler warily announced breakfast served, the company was bright-eyed, bushy-tailed, and ready to board a fast train to the Abode of the Damned.

"Let's do a spot of hunting after this," Millie the Monster suggested as she dipped toast into a soft-boiled egg.

"Jolly grand idea!" Frederick exclaimed. "Just the thing to stir the blood!"

"I'm glad you agree," Millie said. "Your footmen look like sprightly chaps—my blood is stirring already. How much of a head start shall we give them?"

Across the room from her, two footmen shuffled nervously.

"Ah," Frederick said with a startled laugh. "I supposed you meant out in the fields, shooting grouse and whatnot."

"How barbaric, killing defenseless animals in such a manner!" Mrs. Ogden exclaimed through a mouthful of bacon. "It behooves us as ladies and leaders of society to be more civilized. I for one will not be hunting any small, fluffy creature. It's dignified indoor pursuits for me, thank you." She scrutinized the footmen with a widow degree of interest. "I say five minutes should be enough. I'll take the one on the left."

Alice tried not to tap her fingers against the tabletop with frustration. She did not want to be caught up in mindless games all day. There was a weapon to be found, the Queen to be saved, and the rest of her current reading to be finished in peace and quiet back in London. Leaning closer to Daniel, who sat beside her, she murmured, "I fear I have not much appetite. Would you like my crumpet?"

She watched his eyes darken as he stared back at her, and understood that he had recognized the code for *Let us escape the company as soon as possible and scour the damned castle in hopes of finding the weapon, for the sake of Her Majesty's life, not to mention my sanity.*

"It is shaped rather like a cat, don't you think?" she added—i.e., *I have an enchanted petticoat on today in case we need to be like cat burglars and climb in through windows again.*

Daniel blinked rapidly at this—but before Alice could decipher what he meant, Jane tapped a spoon against her teacup.

"How clever is Mrs. Blakeney?" she said. The company paused in their eating to stare nonplussed, first at her, then at Alice. "I will be busy this morning in conference with the housekeeper—which reminds me, Frederick, where did you put my thumbscrews?—but why don't you all take inspiration from Mrs. Blakeney's creative vision and tour the castle's artworks?"

The excellence of this idea was generally agreed upon, and Alice congratulated for it. Her nerves twitched at the attention—but since the sober contemplation of art was second only to reading in her esteem, by the time she left the table she was prepared to be happy indeed.

Had she instead prepared to be exhausted, confused, and nearly stabbed to death, that might have been more helpful.

The company tramped through corridors and galleries, not so much *contemplating* the art as calculating its value, measuring it for theft, and, in the case of smaller pieces, stashing it inside hidden pockets. (They weren't particularly sober either, since Millie the Monster had secretly spiked the breakfast tea with rum.) Several gaps in the collection caused irritation, as pirates do not like having missed out on anything. Daniel and Alice hovered awkwardly at the edges of the group, receiving suspicious looks for their law-abiding behavior.

"Perhaps we should try to steal something," Alice whispered.

"Or perhaps we should sneak off," Daniel whispered back. "We could search Frederick's office while everyone is busy."

"Very well," Alice agreed. "Let's go now, bef—"

"And that is why I consider Rembrandt a fraud!"

Their heads whipped around.

Mrs. Rotunder was sneering at a group of oil paintings. "Complete fraud," she averred.

"Surely you jest," Miss Darlington said sternly.

"Why should you think so?" Mrs. Rotunder answered. "Just look at this portrait of Danaë. Leaving aside the matter of her outrageous nudity (which, you may be sure, I do not approve of), where is the golden shower come to have nooky with her?"

Miss Darlington gasped. "I cannot believe you said such a rude word, Gertrude! A lady never mentions"—she whispered loudly—"*nudity.* I must protest. En garde!"

Mrs. Rotunder scoffed at the rapier Miss Darlington had drawn from inside her walking stick. "Really, dear? Before ten in the morning? How déclassé."

Now the entire company gasped. Metal rang out as swords and daggers were presented. Forget contemplation: the art was now catapulted across the room to emphasize various point of debate.

"Such offensive language is unacceptable in our polite company! I'm going to teach you a bloody lesson!" *Thud!* Miss Darlington smashed a painting over Mrs. Rotunder's head, denting the hat thereon.

"The 'impasto technique' just means the artist ate a lot of spaghetti while he painted, do you know nothing?!" *Clang!* Hadiza the Horrible sent a miniature landscape bouncing off the edge of Mrs. Etterly's sword.

"Look you, the woman is wearing a wedding ring, therefore cannot be Danaë!" *Smack!* Bloodhound Bess applied Danaë's portrait emphatically to the face of Essie Smith.

"Your dress is ugly! Oh yes, and I also disagree with whatever you said about the painting!" *Crash! Ping! Ping! Ping!* Millie the Monster smashed a vase against a wall, causing shards to ricochet about the chamber.

Daniel watched in a state of silent disapproval. But Alice found herself tapping her fingers and clicking her tongue. "Really," she declared at last, to no one in particular, "it is *obvious* the illumination of Danaë's figure alludes to the golden shower."

Bloodhound Bess took exception to this (on general principle, since she did not know what *illumination* meant, although she suspected it was another rude word), and moments later Alice found herself stumbling back so as to avoid the lady's sword. She collided with Mrs. Ogden, who was disputing the pronunciation of *Baroque* with Lysander Smith by means of shouting *"Barro-kew! Barro-kew!"* and bashing him around the head with her purse.

"Hey, watch it!" the elderly pirate complained as Alice knocked against her.

"I beg your pardon," Alice said. But Mrs. Ogden swung about, aiming her purse toward Alice's head even as Bloodhound Bess moved closer—

And suddenly Daniel was there, standing between Alice and the two pirate women, his arms crossed and his disapproval more daunting than a drawn weapon.

"Ladies," he said. "I'm sure you do not mean to threaten my wife."

At that moment, a freak lightning storm occurred inside Alice Dearlove's circulatory system.

"My goodness," Bess remarked dryly as she lowered her sword. "What a romantic gesture!"

"I can look after myself," Alice said—since, according to the mission dossier, a statement of feminine independence was required at such moments, not dreamy music and a dozen roses displayed by candlelight in her brain.

Bess gave a short, crisp laugh. "Come now, every pirate adores romantic gestures. A man risking life and limb for you? So thrilling! And let us be clear—" She pinned Daniel with a hard look. "Life and limb *are* at risk here."

Daniel looked back unflinchingly.

"Frankly, I didn't think he had it in him," Mrs. Ogden commented.

"Oh, I suspect there is a great deal of interest under Mr. Blakeney's cover," Bess replied. "Come, my dear, let us go attack each other over in that corner, and leave Mrs. Blakeney to handle her—" She broke off, clearing her throat.

"Husband," Mrs. Ogden supplied.

"Hm," Bess agreed, and with a smirk she drew the other lady away.

Alice and Daniel stood for a moment in awkward silence, not

meeting each other's eyes. Finally, Daniel shifted, straightening his already perfectly aligned spectacles.

"Yes. Right. Where were we?"

"Going to search Frederick's office," Alice said. "But if we leave now, they'll assume we're being—you know."

"Antisocial?"

"Romantic," she whispered fiercely.

He gave her a smile so wicked it was as if he'd put on a feathered hat and fascinating boots. Remembering that he'd been butler to a notoriously rakish pirate, Alice wondered just how many vices he had picked up along the way . . . and whether he might be persuaded to show some of them to her.

"Good," he said, and tucked her arm around his.

Alice strove to remain tranquil. Over the years, she'd wrestled with men during training, been helped by men into carriages and trains, and even been groped by men who thought she was a naive, powerless servant (and who afterward had much time to dwell upon the error of their ways from a hospital bed). But Daniel Bixby's physical presence always made her feel like a book whose pages were being riffled.

Now, with *my wife* echoing in her brain as they walked together from the gallery, Alice had to admit herself feeling indeed riffled—by a tornado.

The moment they left the pirates' sight, Daniel released her. They did not speak as they strode through the castle corridors, and by the time they arrived at Frederick's office, Alice was sensibly tranquil once more.

"The door is locked," Daniel reported, tugging on its handle.

"I'm wearing my lockpick as a hairpin today," Alice said, and patted her coiffure in search of it.

"Allow me."

Before she understood what he was about, Daniel set a hand against her cheek and used his other hand to slowly withdraw a long copper pin from her hair.

Sticks! Fiddle! The tornado swooped back in again, riffling her so vigorously her brain fell down and had to struggle to get back up again. Her heart tried to outrace the storm. But her eyes were riveted on the sight of Daniel's temperate face, his lashes casting delicate shadows as he watched himself release the pin. A lock of hair tumbled loose against her throat, and she shivered at its light, stroking touch.

Pressing the sharp point of the lockpick to his fingertip, Daniel smiled. "I should have no problem sliding it in," he said.

And Alice's brain, having restored itself, collapsed again.

"Uhngh," she said.

Daniel gave her a slightly perplexed look, then turned to insert the pin into the door. Alice hastily tidied her consciousness yet again. She did not tap even one finger. She was after all a master spy! Her entire focus remained on the mission's sex.

No, wait—the mission's *success*.

Suddenly, footsteps sounded.

"Quick," Daniel whispered, turning to Alice and angling himself so the door's lock was hidden. "Act married!"

Someone appeared around the nearby corridor . . . Daniel reached for her . . .

"*And furthermore,*" Alice said in a strident voice, slapping his hand away and shoving her fists against her hips. "When you take off your shirt at the end of the day, you should leave it in the hamper, not on the floor!"

Stunned, Daniel opened his mouth to reply, but closed it again wordless. There would have been no time for him to respond in any case, for the person was upon them.

"I say! Fancy seeing you here, what!"

"Snodgrass." Daniel directed a chilling stare at the scientist, who grinned back cheerfully. Behind him came a footman carrying a ladder. "What are you up to, Doctor?"

"Up to?" The scientist's limbs jerked slightly, as if they'd taken the question as a command to jump.

"Why do you have a ladder?" Alice specified.

"Oh! It belongs to this fellow. We simply happen to be going in the same direction and fell into chatting, ha ha. I say, what are *you* up to?" He peered at the door behind them. "Trying to open that? Ah! I can help! I have a specially designed key here somewhere." He patted his various pockets; something buzzed, and smoke puffed from the hem of one trouser leg.

"We don't need it," Daniel said hastily.

"No, no, I'm sure I have it, my own particular invention, what, and it's the perfect gadget for a—"

Daniel closed his eyes. Alice flapped a hand at the scientist, mouthing *Go! Quickly!*, and the man finally had enough sense to do as he was told. By the time Daniel opened his eyes again, Snodgrass was almost to the end of the corridor, out of the range of assassination.

The footman lingered, however. Biting his lip nervously, he glanced along each direction of the corridor, then leaned forward.

"I heard you brought down a pack of thieves in St. James using only two fingers and a hat," he said. "Don't suppose you could teach me how?"

He was allowed to leave in full possession of his life and limbs because killing a man who held a ladder would inevitably be noisy.

Watching the footman run after Snodgrass, Alice exhaled. "That was a close call. I feared if Dr. Snodgrass patted one more pocket he might explode."

"Hm," Daniel said, packing into one syllable a fervent monologue on how much he wished such a thing would happen. He unlocked the door to Frederick's office and peered inside.

"Clear."

They entered and, closing the door behind them, began searching the room. But no weapon lay hidden behind its several mirrors, nor amongst the colognes and hair-care products cluttering its desk, nor inside the mannequin dressed in a white shirt and pink silk waistcoat.

"Ned Lightbourne has a waistcoat just like this," Daniel remarked, inspecting the garment's pockets in case a catastrophically dangerous assassination device was hidden inside their two inches of space.

Alice set down a locket containing Jane's portrait and, turning, noticed several marks on the floor. "What are these?" she asked, bemused.

Daniel regarded them thoughtfully for a moment, then began to follow them with his feet.

"It's the tango," he said, moving with the easy, fluid grace of a man whose body was a finely honed weapon. "Frederick must be trying to learn."

"He doesn't seem the type who would dance well," Alice mused.

Daniel turned on his heel and followed the marks back again. "What type would that be?"

"Self-confident," she said. "Good spatial awareness. Firm hips."

A sharp little silence followed this statement. Alice realized she was staring at Daniel's hips. "*Um*," she said, lifting her gaze—and immediately became caught in his.

He was staring right back at her, transfixed. Alice did not even try to look away. She was going to set up camp in this hot, silent moment; she was going to build a house and grow old here. The world beyond turned as dark and vague as smoke. The mission vanished altogether. Daniel took a step closer, and something rattled—her heart maybe, or the office door's handle.

She blinked just as Daniel did, yanked violently back into clarity. The office door's handle rattled louder and began to turn.

There was no time to hide. All they could do was dash to the end of the room and press back against the wall, where they were concealed by the door as it slowly opened.

"I know you're in here," came a cold, hushed voice. "I have a gun intended for you."

A brown-haired woman dressed all in black entered cautiously. Daniel moved toward her with silent swiftness, grasping her by the neck. She had no opportunity to react: within seconds, consciousness abandoned her, and she collapsed to the floor.

"Dead?" Alice asked as she closed the door again.

"I hope I am not so clumsy as that," Daniel answered dryly. Crouching before the woman, he checked her pulse. "Alive."

"Do you recognize her?"

"No. The housemaid's uniform would indicate she's a servant, but these manicured fingernails suggest otherwise. Whatever the case, better safe than sorry." Taking string from his trouser pocket, he began tying the woman's wrists.

"You are using the wrong knot," Alice advised. "She'll be able to slip out of that easily."

"It's a sledge knot. Entirely suitable."

"You should use a constrictor knot."

"Uh huh." He continued applying a sledge knot to the woman's wrists.

"*I* would rather take advice than risk a suspect escaping," Alice noted.

Daniel paused, his forearms resting on his thighs, and looked up at her with an unblinking sternness that would no doubt have daunted someone not raised by spymasters. "Are you questioning my professionalism?"

"Of course not."

He nodded.

"I am impugning it outright."

A muscle in Daniel's jaw leaped. Alice did not smirk, for that would be undisciplined, but her mouth did slant a little at one edge as she bent to pick up the woman's pistol.

Bzzz. Bzzz.

She almost dropped it again as it vibrated in her hand.

"Oh dear," Daniel murmured.

Bzzz. Bzzz.

Alice pressed the facing of the pistol's handle, then caught her breath as it slid up, revealing a metal interior etched with Latin. With a trepidatious glance at Daniel, she held it to her mouth.

"Hello?"

"Agent A?" came a tinny reply from within the pistol. Alice winced, recognizing Mrs. Kew's voice. Daniel bit his lower lip and glanced guiltily at the woman lying bound and unconscious before him.

"Yes, this is A," Alice replied.

"Kew here. Glad to . . . Agent M found you . . . disguised communication device. I have important information . . . you."

"Go ahead," Alice said, watching as Daniel untied ~~the suspicious housemaid~~ Agent M.

"We have discovered . . . will . . . absolutely ghastly! . . . you must . . . at once, before the whole . . . crashing down! . . . disaster!"

"It's a bad connection," Alice replied. "Say again."

"Imperative that you . . . stop . . . or else . . ."

Sparks began flashing from the gun's barrel. Alice instinctively tossed it from her, and even before it reached the floor, the whole thing erupted in flames. Alice grabbed a nearby blond wig and applied it to extinguishing the fire. She managed to do so quickly, but there was no hope of using the device again.

"Any idea what Mrs. Kew was saying?" Daniel asked.

"None. You?"

He shook his head. Then Agent M began to stir, moaning a little. Daniel immediately attended to her.

"You attacked me!" she gasped as he helped her to her feet.

"Er, yes," he confessed. "Sorry about that."

"You actually used a choke hold on me!"

"Well, something of the sort. Apologies."

Her dark eyes widened. "Agent B rendered me unconscious using a specialist maneuver! I cannot believe my good fortune! Just wait until V-2 hears, she will be so jealous! Would you autograph my—my—" She looked about her person for something to be signed, and finally rolled up her sleeve, revealing a decidedly un-housemaid-like tattoo of a bird. "Just sign my arm," she said. "The name's Mia Thalassi, and if you wanted to fold—"

"Listen, Mia," Alice interjected before Daniel could get *calm* again. "Do you know why Mrs. Kew was calling?"

"No, ma'am. Shall I ask Dr. Snodgrass for another device?"

"No!" the agents answered in immediate unison, causing Mia to take a cautious step back from them.

"No," Daniel said more sedately. "We must get that information. But we can't risk sending a telegram—the network is completely infiltrated with enemy spies."

"You mean employees of the British government," Mia said.

"Exactly. Someone will have to go to London and speak to Mrs. Kew in person."

Mia thrust her hand into the air. "I volunteer as traveler!"

"Hm," Daniel said, crossing his arms as he regarded her.

She stared right back. "If you're trying to daunt me, just know that I currently share quarters with Agent V-2 and have to spend half the night listening to her read out scenes from the *Moby Dick* retelling she's working on, written from the perspective of the whale. It starts with, 'Call me Dick, Moby Dick. I am a sperm whale.' As a result, not much unnerves me these days."

"Fair enough," Daniel said, easing his stance. "Very well, return to headquarters and bring us back the information. But be quick about it. Any moment now, the Wisteria Society might—"

"Find the weapon and use it for nefarious purposes," Mia said, nodding somberly.

Daniel frowned. "I was more thinking they might—"

"Discover your identity and force you to walk the plank?"

"Make us play another parlor game," Alice said, and both she and Daniel shuddered.

They sent Mia off, but any further searching they might have undertaken was forestalled by the ringing of the luncheon bell.

"It would help if we'd been told who exactly amongst the staff is on mission support," Alice complained as they headed for the dining room.

"I trust no one," Daniel said. "Except you, of course."

Alice's stomach did a small flip at this statement, and she immediately scowled in self-annoyance. Her stomach was not the flipping kind. It was the disinterested, unemotional kind, entirely professional. Her mind was well regulated. And her eyes did not keep glancing at a gentleman's buttocks like some shameless hussy, *thank you very much*. She needed to pull herself together, or else by the time this mission ended she'd practically be a pirate.

"At least the ladies will be exhausted after this morning," she said. "They'll want to spend the afternoon resting on your bottom—er, on their—er, sitting down—which means we can continue our search."

Bang!

A porcelain vase flew out of the dining room and shattered against the opposite wall. Hollers and cheers followed it.

"You were saying?" Daniel asked.

"Oh God." Alice pressed a hand against her stomach, which had advanced from flipping to twisting. "It's going to be *fun*, isn't it?"

"I'm afraid so." Daniel tucked her arm in his, and they entered the fray.

❊ 12 ❊

One crowded hour of glorious life might be worth an age without a name, but Alice would gladly have traded it for even thirty minutes of anonymous, empty peace. Balancing on a high parapet of Starkthorn Castle, she breathed hard and fanned herself with a tennis racket while overhead several houses floated. On the roof of each stood a pirate, playing what they termed a "fun" game of aerial tennis. Alice considered this a crime against language.

"Look sharp, Mrs. Blakeney!" shouted Millie the Monster, pink skirts flouncing as she ran the length of her ridgepole to whack a ball in Alice's direction. Alice raised her racket without much hope, but Millie's aim was true—thankfully, considering the aforementioned ball was in fact a grenade. It bounced off Alice's racket and flew randomly across the sky. Miss Darlington, seated on a wicker chair with a blanket over her lap and cup of tea in hand, pointed to it with her cane. Immediately her maidservant, Competence, jumped, racket swooping efficiently. There came a businesslike *thwack*, and the grenade-ball spun away toward Mrs. Rotunder's conservatory.

Boom!

Glass exploded. Pirates cheered and then, as smoke billowed through the trembling air, began to cough. Alice ducked as something shot toward her. It clattered onto the walkway behind the parapet. Turning carefully, Alice looked down to see a wooden arm, splintered and flickering with flames, roll across the stone.

"Sorry, Mr. Rotunder!" Competence called out.

"No worries!" the gentleman replied sunnily from the conservatory's shattered doorway, waving what remained of his limb. "I always bring a spare arm when visiting with the Society, just in case."

"That was the last ball," Mrs. Etterly announced from atop her chimney. "Shall we have a tea break?"

"Thank goodness," Alice muttered.

"Excellent idea!" Mrs. Ogden shouted. "I'll get my butler to bring up some old cups. But we'll need bats instead of rackets."

Alice groaned. While the pirates busied themselves changing equipment, she slipped down from the parapet and leaned back against its stone wall, hoping that out of sight would render her out of mind. The pirates' minds, that is. Alice felt fairly certain she was already out of her own mind following an afternoon of aerial tennis, aerial calisthenics, and other mundane activities that became terrifyingly manic once the word *aerial* was attached to them. She could do with an actual tea break—preferably with wine instead of tea in the cup.

In fact, forget the cup. Just hand over the bottle.

Pushing back the wide-brimmed hat Miss Darlington had loaned her, she ran a hand across her damp face, not even bothering to tidy the strands of hair hanging loose about its edges. Remembering that Daniel still had possession of her hairpin from earlier, she closed her eyes and indulged in a small, pleasant daydream about reaching into his trouser pocket to take it back . . .

"Ahem."

At the sound, her eyes flung open—then attempted to open even wider still as they saw Daniel walking along the battlement toward her, a mild expression of disapproval upon his face. Watching him, Alice realized she was probably going to have to report herself for mental dereliction of duty. Her secret thoughts about Agent B broke several rules of professional psychological conduct—then ground the pieces into the dirt and set them aflame. She knew she could not have him, knew equally that he did not want her, he was just particularly good at taking on the role of husband. But that did not stop her from fantasizing a great deal about *having*, and *taking*, and other risqué verbs.

She fanned herself vehemently with the tennis racket. Daniel, on the other hand, appeared utterly cool in a dark gray suit, his spectacles glinting with afternoon sunlight. Not a single crease blemished the trousers encasing his thighs. *Six rules broken*, Alice thought as she contemplated those thighs. *Seven rules*, as she imagined them between hers while he pinned her to a bed.

Fiddlesticks. She was approaching hooliganism with such speed she might as well just give up and become a politician.

"I trust you are not leaning while on duty, Miss Dearlove?" Daniel said as he drew near.

His expression was stone. His demeanor, controlled. And his voice, cold like something sliding against her skin—a chocolate-dipped strawberry, for example. Alice hastily summoned a frown. "Where have you been? And why is your jacket sleeve torn?"

He shrugged. "Someone shot a crossbow bolt at me from the shadows."

"Someone tried to kill you? That is good news."

"Indeed. It proves we have been accepted into the group." He cocked his head. "You are in a most unseemly disarray."

"I have been playing tennis. As you were supposed to be also. And yet you departed without notice after aerial duck-duck-goose, which you can be sure I will be mentioning in the mission report."

He leaned close, his voice fluttering against her ear. "Go ahead, write me up."

Crash! The pirates had begun breaking crockery. Or possibly Alice's nerves were breaking like an explosion of rose-painted porcelain.

"You are living dangerously, sir," she managed to say as she tried to push him away. Oddly, however, her hand seemed to have lost all understanding of force, and was instead lingering against his waistcoat buttons, thrilling at their texture.

"Living dangerously is the job description," Daniel said. His gaze slid with languid slowness down her form. "What are you wearing?"

"Bloomers," she said.

"There is no need to swear."

"No, bloomers. Turkish trousers. Mrs. Rotunder loaned them to me so I could play tennis without the inconvenience of tripping over a hem and plunging one hundred feet to my death. And Miss Darlington gave me the hat, which apparently protects against the Great Peril. I have no idea what she meant."

Daniel considered it with some bemusement. "Perhaps it's a shield against aerial weapons?" He reached out and tugged it more properly into place. "I found a barricaded room on the second floor that we might be able to access via a window," he said as he straightened the hat's brim. "I also spoke with Agent M before she left to catch a train from the nearby village. I've requested new premises, which she can fly back along with Mrs. Kew's message. Might as well kill two birds with one stone."

Alice stared at him wide-eyed. "Why would you kill birds? That is despicable, sir! And where is this stone of which you speak?" She looked around for it without success; returning to his face, she found it perfectly inscrutable.

"I beg your pardon," he said. "It was merely an idiom."

"Oh." She sighed. "Sorry. This is why I work alone. Conversation is beyond me."

"Don't worry on my account," he said, tucking a loose, damp strand of hair behind her ear. "God knows I often have my foot in my mouth." And, as Alice drew breath to answer—"Idiom again."

"You cannot be worse than I am," she insisted. "For example, I once called Mrs. Kew 'Mrs. Cute' by mistake."

Daniel did not look up from tidying a strip of lace that had become slightly folded on her bodice. "I once called a cutthroat band of smugglers 'snugglers,' and barely made it out of their company alive."

"Oh dear." Alice bit her lip in an effort to repress her amusement, but Daniel only stared at the lace strip.

"It would be nice to feel safe with someone," he said quietly.

Alice's heart stirred. "You—" she began.

Toot! Toot!

They jolted, reaching for weapons.

"Blakeneys!" Mrs. Ogden leaned out of her attic window to wave at them. "They've just rung the bell for afternoon tea! I'll race you to the field behind the castle!"

Her house swooped away before they could answer, and Daniel and Alice both shook their heads in silent condemnation.

"I am not going to race," Alice said airily.

"Nor I," Daniel agreed.

They glanced at each other for half a second.

And then they were running along the battlement—vaulting a cannon—yanking open a door—clambering down a tower of stairs—avoiding servants wanting their autograph—pausing to check inside a sideboard for the hidden weapon—racing through the central hall—skirting a trolley of silverware—pointing out a cobweb to a housemaid—leaping over a sudden cat—and arriving at the castle's main rear exit with only the merest acceleration of their breath. Dashing over the threshold, they scanned the collection of white-clothed tables and parasols that had been set up on the grass—

And stopped.

"There you are at last, Blakeneys!" Mrs. Ogden called from where she sat at a table with a plate of tiny sandwiches and cakes in front of her. She lifted a cup of tea in salute.

Alice and Daniel just looked at her.

"I am inspired to recollect paragraph seven in the mission dossier," Alice murmured to Daniel as he took her by the arm and they proceeded across the grass toward Mrs. Ogden.

"'Make sure you have a good view before you kill,'" Daniel recited.

"No, the second sentence," Alice said. "'Pirates always cheat.'"

Daniel huffed a dry laugh. "I didn't need a dossier to tell—"

"*Imposter!*" came a sudden shout.

The agents froze immediately.

"Well I never!" Miss Darlington marched into sight across the grass, pointing her cane at Alice in an accusatory manner. "I am shocked, young woman. Shocked!"

Alice felt Daniel's fingers tighten on her arm. But she just smiled in a mildly inquiring fashion. "Ma'am?"

"You presented yourself to me as a conveniently reasonable woman!" Miss Darlington declaimed for all to hear. And indeed, pirates began appearing from inside the castle and around various corners, bristling with fascinators, glinting with the swords and guns strapped against their bright dresses, looking altogether like elegant, gilded, and extremely well-armed vultures.

"Reasonable," Miss Darlington reiterated. "And yet here you are, in broad daylight, being *unreasonable* indeed! Do you not care *at all* about the broad daylight, gel? The burning sunlight?"

"Um," Alice said.

Miss Darlington gesticulated. "You are not wearing your hat!"

"Oh!" Alice lifted a hand to her head and discovered the hat Miss Darlington had loaned her was missing. "I beg your pardon, ma'am. I must have dropped it along the way."

"I'm sure a servant will have picked it up," Daniel said. "We can inquire later."

"Later? Later!" Miss Darlington turned an incredulous stare at Mrs. Rotunder, who was just then coming up beside her. The lady gave an obliging murmur of disapproval.

"Even *Ned* understands that Cecilia must have a supply of three stylish hats for each day of the week if she is to protect herself from the Great Peril," Miss Darlington told Daniel. "Perhaps you ought to read a book on husbandry, young man."

"That would inform me about farming, ma'am," Daniel answered—and did not die on the spot only because Miss Darlington's stare was not *literally* a flaming sword.

Alice hastily intervened. "What exactly is the Great Peril?" she asked.

The pirates answered in fervent accord. "Freckles!"

Miss Darlington bustled her away from Daniel, tucking her into a chair at Mrs. Ogden's table, sheltered by a large parasol. An emergency hat was brought forth and a footman established nearby, his purpose being to stand at any angle necessary so as to block the slightest hint of sunlight attempting to fall upon Alice's skin.

"There," Miss Darlington said finally as she sat. "We have you nicely undercover again."

Alice tried to thank her but could not summon words. No one had ever before cared that she might freckle in the sun. No one had fussed over her in this manner—or indeed any manner, unless "caning with a birch rod" constituted fussing. It felt decidedly strange. Not helping matters was the mysterious watering of her eyes. Perhaps she was developing spontaneous hay fever. Frankly, she would not be surprised—she'd put nothing past this mission.

"Pardon me infiltrating the conversation," Mrs. Rotunder said, sliding into a chair beside Alice, "but you don't want to be a sleeper when it comes to the Great Peril, my dear. While no one is suggesting you act like a mole, you should nevertheless conceal your delicate skin at all times."

Alice could only smile, still too dazed (and cold in the shadows) to reply.

There followed a pleasant chat over tea and cake about the latest guns being imported from America. Alice knew she should subtly interrogate the ladies about what they might do with those guns, but could not judge how to enter the conversation without literally shooting her way in. Waiting for pauses, starting a question only to find someone else starting their own more quickly, and trying to keep up with a barrage of idioms made her so tense that, when Frederick announced a game of croquet had been prepared—"fair ladies, come and join me in a stirring contest of brain and balls . . . O! croquet, once a sport of kings, now beloved by the most discerning of lawn athletes!"—she could have employed herself as a mallet.

The game led to wholly expected results, i.e., several smoking craters in the field, the entire set of mallets broken, and Frederick being rendered unconscious when three croquet balls and a hoop struck his head at the same time in a remarkable coincidence that *absolutely astonished* the entire company. By the time darkness and dinnertime brought a halt to the ~~violence~~ entertainment, Alice was exhausted, but she barely had time to wash, change her clothes, and read a page of *Prometheus Bound* for some light comfort before being faced with the arduous trial of eating stew despite not knowing exactly what it contained.

After dinner, the ladies sat around on sofas, drinking sherry while Mrs. Etterly tried to persuade them to buy a collection of nifty storage containers for their grenades and knuckle-dusters. Meanwhile, in another room with the men, Daniel suffered being blinded (for a jolly game of pin the tail on the donkey) and beaten (in several rounds of chess, which he lost on purpose for the sake of the mission). Finally, Alice pleaded a headache and thus effected her escape. She found Daniel already in their bedroom, muttering *"pawn to queen bishop four"* furiously as he did one-armed push-ups.

"All well?" he asked, jumping to his feet and looking around for his spectacles.

"The ladies are still downstairs, but I could not bear another moment," Alice confessed.

"I felt the same way."

The expression of empathy took Alice by surprise. Her heart softened, and she began to think herself removed from the verge of combustion—albeit still within walking distance.

"It's just all the noise," she said. "You know?"

"I know," Daniel said, and her heart softened even more. He put on his spectacles, and his fingers lingered against his brow. "The different perfumes."

"Frederick Bassingthwaite's laugh."

"You win," he said wryly, and Alice's heart grew so soft it was almost easygoing. She found herself smiling at him. The realization shocked her, and she quickly straightened her expression back into professional sobriety.

Daniel sighed. "This mission is exhausting. Miss Darlington has diagnosed me with both rabies and a fatal case of tinnitus in my liver. Someone stole my pocket watch. And there were *raisins* in the ice cream tonight."

"We are also still getting comments about our relationship," Alice said. "At dinner, Mrs. Etterly declared herself amazed I managed any sleep with a husband like you. I think she was suggesting you might try to assassinate me in my bed."

"Hm," Daniel answered in such a bland tone it could have been served for dinner in a hospital.

"Perhaps we ought to choreograph some marital gestures," Alice said, "to strengthen our disguise."

"What exactly do you mean?" Daniel asked, caution shadowing his eyes.

"I noticed the Rotunders holding hands earlier today."

"Holding hands." He made it sound as if she had asked him to unblock a lavatory.

"It should be easy enough." Advancing her right hand, she waited, and after a moment of reluctance Daniel took it with his left.

"Er, I think the palms go together," she said. "And you should probably not brace yourself in that manner, as if you are about to pull me into a headlock."

He released her hand, tried again.

"There," she said, nodding in satisfaction. Something a little wilder than satisfaction shivered through her body, but she ignored it. "Now we look entirely married."

Daniel considered their clasped hands with some doubt. "There may be more to it than this."

"Try holding a little tighter."

He obediently hardened his grip. "I am not hurting you?" he asked, hearing her breath catch.

"No." She inhaled more carefully. His hand was larger than hers, stronger. She could see faint scars across his tanned skin, and the wedding ring on his finger thrilled her inexplicably. Deep inside came a tug of sensation, as if he was pulling dreams out, old secret dreams she had long forgotten. Withdrawing her hand carefully, she curled its fingers. Daniel pressed his own hand against his midriff as if it burned.

"That's probably sufficient hand-holding practice," Alice said rather faintly. "What else can we try?"

Daniel frowned in thought. "Perhaps some mild caressing?"

"I am unsure what you mean. Please demonstrate."

He lifted a hand toward her again, and Alice had all she could do not to catch it, twist it around his back, and force him to his knees until he begged for mercy. But she restrained her professional instincts, staying still—at least until he brushed a stray lock of hair from her temple. Then she shivered all over.

"I'm sorry," he said, jerking his fingers away. "No light touches."

"It's all right, I accept this is necessary," she said. "Husbandly. It did tickle, but this is why practicing is a good idea. I can build up my endurance. Ultimately, I should feel nothing when you touch me."

"I'm not sure that's how it works between a husband and wife. You should probably always feel something."

"Are you certain? That doesn't sound very comfortable."

"From my observation, marriage seems to have little to do with comfort. Anyway, I think we've done enough for—"

"You need to kiss me."

Tilting his head, Daniel gave her one of his gorgeous smiles, tender, quizzical, all too brief. "I beg your pardon?"

Alice gestured vaguely. "In case of further parlor games."

Daniel considered this, then nodded. "Seems sensible. Very well, then."

"Wait." She rummaged in a skirt pocket for pen and notebook. "I should take notes."

An odd noise emerged from Daniel's throat. "That is probably not necessary."

"What if I forget how it was?"

He looked at her intently. "I promise you will *never* forget how it was."

"Huh. Very well, shall we proceed?" Clasping her hands together before her, she presented her face for kissing. "And not another a peck on the cheek. Something marital."

Daniel gave a brisk nod. "I am at your service, madam."

❊ 13 ❊

THEY ARE EXTREMELY PROFESSIONAL—
HAND-HOLDING PRACTICE PAYS OFF—
OCCUPATIONAL HEALTH AND SAFETY—
DANIEL IS MESSED UP (MENTALLY AND LITERALLY)—
ECHOES—ALARM!

Nothing in Nature stands still; everything strives and moves forward—with the exception of Daniel Bixby. Alice waited, and waited, while he looked down at her so heatedly her nerves began to sizzle. Was he actually going to kiss her? Perhaps he did not know how to do it after all and was trying to recollect the procedure?

She had been wishing for this from the first moment she saw him in the dress shop, his posture so impeccable she would have defied anyone not to lust after the man. Since learning he was Agent B, she'd struggled to reconcile their professional rivalry with attraction. But she expected now to solve that dilemma, for surely nothing simplified things more than a kiss. If only Daniel would make haste. She restrained herself from glancing at the nearby clock.

Finally, he bent, and Alice caught her breath.

He gently pressed his mouth against her forehead.

Alice was bewildered—did he not know the correct zone for kissing?—and annoyed! And *oh*, melting warm and slow all through her body until she found herself swaying helplessly against him. He kissed next the edge of one eye, her eyelashes sweeping against his lips.

No one had mentioned this variation of the activity. They had talked about mouths and knuckles and not doing it unless you were prepared to get married. But now Daniel was kissing her cheek, and not at all like he had the night before; this time, it was slower, softer, his breath fanning her skin and intensifying the warmth inside her. Alice felt sure this must be highly inappropriate even for the most married of couples.

A sound shuddered from her unkissed mouth. It said nothing, but it meant *please*. At this point, she would have levitated a dozen tigers and assassinated Queen Victoria herself if only he would make haste. *Please*, she wished again.

At last, taking her chin between thumb and forefinger, he tilted it up, lowering his mouth to hers.

And she combusted into flames.

It was not like this in books, she thought in the fleeting moment before all thoughts burned away. Not even Primula Tewkes's penny-dreadful novels had described the sense of intimacy. After a lifetime of seldom being touched, she now had a man touching her in a way that, although confined to their lips, felt like caresses all over her skin. Daniel kissed her gently, yet with authority, and it was clear he knew exactly what he was doing after all. Alice found herself clutching at him as her knees began to tremble. Her heart was already at ten on the Richter scale.

She had no idea how to kiss him back. Overcome with sensation, she could not even evaluate his tactics and attempt to replicate them. But Daniel did not seem deterred by this. He did not slow to let her catch up, nor offer instruction, nor expect anything from her but surrender. And so she let go completely, requiring him to set an arm across her back so as to prevent her collapsing.

She remembered tumbling through the storm the other day. This was a dizzyingly similar experience, although with the defect of her skirt still being on.

Gradually the kiss eased, providing her with the opportunity to breathe and to analyze the event. (1) She had not expected so much involvement of the tongue. (2) Cardiac side effects may present some concern. (3) —

But it had not been an ending after all, only a trap to lure her further in. Suddenly he kissed her even more deeply, stroking against secrets she never knew she had. He pulled her close, cupping a hand against the back of her head, wrapping his arm more securely around her waist so their bodies were pressed hard together. Everything began to pulse—lips, heart, loins. Alice felt an echo of it in him too, through her clothes, behind his bones.

Good heavens, no wonder people married!

At last—too soon—Daniel pulled back with an effort. He seemed dazed. His eyes behind their slightly crooked spectacles blinked past her at some vision that darkened his expression.

"Perhaps this should not go in the mission report," he said.

"I agree," Alice replied through throbbing lips. She resisted the urge to rub them, for Daniel was not rubbing his, and she possessed no other guide to correct post-kissing behavior. "Nonetheless, I do feel. Um." What did she feel? Where had her brain gone? Groping incoherently through her overheated inner darkness, she found it at last surrounded by metaphors and rose petals. Sighing, it came to attention. "I feel that my portrayal of a happily married wife will be improved from here on. And I must say, already you look more like my—um, like *a* husband. So. There we have it. Excellent work. I suppose we should go search some rooms—?"

"Uh huh."

Neither of them moved.

"It would behoove us check in with Agent V-2 also." Her voice shook a little. Daniel was staring at her mouth now as if he wanted to lick the words coming out of it. "There may be an update from the servants' quarters, and—"

"Your stance was incorrect," he interrupted abruptly.

Alice frowned in perplexment. "My what?"

"A married woman would never stance—um, stand in that manner while she was being kissed." He made a vague gesture.

"Oh." Alice felt a blush warm her face. "What manner?"

"Er—angled too much to the left. Yes. And I got the—er, the middle bit wrong."

"You did?"

"I think we need to practice a little longer," Daniel said. "For the sake of the mission."

A thrill shot through Alice's blood. "That is an admirably professional attitude."

"Diligence is key to being a good secret agent." Taking her hand in his, just like they had rehearsed, he tugged her across the room in a manner that felt less marital than salaciously premarital.

"Where—?" Alice began to ask, but before she could further the query, they arrived at the bed and Daniel arranged her so she was sitting at its edge. He sat beside her and, removing his spectacles, laid them neatly on the bedside table.

"Occupational safety measures are important," he explained. "By continuing to stand, we risked falling and wrenching a knee or ankle."

"Ah, good point," Alice said. "I shall write in my report that you were assiduous in maintaining the welfare of all mission operatives."

He brushed the words from her lips with the pad of his thumb, and Alice gasped as sensation rampaged through her. Immediately he took advantage, sliding the thumb along the inside of her lower lip in an action so scandalous Alice would have gasped again were not her tongue, operating under its own instruction, busy swirling around that thumb, trying to draw it farther in. He tasted like salt and unsweetened tea. Alice swallowed as he shifted his hand away to cradle her cheek.

"And now I am going to kiss you until you see stars, Mrs. Blakeney."

"For the sake of the mission," she added.

He smiled. "Exactly."

"Very well then, Mr. Blakeney. You may proceed."

Daniel had spent his entire life devoted to duty. Literally. Raised in one of A.U.N.T.'s feeder orphanages, he had been selected for Elite Force training after he corrected the headmistress's caning technique in the middle of her punishing him. Slowly, inexorably, the nurses and instructors had drawn him out of his all-consuming desire for exactitude until he learned to find it again through obeying orders. Whenever the world seemed an impossible mess clattering against his senses, they taught him to clean it by sweeping, folding, assassinating. Whenever his own internal world threatened to explode, they taught him to become a precision bomb.

He had never viewed himself through any other lens than that of secret agent for the downstairs government. And he excelled at his work. To do less would chip away at his identity, threatening him with disorder, uncertainty, fear.

Daniel could not abide fear.

Alice Dearlove frightened him more than anything else had in all the years of violence, piracy, and dirty kitchens. Just looking at her stirred emotions and sensations that would shatter his carefully wrought control if he dared to allow them. Touching her felt like skimming his hands across a live electrical wire. Even were she not the most alluring thing he'd ever encountered, he'd fall for the charm of her stern disapprobation and the incredibly sexy way she talked about rules. He could not seem to chide himself out of wanting her, despite knowing it was hopeless. He longed to incinerate himself against her naked skin—to let the whole universe storm with the force of her breath on his tongue—and to sit cuddled up with her on a rainy night, reading aloud from Pushkin.

But that would be terrifying, agonizing, and inappropriate under the circumstances. So he just kissed her with such cool mastery, she swooned back onto the bed.

It went exactly how he intended. He could have written the process down on paper and ticked it off as he went along. After all, kissing a woman was no different from putting a gun together. If one fit the pieces properly, in the right order, it resulted in an effective bang. Daniel had done enough research to know this—textbooks, novels, and a few ladies who had volunteered as willing subjects for experimentation. In addition, living with a pirate for three years had provided a wealth of data. Before marrying, Captain O'Riley had been a notorious rake whose mere smile was worth several volumes on the art of seduction. Daniel applied the most interesting details of his research directly to Miss Dearlove's lips.

And then he struck a problem.

He had her right where he wanted her: soft and warm beneath him, in an appropriate disarray of lace and silk.

And she had him in chaos.

She tasted like hunger in his mouth. She felt like loneliness against his body as they lay on the pirates' bed, practicing how to be piratic. His precise list of tactics began to burn away as if written on Snodgrass's self-destructive parchment. His heart pounded so hard, he was the one seeing stars. And it is best not to mention what was happening inside his underwear.

Stop, he told himself.

Hm, his hand replied, sliding up under her skirts.

Alice gasped, and Daniel found himself shaken abruptly out of derangement by the sound. Lifting his head, he looked down at her carefully. Bloody hell, but she was beautiful. And almost unbearably valuable to him. He should never have started this.

With an effort, he forced his hand to stillness against her knee.

"I beg your pardon," he said.

Her eyes, hazy and dark, tried without much success to focus. "No, I am sorry. It tickled, that is all. I assume—I suppose—touching the leg is a marital maneuver?"

He shifted back a little, wary. "You do understand about, er, marital maneuvers, don't you?"

"Of course. I read a postdoctoral thesis on the subject."

The vision of her sitting in a hushed and solemn library, reading about sex while all around her students and librarians sat oblivious, so aroused him he fell to kissing her again without another thought. She drew him in, tiny wordless sounds emerging from her throat to tremble against their tongues, fingers tapping without rhythm against his back. Daniel forgot every rule of proper conduct as he lost himself in the desire that had been lying like dust in his heart, begging for a good sweeping up this past year. His hand continued sliding closer to the hot, dark euphemism that lay so secretly between her thighs. Every finger ached to be the first to enter her.

His self-control began to plummet once again.

With a great force of nobility, he pulled his hand back—but immediately it propelled itself to her bodice instead. Ripping was too messy to be indulged, but his fingers fumbled with the pearl buttons, shoving them through buttonholes, reaching through to tug at the embroidered trim of her chemise—

Beeeeep! Beeeeep!

They flung away from each other in shock. Tumbling off the bed,

Daniel was on his feet again in a matter of seconds, gun in hand, blood flaring through his veins as he ricocheted from sexual arousal to homicidal arousal. But the only hazard he saw was Miss Dearlove sitting rumpled on the bed, clutching her open bodice. His breath trembled as he stared at her. She was so flushed, he wanted to cool her down by licking her all over. She had lost her hairpins, and long, fine brown hair cascaded over her shoulders in a sultry mess that gleamed red where the lamplight stroked it, making her look like a portrait of some alluring heathen goddess. (Albeit not painted. Nor on a canvas. Nor even framed. Daniel's grasp on metaphors tended to have all the strength of a slippery thing trying to hold another slippery thing.) He struggled to recollect that she was a colleague, a highly trained agent of the secret government.

And then she straightened, her mouth tightening and her eyes becoming narrow—and memory snapped back into place. With it came an image of what she'd done to the men in the alleyway outside A.U.N.T. headquarters—and although Daniel briefly wondered if he could convince her to do the same to him, he sensed she no longer was in an amorous mood.

The scowl provided something of a clue.

"Kindly stop pointing that weapon at me," she said.

For one wild, blushing moment, Daniel looked down at his trousers—but then realized she meant his pistol, and sheepishly holstered it. "I beg your pardon," he said. "But what on earth was that appalling noise?"

"I have the incantation's collision prevention phrase sewn into my chemise," she explained. "It is a special precaution for female agents, especially those working in the households of rich men. I forgot it was there."

"I see." He ran a hand through his hair, unsure whether to be more appalled about the necessity of such a precaution or the fact that his own behavior had tripped it. Snatching his spectacles from the bedside table, he shoved them on and turned to stare at the wall.

Twenty white bouquets decorated the pale blue wallpaper in each vertical row.

Nineteen and a half in the third row from the door, someone having misaligned the paper.

Daniel's jaw twitched. He wanted to rip the wallpaper away to be rid of that one small error. He wanted to burn it, and beat the ashes, and absolutely stop envisioning himself teaching Alice Dearlove his own thesis on sex. Tightening his hands into fists, then stretching out the fingers, he breathed.

One, two, three.

Four, exhaling.

Behind him, Alice exhaled at the same moment. Daniel was unsurprised. As she inhaled again, he could practically hear the numbers being recited in her mind. No doubt they would sound just as they did in his, echoing the stentorious voice of Academy headmistress Mrs. Aberfinch—which was not exactly something he liked hearing so soon after kissing a woman. He wished he could take Alice in his arms once more and hold her, just hold her, drawing warmth from her body to dispel the endless chill of that voice. But he did not dare.

"Fiddlesticks," she muttered.

Daniel looked sidelong at her again. She was frowning as she searched for her hairpins across the crumpled bedspread.

"Sorry," he said on general principle.

"Why?"

He opened his mouth to explain before realizing doing so would probably lead to further kissing in order to prove his point. "Never mind."

"Have we reached the conclusion of our practice?"

"Yes. No." He shook his head. "Yes, but no, I—"

"Yes?" she prompted when he fell abruptly silent.

No, he thought, *I want to keep going. I want to kiss more than your mouth. I want to fit myself against your lovely, flawless being until all the fractures and jagged places in the world are eased. And I want to hold you, breathe you, as we move together into a moment of transcendent perfection.*

"Nothing," he said. "It's been a long day. I do believe I will retire." And giving her a pleasantly bland smile, he turned away, thereby missing the wishful expression in her eyes as he went to hide in the washroom and recover his good senses piece by piece.

✳ 14 ✳

DESPITE A THESAURUS, ALICE IS RENDERED WORDLESS—
THE NAKED TRUTH—THE BECHDEL TEST IS FAILED—SPY CENTRAL—
JUST DESSERTS—KNOCK ON WOOD—*LECTIO INTERRUPTUS*

It is better to have kissed and been interrupted than never to have kissed at all. This Alice reminded herself as she rebuttoned her bodice. Even so, her heart drooped miserably, despite the carefully nonchalant disguise upon her face. With a sigh, she reached for the emergency thesaurus she kept in a skirt pocket, seeking comfort. A quick, expert flick through the pages brought her to an altogether familiar list of words.

Chaste, celibate, pure, virtuous . . .

A knock on the door saved her from further sighing. She returned the thesaurus to her pocket and was proceeding toward the door when Daniel emerged from the washroom.

"Was that someone knocking?" he asked.

Alice stopped mid-step to stare at him. He was dressed only in trousers and shoes, his braces hanging loose, as he applied a towel to his naked torso. This was not the first time Alice had been made privy to what existed beneath a man's shirt; after all, she'd been raised in a coeducational facility and had worked undercover as a chambermaid. But Daniel's torso was not like all the other torsos. It was *special*. It had clearly been honed into a model of efficiency rather than brawn: not one inch was superfluous to its purpose of neutralizing whatever A.U.N.T. deemed a threat. Interesting ridges of muscle banded its tanned surface. An even more interesting patch of fine dark hair dusted between the pectoral muscles. And a vertical line of hair below the navel, descending into his trousers, was so extremely interesting, Alice's brain had to go have a wee lie-down.

"Uughhngh," was her response to his barely recollected question.

He gave her a bemused look. She did not see it, however, because she had fixated on his forearms and was busy trying to consult her internal thesaurus for just the right adjective . . . only the pages kept catching alight . . .

"Shall I answer it, then?" he said, and Alice dimly realized that the knock had sounded again.

"Um-hm," she managed to say.

His expression deepened from bemusement to concern, but he crossed the room and opened the door. Veronica stood in the corridor.

"Yes, what is it?" Daniel asked in a brusque voice.

The junior agent stared at him. "Unghghn," she said.

With a weary sigh, Daniel ran a hand over his brow. At the revelation of a hairy armpit, Veronica dropped her duster. Stepping aside, Daniel made way for the young woman to enter the room. As his back presented itself for Alice's view, she dropped her own internal, metaphorical duster.

There was the tattoo that had been hinted at above his collar: a barbed rose vine winding up his spine, beautiful, elegant, vicious. That he had the symbol of A.U.N.T. etched into his skin troubled Alice, although she could not quite grasp why. A rose against his breast would have been one thing (she paused to imagine it); a tangled vine with more thorns than roses, superimposed on his backbone, suggested a deeper, harsher meaning than she dared to contemplate.

"What do you want?" he said.

Alice drew breath to ask if she could touch the tattoo, but then Veronica spoke, alerting her to the fact that Daniel's question had been addressed to the junior agent, not her. Which was just as well. Further practice of marital touching might behoove the mission, but *actually participating in* the mission would no doubt behoove it even more.

"You must come at once, sir!" Veronica urged. "There is a calamity in the kitchen."

"What kind of calamity?" Daniel asked, folding his towel serenely. "Has someone been murdered?"

"No, sir," Veronica said.

"Has Mrs. Etterly's tiger got free and gone on a rampage?" Alice asked.

Veronica frowned. "No, ma'am."

"Has—"

"The cake for tomorrow's morning tea has been ruined!"

Daniel looked at her until she flinched. "Please, sir. Just come and see."

"Fine."

As Daniel returned to the washroom to dress again, Alice and Veronica shared a speaking glance. "Oh my giddy aunt," Veronica whispered.

"Your giddy A.U.N.T.?" Alice whispered back, confused.

Veronica's eyebrows gave a suggestive dance. "I'll bet that man has a golden gun, if you know what I mean."

"No, it's metal, with—"

"And balls of steel."

Alice felt like she had fallen entirely off the roller coaster of this conversation. "Do you refer to some variation of cricket?"

Veronica fanned herself with her apron. "I wonder if he would shoot me if I asked?"

Alice stared with concern at the girl. She was rambling incoherently and expressing suicidal ideation; clearly, A.U.N.T. had overworked her!

At that moment, Daniel returned to the room—alas, covered once again by a shirt. He was, however, affixing the link of one cuff as he walked, and at the sight, Veronica and Alice both gave rapt sighs.

Daniel looked up with impatient confusion. "Are you quite well?"

"Just dreamy, sir," Veronica said, her eyes unfocused as if she was looking right through the white linen of his shirt.

"Hm. Kindly wake up, Agent V-2, and take us to this *calamity*."

They left the room. "Besides," Alice murmured to Veronica as they waited for Daniel to lock the door, "gold is too soft for a gun. It would explode in your hand as soon as you pumped the trigger."

The maid choked on a laugh. "I didn't know you had a ribald sense of humor, Agent A."

Before Alice could explain that she most certainly did not, Daniel glanced irritably at the women, and they fell into a prudent silence.

Veronica led them along the corridor and down the narrow service stairs. Entering the kitchen, they found half a dozen servants at work amongst the benches, sinks, and worktables. Everyone watched furtively, whispering amongst themselves, while Alice and Daniel crossed the room.

"There," Veronica whispered, pointing to a crumb-covered sideboard as if it were a ghastly murder scene.

An elderly butler in an impeccable black suit turned to skewer them with a casually despotic look as they approached. "What?" he demanded, his gaze flicking over Daniel's lack of jacket and Alice's unbound hair. "If you're the musicians, you're late."

"No, sir," Daniel replied. "We're on a mission from A.U.N.T."

"Mr. Cranshaw, this is Agent A!" Veronica said excitedly. "And Agent B! Can you believe it?!"

Cranshaw frowned. "Keep your voice down, girl! Not everyone in this room is an A.U.N.T. operative. Annie over there washing the pots is a spy for the Wicken League of witches. The sous chef is a spy for Mr. Bassingthwaite's uncle. Daisy the scullery girl is a spy for the real estate institute. And Jen the dairy maid is an innocent dairy maid."

"Sorry, sir," Veronica said, abashed.

"And *someone* is the enemy of us all," Cranshaw added, turning his frown to the sideboard.

"What happened?" Alice asked, stepping closer to inspect the mess of cake crumbs. It lay in an almost exact rectangular shape, littered through with raisins, cherries, and those gummy yellow blobs you find too late in a mouthful and are forced to swallow. A rich odor of brandy wafted up. *Fruitcake*, she thought, wrinkling her nose.

To her amazement, the cake had been entirely flattened. While Alice could not regret its loss from tomorrow's morning tea table, she was curious about how this might have occurred. As an Englishwoman, she had been subjected to traditional fruitcake every Christmas, and therefore knew the near impossibility of digesting it, let alone crushing it as a whole. Furthermore, the cake had been large, and yet the effect on it entirely uniform. She looked about for an object someone might have dropped on it, but saw nothing except a few crumbs that had made it all the way to the ceiling, and a large cake knife lying on the floor.

"What happened is that we were ruthlessly attacked!" Cranshaw declared, stabbing a finger at the crumbs.

From the corner of her eye Alice saw a brief, weary flicker across Daniel's otherwise inscrutable expression. "Perhaps someone dislikes fruitcake," he suggested.

The butler scoffed with all the derision of a man to whom a digestive system is but a fond memory. "To dislike fruitcake is unpatriotic. Besides, this was more than cake; it was a work of art. A perfectly to-scale replica of Starkthorn Castle. You have no idea the amount of effort that goes into such things. I spent *an entire week* supervising it being made. This brutal violence represents a serious threat! Queen Victoria's life is not the only one in peril."

"Hm," Daniel said. Crouching, he withdrew a handkerchief from his trouser pocket and used it to pick up the cake knife. Veronica watched him avidly.

"Are you using the handkerchief so as to not transfer your fingerprints to the knife?" she asked.

"I am doing it because there is blood on the handle," he told her, "and I do not wish to soil my fingers."

"Blood!" Cranshaw said with dismay.

"Blood!" Veronica said with delight.

"Or perhaps only cherry juice," Alice countered. "A good agent does not jump to conclusions." Touching a fingertip to the knife, then to her tongue, she grimaced. "Blood. Ugh. Ugh." She rubbed the heel of her hand against her tongue. "Can someone get me a glass of water? Ugh!"

As Veronica rushed to do so, Daniel passed the knife to Cranshaw, handkerchief and all. The butler took it gingerly.

"Do you have any suggestions as to suspects?" Daniel asked.

Cranshaw exhaled a laugh through his nostrils. "Boy, we are in a kitchen surrounded by double agents, in a castle filled with pirates. Everyone is a likely suspect."

"Hm," Daniel said. As a professional courtesy, he did not assassinate the butler for calling him "boy."

"It seems unlikely a person could destroy a cake of this size, to this degree, without being observed," Alice pointed out.

"We were all distracted," Cranshaw explained, "watching the fireworks."

Alice and Daniel blinked. "Fireworks?" Daniel asked.

"Yes, there was just now a fireworks show outside." He paused, but the agents' expressions remained vacant. "Lots of flashing light and noise? People cheering? You must have noticed!"

Alice and Daniel carefully did not look at each other. "We were busy," Daniel murmured.

Cranshaw's eyebrows rose in silent eloquence as he turned away to brush at a few raisins. Veronica returned with a glass of water, and while Alice gargled, Daniel surveyed the kitchen and its occupants.

"Nothing else was damaged? No actual— I mean no *other* suspicious incidents?"

"None."

"Very well. Inform us if you have any further concerns."

"Is that all?" Cranshaw practically vibrated with outrage. "Someone intends harm!"

"Trust us, sir. We will find the culprit."

"So long as she isn't standing in front of a fireworks display," the butler muttered facetiously, but Alice and Daniel had already moved away. Veronica followed them back across the kitchen.

"What do you think?" she asked, her voice skipping like a little girl.

"I think we just wasted our time," Alice said.

"Oh." Now Veronica's voice became a teenager in a black-walled bedroom listening to Leonard Cohen on the record player. "Mr. Cranshaw seemed so convinced."

Daniel gave her a kind smile. "Perhaps, but we are the experts. Good night, V-2."

They turned to the stairs.

"*Hi-yah!*"

A man dressed in black leaped wildly from the shadows, hands raised like weapons. Veronica yelped in shock. Daniel took a quiet step back, exasperation lining his brow. And Alice, being nearest, caught hold of the assailant, twisting his arm to restrain him.

"Who are you?" she demanded.

"Ow!" he squealed. "I'm Hakim Evans, underfootman and junior A.U.N.T. agent. Ow, you're hurting me!"

"Evans, are you mad?" Veronica whispered, jerking her head toward where the kitchen staff were watching in fascination.

Daniel crossed his arms and looked over the rim of his spectacles with the terrifying authority of a high-ranking agent and experienced butler. "Yes, please do disclose your mental status," he said as Evans cowered. "Or give some other reason why you attacked a senior officer."

"Mia Thalassi said you put her in a choke hold," Evans explained tremulously. "She's pretty much famous now because of it. I—I hoped you'd do the same with me."

Alice released him with a disgusted exhalation. Daniel muttered something about twits. They turned away, heading up the stairs.

"Maybe just a punch to the jaw?" Evans called after them. "Or a bruised rib?"

Daniel said nothing, merely paused between one stair tread and the next.

The two younger agents fled.

"Juniors these days certainly are excitable," Alice said as they continued up the stairs.

"I imagine you are used to it," Daniel said. "Being A.U.N.T.'s second best agent and so beau— Um, I suppose you are often surrounded by admirers."

"First best," she answered automatically. But in fact she doubted anyone beyond Mrs. Kew and the Academy assessors had regarded her long enough to form an opinion of her, let alone an admiration. Some undecipherable emotion trembled within her at the thought, and she repressed it with brutal tranquility. "However, I am a master of disguise, so—"

Thwack!

Both agents drew their guns at the sudden sharp sound from the corridor above. They hurried up the stairs. At the top, Daniel placed a cautioning finger on his lips before stepping into the light of the corridor.

"*Watch out!*"

He ducked. A crossbow bolt flew over him and buried itself deep in a framed portrait of Queen Victoria hanging at the end of the corridor.

Thwack!

"Bull's-eye!" someone shouted.

Alice turned, raising her gun in a double-handed grip—

And lowered it again as she saw a group of pirate ladies farther along the corridor.

At their forefront, Mrs. Etterly casually propped a pink, bejeweled crossbow against her hip. "Good heavens! What are you two doing on *the servants' stairs?*" she asked, and turned wide-eyed to the other pirates. They murmured that this was indeed utterly, utterly déclassé behavior.

"We just went down for a late-night snack," Alice said.

"Did you rob the kitchen?" Millie the Monster asked, eyeing their guns.

"No, of course not."

"Huh." The pirates exchanged meaningful glances again; apparently this had been the wrong answer. Mrs. Etterly loaded another bolt into her crossbow.

"What are you doing?" Alice asked warily. She noticed several bolts impaled in the corridor walls at random.

Millie grinned. "Testing for secret hiding pl—"

"Sh!" Mrs. Etterly hissed. She smiled at the agents. "Testing for dry rot. Old castle like this, terrible problem. Would you like to help?"

"No, thank you," Daniel said. "It's been a long day. I am quite stiff. Coming, Mrs. Blakeney?" As the pirates inexplicably laughed, he grasped Alice's wrist and tugged her along the corridor. The crossbow seemed to veer in their direction, but that may just have been a trick of the lamplight. They edged past the group and managed not to outright run toward their bedroom.

"Have a good night, Mrs. Blakeney!" someone called out.

"Thank you," Alice said without daring to look back. "You too."

The pirates laughed again. *Thwack!* went a bolt into the wall behind them.

Locking the bedroom door, the agents looked at it for a moment, then Daniel silently wedged a chair beneath its handle. Alice pushed one of their book-filled suitcases over and Daniel hauled the other on top. Standing back, they regarded the barricade wearily.

"We probably should continue searching for the weapon," Daniel said with reluctance. "We could try the library—"

"No point," Alice told him. "According to my literary sources, at night during a house party the library is *always* occupied by trysting lovers."

He glanced at her sidelong, and Alice shrugged. "What?" she said defensively. "I like to be familiar with a breadth of literature."

"I—"

"It is misogynistic of you to take that attitude toward romantic novels, Mr. Bixby."

"I—"

"They are rich with psychological and sociopolitical themes pertinent to—"

"I was merely going to say that you're right. Let's just go to bed, and preserve our energy for tomorrow."

"You mean the sofa," Alice said.

Daniel frowned a little. "Mrs. Rotunder seemed to find it odd that we were on the floor this morning. Perhaps married couples never—er, lie together anywhere but a bed."

"That is a concern," Alice conceded.

"As professional people, I believe we can manage sharing one bed."

Alice considered just how professional they had been half an hour before on that bed, and started blushing. But the mission was all, so she relented. Allowing Daniel first use of the washroom, she then took her turn, and when she emerged, dressed in a nightgown and robe, he was already in bed, propped up against the pillows and reading a book. His spectacles were off and once again he wore his sleeveless vest. Gritting her teeth and girding her loins, Alice climbed in beside him.

He did not look up from his book as she arranged herself rigidly against the pillows.

He did not glance her way as she pulled the quilt up high and smoothed it.

Nor did he even blink as she untied her robe and attempted to wrangle it off beneath the quilt, in the process smacking his book with her elbow, almost knocking a pillow to the floor, before at last liberating herself from the wretched thing. She attempted to fold it but ended up in a wrestling match with the silky material until finally Daniel set down his novel, took the robe from her, and folded it into a precise square with what appeared to be only three moves. He placed it at the end of the bed and went back to reading.

Alice sat for a moment considering whether or not to shoot him. Then she took her own book, Shakespeare's *All's Well That Ends Well*, from the bedside cabinet.

There, she thought as she opened the book and felt the familiar calm of typeset words seep through her. *We are just two people sitting on an item of furniture, reading. It is perfectly fine.*

Daniel shifted slightly. His scent of fresh soap wafted about Alice. She frowned determinedly at her book.

"Man is enemy to virginity. How may we barricado it against him?"

Her frown deepened. Just then, Daniel turned the page in his own book. Alice glanced at him for the merest second. His right hand cradled the book. His left hand, with its wedding band, lifted to scratch his jaw, where a promise of beard shadowed the firm curve. Alice swallowed hard.

"Is something wrong?" he asked, and she realized her brief glance had become a long, intense stare.

"No, no, not at—no, nothing," she said and returned to her reading.

"There is none. Man setting down before you will undermine you and blow you up."

Alice slammed the book shut so forcefully, Daniel jolted.

"Those women in the corridor were mocking us," she said. It was the first thing that had come to mind but would suffice as reasonable conversation.

"Mockery is part of a pirate's job definition," Daniel answered. He turned the page in his book.

"I fear they *still* don't believe us happily married."

"Well, we are. Professionally speaking, I mean." He turned another page.

"Our practice must have been inadequate."

"It was perfectly adequate." He turned the page with more vim this time.

"You are going through that book remarkably fast."

His hand paused in the process of reaching for the next page corner. "I've read it before. I am a speed reader. It is only boring description of sunset. I don't see why you are interrogating me in such a manner." He smacked the page back against the preceding one.

"What book is it?"

He held up the cover for her to see. *Madame Bovary.* Alice's heart flipped and did a nosedive into her stomach. "Did you read in bed with Princess Louise?" she asked before she even realized what she was saying.

The question startled her, but apparently startled Daniel even more: he tore the page he was in the process of turning. Alice gasped. Daniel stared bleakly into the middle distance for a moment, his jaw twitching as if he had just killed a man. Then he closed the book and turned to look at her with eyes that had become so dark she could see herself reflected in them.

"That is a rumor."

Alice waited, but he did not further explain that it was a *baseless* rumor. As the silence lengthened, growing heavy with overtones, undertones, and implications, the air between them blushed, made up an excuse, and departed the room in awkward haste.

"You're right," Daniel said at last. "We ought to further our marital practice, due to safety concerns."

"Uh huh," Alice answered—which represented a high degree of eloquence considering the storm of blood thundering through her. "Perhaps a few more kissing exercises would be wise," she managed to say.

"Not kissing," Daniel said. "Lie down."

Alice frowned in suspicion. "Why?"

"Lie down, Agent A."

The cool authority in his voice strangely delighted her. She wriggled lower, clutching the quilt against her with one hand while trying to keep her nightgown from rising up with the other. Staring at the ceiling—goodness, they ought to bring in a long mop and give it a thorough wash—she waited, hoping she did not drift asleep before Daniel began doing whatever it was he intended. It had been such a long day . . .

Then his hand slipped under the quilt to her thigh, and she was abruptly wide awake indeed.

❧ 15 ❧

CHEMISTRY MOVES ON TO PHYSICS—
BREAKING THE RULES (AND POSSIBLY THE WRISTS)—
INTERESTING SYNONYMS—ALICE TAKES A STANCE

To squirm or not to squirm, that is the question Alice posed herself as she lay gazing at the ceiling while Daniel pressed his hand against her thigh. Although the weight was comfortable, its warmth ignited nerves even through her nightgown and drawers, making her restless. She wanted him to move that hand—but in which direction, she could not decide.

"There is an advanced exercise which may help us get more into character," he explained. "Shall we attempt it?"

"By all means," Alice agreed. "I am always in favor of professional development."

"Are you sure? It will go against Regulation 32. And possibly Regulation 17 also."

Alice frowned in bemusement. "'No forward reconnaissance into closed-off spaces without first advising headquarters of your intentions'?"

"Hm."

"Well, Mr. Bixby, regulations exist for a good reason and ought to be respected. Nevertheless, these are exceptional circumstances. I authorize you to proceed at will."

She felt proud of these words. She admired their straightforward vigor in much the same manner she might admire a jolly good Marmite sandwich. Not one single tremble or high-pitched vowel existed anywhere amongst them.

Her heart, however, represented nothing more than jam dolloped haphazardly atop a crumpet. If Daniel ever realized how smitten she was with him—how deeply vulnerable she really felt—he'd be appalled.

"Very well," he said, and kissed her.

It was a tender kiss, softening her lips, soothing her nerves. She returned it in the way she remembered from their earlier practice until slowly, delightfully, theory dissolved, leaving only pleasure. Reaching up, she stroked fingers through his hair and down along the strong curve of his jaw. She had never touched another person like this, never known it was possible to feel tingling enjoyment rather than discomfort in doing so. Just as soon as he stopped kissing her (hopefully many long minutes from now), she would assure him that his advanced exercise was a great success.

And then he began to lift her nightgown.

Good heavens, she was about to be utterly exposed! This was hooliganism at its most outrageous! Agent B would see her drawers!

Daniel paused, somehow divining her alarm from the widening of her eyes, or the cessation of her breath, or the way she was holding his wrists in a white-knuckled grip.

"I'm sorry," he said.

Alice blinked. Releasing his wrists, she exhaled slowly. "It's fine. A mere reflex on my part. Kindly move on with all promptitude."

"Are you su—"

"I can complete the A.U.N.T. level three obstacle course; I can do this."

He paused, shifting back with a concerned look—

"If you stop," Alice told him, "I will write you up for dereliction of duty."

"Yes, Mrs. Blakeney." He regarded her with a thoughtful expression, trying to decide the degree of her vulnerability or the chances of her murdering him. "Perhaps I should just get straight to the point?"

"Yes. I dislike fiddling about unnecessarily. In most ventures, brisk penetration of details and a straightforward thrust to the core of the matter is the best tactic."

Daniel made a small, odd sound. Alice wondered if he had developed some sudden malady of the throat, but he pulled himself together and returned her gaze implacably. She felt a sudden thrill. Not even the Academy instructors had looked at her with such unwavering dominance. This was a man who knew exactly what he was doing and who felt not one shred of fear about what she might do in turn. It made her feel safe in a way she never had before.

Somewhere in the brightly lit, well-polished lobby of her mind, Memory tapped the mission dossier pointedly. But Alice was moving through low, dark tunnels of instinct and desire, and if anyone had asked her about the dossier, she wouldn't know it.

"Spread your legs," Daniel ordered.

The instruction was simple enough—and yet somehow akin to a passage from *Les Liaisons Dangereuses*. Swallowing dryly, Alice did as she was told. Daniel moved his hand beneath her nightgown and through the silk-hemmed center opening of her drawers, placing it firmly upon the warm, damp place it found there. Such a jolt went through her, Memory flung the mission dossier aside and ran to hide under a stack of Bible verses.

"Try to relax," Daniel said.

"I am relaxed," Alice replied in a voice so taut the final syllable cracked under its strain. After all, what could be more restful than lying in a houseful of maniac pirates while a man to whom one was ridiculously attracted inserted his hand into one's drawers?

"Hm," Daniel murmured doubtfully. And then he stroked a finger . . .

And stopped, consequent to having been shoved onto his back while Alice knelt astride him, two of her own fingers pressed sharply against his windpipe.

"Um," he said.

She moved her hand back. "Oh dear. Another reflex. Light touches, you know? My apologies, Mr. B-Blakeney."

"No, the apology is mine," he answered somewhat breathlessly. "I propose—er, I mean, I suggest we postpone this exercise until another night."

Alice frowned. Postponement was the last thing she wanted. She had not reached the pinnacle of A.U.N.T.'s ranks by postponing difficult tasks or shirking her professional responsibilities. And plainly her responsibility to A.U.N.T., the Queen—nay, *all of humankind*—was to have Daniel Bixby continue fondling her. Preferably without her killing him in response.

"I'm sorry, I must insist on begging your pardon," she said. "It seems duty acquaints a man with strange bedfellows."

"You are not strange, merely sensitive, like the most finely constructed pistol."

He smiled up at her, and Alice became aware that his center of marital activity was aligned directly below hers, with only a few inches of hot, empty space providing a bulwark against depravity. *Get off the man*, she told herself sternly.

Make me, her body answered.

"We must have done enough now to pass as married," she said, although it was less a statement than a tentative reconnaissance. Secret question marks lurked behind every word.

"Hm," Daniel said. And taking hold of her hips in a firm grip, he lowered her so that their bodies met.

Alice gasped. The open crotch of her drawers left her exposed to something for which *depravity* seemed far too mild a word. *Sinful* would be more appropriate. Or better yet, *throbbing*.

Daniel guided her a few inches forward and then back, dragging her against the hard ridgeline of him. The texture of his linen underwear scraped her bare flesh. The sensation was even more electrifying than if she had drunk tea with several tablespoons of sugar. Suddenly she apprehended the vast field of experience she had yet to cross —and how many land mines it contained.

Keep going, her heart pleaded.

Tap tap, her fingers replied against the air.

Seeing this, Daniel frowned with concern. He stopped their activity at once, and Alice felt herself being lifted away from him.

Frustration rushed her senses. She'd always found physical contact difficult, and in response, others had invariably stepped back, walked away, leaving her untouched rather than helping her to find a manner in which to experience it safely. Daniel Bixby had promised to be different. And now here he was, being considerate, *taking gentle care*.

Well, she would just have to show him what she needed.

She grasped his hands and, in one swift, firm motion, removed them from her hips to pin them instead to the mattress on either side of his head. Glaring down at him from within curtains of tumbled hair, she saw his eyes flash bright, and her own responded in kind, as if a current of electricity ran between them. He gave her a smile so thoroughly wicked, he might as well have gone through her book collection and dog-eared all its pages.

Alice thrilled. She had him restrained but knew that at any moment he could overcome her without even taking a breath. She paused to imagine it, and the pulse in her wrists and between her legs grew more fierce. Lowering herself again, she restarted the slow, rocking motion.

Where Daniel had been hard before, he now felt like granite against her softness. Tiny sparks of pleasure began to shoot through her nerves. Panic began to rouse itself within her at the overwhelming stimulation—but, as if he sensed it, Daniel curled his fingers tightly around hers. He held her protected even with her kneeling over him— kept her safe as she took what she wanted from his body. Alice tugged a little, testing if she could escape, but he would not relent. He had her.

She exhaled with relief.

Sparks turned into flares, and flares kindled fires. Suddenly Daniel lifted his hips, introducing a new angle as he rubbed against her, and the fire soared until it was a raging conflagration that scalded her breath and threatened to turn her self-control to cinders. Alice sought in vain for the cooling, calming modulation of old poetry . . .

And the whole alphabet exploded through her body.

At the same moment, Daniel's body shuddered beneath her. Alice wondered dimly if he felt the same ecstasy, but could not ask, all her language lost and most of her breath along with it.

"Holy Mother of God," he gasped.

Seeing his stunned expression, Alice felt suddenly, oddly shy. She would have moved away, but a heavy lassitude came over her, obliging her to remain where she was, her fingers damp in Daniel's grip, other parts of her body damp also, as if she'd been a fire indeed, and now was doused. She did not know what to do next. Her gaze slipped away into a vague middle distance just as Daniel's did the same, but they breathed in unison, heavily, a little shakily. Their bodies lingered together with a mutual longing that not even acute pleasure had satisfied.

"Does that answer your question?" he asked.

"Yes, it was most informative," she replied. "I am now a little concerned about my heart rate, however."

He laughed. Their eyes met accidentally, and intensity tightened the space between them, as if each was the other's moon, subject to a private gravity. They looked away again, fast. Alice climbed off Daniel, her legs trembling almost as much as her pulse. A.U.N.T. regulations began firing rapidly through her brain. *Damn, damn, damn,* ricocheted in consequence. *I should not have done that.* Kissing was one thing, but she'd just crossed a line that felt very dangerous indeed.

As panic began to swell, she shut everything down with well-trained ruthlessness. Physical pleasure—gone. Desire—gone. A robust connection to her sense of self—just gone, so that she felt like an observer of Alice, rather than the woman herself. She stacked pillows before the wrought-iron headboard, then arranged herself in a stiff, upright pose against them, knees drawn to her chest and nightgown hem tucked firmly beneath her toes. Yanking the quilt until it covered her knees, she swatted briskly at a few wrinkles.

"Good night, then, Mr. Blakeney," she said, and closed her eyes.

A moment's silence was followed by Daniel's hesitant voice. "Er, yes. Um. Perhaps I shall retire to the sofa again, so that you may feel comfortable lying down."

"I am entirely comfortable," Alice said without opening her eyes. "This is my regular position in bed."

Although she could not see him, she absolutely felt his doubtful sidelong glance. "I'm not sure you're being—"

"Sir. Do you mind? I am trying to sleep."

Silence fell again.

Daniel lay carefully motionless, listening to Alice count beneath her breath. He wanted to cuddle her, kiss her, softening all those damned numbers into poetry. He wanted to remove her nightclothes and continue practicing marital exercises with her until they both graduated several times over. But if he did not repress his desire he might just destroy the mission—and Alice's heart—his own heart—the whole entire bloody world—along with it.

Worse, he could be fired if A.U.N.T. learned about what had just happened.

Not to mention how appalled Alice would be if she learned the degree of his attraction to her. He could just imagine the stacks of Human Resources complaints she'd write on the subject. Well, not *imagine*, but at least extrapolate the likelihood from known facts.

So he stared up at the ceiling (good grief, someone really ought to clean it) and started counting beneath his own breath. But the tidy rhythm broke apart again and again under the force of his pulse, and the silence in the room shivered like a shy girl—or, indeed, a shy man who lay beside a woman with whom he was hopelessly enamored.

Damn, he thought. *Damn, damn. This is not safe.*

"I think—" he began.

"Sleeping," Alice snapped in reply.

A melancholy sigh threatened to rise in his throat. Horrified at the prospect, he climbed out of bed, obtained new underwear from his bag, and employed the washroom to refresh himself. Upon returning, he paused for a while, regarding Alice's finely wrought face within its tumbled frame of hair. She looked like an angel—granted, an Angel of Death, considering her abilities with an umbrella or merely the heel of one hand, but that was beside the point. He was obsessed with her beauty. Part of him wanted to bring out a ruler and measure the width of her cheekbones. Another part began to raise more ribald suggestions.

"I cannot sleep with you staring at me like that," Alice said without opening her eyes.

Daniel actually felt himself blushing. "It's probably unwise for us to share the bed."

"Nonsense. Besides, my reputation would be ruined if a servant or pirate entered the room and found you sleeping alone on the sofa. Come now, you are making much ado about nothing."

He almost laughed at that, but judging from Alice's cool expression, she'd not had the same literature professor as him. With a shrug of surrender, he climbed into the bed and settled down with his back to her. Reaching out, he doused the bedside lamp.

"Good n—"

"Sleeping."

He did sigh then. At least with her rigid attitude, there was no danger of waking to find her head in his lap like he had this morning.

Which was not the best thing to remember, under the circumstances. He cast the provocative image from his mind and began a slow, resolute count backward from one thousand until at last, somewhere around sixty-nine, he drifted thankfully into sleep.

And woke at dawn with Alice Dearlove dreaming in his arms, her breath like poetry against his hard-pulsing throat.

❈ 16 ❈

ALICE WISHES FOR SILENCE—SHE GETS SOMETHING FAR BETTER—
THEY TAKE THE PLUNGE (IN MORE WAYS THAN ONE)—
POETIC INTERRUPTUS—OUT OF THE WOODWORK—AS THICK AS THIEVES

For all evils there are two remedies—time and Daniel Bixby's muscled arms.

Wait. No.

For all evils there are two remedies—time and *silence*. That was the correct quote, and Alice liked being correct in all things. Almost as much as she liked the tanned skin of Daniel's forearms when he folded up his sleeves and—

She scowled. Since waking this morning embraced by those arms, she'd found it difficult to think about anything else. Except perhaps the man's jawline. And his torso. And the way every sweep of his eyelashes seemed to stroke her inside. She tried to counter this with reminders of the mission, but it was really quite amazing how her brain could take "the impending murder of Queen Victoria" and translate it into "the thrilling breadth of Mr. Bixby's shoulders."

Besides, silence as a remedy for the evil in this house seemed beyond hope. She and Daniel had excused themselves after breakfast,

claiming a desire to rest, only to discover everyone else resting too—
i.e., searching the castle for Jane's secret weapon. Crowds jostled,
thumped against walls, and stabbed cushions (as well as the occasional
bustle of a passing lady). Daniel did find his pocket watch tucked behind a powder box in Mrs. Rotunder's bedroom, but since it was stolen
from him again ten minutes later, they felt unable to call this a success.

At least no more kissing had taken place. Thank heaven for that! In
absolutely no way whatsoever did Alice wish for further kissing. About
this, she was adamant.

Daniel's voice broke through her thoughts. "Do I have something
on my face?"

"Pardon me?" she asked rather dazedly.

"You are staring at my mouth."

"Oh." She looked away, glaring at the wall of the corridor in which
they stood. Several holes had been bashed in it. Farther along the corridor, Millie the Monster was using her sword to rip apart a framed
portrait of Beryl Black, as if the secret weapon might have been hidden
behind the lady's painted smirk. Mrs. Rotunder kept trying to wedge
her husband's wooden hand into a gap between floorboards, so as to
lever them up, while the gentleman himself dozed in a chair nearby.

"I was thinking about that barricaded room you mentioned yesterday," Alice lied. "Shall we attempt it now, while everyone is busy? I am
wearing my petticoat parachute."

"Good plan," Daniel agreed.

They hastened to the castle roof and, climbing onto the parapet,
surveyed the hundred feet below them. "That window," Daniel said,
pointing to one nearby.

"Right," Alice said briskly. As she began unknotting the ribbon for
her parachute petticoat, she gazed out across the fields and woods, the
vast, lonely sky soaring untouched above them. "Hampshire is so tranquil," she remarked, a strange dissatisfaction rippling through her mind.

Daniel glanced at her sidelong. "Hm?"

"Do you know Jane Austen lived here?"

"Of course." He sounded rather offended that she'd even asked. "Now, I think if we angle ourselves during the descent, we should—"

"I wonder how much of an influence scenery like this had on her writing."

Daniel stood in blank silence. Alice expected him to chide her for not focusing completely on the mission, but then he shifted a little on his feet, as if he experienced the same dissatisfaction as she.

"Interesting question," he said, his voice low. "If I recollect correctly—"

Alice snorted, since they both knew that of course he did.

"—in *Persuasion* she used the autumnal countryside to represent Anne and Wentworth's lost love."

"I believe you're right," Alice said. Then, shaking her head, she forced herself back on track. "We ought to—"

"But," Daniel interjected, taking a step toward her, "it was in *Emma* that Austen most excelled at using setting metaphorically."

Alice's brain went so fast off track again that she swayed, and only by stepping closer to Daniel could she maintain her balance. "That's true! *Emma* is luxuriant with metaphor, allusion, and symbolism."

"It is the most perfectly constructed novel ever written," Daniel opined.

Alice almost fell from the parapet with sheer delight. Really, was it any wonder she cherished this man, considering he said such things?

Cherished? Her inner dictionary slammed open, pages fluttering urgently in hopes of an innocent definition for the word. But there was no reprieve from the realization that she harbored feelings for Agent B beyond mere physical attraction. Alarmed, she leaped back on track with a determination so fierce, she probably would have whipped herself with a birch rod, were one present. Shoving a hand beneath the waistband of her bustled skirt, she yanked the ribbon hard.

Her petticoat ballooned instantly, setting her truly off-balance. She stumbled, tilting over the edge of the parapet—

At once, Daniel grasped her, pulling her back against him, wrapping his arms around her waist. It was like being embraced by Michelangelo's *David*, only human-size and with no museum security guards involved.

"All right?" he asked. Or, at least, Alice thought he asked it. Hearing was rather difficult over the pounding of her heart.

"All right," she lied.

His embrace grew tighter, and Alice's corset stays dug into her skin with little bursts of pain, like love bites. He pressed his cheek to the side of her head. Alice heard his sigh—or perhaps it was her own: a soft, wistful sound.

Then he threw them off the roof.

Angling carefully, they reached the window in seconds, and Alice clutched the edge of its alcove with one hand to hold them steady while with the other she searched her dress pocket for a small knife to jimmy open the window frame. Finding none, she twisted so as to try a different pocket.

"Unngh," Daniel said in a taut voice.

"It's here somewhere," Alice assured him, bending forward to check inside her boot.

"Bloody hell," he gasped.

"Sir! Language! You are in the presence of a lady!"

"Yes, I am painfully aware of that." He kicked out, smashing the window frame with the heel of his shoe. Wood splintered, and the window flung ajar. Taken by surprise, Alice lurched forward, and they fell together onto the hard floor of the room.

Daniel had twisted them in midair so he landed first, receiving the brunt of the impact and cushioning Alice from harm—although *cushion* was perhaps the wrong word, considering the solidity of his body. Lying atop him, Alice told herself to move and got a brusque, itemized reply: (1) My balance is not yet restored. (2) The petticoat is still deflating. (3) He smells so damned delicious.

"Are you hurt?" Daniel asked, wincing behind his crooked spectacles.

"No," she said. "Did you knock your head? What is my name? Can you recall the date?"

"Time has ceased to have all meaning on this diabolical mission, Mrs. Blakeney." A flush swept over his face. "We should get up. Now. *Immediately.*"

"I beg your pardon," Alice said, realizing she had been practically lounging on him.

"Not at all; my fault," Daniel answered in a rather strained voice. Clambering to their feet, tidying their clothes, they looked around—

"Egads!" they exclaimed in horror.

If Jane Fairweather's weapon was indeed present in this room, it could not be detected amongst a clutter of broken furniture, grimy knickknacks, and piles of clothes so filthy they were on the verge of becoming a whole new life-form.

"*Hm,*" Daniel said.

Alice recognized his tone. "We are here to search, not clean," she chided. Peering into a box of books, she almost wept at their moldy covers. "My God, these people really are criminals."

Daniel shifted aside a broken suitcase to reveal a painting of a riverside city. "Bah," he said with a frown. "Hamburg."

Alice laughed. The noise so startled her, she clamped a hand against her mouth. Daniel turned to stare at her amazedly.

"Please excuse me," she gasped. "I have not been amused in years."

"No, I apologize," Daniel answered. "I should not have referenced Dickens in such an offhandedly witty fashion."

"The apology is mine," Alice argued. "I fear I'm devolving into hooliganism."

He stepped toward her. "I insist on being to blame."

She shook her head. "Begging your pardon, but I demand to be forgiven."

Shadows filled his eyes as he regarded her with an expressionlessness that took her breath away. She found herself moving closer without thinking—and, alas, without looking: she tripped over a candlestick lying on the floor and staggered. Daniel immediately caught her.

"Sorry," she said, staring up at him.

"I'm sorry," he said at the same time, holding her close.

And then they ~~continued on with their search for the weapon like exemplary professionals~~ kissed.

The force of their sudden passion sent them stumbling back. They impacted with a cluttered shelf, and a small vase toppled over. Without pausing in his romantic industry, Daniel reached past Alice to set it upright again. He bit Alice's lower lip. She rose onto her toes to get even closer, and they stumbled again.

Tongues clashing, they moved a coat rack aside . . . swaying into a stack of boxes, they aligned it neatly, each using one hand while the other remained busy thrusting into hair or grasping clothes . . . then they straightened a painting on the wall before Daniel pinned Alice against that same wall. "Why are you doing this?" she breathed as he kissed the dent at the base of her throat and she rearranged a bonnet hanging crookedly on the rack. "There's no need—no one is here to witness it."

"By my troth, I kiss thee with a most constant heart," he murmured, the words humming against her skin, making her sigh. She felt disguise after disguise slide away until she was no more than a shy, unamiable woman who, even long out of childhood, still hugged books and dreamed of having a family. It was a frightening nakedness, and she fluttered anxious fingers against the unrelenting solidity of Daniel's back. He did not even flinch.

"But—" she tried to say, to no avail. He was kissing her mouth again. He was holding her so near, she could feel the *tap-tap* of his heartbeat.

Oh God, please, her soul whispered. *This one. This man. Mine.*

She made one last, weak effort at cynicism: "At the touch of a lover, everyone becomes a poet."

Daniel shifted back a little to cup her face in both his hands. His smile could have unfolded sheets and dirtied dishes. "Doubt thou the stars are fire," he said emphatically. "Doubt that the sun doth move; doubt truth to be a liar; but never doubt I—"

Crash!

Now was the moment of Alice's discontent. Daniel pulled her behind the coat rack, into what appeared to be an ancient spider civilization. To have gone from the verge of receiving a romantic declaration to being draped with a veil of cobwebs might have been appropriate, considering Daniel had been quoting *Hamlet*, but it left Alice rueful.

Less than a second after they hid, a section of the wall flung open, knocking a taxidermied dodo to the floor.

"Bloody hell!" Alex O'Riley strode into the room, brushing dust from his long black coat. "Why must secret passages always be so dirty? God knows they're used so often in pirate houses, people ought to keep them swept."

A laugh sounded as Charlotte emerged behind him. It was dry, brief; the kind of laugh that has eyes in the back of its head and just *knows* when you're about to do something stupid. "This coming from a man who didn't realize one has to use a mop with water."

"Don't try being supercilious with me, darling," Alex replied. "We all know who mopped our floors. And that it hasn't been done since he left, water or not."

Alice heard Daniel gasp. She gripped his arm to prevent him from leaping out with an offer to commit housework. Alex and Charlotte might be his friends, but Alice considered them as wayward and dangerous as every other pirate and witch of her acquaintance. Furthermore, she suspected Charlotte would take one look at her and know exactly what she'd just been doing.

"Witches tidy," Charlotte said. "They do not *clean*. We really must procure a new housekeeper. Perhaps when we return to London we should— *Sufflamino!*"

Alex jolted to a sudden halt.

"Really?" he said from his rigid posture, one arm reaching toward a sword that leaned against a grimy old bust of Wordsworth. "You couldn't have just *told* me to stop?"

"Don't touch that sword! You'll probably get tetanus."

"I can't touch it, can I? You've bewitched me. I can't bloody move at all."

"Oh dear." Charlotte's voice swayed in rhythm with her body as she crossed to where he was standing frozen. "Poor lad."

"Lottie," he murmured in warning.

She ducked beneath his arm and came up smiling. "Alex."

Suddenly Daniel's hand clamped over Alice's eyes—but not before she saw Charlotte grasp hold of Alex's shirt and tug him out of magic, into her wry smile. Furious, Alice tried to pry Daniel's fingers away. He was not the master of her, to determine what she was and was not allowed to witness! He was—

Well, he was currently featuring in a mental vision of how precisely he might master her, and it proved a great deal more salacious than a husband and wife kissing. The fact that this vision also included his hand over her eyes only served to make matters worse. Alice began to perspire more than the autumn temperature justified. Finally, as she feared herself on the brink of hyperthermia, Daniel moved his hand away and started pulling her farther into the shadows. She frowned, and in response he put a finger against his lips, then pointed it to the ceiling. Glancing up, Alice realized she could hear shuffling footsteps and voices murmuring beyond the grimy plaster above.

Charlotte and Alex heard it too. They abruptly ceased their marital endeavors and ducked behind the coat rack, almost crashing into Alice and Daniel.

"You again!" Alex hissed.

"I beg your pardon," Daniel said disapprovingly.

"What are you doing here?" Charlotte asked in a tone that would have seen A.U.N.T. offering her a job at once.

Alex clicked his tongue. "No doubt they're searching for the weapon in efficient fashion—unlike you, who showed more interest in hanky-panky."

Upon hearing this phrase, Alice's inner dictionary opened its pages excitedly. "What does hanky-panky mean?" she whispered to Daniel.

"Witchcraft," he whispered back.

"Oh." Alice felt inexplicably disappointed.

"You have corrupted me," Charlotte told her husband. "You are nothing more than a reprobate."

"True," Alex agreed. "And you're a harridan."

Alice gasped—but Alex had spoken in a genial tone and Charlotte was gazing at him with an expression Alice believed was Adoration (Female, Type Three: Married/Long-Suffering but Nevertheless Smitten). She began riffling through the aforementioned inner dictionary confusedly, but she was interrupted by laughter rippling out from the shadows behind them.

Immediately, all four drew their guns and aimed into the darkness. In response, a hand emerged, containing a bag of lollies.

"Peppermint?"

Two figures came forward, smiling cheerfully. Alice recognized Essie Smith and her husband, Lysander. They were a pleasant couple, notwithstanding a shared criminal record that would take hours to relate, and Alice felt appalled that they must have witnessed her and Daniel kissing. She tried to recollect if she'd said anything to jeopardize the mission but found only a haze of passion and poetry. Fiddlesticks!

"Have a peppermint," Essie urged. "I don't know a pirate who doesn't love them."

"Er," Alice said. Her very soul shrank at the thought of eating something from a bag in which others' fingers had been rummaging. She glanced at Daniel, hoping he would provide some clever excuse as to why she was exempt from peppermint consumption, but he appeared as horror-struck.

"'Scuse me," Alex O'Riley said, reaching between them to scoop several lollies from the bag and deposit them in his mouth.

"Sh!" Charlotte hissed suddenly. "They're coming."

The group settled into cautious silence as a trapdoor flipped open in the ceiling and a ladder angled down. "Allow me to go first, precious petal of my heart's summer rose," came Frederick Bassingthwaite's voice. "I will be your preservation should you fall, although it would mean crushing the very life from this meager but devoted body, a sacrifice I gladly—"

Shoe heels smacked against wood as Jane Fairweather descended the ladder. The hidden group shuffled back even more. Alice felt ripples against her skirts as the pirates reached around her to pick each other's pockets. Reaching the floor, Jane looked about with shrewd calculation.

"There must be enough saleable goods in here to pay for the new oven."

The pirates exchanged confused looks. *Pay?* Alex mouthed; Lysander shrugged in bewildered reply.

Frederick joined his wife. "Whatever you wish, cream of my crop, it shall be—"

"Focus!" Jane snapped. "Where did you leave it?"

Frederick pointed. "On yonder box, dearest."

The group craned their necks to see more clearly, but Jane snatched the object and hugged it close to her bosom, allowing only an impression of whiteness.

"With this, poetic justice shall be served!" she declared.

"Indeed, it shall be a veritable cataclysm of—"

"Let's go. We must take it downstairs at once, before anyone notices we've disappeared."

"Of course, dove of my cloudless sky."

They ascended the ladder, pulled it up behind them, and shut the trapdoor with a thud and a shower of dust.

"Have they gone?" someone asked from across the room.

In reply, guns were drawn yet again. The group emerged from their concealment and stared across the piles of junk.

Bloodhound Bess stared back. She was grinning, albeit only as a consequence of the scar that curved from her mouth to her left ear. Cobwebs draped from her purple hat feathers; dusty sunlight glistened against the long, heavy blade of the sword she employed like a walking stick.

"That was the most outrageous thing I have ever been made witness to!" she pronounced.

"You mean Mr. and Mrs. Blakeney nearly doing themselves an in-jury snogging?" Lysander asked, winking at Alice as she blushed.

"No. Although I spied them doing so, I have enough intelligence not to bug them about it."

"Then you mean Captain O'Riley kissing his wife?"

Bess bristled. "No. But you can be sure my mind is a bonfire at the sight of a witch in this room."

"Then you mean—"

"Jane," Bess snapped. "I meant Jane. What kind of pirate suggests *paying* for something?!"

The group murmured in troubled agreement.

"Did anyone see what she took from the room?" Daniel asked.

No one had.

"The obvious solution is to waylay her before she hides the item elsewhere," Charlotte pointed out with witchlike rationale. Then, catching a vexed glance from Alex, she hastily added, "Not that the item is of any importance. Merely if one was curious."

"I have no curiosity whatsoever," Bess said. "However, I must be on my way. I only came up here for—er—" Looking around, she snatched up a stained ashtray in the shape of an open-mouthed bulldog. "This. Yes. Extremely valuable antique. Have a customer wanting this exact—er—thing. Tally ho!"

She backed into a section of the wall, causing her hat to tilt pre-cariously, and kicked out with her heel. Nothing happened; she side-stepped, kicked again, and almost fell through a suddenly opening secret door. The others would have heard her running along the hid-den passageway beyond were they not busy making their own excuses to immediately depart. With a *"descendeo,"* Charlotte summoned the ladder from the ceiling, and there followed a skirmish as Alex and Ly-sander both attempted to climb it ahead of each other. Essie intervened, peppermints exploded everywhere, and, as all three pirates drew their swords, Charlotte sighed with exasperation and levitated over them.

Alice and Daniel hastily departed by way of the door through which Alex and Charlotte had entered. Racing along a dark passageway, they found stairs leading down, at the bottom of which was a door opening to a service corridor. Following this led them to the entrance hall at the same time Lysander and Essie Smith arrived from another direction; seconds later, Bloodhound Bess and Alex ran down the grand staircase, shoving at each other.

"Ah, there you are," said a laconic voice. Everyone turned to see Jane stroll in. She was carrying several books and, with a placid expression upon her narrow, bespectacled face, she looked for all the world like a fierce piratic heroine's dull governess. Frederick followed two paces behind.

"Is everyone having a nice day?" she asked, smiling blandly.

They all stared at her in dumbfounded silence. Then Alex gave an insouciant shrug. "Very nice, very relaxing," he said, sheathing his sword.

Jane's eyes widened at the sight of him. "Rotten O'Riley! I did not realize you were visiting us."

"Oh, I'm just passing through," Alex answered. "Taking a shortcut to Dublin. Cheerio, then." He saluted her, winked at Daniel, and ambled away out the front door.

"Good heavens!" Frederick exclaimed. "Do you think someone should run out and tell him Dublin is in the opposite direction before the poor chap goes too far?"

Jane sighed, and Alice recognized on her face the Married/Long-Suffering expression, albeit without any Adoration. "Luncheon is being served, should you—"

Staggering back, she only just saved herself from being trampled by

Essie, Lysander, and Bess as they rushed to the dining room. She hurried after them, muttering about having barely any spoons left for stealing. Frederick scampered behind.

"Wait for me, sweetest nectar of my vine!"

Alice and Daniel found themselves alone in the entrance hall. They inhaled—

"Tsk." A voice echoed through the wide marble space. The breath went out of them wearily.

Charlotte marched down the stairs. "Where did he go?" she demanded.

Alice and Daniel pointed out the front door and she strode toward it, bootheels sparking, voice muttering as she went. "'Hide in the secret rooms and passageways,' he said. 'Steal the weapon, easily done,' he said. Did he mention dust and cobwebs? No!" (A flower vase trembled on a sideboard.) "Did he mention not being able to get a decent cup of tea?" (The vase rose three feet in the air.) "Just as well the man is lovable, or else—"

Crash. Carnations scattered all over the floor.

"Will you leave now, Miss Pettifer," Daniel asked her sternly, "since the pirates know you are here?"

"Of course!" Charlotte answered so readily, even Alice could tell she was lying. "Oh, and a word of advice," she added as she passed them. "Married pirates tend not to cling to each other quite so much."

Glancing down, the agents realized they were holding hands, and hastily snatched them apart. With a laugh so dry it made the Sahara seem like a beach, Charlotte departed. They watched her go, then turned to each other.

"These people are enough to try the patience of an oyster," Alice said grimly.

"They're all mad here," Daniel agreed, making her smile. He lifted his hand as if he would touch the rare curve of her mouth, but lowered it again without doing so. "We should retrace Jane's steps to see if we can find where she left the weapon," he said.

"We should join the company for luncheon," Alice said at the same time.

Their mutual gaze grew heavy.

"We should . . ." Alice murmured.

"We should," Daniel agreed vaguely.

They swayed toward each other.

Boom!

Smoke billowed out from the dining room. "Ahoy!" someone shouted.

The agents sighed and went to do their duty.

❧ 17 ❧

There are few hours in life more terrifying than the hour dedicated to the ceremony known as afternoon tea, when partaken in piratic company. After two cups of Earl Grey, a slice of coconut cake, and "amusing conversation" with the matrons of the Wisteria Society, Alice feared she had become insane, without any intervals of sanity, horrible or otherwise. Not only was she unable to focus on the book in her hands, but she felt actually tempted to slouch on the sofa upon which she sat! Only her corset, and the much-ruffled posterior of her yellow and purple afternoon dress, saved her from such a derangement of good manners.

And only the imperatives of the mission saved her from removing said dress and stuffing as much of it as possible down Frederick Bassingthwaite's throat so he would stop reciting Keats's "Ode to a Nightingale" in a voice that turned the exquisite poem into something alike to Wordsworth's "Ode to Duty."

Once, a few years ago, she had infiltrated a gang of lady smugglers who were terrorizing the law-abiding gentlemen of the west coast with their guns, their secret basements full of explosives, and the interesting sway of their hips as they strolled Cornwall's cliffs. After her cover was blown, Alice had hidden behind a barrel of stolen rum while the gang drank masala chai (for what self-respecting smuggler drinks ordinary English tea?) and discussed exactly what they would do to her when they caught her. (After hearing their decidedly inventive plans, Alice had never been able to look at a Cornish pasty the same way again.) That was an interesting tea party, to say the least.

The one today had been worse.

Alice would never have believed it possible for a teapot to endure the uses to which Mrs. Ogden put it, had she not seen it with her own eyes.

And she'd always thought a lady did not expose her ankles in mixed company, let alone her knees, thighs, and knickers, by performing a handstand on a table cluttered with cups and plates, such as Eureka Selassie (her *nom de pirata*: Eek!) had done.

And after hearing the story Millie the Monster told about how she'd employed a coconut in her youth, Alice had sorely wished she'd not eaten that slice of cake.

Now the pirates were enjoying a quiet period, much in the same way the eye of a hurricane is quiet. Settled in the Ecru Drawing Room, they engaged in ladylike occupations such as needlework—*"oh, stop sniveling, Olivia, I'll have this tattoo finished in one minute"*—sipping a few extra cups of tea—*"dearest, could you pass me the milk jug, and by milk jug I mean rum bottle"*—and attending to their correspondence—*"I say, Hadiza, how do you spell 'extortion'?"*

Alice wanted nothing more than to get Daniel out of the room so they could have some respite from the grim work of socializing by instead searching up chimneys and in cisterns for the hidden weapon. But he was trapped beside the hearth, staring blankly at Miss Darlington while that good lady lectured him on the risks of encephalitis for young married men. One sleeve of his suit jacket needed straightening, and he had not even noticed a loose thread on the upholstery of the chair in which he sat. He looked like a man who needed a ~~holiday~~ thorough debriefing from his superiors prior to being assigned some new, more gentle mission, such as assassinating the Russian emperor.

Watching him, Alice sighed with melancholy.

Egads! This blatant evidence of her eroding mental well-being so alarmed her, she did not notice someone sit beside her on the sofa until they reached out to take the book from her hands. That they survived doing so speaks to how discombobulated she had become; looking up belatedly, she saw Essie Smith.

"*All's Well That Ends Well,*" the pirate lady said, reading the book's gilded cover. Her tiny skull earrings glinted as she lifted a smile to Alice, who blinked warily in response. "I do so love a happy ever after, don't you, Mrs. Blakeney?"

Oh God, another conversation. Was there no end to the misery of this mission?

"Indeed," Alice said. "A happy result to any investig—er, interesting event—is always pleasant." Her stumbled answer illuminated to her that she had no life outside work. The thought brought another sigh from her lips.

"You sound happy," Essie noted.

"I am," Alice answered. After all, service is a fine heritage. She could have written her own ode to duty had she been given enough time with ruled paper and a thesaurus. At least, she could have last week. This week's bewilderments had left her barely able to recollect the A.U.N.T. motto (*Semper Octopus*—i.e., Really Needing Eight Arms All the Time Just to Get Everything Done).

"It does not surprise me," Essie said, flicking through the pages of the book in a carefree manner that made Alice want to snatch it back and hold it safe against her heart. "You are young, attractive, with excellent taste in fashion, and clearly you and your husband cherish each other."

"We do?" Alice said, perplexed. Then, recollecting her mission identity: "We do!"

Essie's smile deepened. "In this house full of huggers (and muggers), everyone privately has their eyes on you and Mr. Blakeney. We feel quite arrested by your romance. Someday you must tell me your secrets, for I confess, keeping order in my own relationship is not always easy. As Shakespeare says"—she tapped her long fingernails against the book, and Alice barely managed to restrain herself from breaking those nails and the fingers attached to them—"if only men could be discontented to be what they are, there would be no fear in marriage. But so few of them seek self-improvement!"

Alice's brain, distracted by the misquote, hastily searched itself for some reply. It flung phrases out of boxes, grabbed her imagination and shook it, all to no avail. Fortunately, Essie continued.

"I am, of course, fond of my dear husband. He is good with his hands, if you know what I mean."

Aha! Alice's brain snapped to attention, for it knew how to respond here. "Yes! Mr. Blakeney is also good with his hands," she said. "He can kill with just one punch."

"Indeed?" Essie blinked rapidly down at the book. "Goodness me. That is . . . charming, I'm sure. I suppose he is more careful when touching you, though."

Alice's expression darkened. "Indeed, he has become prone to gentleness of late." Even the thought of it made her skin tingle in the most disconcerting manner.

"Oh dear," Essie murmured.

Alice looked across to where Miss Darlington was now prodding Daniel's temple and explaining how a freckle proved him to have a raging case of brain inflammation. The elderly pirate seemed oblivious to how close she came to assassination for the crime of being concerned about him. Alice, however, could discern from Daniel's polite smile that he was clearly on the verge of homicide. She had to clench her muscles to keep from shooting Miss Darlington herself.

Fiddlesticks. When had Agent B, her absolute archrival, become so dear to her that she'd kill to protect him from mild discomfort? If only this mission would finish soon so she could have *her* happy ending: a whole new mission, assigned to her alone.

At this thought, her heart flinched oddly. Almost as if it would miss Agent B. Almost as if it wished with all its, er, heart to stay with him. That, of course, was nonsense. Falling in love with one's mission partner contravened several rules and

Excuse me. *Falling in love?*

Alice frowned. She was willing to admit *stumbling in fondness*, perhaps even *tripping in lust*, but anything further represented an unprofessionalism that could not be countenanced.

"Were I his lady, I would poison that vile rascal," Essie commented, and Alice turned to stare at her.

"A line from the play," the woman elucidated, tapping a fingernail again on the open page. She then *licked the finger* before using it to turn to a new page, and Alice felt the North Pole's ice caps relocate suddenly into her body.

"You know," Essie mused, "I suspect Shakespeare may have been a pirate."

Alice did not reply, her whole attention fixated upon the book for fear of what Essie might do to it next.

"He wrote much that inspires me," the woman added. "For example, 'to thine own self be true.' That is the best advice anyone might receive."

"And yet it originates with Polonius," Alice said, "who was a pompous hypocrite."

"The problem with that being——?"

Alice blinked in bemusement. "Why, a pompous hypocrite is—is—"

"Piratic?" Essie suggested, laughing. "You know, when I was young, I despaired at how different I was from others. No matter my efforts, I could not seem to manage proper behavior. It would have been bad enough had I been a wallflower, but I actually *climbed* the walls, from a burning curiosity about what was on the other side. Luckily, I met Gertrude Rotunder, who taught me the flight incantation. I stole my first house and never looked back. Now I am to my own self true, and it's brought me love, friendship, and a rather delightful hoard of treasure. Maybe one day uniqueness will be considered acceptable in women; until then, I pass on Polonius's advice whenever I can. We pirates know that not even the sky needs to be the limit. Wouldn't you agree, Mrs. Blakeney?"

Crash!

It took a moment for Alice to realize the sudden loud agitation was not her brain imploding from conversational stress. Mrs. Rotunder had overturned the small round table at which she had been playing whist with Mrs. Ogden and Millie the Monster, and now all three ladies were on their feet and glaring at each other.

"Are you cheating, Mrs. Ogden?!" Mrs. Rotunder shouted, drawing her sword.

"I most certainly ain't!" Mrs. Ogden said, bristling with outrage.

"Well, why not?" Mrs. Rotunder demanded. "Do you not believe me a good enough player that you need to cheat?"

"Um . . ." Mrs. Ogden was momentarily flummoxed. "Of course you are, dear. The best! I was absolutely on the verge of cheating, I can assure you."

But it was too late. The brief hesitation had sealed her fate.

"En garde!" Mrs. Rotunder declared.

Around the room, chairs and small tables clattered to the floor as several other ladies jumped up, drawing their swords automatically, before realizing the challenge had not been for them. Whereupon, they shrugged . . .

"En garde!" they shouted in reply.

Metal clashed against metal. Cries of *Take that!* and *Die, fiend!* and *Watch out for the teapot!* resounded throughout the chaos.

Essie stood, tossing *All's Well That Ends Well* onto Alice's lap before hurrying over to join the melee. Stunned and aghast, Alice took the book into her hands and stroked it, then checked the pages for tears and creases. The fact that she found none was not appeasing, for her private intimacy with the book had been disturbed. She was beginning a careful four-count of breath when a hand appeared in her line of vision, presented quietly, as one presents their hand to a dangerous animal of whose temper they're unsure. Looking up, she saw Daniel regarding her somberly.

"You seem fatigued, dear wife," he said. "May I escort you upstairs for a rest?"

Alice gratefully took hold of the hand, so strong and steady, so cool and dry, with its gold ring and an interesting small scar across one knuckle that she wanted to—

"Mrs. Blakeney?" he prompted.

Blinking rather dazedly, she stood.

A lady spun past, skirts a-whirl and ringlets flapping, as she whacked her sword against that of an elderly gentleman who puffed a cigar while fighting back. The foul whiff of smoke made Alice blanch with sudden nausea. Daniel held her still for a moment, his hand remaining around hers, his other reaching across her front like a shield, as though she was some fragile creature requiring his manly protection.

Outrageous! declared her brain. *I am a powerful, professional woman!*

Do you think if I swooned, answered her body, *he'd lift me in his arms?*

A gap opened up in the tumult and they hurried through, weaving between pirates, ducking blades, until they reached the corridor outside. Servants ambled past unperturbed, busy with their various duties (dusting, carrying laundry, making secret floor plans for the government). The calm soothed Alice's nerves, but she could feel Daniel's grasp on her hand tightening, and knew that if anyone so much as nodded a greeting to him, all hell would break loose. Now she was the one to protect and guide, practically towing him along the corridor and upstairs.

"We should search—" he began to suggest.

"We should take a quiet moment to restore our balance," Alice countered, and strode for their bedroom before he could argue. Opening the door, they stepped inside . . .

Boom!

The world filled with smoke.

"I say," Dr. Snodgrass murmured from beneath a quivering mustache. "It wasn't my fault."

They stood contemplating the charred wreckage of the washroom door. Daniel and Alice were composed to such a degree of tranquil perfection, Snodgrass and Veronica trembled at the sight of them. Alice was not even tapping her fingers. And if Daniel had blinked once in the past five minutes, they'd missed it. Veronica was beginning to fear exactly what it took to be a premier A.U.N.T. agent; Snodgrass, who had more experience with them, was mentally composing his last will and testament.

"I didn't suspect you, Doctor," Daniel said. "No doubt this was just another of the Wisteria Society's friendly attempts to assassinate us."

"Friendly?" Veronica echoed incredulously.

"They wouldn't try to kill us if they thought we were civilians," Alice explained.

"Besides," Daniel said, "we have something more important to worry about."

"The next assassination attempt?" Snodgrass said, looking around as if he expected it to happen at any moment.

"No, I mean the announcement Frederick Bassingthwaite made at afternoon tea. There will be a ball tonight."

Veronica gasped. "Oh my!"

"Exactly," Daniel intoned grimly.

"How wonderful!" The junior agent's eyes lit with shimmery dreams as she clutched her hands to her breast.

"What? No." Daniel shook his head. "There will be dancing. And as supposed pirates, we will be expected to join in."

"How is that worse than people trying to kill you?" Veronica asked.

"I have spent the past several years in Rotten O'Riley's company with people trying to kill me. That is regular pirate culture."

"It is also regular life for a secret agent," Alice pointed out. "If you do not find yourself on the verge of being murdered at least once a week, you are not doing your job properly. Rather that than attend a ball."

Daniel nodded in agreement.

Veronica's shimmer began to dim. "But—"

"I do not dance," Daniel said in an end-of-conversation tone, which from a professional assassin also threatened end-of-life.

"Nor I," Alice added.

The junior agent continued staring at them bemusedly. They were side by side, arms crossed, expressions stony, postures on the brink of reaching for a weapon. Veronica proved either her stupidity or her fitness as an A.U.N.T. agent by asking one more question. "Surely you were taught how to dance at the Academy?"

Both agents stiffened even more. "There was an—incident," Daniel murmured.

"There was an—accident," Alice murmured at the same time.

"*I do not dance,*" they reiterated in unison.

"You did the conga the other night," Veronica pointed out.

"Under duress," Daniel said. "And that was more a matter of accessorized walking."

"Well, you must dance tonight," Veronica persisted in what was perhaps the most death-defying action of the entire narrative. "Suspicion will fall on you if you don't."

"Cannot a chandelier or ceiling panel fall on me instead, thus excusing me from the evening?" Alice asked.

"Ha ha ha!" Snodgrass laughed heartily. "What a funny joke, Miss Dearlove!"

Alice stared at him with such icy intensity, it was remarkable he did not freeze on the spot. But instead he flushed, his mustache bristling. "I have just the solution!" he declared. "A little thing I've been working on in my spare time—self-dancing shoes! Why, put them on and you'll be doing the can-can in no time!"

"More likely the crash-bang," Daniel muttered.

"There is a far easier solution," Veronica said. "You must practice!"

Before the agents could react, she reached out, grabbing Daniel's hand and tugging him toward Alice. Only his utter bewilderment saved her from the tedium of three weeks in a hospital bed.

"Now, Agent B, place your hand on A's upper back—thusly. And Agent A, place your hand on B's arm. No, higher up—higher—just let me put it there for you. That's it. Now, each hold the other's free hand . . . Oh dear."

She bit her lip as she regarded the two pistols aimed directly at her.

"You'll need to put those away if you wish to waltz," she said in a cautious tone.

"There will be no waltzing," Daniel said.

"No can-can," Alice added.

"*No dancing*," they both emphasized. And holstering their guns, they took a professional step away from each other.

"The discussion is over," Daniel said. "We will simply intensify our search efforts, defy the odds, find the weapon, escape the pirate hordes, and depart this insane asylum before the band even begins to play."

"Very well," Veronica relented with a sigh. "It does not sound particularly romantic, however."

"This is a mission, V-2," Daniel chided. "Romance plays no part here."

"None whatsoever," Alice agreed.

They glanced at each other, and if Veronica was temporarily blinded by the heat passing between them, she finally retained enough good sense to say nothing about it.

"I can organize more servants to help in the search," she offered instead.

"Definitely not," Daniel said. "There are too many double agents downstairs. And the walls have ears." He paused, seeing Alice look around the room in startlement. "Idiom, Mrs. Blakeney. No, I trust no one at this point."

"Except us!" Snodgrass piped up.

Daniel frowned in response. "Now, listen. Mrs. Blakeney and I will change our clothes for dinner—*not* for dancing—and then continue the search. V-2, return to the kitchen, but remain alert for any news and—"

"Guard against exploding cakes," she added.

A moment of silence followed, in honor of Daniel's deceased patience.

"Good idea," he said eventually. "You do that. And Dr. Snodgrass, stay safe in your room."

The scientist sputtered. "But I have the perfect device, what, which when I—"

"Stay. In. Your. Room."

Snodgrass's mustache drooped. "I say."

Daniel shifted his frown to each of them. "If we all remain in our circumscribed roles, we will have this mission done with no more complications. It's as simple and easy as that."

Alice nodded in approval.

Two hours later, they were running for their lives.

✻ 18 ✻

HOW NOT TO OPEN A DOOR—A LITERARY ENCOUNTER—
DANIEL'S PATIENCE GOES UP IN FLAMES—A BUCKET OF COLD WATER—
NOT STRICTLY BALLROOM—AN IMMOVABLE OBJECT

W hen life itself seems lunatic, who knows where madness lies?"
In the attic, that is where.

Or, rather, madness crouches on an old sofa in the attic, and when disturbed by A.U.N.T. agents searching for a mysterious secret weapon, it leaps forth with quixotic energy. There is no reasoning with it, no soothing it, and apparently no getting close enough to whack it round the head and subdue it.

"Simple, you said," Alice complained to Daniel as they sped along a corridor. "Easy."

"What is your point?" Daniel replied tetchily.

"My point? That would be the screaming madwoman with a flaming torch chasing us."

They glanced over their shoulders and, upon seeing again the tangle-haired woman in a filthy nightgown bearing down upon them with uncanny speed, they increased their own pace.

"How was I to know we'd encounter someone like that in the locked attic of a Gothic castle?" Daniel asked. "Really, madam, I find you overly fastidious."

"Now I *know* this mission has been too much for you!" Alice retorted. "No agent in their right mind would consider it possible to be overly fastidious."

He frowned at her. She frowned in reply.

Alas, this state of relationship was entirely different from how it had been even five minutes ago, before the graceless moment that saw them confronted by the madwoman. Searching the upper floors of Starkthorn Castle, they had been entirely companionable.

For example, they had assisted each other in picking door locks.

(And if their hands had touched each other briefly in doing so, why, that was just an accidental consequence of professional behavior.)

They had explored shadowy, barely furnished rooms.

(And if Daniel's fingers, firmly brushing a scattering of dust from Alice's shoulder, had continued to linger at the nape of her neck—and her fingers in turn had stroked their knuckles against his thigh—one can only attribute this to the innocent effects of physical proximity.)

They had stopped to discuss their search route, marking off room numbers in Daniel's mental map.

(And if they had caressed each other's faces while doing so, that was due to—um—oh yes, the poor lighting in the corridor, requiring them to *feel* as well as listen to their speech.)

Finally, they had reached the last door and, after unlocking it, had paused outside to—to—

Oh, fiddlesticks. They had grasped at each other with such an abrupt and complete rejection of professionalism that A.U.N.T.'s Code of Conduct burst into hot, metaphorical flames between them as they kissed. Daniel had pushed Alice hard against the door, his lips bruising hers, his hands hauling up the layers of her skirts, while she'd clutched at his hair so he could not relent. With a careful degree of ungentleness, he had breached the gap in her drawers, and she had invaded the front of his trousers, and he'd pressed her harder against the door, causing her to knock the handle, the door to thrust open, and them to stagger through it, still holding and clutching and kissing, whereupon they had immediately become diverted by the question of *what the hell was that screeching?*

For two people who had read *Jane Eyre*, the answer really ought not to have been a surprise.

Now, skidding around a corner, they entered a wide, well-lit corridor. Music swamped them, and laughter tumbled from a double door opened farther along. Instantly, they halted.

"The dance," Alice said in horror.

Turning on their heels, they reared back from the madwoman as she waved the flaming torch at them.

"The devil," Daniel said disapprovingly.

"Aaaaarrgghhh!" contributed the madwoman.

Trapped, both agents drew their guns in a synchronous movement, aiming at the woman's heart.

It was a tense moment, requiring only dark sunglasses and a more dramatic kind of music playing in the ballroom in order to flip the narrative into something closer to a thriller than has thus far been its tone. Alice's tranquil layers knotted up in her digestive system as she strove not to flutter her fingers—arms—entire body.

This should never have happened. She'd been unprofessional. She'd lost focus on the mission, falling instead into obsessing over Daniel's strong, competent body—and, more especially, the way he employed that body to touch her as no one ever had before. Prior to meeting him, she'd felt only mild desires: to obtain secret information, to thwart criminals, to find a Latin edition of *Utopia*. Now it seemed as though her entire being was comprised of longing. Even in this moment, facing down the madwoman in the corridor, her senses kept veering to Daniel beside her. The height of him made her feel dainty. The trusting calm of him made her feel powerful. She was not just Alice pointing a gun at some raging threat; she was part of a couple— a mission team, a friendship.

At that dangerous thought, she winced. Alice Dearlove, Agent A, did not have friends. She had associates. The fact that, not five minutes ago, this particular associate had been slipping his hand into her underwear signified nothing more than an overenthusiastic enactment of their mission cover. Most certainly, it did not signify any involvement of her heart. Agent A possessed no heart.

The aching in her chest region was probably indigestion.

"Good gracious!" came a sudden high-pitched voice, sending a shudder through her awareness in much the same way fingernails down a chalkboard might have done. From the corner of her eye, she noticed Frederick Bassingthwaite standing nearby, dressed in orange velvet, his mouth even more agape than usual.

"Why are you holding Evelina at gunpoint?" he asked.

Neither agent looked away from the madwoman, whose wary expression upon Frederick's arrival suggested she retained at least some glimmers of sanity.

"She is threatening us with the flaming torch you might notice in her hand," Alice explained.

"Of course she is," Frederick said with a tinkling laugh. "That is what we hired her to do."

The madwoman bared her teeth.

"She is our resident Lunatic," Frederick continued blithely. "One can hardly own a properly decent Gothic castle without keeping an Attic Lunatic. We also have a Mysterious Scar-Faced Man lurking in the cellar, and the famous medium Mrs. Zhu comes in quarterly to refresh our ghosts."

Alice's eyes narrowed as she attempted to process this information. "So this woman is—?"

The madwoman held out her free hand in the offer of a handshake. "Muriel Happely," she introduced herself in a polished voice. "You may have seen me onstage in the Adelphi Theatre, playing Desdemona. Prince Edward himself called it 'a tour de force of suffering,' and it is generally agreed that he meant my performance, not the watching of it. I hope you have enjoyed your immersive experience of Evelina this evening."

"Enjoyed," Alice echoed with the hollowness of someone for whom all inner dictionaries have self-combusted in despair.

Ms. Happely withdrew her hand, which not only had gone ignored but hadn't even encouraged the slightest lowering of guns. Her smile wavered slightly at its edges, but she'd clearly dealt with critics before. "Thank you for watching! Please do consider leaving a review in the guest book before you go home."

Alice turned her head to look at Daniel. He met the stunned gaze with one of his own. If Mrs. Kew could have seen them at that moment, she'd have thrown away her sugar canister and just handed them a whole pot of black tea.

"Tremendous!" Frederick declared. "Kudos to you, Evelina, it was a master class in dramaturgy! That will be all for now."

"Actually," Ms. Happely said, "while I have you, Mr. Bassingthwaite, perhaps we might discuss the small matter of my outstanding wages, which—"

"Yes, yes, of course," Frederick interrupted, dismissing the question with a wave of his hand. "The check is in the mail!"

"*Arrrghh!*" Ms. Happely gave the flaming torch one last maniacal shake, then turned and ran back along the corridor, hollering as she went. Slowly, the agents lowered their weapons. Alice smelled something acrid; noticing a scorch mark on her bodice, she brushed at it and—

Abruptly, Daniel caught her hand in his. "Mrs. Blakeney," he said in a taut voice. "You have been harmed."

"It's nothing," Alice assured him, but as she looked up her blood chilled at the sight of his expression, so still, his eyes gone silver with fury.

Oh dear, she thought.

"Starkthorn Castle is proud to offer the best, most authentic entertainment," Frederick was saying cheerfully. "An elevated heart rate, a singed bodice, and as many thrills as you—*eee!*"

The butt of Daniel's pistol slamming into his temple caused him to squeal for the short duration of his passage to the ground, a journey that ended in unconsciousness. The agents regarded his heaped form with cool distaste.

"I think you are supposed to say something pithy at this moment," Alice advised.

Daniel frowned slightly. "Such as?"

"The jig is up," came a voice behind them.

Turning, they saw Miss Darlington stride along the corridor with a vigor surprising in one so encumbered by lace, pleats, puffs, and pearls that the fact of her even remaining upright was remarkable. Her walking stick tapping against the floor sounded eerily like a matronly *tsk-tsk*. Behind her lumbered Jake Jacobsen, who might have been described as her shadow were it not for the considerable substance of his body. And behind him came Mrs. Rotunder, bringing up the rear with a dress whose bustle made her own rear seem enormous.

"Surely it would be more appropriate to say the jig is down," Alice countered, "since Frederick is on the ground."

Daniel lifted his hand with the gun in it and pressed the thumb knuckle against his brow, where a headache lurked menacingly. "I believe Miss Darlington is referring to our cover being blown," he said.

"I am indeed," the pirate lady confirmed. "You made a good effort, but to be proper, after rendering Frederick unconscious you should have immediately robbed him."

"We were just about to," Alice tried—but Miss Darlington shook her head pityingly.

"It's no use, dear. There's also the fact you did not join in the melee in the art gallery."

"And you take your tea without sugar," Mrs. Rotunder added.

"And you don't stand like pirates."

"Or know about the Great Peril."

"Or have enough luggage."

"Or ever tried to assassinate any of us."

"And neither of you wears perfume."

"Not to mention getting frisky on the floor of your bedchamber instead of the bed," Mrs. Rotunder concluded. "A pirate would never!"

"Er." Miss Darlington very overtly did not look at her husband. "Exactly right, Gertrude. Shocking behavior! Besides, young lady, I realized what you were the moment I saw the butterfly on your hat. As if a pirate would be caught dead with such ridiculous headwear."

She nudged Jake, who laughed obligingly. (And such was the degree of his love for her that he didn't look, not even for the merest second, at her purple, ostrich-feathered, lace-swathed turban.)

Alice and Daniel exchanged a weary glance. Then, as one, they raised their guns at Miss Darlington.

She rolled her eyes. "Dear me, how tedious. This illustrates what I was saying before, Jake."

"What's that, my dear?" Jake asked, smiling tenderly at her.

"If only the authorities trained their operatives to have a sense of imagination, they might enjoy more success in overcoming piracy. As it is, these poor two souls were sent here like lambs to the slaughter. Note them standing there before us, wretchedly vulnerable."

"Madam," Alice said, "please note we are aiming guns at you."

"Yes, yes, but those guns have not contained live bullets since an hour after you arrived in the castle. We are *pirates*, 'Mrs. Blakeney.' Most of us have been dealing with spies and secret police for decades longer than you have been alive. You did provide us with much entertainment, however, so we won't kill you—"

"You have attempted several times to kill us!" Alice protested.

Miss Darlington bristled with outrage. "We most certainly have not. That would be uncivil—and worse, boring. Besides, why would we want you dead? I am sure your superiors will pay a fine ransom to have two such expert operatives returned to them."

Alice raised her chin proudly. "Our organization does not pay ransoms."

Beside her, Daniel sighed. "You probably should not have mentioned that," he murmured.

"You *definitely* should not have mentioned that," Miss Darlington said with a grin. "Jake, do me a favor and tie them up, then put them in a cupboard somewhere so I can enjoy a glass of sherry in—oh look, they've run. How amusing!"

Indeed, Alice and Daniel had tossed aside their useless guns, leaped over Frederick's body, and plunged without hesitation into the nearest available escape route: the ballroom.

And stopped, instantly overwhelmed.

A paso doble was being played with vigor by a band of Spanish musicians Jane had kidnapped for the event. Pirates strutted and swirled in pairs around the polished floor, their jewels and sword hilts glinting in the chandelier light, their frothy skirts creating a maelstrom of color that seared across Alice's vision. She took a deep breath, trying to steel herself.

I can do this, she averred silently. *I am a profess* . . .

The words disintegrated within the turgid swirling mass of color and sound. For one terrifying moment she herself became nothing more than a blur of light, guitar strums, bright twirling dresses, nameless and without reason.

Then pain grasped her, hard and sharp. Looking up dazedly, she saw Daniel's brief, unemotive smile. He held her hand so tightly, their fingers turned scarlet.

"Miss Dearlove?"

She gave him a brisk, professional nod.

Letting go of her hand, he began to remove his jacket. Alice tugged on the emergency release ribbon of her skirt. The heavy, layered material parted, revealing a ruffled, red satin petticoat beneath and, peeking out from under its flounced hem, high-heeled ankle boots embroidered with *libra*, an incantation phrase to help her maintain her balance. Even just the sight of those boots made her feel stronger. Kicking the skirts aside, she raised her chin to face the ballroom with determin . . .

No, still with a vast, trembling sense of overstimulation. Fiddlesticks.

Then Daniel grasped her hand again. As she swung around to face him, he pressed his other hand firmly against her upper back.

Their eyes met. Chandelier light flashed between them, and the music beat fast, imperative.

"I never thought I'd say this, but shall we dance?" Daniel suggested.

"I fear there is no hope for it after all," Alice said with a regretful wince.

He shrugged one shoulder. "Frankly, they had it coming."

They smacked their heels against the floor, bringing them into rhythm with the music. Daniel smiled, and a whole paragraph of interesting French literature burst through Alice's heart.

"Stop!" shouted Jake Jacobsen as he lurched into the ballroom. "Police!"

Pirate heads instantly turned. But the musicians, in indomitable Spanish fashion, sensing a moment of passion, intensified their playing at once. Daniel danced Alice backward across the floor. Mr. Rotunder rushed at them, waving his wooden arm. Without even glancing the pirate's way, Daniel lifted Alice's hand in his, while at the same time lowering his other hand to her hip to spin her.

The red petticoat swooped around her legs. She thrust out with her free arm and effected a brisk karate chop to Mr. Rotunder's neck. As he stumbled, she spun again beneath Daniel's arm, brought her foot up, and planted its bootheel with force against the pirate gentleman's midriff. He went down with a *thud* (and a clatter) that shook the floor.

Alice completed her spin and Daniel caught her, turned them together, and danced them through a gap in the crowd. Mrs. Etterly attempted to stop their progress, but Alice kicked backward, her bootheel smacking into the woman's legs. Then she and Daniel spun, and he applied a fist to Mrs. Etterly's waist (causing him more pain than the lady, due to her whalebone corset). She crashed against Mrs. Ogden, who staggered in turn, her hefty bustle taking down two other nearby pirates.

Daniel and Alice spun again. They clasped hands and fixed a center of focus within their calm, mutual gaze. Dancing around the heap of fallen ladies, they made for an open door at the far end of the chamber.

Bloodhound Bess rushed behind them, sword raised. Daniel, sensing the woman's approach (possibly due to her furious hollering), released Alice and turned.

"Pardon me," he said disapprovingly, then grasped Bess's wrist, twisted, and caught the sword as she dropped it. He flipped the grip around his hand with unthinking professional grace before thrusting the blade's point into the polished wooden floor. The blade shuddered. Bess did not have even a moment to react before Daniel tugged the puffed brim of her headdress down over her eyes and shoved her away.

A second later he had turned back, taken hold of Alice, and propelled her into a new spin. Arm extended, fist coming into play, she felled two more pirates, and they hit the floor in time with a fervid beat of music. Daniel gathered her to him once more, and Alice locked her hand with his. *Tap tap* went her heels as they skipped forward. The sense of overwhelm had gone. Old training routines took possession of her nervous system, and she felt like she could dance the night away.

"I've never known a woman as competent as you," Daniel told her over the rushing, rollicking music.

Alice thrilled at this effusive compliment. "You also are proficient to an admirable degree," she replied.

He lifted her, and she set her arm around his shoulders, and as they turned in a mutual dream of absolute professionalism, her outflung legs knocked Essie Smith, Lysander Smith, Millie the Monster, and a passing waiter all to the ground. The light swirled, shimmering with a thousand tiny reflections of crystal and glass, stirring the scene into one of fairy glamour. The music spiraled toward a crescendo. It was a perfect moment.

Finally Daniel set her on her feet and they fled the ballroom into the corridor beyond. Behind them, voices roared as a counterpoint to the music as the pirates realized the chase was on.

"Left," Daniel said tersely.

They turned a sharp corner. Servants carrying trays of champagne glasses hurried aside, their loads trembling perilously.

"Right," Daniel said. They turned another corner. "Left," he ordered almost immediately. Descending a narrow, shadowed stairwell, they did not dare glance back as the sound of pursuit raged behind them. It was surprisingly tuneful. Apparently the pirates were not only making chase but had brought the musicians with them.

Arriving at the foot of the stairwell, they paused briefly as Daniel consulted his mind map. "Left," he said, and they set off down a long corridor.

"Is that room ahead of us what I think it is?" Alice asked, noting a closed door.

Daniel flashed her a smile. "I thought about how Jane was carrying books when she reappeared after taking the weapon from storage. And I realized the one place we've not yet searched is—"

"—the library," Alice joined him in saying.

They increased their pace. A furious clatter of shoe heels, curses, and drumbeats echoed from the stairwell as the pirates gained on them.

"Faster!" Daniel urged.

"Hi-yah!"

Suddenly, Miss Darlington's maid, Competence, leaped from a side corridor into their path. Grim-faced, she wielded a broom in each hand.

Daniel and Alice halted before her. They stared dumbstruck as she spun her weapons with such ferocity they seemed to blur. Her feet jumped back and forth beneath her plain black dress, and the long yellow feather on her mobcap swooped. Finally she stopped, setting the brooms at a sharp angle to cross each other, and displaying a fierce grimace between them.

Daniel stepped forward calmly and punched her in the face.

She dropped with a clatter of broom handles to the floor.

"How cliché," Daniel said in disapproval.

Alice raised an eyebrow at him.

"What?" he said defensively. "It was pithy."

"I believe it should also have been witty."

He gave her a look so expressionless, so impeccably bland, Alice very nearly swooned. But she'd already made a mess of this mission and was determined to be more sensible from here on. Daniel Bixby's cool self-control would not be the focus of her attention, any more than his deep-seeing eyes, or his magnificently honed physique, or those forearms, which—

No, *the important thing* was the Queen's life (and completing the mission with distinction) (and staying alive) (and the thick, dark lashes fringing Daniel's *no!* the security of the realm). Stepping over Competence's semiconscious body, she continued on toward the library, Daniel close behind.

"Stop!"

"Fiends!"

"Blighters!"

Alice glanced back as she ran and saw the pirates had spilled in a jumble from the stairwell into the corridor. Their shouts were not directed at her and Daniel, however, but at each other as they wrestled and shoved to get precedence. Weapons were drawn, hats flew. A shuttered lace fan shot down the corridor, sparks flying. Daniel opened the library door, stepped back in a gentlemanly manner to allow Alice precedence, then entered behind her, turning to lock the door. Shadowy quiet filled the scene.

Alice had come to an abrupt halt, her breath vanishing.

A red-haired, fashionably dressed woman stood in the middle of the room, cradling an infant in one arm. The other arm was extended before her, a pearl-handled revolver in her lace-gloved grip. She pointed it directly at Alice's heart.

"Cecilia Bassingthwaite," Alice said tonelessly.

The woman raised one fine, terrifying eyebrow.

And the pirates began to thump against the library door.

❧ 19 ❧

A CAMEO APPEARANCE—TRAPPED—MAYHEM! MURDER! DUST!—
PERSONAL TALK—IMAGINATIVE REGRETS—
INTO THE DARK CHAMBERS OF DEJECTION RETURNED

Alice's impression of Cecilia Bassingthwaite resembled the eternal
rocks beneath a woodland: a source of little visible delight, but
necessary to behold, considering that any moment now the infamous
pirate might shoot her dead. Miss Bassingthwaite looked a great deal
more vivid than her portrait, although this may have been due to the
silvery light reflecting from her gun onto her elegant visage. Alice immediately sensed that, while the pirates she'd been dealing with this
week were deadly, Cecilia was *deadly serious*, and that represented a
whole new level of threat.

Behind her, Daniel turned and, upon noticing the pirate, said,
"*Hm,*" in a mild tone.

"Bixby!"

Blinking, Alice dared to glance away from Cecilia to where a handsome blond man arose from behind a desk farther back in the library,
his hands filled with checkbooks and gold pens. "What are you doing

here?" the man asked, grinning as if they were standing at the counter of a coffee shop, awaiting their turn to rob it.

The thumping on the other side of the door grew louder, causing the man's grin to tilt wryly in comprehension. "Ah, I see. Cecilia, sweetheart, it's probably not advisable to shoot Bixby. Alex might be a little put out if you kill his butler."

"I am no longer in Captain O'Riley's employment," Daniel advised, the mild reproach in his voice suggesting that he deemed it entirely proper for Cecilia to go ahead and shoot him under the circumstances.

"Even so." The man turned his grin to Alice, who rocked on her heels as if she'd been struck by a cannonball of sparkling delights. Were she carrying a purse, she'd hand it over to this fellow without a second thought. His blue eyes glinted as if he knew it very well. "And who is your companion, may I ask?"

Daniel did not take a small, protective step closer to Alice, but he so clearly *felt* one that the air shifted between them, and the blond man's smile quirked.

"Miss Dearlove," Daniel said in a rigid voice, "allow me to present Miss Cecilia Bassingthwaite and Captain Ned Lightbourne of— well—of wherever they want to go, quite frankly. In addition to being a blight on the lawful peace of England, Miss Bassingthwaite enjoys reading and Captain Lightbourne has a talent for dance. Miss, Captain, this is Miss Dearlove, my professional acquaintance."

"Is that what you're calling her now?"

Everyone turned to see Charlotte enter the room through a secret doorway in the wall of bookshelves. She threw Daniel such a knowing look it could have been awarded a master's degree from Oxford University. Behind her came Alex, wincing with caution as he pulled a cobweb from his wife's hair before she noticed. Upon seeing the occupants in the room, his eyes flashed with an emotion so intense, yet so indescribable, it would have been expelled from university in its first term. Immediately he strode across to Cecilia, his weapons glinting beneath the heavy shadow of his coat, his high, buckled boots thudding against the wooden floor. Without a word, he removed the infant from her hold.

"Ahoy there, Evangeline," he said, and lifting the golden-haired child, he kissed each tiny, bootie-covered foot emerging from her white lace gown. "Coochy woochy coo."

Cecilia closed her eyes briefly, shaking her head. "You know we are determined against using baby talk, Alex."

He grinned at her. "'Coochy woochy coo' is formal Irish," he said, and blew a raspberry against Evangeline's tummy. She laughed and tried to steal his earring.

Suddenly, the library door shuddered violently, splinters flying. Alice found herself being shoved aside by Daniel, less than a second after which the door flung open, crashed against the wall—and, as Mrs. Rotunder began to lead the charge into the room, slammed back in her face. A moment of stunned silence followed, during which everyone in the library stared at the door in wary astonishment. Then the handle turned, and the door glided quietly ajar. Ladies jostled to enter.

"Ahoy!" Miss Darlington declared. Then her eyes widened. "Cecilia!"

"Cecilia!" chorused the other pirates in joy.

("And Ned," Captain Lightbourne called out, waving, but everyone ignored him.)

"You brought The Baby!" Mrs. Rotunder said delightedly.

Another scuffle broke out as ladies began to rush toward Evangeline with such babbled cries of *coochy coo* and *itty bitty pretty* that even the baby seemed aghast. Ned strode forward to take her before the suddenly pale-faced Alex could draw his sword in a wild, overprotective instinct. Evangeline reached for her father, nestling against his broad shoulder as he murmured soothing words.

"Stop!" Cecilia said in a clear, ringing voice. She raised her gun in both hands, and the ladies staggered to a shocked halt.

"It is so very lovely to see you all," she said. "However, I require you to step back. Captain Lightbourne and I are here on business, and I will regretfully (but unhesitatingly) shoot anyone who gets in our way."

"If you've come for the weapon," Mrs. Rotunder said, "you should know this room has already been searched. It's not in here."

"Weapon?" Jane Fairweather's tremulous, high-pitched voice rose from somewhere within the crowd. "Goodness me, what weapon, ha ha?"

Everyone in the room, including Alice and Daniel, rolled their eyes.

"Thank you, Mrs. Rotunder," Cecilia said, "but I behold with perfect clarity the weapon of which you speak."

The pirates looked around excitedly. Alice, however, kept her focus on Cecilia. The young pirate had lowered her gun and turned toward the left side of the room. Following her gaze, Alice saw only a wall of books, a purple velvet armchair, and a small round table upon which stood a marble bust of the poet Wordsworth, decorated with a black bow tie. Above it, snagging her vision, a black thread hung untidily from the join line between ceiling panels.

All at once, her thoughts rushed together with such speed they seemed to meet instantaneously. She remembered finding a volume of Wordsworth's poetry that had been tossed behind the sofa in Jane's sitting room . . . remembered the marble bust originally being in the storeroom from which Jane and Frederick had removed the weapon . . . and remembered the flattened cake that had so distressed the castle's butler . . .

Cecilia stepped forward, reaching for the marble bust.

. . . And Alice saw again in her mind's eye the incongruous smattering of crumbs on the kitchen ceiling above that flattened cake. Even before she understood the vision, she was moving in response to it. Ignoring shouts from others in the room, she bashed into Cecilia just as the young pirate placed a hand on Wordsworth's noble head. Both women slammed to the floor.

Cra—!

Click.

Huddling protectively atop Cecilia, Alice felt a gentle shower of dust sprinkle onto her back. She tensed, but nothing further happened.

"*No!*" Jane cried out in anguish.

Tilting her head up, Alice noted one of the ceiling panels had cracked. Then she glanced at Wordsworth, tumbled on the floor. The dangling thread, on closer inspection actually a ribbon, now lay across his face, lending the poet a rumpled mustache that made him appear far more dashing than he'd ever have appreciated.

Bbbrrmmbbbrrmmbbbrrmmmm!!

She ducked her head again—but experienced nothing worse than the sound of Miss Darlington's strident command: "Give the señor back his drum, Mrs. Ogden!"

"I just thought the moment required a drum roll," Mrs. Ogden murmured contritely.

"Ahem," came a soft, polite voice closer at hand.

Alice blinked down at Cecilia. "Oh. Sorry. I do beg your pardon for the inconvenience," she said.

"It is quite all right," the pirate replied amiably. "I have the same reaction myself to Wordsworth. But would you mind getting up now? There are several daggers and a baby's bottle stored in my bustle, and they're rather digging into me."

"Of course." Alice hastened to her feet and assisted Cecilia to stand also, guiding her away from the cracked panel at the same time. Then Ned arrived, touching his wife's arm.

"All right?" he asked quietly.

"Yes," Cecilia said, reaching out to stroke Evangeline's hair before smoothing back a loose strand of her own. She glanced up, directing Ned's gaze to the ceiling; he maintained a placid expression, but anger darkened his eyes.

"It's fine," Cecilia said, laying a hand against his chest. "Thanks to Miss Dearlove, I am well."

"Miss Dearlove, hey?" Miss Darlington interjected, her eyes narrowing. She pointed her walking stick at Alice. "Just what is going on here, gel?"

Alice looked to Daniel. He frowned slightly, which she interpreted to mean, *You might as well inform them of our business, since the only hope now for us surviving the piratic horde is to persuade them you did not just assault Cecilia Bassingthwaite but in fact saved her life— although I do suggest you talk fast and get ready to run.* She opened her mouth to convey the gist of this—

"It was me!" Jane interrupted with a desperate shout.

Everyone turned to stare at her. She flushed, nudging her little round spectacles higher upon her nose in a futile effort to hide the crimson wash of emotion. "I lured you all here under false pretenses."

A shocked gasp burst from the company.

"The weapon does not exist!" she declared.

Another gasp.

"Queen Victoria is safe after all!"

Silence; a few shrugs.

Jane stiffened her shoulders with determination. "I felt certain Cecilia would guess my supposed weapon involved Wordsworth. She and I have long discussed his genius. Debated it. Had sword duels at sunrise over it. When she did not attend the party, I bade Frederick hide the bust away again, in case it became damaged in one of the games. But then word arrived that Cecilia's cottage had been seen flying nearby. So I brought out the bust once more, reset the plan, and waited for dearest Cecilia to succumb to my murderous trap."

Cecilia looked at her coolly. "I always knew you to be truly degenerate."

Jane's eyes shone with tears as she pressed a hand to her heart. Bemused, Alice consulted her inner manual of Facial Expressions, for she thought the lady looked *pleased* by Cecilia's words, and surely that could not be right. But she found the manual burned, mangled, and with a pirate dagger stabbed right through. These people were simply beyond comprehension.

"I knew I could rely on you, Cecilia," Jane continued. "The very second you took hold of Wordsworth's noble form, the panel above should have collapsed, along with several weights stored in the crawlspace." She eyed the ceiling with annoyance. "You'd have been instantly killed—assassinated by me, in front of our peers! I would at last succeed you as the most *daring!* the most *dangerous!* the most *nefarious!* pirate of our Society!!"

Alice waited for the company to gasp yet again, but a taut silence followed this speech. Cecilia's expression was inscrutable. Ned's jaw twitched.

"And what if I had been holding Evangeline at the time?" Cecilia inquired mildly.

Jane's blush reignited. "Why, I'd have stopped you, of course! I would never harm a child. 'Trailing clouds of glory do we come / From God who is our home: / Heaven lies about us in our infancy!'"

Cecilia raised one of those perilous eyebrows. Alice held her breath, anticipating explosions. Out of the corner of her eye, she saw hands grip sword hilts all about the room.

Then—

"Well done, Jane dear!" Cecilia declared with a smile. "Such an excellent scheme! I am naturally glad it's execution (pardon me) did not succeed, but I cannot fault your inventive planning. And I am truly honored that you'd try to kill me."

Jane lowered her eyes shyly. "I only ever wanted to be your friend—and murder you, too, of course."

"Of course," Cecilia said.

"There is also the small matter of a fortune being on your head," Jane continued. ("Idiom," Daniel whispered to Alice, saving her from a moment of significant confusion.) "I am determined the fortunes of the Bassingthwaites of Starkthorn Castle shall be restored, even if I have to sell heirlooms and steal from my guests" (indignant cries of *Excuse me?* and *Well I never!* arose from the crowd) "and take up a number of contracts on your life, dearest Cecilia."

"Completely understandable," Cecilia replied. "I shall assist you however I can—er, not by offering myself up for murder, you understand, but I can rob a bank or two if that would help."

She stepped forward, and as Jane opened her arms to welcome an embrace, instead took one hand and shook it. Jane's other hand flopped awkwardly down, but she smiled as if she was not in that very moment entertaining new schemes for assassination.

Cheers rang out from the crowd. Alice's brain spun in confusion. The pirates were *happy* Jane had tried to kill Cecilia? She looked instinctively again for Daniel, needing his steadiness and good sense—only to find him staring expressionless into the middle distance as if refusing to acknowledge the existence of the scene before him.

"This calls for sherry!" Mrs. Rotunder declared.

"Hurrah!" the crowd agreed.

Ned stepped forth and, masterfully avoiding a dozen eager, grandmotherly hands, presented Evangeline to Miss Darlington. She hesitated, looking for all the world like he was trying to hand her a sack of infested opossums. Reaching out, she patted the child's head, then clicked her fingers peremptorily. At once, Jake was at her side. He took Evangeline in the crook of one massive arm, Miss Darlington set her hand on his other arm, and they proceeded toward the door.

Alice saw Cecilia cast Ned an amused but weary look. Then suddenly, without warning, the red-haired pirate was staring directly at her. Alice's senses went immediately to battle stations.

But Cecilia smiled. "Thank you again, Miss Dearlove."

"Just doing my duty," she replied brusquely.

Cecilia's smile softened, as if she saw right through Alice's disguise and rather liked what she found there. *Impossible!* Alice urgently stamped down the idea and its attendant shadow of longing. After all, A.U.N.T. had worked on her for two decades to ensure she was neither seen nor liked.

But Cecilia went on with ruthless goodwill: "Anytime you wish, you are welcome to visit me and borrow a book from my library."

Beside her, Ned widened his eyes with amazement. Alice felt the shadow of longing grow stronger, and she suppressed it so definitely this time that the stone-cold look she gave Cecilia made the pirate take a step back. They exchanged polite nods, murmured, "Good evening," and Cecilia moved away. Alice inhaled with ~~regret~~ relief and—

Crash!

Abruptly the ceiling panel collapsed, sending oak and bricks thundering down. Wordsworth shattered into a thousand pieces. Dust billowed. Alice barely had enough time to inwardly exclaim a fiddlestick before she found herself being yanked back against a hard surface—namely, the full frontal region of Daniel Bixby's body. As his arm clamped protectively around her, she said a fond farewell to her breathing process, but this was a small loss compared with the gains made by her nerves. *They* were alive with excitement.

But the dust cleared with a disappointing rapidity, whereupon Daniel released her, murmuring an apology. Everyone proved to be unharmed; indeed, the pirates were regarding the horrifying mess with professional interest.

"Well, that certainly would have been effective had the timing worked," Miss Darlington remarked.

"I'm impressed," Cecilia added.

"So all's well that ends well," Mrs. Rotunder said, brushing dust from her bodice. "Now we need a new entertainment."

Silence slammed down with even more terrifying force than the ceiling had done. The pirates turned as one to regard Alice and Daniel.

"Ladies," Cecilia chided. "Miss Dearlove just saved my life."

They immediately pivoted to study Charlotte with the same calculating stare.

The witch raised her chin. "Yes?" she asked, fearless.

"We are just wondering, dear," Mrs. Rotunder said in a genteel, grandmotherly voice, "how much of a head start would you like?"

Charlotte paused to consider this, but before she could reply, Alex drew his brutally long sword, grabbed Charlotte around the waist, and escaped with her into the secret passageway. As the bookcase slammed shut behind them, the pirates shook their heads with disapproval.

"Such manly heroics for the sake of a *witch*," Mrs. Rotunder muttered. "And in front of The Baby, too."

"Now what do we do?" Mrs. Ogden grumbled.

There followed a whoosh of silk and hat feathers as everyone turned again to stare at the A.U.N.T. agents.

"We'll take a five-minute head start," Daniel said promptly.

Mrs. Rotunder gestured at the library's open door. "By all means, Mr. Blakeney. Good evening, Mrs. Blakeney. We wish you well in your endeavors to escape our terrifying pursuit."

Without looking, Daniel took Alice's hand. They walked through the crowd, eyes forward, breath in abeyance. Not one pirate moved, but the silence seemed to echo with a promise of screams and drawn swords. Exiting the library, Daniel shut the door behind them, and they immediately began to run.

"To the mission house!" Alice directed.

"No, we wouldn't get there in our two-minute head start," Daniel argued.

"But they gave us five minutes."

Daniel laughed brusquely.

A second later, the library door burst ajar.

❋ 20 ❋

THE CHASE—DANIEL IS CAPTIVATED—LIES AND ILLOGIC—
TAKING A MOMENT TO APPRECIATE ART—
DANIEL RESORTS TO MATHEMATICS

Pirates are almost always better than their neighbors think they are. They attend church (do you realize how many silver candlestick holders and golden plates are in a church?). They respect the law (as one does respect a powerful enemy). And they can be counted on (to do the wrong thing).

As they spilled into the corridor four minutes and thirty seconds before the head start was completed, a chorus of *Tally ho!* announced that the hunt was on—for while pirates might embody Shakespeare's "to thine own self be true," they cheerfully skipped the "thou canst not then be false to any man" part.

Daniel could not help but feel a rush of exhilaration as the ladies roared in pursuit. Danger was, after all, what he had been constructed for. Even as he ran, he calculated risks, scanned for potential weapons, and consulted his mental map for the best escape routes. The Wisteria Society might be wicked villains, but he was something far more dangerous—a professional hero. They would not catch him. And he would kill every single one of them before they even touched Alice.

The name fluttered softly, like fine, rose-scented fingers, beneath his heart. He almost stumbled. *Alice?* Since when had Agent A, Miss Dearlove, rival and mission associate, become *Alice?* And why did his pulse shiver when he glanced at her, seeing several locks of hair tumble from her coiffure as she withdrew the miniature dagger concealed therein?

A shadow loomed at the corner of his eye and he looked over just in time to realize he was about to collide with a tall vase at the edge of the corridor. *Focus on where you are going*, he reminded himself sternly.

Alice reached inside her bodice to withdraw another dagger.

He crashed into a statue.

"Are you all right?" Alice asked, glancing at him.

"Left," he snapped in response. They turned into a narrow corridor leading to a rise of stairs, and Daniel pushed Alice ahead of him. Her red petticoat swirled around her like a—a—red swirly thing. Her hair fell completely from its pins in the manner of—of—

Damn. He almost wished for the pirates to catch him before the urge to romantically similize completely destroyed his brain.

Besides, Alice Dearlove was truly incomparable.

"Left," he said again at the top of the stairs. As they ran, the pursuers shouted advice:

"Just give up!"

"Surrender!"

"At least slow down, I'm getting too old for this kind of thing!"

But their voices were diminishing, and Daniel began to think escape was just around the corner.

Then he turned the corner.

"Damn," he swore with uncharacteristic passion, coming to a halt as he stared at the dead end ahead of them.

"Well, that's a nuisance," Alice remarked. "And no door, no window, to escape through."

"*Aaaaaahhhh!!*" added the approaching mob.

Turning to face the way they had come, Alice set her feet apart and spun the tiny daggers in her hands. Daniel himself had no knives, and the spare gun in his concealed holster was obviously useless if Miss Darlington had been telling the truth about stealing their bullets. But he did have his bare hands, which were registered weapons (the paperwork had taken him hours). He and Alice did not need to glance at each other to share a battle plan.

Go Down Fighting.

Alice squinted as she aimed her dagger at an imagined foe, then spun it again with casual proficiency and used the tip to scratch at her eyebrow. Daniel considered whether he had enough time to push her against the wall and kiss her until they both swooned.

The floor began to tremble. The horde was growing closer. Probably no, in that case. He took a step forward.

Suddenly a panel in the wall swung ajar. A hand emerged, beckoning.

"Quick," someone urged from the shadows. "In here!"

Immediately Daniel grasped Alice's arm and sent her through the doorway, hurrying in behind her. They found themselves in a tiny, bare room only just discernible in the faint light coming through the open door.

"Thank you," he whispered to their rescuer.

"My pleasure," the mysterious figure said. Then she shut the door—having first exited through it.

Darkness clamped down.

"I've got them!" the ~~rescuer~~ villain shouted. "They're in here!"

Daniel cursed beneath his breath. How could he have been so stupid as to trust someone in a pirate's house?

Jostling him aside, Alice crouched down. Daniel heard a scraping noise, then she rose.

"I've jammed a dagger beneath the door," she explained in a whisper. "But it won't keep them out for long."

Even before she finished speaking, the door shuddered as the pirates tested her theory.

"Let us in," Mrs. Rotunder called out in a voice as sweet as Mrs. Kew's tea. "We only want to chat!"

"Chat you right off the plank," Millie added, chuckling.

"Millie!" Mrs. Rotunder *tsk*ed with exasperation. "I'm trying to fool them into a false sense of security."

"They're spies, not idiots," Millie retorted. "Well, not *complete* idiots."

"Fair point," Mrs. Rotunder said, and the thumping against the door grew louder.

Daniel began to shove at the walls. "It's a secret room," he whispered to Alice, "therefore it must have a secret exit."

"That is a fallacious statement if ever I heard one," Alice said, but she joined him in his efforts. "I must say, Mr. Bixby, being in mortal peril is no excuse for illogical—"

She fell abruptly silent. Groping through the darkness for her, Daniel felt her hand catch his. She pulled him forward, and he stumbled with her into a newly opened space. A dim light above indicated she had found a secret staircase. Daniel closed the door behind them, Alice wedged her last dagger beneath it, and they hurried up toward the light.

Thud! The pirates broke through the first door.

"No one here!" came a shout. "Muriel Fairweather, you're a liar!"

"I told the truth!" Muriel replied indignantly. "They were here a moment ago. They must have found the secret passageway!"

"A pirate telling the truth?" The pirates laughed.

"How rude! Edwina Ogden, I demand you apologize!" There followed the sharp sound of a sword being drawn.

"I'm a widow," Mrs. Ogden replied. "That means I never need to apologize again!" Another sword scraped from its scabbard.

"En garde!"

"En garde!"

Metal clanged.

"Take that, fiend!"

"Be careful of my hat!"

The agents reached the top of the stairs and cautiously entered a room that glowed with the soft golden light of dimmed gas lamps. They stared in confusion at an assortment of beds, rocking horses, and tall standing easels displaying art. Not immediately seeing an exit, they grabbed paintbrushes as makeshift weapons and pressed themselves against the wall at either side of the half-open door, listening to evaluate the threat of pursuit.

Thud! The second door below slammed open.

The agents exchanged a grim look and tightened their grips on the paintbrushes.

"More stairs? Really?" came Mrs. Rotunder's cry.

"I am as fit as the next person," replied Millie the Monster (a tiny woman whose age had long ago gone for a stroll in the mists of time and never been seen since). "I could continue this pursuit for hours. But frankly"—she paused for a heaving breath—"it has become boring."

"I'd rather be playing with The Baby," Muriel added.

"Dearest Evangeline! I have never seen a more prodigious child!" Mrs. Rotunder's voice faded as the pirates began to leave. "Only four months old, and yet at luncheon last week I looked away for no more than a second and she stole my teaspoon."

"Ridiculous name, though," opined Millie (short for Verisimilitude).

"It's from a poem, apparently," Mrs. Rotunder said, and the resulting laughter dwindled away.

Daniel exhaled just as Alice did the same. He closed the door, and noticing a chest of drawers nearby, they hauled it over to serve as a barricade. Then leaning back against it, they stared wearily into the middle distance.

"I am just so shocked," Alice murmured.

"Oh?" Daniel asked, wondering which of the screaming women with a torch, terrifying pirate horde, exploding ceiling, or further terrifying pirate horde had troubled her in particular.

"'It's a secret room, therefore it must have a secret exit,'" she said, and shook her head. "Have you read no Aristotle at all?"

"There *was* a secret exit," he pointed out.

"That is beside the point." She shook her head again, as if trying to settle the thoughts therein. "I also cannot believe Jane blew up the library ceiling in an effort to kill Cecilia Bassingthwaite, and everyone *applauded* her. Even Cecilia."

"Pirates," he said.

"And they keep tigers in their bedrooms."

"Just one tiger," he pointed out reasonably.

She impaled him with a look that ought to have been given its own entry in the A.U.N.T. index of weaponry. "They are . . . are . . ." She cast about for the worst insult possible. "*Utterly inexplicable.* At least we can now leave this place, since the weapon does not exist. Our mission is complete. We can take the cottage and be back in London before dawn."

"I'm not flying that alleged building at night," Daniel countered. "We're safe here; we should take a break."

That idea perked Alice up at once. "Good idea! Break what, though? Frederick's bones? Windows?" She looked around the room. "Where exactly are we?"

"The castle nursery, I think," Daniel said. "But it seems someone has turned it into an art studio."

Drifting over to one of the easels, Alice tilted her head as she contemplated the large charcoal sketch on display. Then she tilted it in the other direction.

"The artist appears to have a poor understanding of gravity," she commented.

Daniel went to stand beside her. One glance at the sketch and he swallowed dryly, shoving his hands into his trouser pockets. "No, I think they understand altogether too well."

Alice peered closer. "Is that supposed to be Jane?"

"Mm-hm."

"Why is she wrestling that gentleman? He— wait, that's one of the Bassingthwaites' footmen, isn't it? Why is he not wearing trousers?"

Daniel raised his eyes heavenward. "Miss Dearlove, I cannot believe you are *that* innocent."

She jumped back as if the sketch had tried to assault her. "Oh. Well, goodness me. Of course I am worldly to the correct, ladylike degree. It's only . . ." She tilted her head again. "Surely that is not normal practice?"

Daniel regarded the image thoughtfully. "Actually, it's not abnormal, as such. Just not very safe for her neck, I should think."

"Well. Fiddlesticks." A delicate flush warmed the frown on her face, making her practically luminous with disapproval. Daniel's brain informed him tersely that he was staring at her and, if he did not stop, it would send an official complaint to his nerves. He ignored it.

Was there a more exquisite woman in all the world than the one standing before him? If so, Daniel had not met her, and never expected to. Alice Dearlove defied even his ability to find a suitable quote from literature; he could only say she was $e^{(i\pi)} + 1 = 0$ in feminine physical form. Her mouth shaped a general, silent reproof with gorgeous perfection. Her eyes were so opulent they might have inspired any amount of poetry were Daniel's imagination capable of bending further than "dark brown." And the memory of her soft, creamy skin pressed against his body as she attempted to strangle him made him ache with longing. He moved unthinkingly, helplessly, toward her.

She took a step back.

"I have questions about how Jane effected the ceiling collapse," she said. "We must debrief."

"Tomorrow." He took another step, and although she did not retreat this time, her fingers tapped a staccato beat against her thigh. Daniel stopped at once, swallowing disappointment.

Then she broke his world apart and pieced it back together with molten gold: she took a step toward him. He drew in a breath he hadn't known he'd been inhaling, and almost choked.

"Tomorrow it's over," he said, his voice gritty. "We go back to headquarters, get reassigned." Gathering all his courage, he offered a dream in disguise: "We could use tonight to professionally expend our residual marital energy, as a way of transitioning out of the mission roles of husband and—"

He got no further before Alice grasped hold of his shirt, pulled him against her, and gave him his wish. She kissed him rapaciously, devastating every barricade and barbed trap he had within. Sensation barreled free, overwhelming him with emotions. It was all he could do not to weep. He desired her with such intensity, the fact he had her in his hands now was a bomb he could not safely defuse. He tried to pull away but was holding her too tightly to escape.

Her hands roamed his back, fingernails digging through shirt linen, making new, tiny thorns amongst his inked roses. The pain was delicate, and it stirred him beyond lust into deep, warm fondness for the woman. Breaking the kiss, he gazed down at her lovely face, tenderly stroking loose strands of hair away from—

Thud. Pain burst through him as Alice shoved him back against a wardrobe, his head smacking on the wood. Stars filled his vision.

Idiot, he cursed himself, even as Alice lifted a hand to strike. *No goddamn light touches.* Blocking her attack effortlessly, he ducked, slipping around behind her, and shoved her in turn against the wardrobe. Twisting her arm back, he pressed his body to hers so she could not move.

She whimpered.

And then—"Harder," she commanded.

Everything in him went instantly, obediently hard, even as he angled her arm further.

"I still have a hand free," she pointed out.

He lowered his head to whisper in her ear. "You don't scare me, Alice."

She went so still at the sound of her name in his mouth, Daniel wondered for a moment if she was going to detonate. But then she gave a soft, quiet sigh. It seemed to echo the yearning he felt, and he closed his eyes, bent his brow to the back of her head, as if she was an altar he would pray on.

"I scare the living daylights out of myself," she confessed. "We should probably stop."

Fine. That was fine. He had no need to caress her, nor kiss her rosy mouth until the razor-sharp edges of his heart began to soften. He needed nothing at all but a gun and a rule to live by. Releasing her, he stepped back—

"*Tsk,*" she said.

And he frowned, feeling more lost than he'd ever been in his life. "Perhaps you could help me understand what you want?" he asked, trying to keep his voice steady, never mind his heart.

Alice turned to face him, leaning back against the wardrobe. Her hair was disheveled, her face almost white in the mingling gaslamp-

and-moon light, except where shadows limned her eyes. Daniel could hardly fathom such loveliness.

"I want to not be ruled by *should* and *ought*," she said. "I want—" She paused, then huffed a brief, sardonic laugh. "I want to be to my own self true. But I cannot, can I? Neither can you. We live to serve."

The sentiment nauseated him, because it was true. Suddenly he burned with a furious desire to destroy every single Academy teacher who had broken Alice Dearlove's will and manipulated her into doing only what benefited A.U.N.T., just as they had to him. But he stayed calm, focused, the way he did when faced with any other monstrous villainy.

"You're right," he said. "My whole life has been in service. Only books have given me any kind of escape. But this week I've been starting to realize I want more than that. For example, I want you."

Alice flushed in a way he loved to see, going all hot for him. But her gaze slipped away over his shoulder. "No one wants me," she said, "except as a fixer. A servant who can fetch their handkerchief, carry their hatbox, disarm their villainous criminal. What can I do for you, Mr. Bixby?"

"Nothing," he said instantly—then paused to think it through, to give her a real answer. She had already said it herself: "Be your own self true. I want *you*."

Emotion rippled over Alice's face—grief, maybe, swamping her eyes with tears; or perhaps it was anger, making her jaw muscles go *tap-tap*; or God only knows—Daniel could have done with an instruction manual on women just at that moment, along with a cross-referencing bibliography and several diagrams.

"I am dangerous," she said.

"You won't hurt me," he answered at once. "I won't let you."

She gave him a cynical look. "Good luck with that, Mr. Bixby."

"I don't need luck." Reaching out fearlessly, he took hold of a satin button on her bodice, and rolling it between two fingers, he recited a slow, sensual line of Latin poetry. The wardrobe behind them lifted, floating across to the door, where it settled to strengthen the barricade.

"Witchcraft!" Alice gasped. "Does A.U.N.T. know you can do that?"

"What do you think?" He slipped the button from its fastening. "You've spent a few days in pirates' company and admit yourself corrupted. I spent *years* with them. Share the night with me, Alice."

"I rather have to," she answered. "There seems no safe way out of here except—"

"I mean," he interrupted with endless patience, "making love together. Just us, Daniel and Alice, not Agents A and B, not Mr. and Mrs. Blakeney. Our own selves true. Only—only if you want, though, of course."

Forcing himself into silence before he could utter a cringing apology, he reached for the next button on her bodice.

"Yes," she said.

Yes! his heart echoed, trembling with sheer, amazed delight. *She said yes!*

"But," she added. Her hand clamped his against the button, stopping him. Her countenance became deadly tranquil once more, and Daniel felt electrified.

"Before we go any further," she said, "let's list some rules for ourselves."

And just like that, his nervous system invented nuclear fusion.

LAWFUL BEHAVIOR—RULE THREE—ALICE IS UP AGAINST IT— RENEGOTIATIONS—MUTUAL ASSASSINATION

Alice was afraid of too much expression on Daniel's part. But after clipping a blank piece of paper to an easel, they listed more than a dozen rules for lovemaking, and her concerns were relieved. Should Cupid have come upon their contract, he'd have gone blind trying to read the fine print.

"Most especially, A.U.N.T. must never learn of what we've done," Alice declared, writing a final exclamation mark then stepping back from the easel.

"I certainly agree with that," Daniel said. But he frowned as, with arms crossed and eyes peering over the top of his spectacles, he regarded the list. "I still aver we cannot regulate the degree of pleasure experienced."

"That is why we have a range," Alice explained. "By all means, induce my physical satisfaction anywhere up to level eight out of ten, but higher than that and I'm liable to strangle you."

"Uh huh."

"And don't forget to employ your tongue when kissing. That was most gratifying."

"Understood." Removing his spectacles, he placed them tidily on the easel's shelf, then turned back to her and extended his hand. "So we have a covenant?"

She regarded him (that is to say, his left shoulder) for a long, cool moment. The evidence was undeniable, he desired to partake in co-ital activity with her—*I want you,* meaning he wanted her body. And equally impossible to deny, she was in love with him. But she felt sure the rules they had formulated would provide a safe, tidy structure in which physical pleasure could be experienced with hopefully a reduced risk of murder.

"We do." She took his hand in a firm grip and gave it a brisk shake. "Now, let us start with—"

He yanked her suddenly. She stumbled against him, her pulse shattering on the hard planes of his chest, and he enfolded her at once in his arms.

"What are you doing?" she asked, her voice as taut as every muscle in her body.

"Hugging you."

Alice frowned. Really, this did not bode well. Restraint was one thing—she had negotiated for that safety measure and had gained an assurance he'd use a constrictor knot if he was called upon to tie her up. She almost hoped it would happen. But this random embrace? It only served to slow the pace of the action.

Well, she would be accommodating. He could have sixty seconds of *hugging* before she brought them back to the schedule.

She began a silent count toward sixty. Daniel rested his head against hers but otherwise did not move. Ten seconds. Alice tapped her fingers against her thigh. Twenty seconds. Her frown eased. Thirty seconds, and her breath slowly loosened. Senses that had been overstimulated for days—years, really—began to gentle within the silent, unrelenting compass of Daniel's embrace. Twenty-five seconds. Wait, no, thirty-five. Or was it forty? Numbers dissolved as she softened, and Daniel's arms grew tighter about her in response.

"Is that a gun in your trouser pocket," she murmured, "or are you—"

"It's a gun."

She stroked it through the dark wool of his trousers. "What model?"

"Smith and Wesson .38. An American weapon."

Her breath caught. "Say it again."

She felt him smile against the side of her head. "Smith and Wesson .38 double-action hammerless revolver with a five-round cylinder and nickel finish."

"Oh." Her tranquil layers began to melt like warmed honey, pooling in the secret dark place between her legs. "I'm going to garrote you," she said, nestling against him.

"Hm," he murmured in her ear. Her nerves trilled just a little—a delicate sensation she was surprised to declare pleasant.

Then he drew her earlobe into his mouth, sucking on the trapped flesh, and "pleasant" flung off its drab-colored cloak with a dramatic gesture, revealing the bright, spangled form of bliss.

Alice gasped. "This isn't on the list!"

"Yes it is," Daniel said. "Rule three. Kissing."

"But—but—" she stammered.

He stopped, moving back slightly. "No?" he asked. "Or yes? Your word is my command."

This sudden requirement to choose sent Alice's nerves into disarray all over again. She contemplated asking for a pause in proceedings so she might read a calming scene or two of *All's Well That Ends Well* but remembered she'd left it in the pocket of her skirt, which was currently lying in a heap in the ballroom downstairs. Bother! That was the second skirt she'd lost on this mission. Very much longer and she'd be entirely naked.

Oh. Wait.

At the reminder that she was in fact going to be naked in—she glanced at the timetable—*twelve minutes*, Alice's nerves jumped out of the frying pan of disarray and into the fire of absolute chaos. "No," she said. "I mean no, it's yes. Yes to all the yes things, unless I say no. Yes?"

"Um . . ."

Frustrated, she kissed him on the mouth—firmly, in the proper regulated manner.

Daniel welcomed her efforts with a response that slowly deepened, turning the kiss sumptuous. She began stroking him, getting tingles from the fine, crisp texture of his shirt. Instructions on how to murder him kept flashing through her brain, even as she slipped her tongue against his. Tiny inner Alices ran around smoothing down her tranquility, only to have the edges curl up and blacken in an intensifying heat of lust. Indeed, so busy was her interior that she didn't even realize Daniel had unbuttoned her bodice until he began removing it.

She gasped. "Already?"

He paused. "This *is* the scheduled time for undressing."

"Good heavens. I now understand the phrase 'time flies when you're having fun.'"

Daniel grinned. Bending, he proceeded to kiss and lick (subclause 3b) and nibble (unnoted, but Alice was willing to let it slide) a path down her throat to her collarbone. Alice trembled. She hadn't felt so good since the time she was allowed to arrange all the desks in the Academy classroom. Daniel's hand slipped down her back, then lower still, tucking itself beneath the waistband of her petticoat. At this new experience of touch, she stiffened.

Immediately Daniel withdrew the hand. "Sorry," he said. "I was moving toward point six on the schedule, but would you like me to stop? Or should I—"

Alice shook her head, not in reply but from sudden, overwhelming anxiety at having to make yet another decision. Aroused as she was by so many strange but pleasurable sensations, these choices felt like bombs in her brain. *Yes! No! Maybe! Slightly! Sometimes! Stop! Go faster!* A hundred consequences of her every possible answer exploded in wild, loud colors. She tapped fingers against her brow in a desperate attempt to regulate them. She tried to count her breath, but the numbers changed depending on whether she said yes or—

"Oh!"

Surprise flooded her mind with white silence as Daniel lifted her abruptly. He walked her two steps backward and pressed her against a wall. Then he set her hands at either side of her, palms to the wood paneling.

"Keep them there," he instructed, and gave her a look—cool, untroubled, *safe*. She swallowed heavily, her nerves thrilling at his mastery but her pulse easing, her mind sighing contentedly now that he had relieved the burden from it.

"You have the right to remain silent," he told her, "but anything you do say will be taken as the word of law. Do you understand this right I have just explained to you?"

"I do," Alice replied—and suddenly envisioned them standing at a church altar, with her saying those words while he slipped a genuine ring onto her finger.

Daniel's eyelashes fluttered, and she wondered what he was thinking. Not one hint of romantic hooliganism threatened his impeccable countenance. But his voice trembled when he asked, "Do you wish to proceed under these conditions?"

She nodded.

Reaching up under the lustrous red billows of satin, he set his hand against her drawers' open crotch. Alice gasped delightedly, clutching at the wall, as he began deploying one finger in such a manner that several rules quit on the spot, instead setting up recliner chairs, sunglasses, and tumblers of lemonade with paper umbrellas in them, so as to bask in the heat.

Although Daniel had touched her *there* before, this time nothing interrupted him, and he progressed further than Alice had known was possible. Indeed, should they make it back to London without being murdered by pirates, killed in a house crash, or electrocuted after using a hairbrush designed by Dr. Snodgrass, Alice would have to nominate him for promotion solely on the basis of his thumb skills. He was not gentle, and the sensations that rampaged through her body did not so much trip her alarms as smash them down and trample them. Moaning, Alice began to flounder. It was too much feeling—too much—she could not breathe. But Daniel did not pause, driving her right to the upper limit of pleasure's level eight, then pounding her against it over and over again.

"Willows whiten," she gasped, to no avail. Her muscles began to quiver more than a whole forest of aspens. Level eight gave a little cry and collapsed beneath the swollen, pulsing weight of levels nine and ten. Alice herself sagged against Daniel, and he stroked her hair with his free hand, whispering fragments of Tennyson until her heart no longer felt like it was going to burst.

"I estimate we're a third of the way through our schedule," he advised.

"I'm not going to make it," Alice moaned into the cool linen of his shirt. Even the scent of laundry soap and masculine sweat threatened to spiral her into confounding bliss all over again. "You go ahead, leave me behind."

Daniel smiled. "I'll wait until you're ready." And he slipped his hand slowly from her drawers.

Alice straightened as if electrified. "It's fine. I have my second wind now. Let's continue."

He looked through his eyelashes at her, stirring that second wind into a storm. "As you wish."

And before she knew what he was about, he'd removed her drawers and knelt before her, and she discovered that the postdoctoral thesis on coitus had been missing a few pages.

Forget hooligan; she was a *delinquent* now. "Um—" she attempted. "What—"

"Rule three," he reminded her. "Kissing." And when she gasped, clutching at his hair—"Subclause 3b: with tongue."

By the time he finished, level eight was a mere speck in the eye of level twenty, and Alice could barely stand. In a haze, she felt herself being lifted, then carefully lowered to a narrow bed. The metal frame creaked; a smell of mold wafted up. Her petticoat had disappeared somewhere along the way, leaving her clad in only a thin linen camisole embroidered with enchantments.

She lay stiff, thighs pressed together, arms crossed. Daniel removed his shoes and trousers, then climbed onto the bed, kneeling astride her legs. Without a word, not even looking at her, he unfastened his tie and began unbuttoning his shirt.

"Don't tell me to relax," she warned, her voice raspy after all its recent moaning.

"All right," Daniel said evenly. His shirt fell open, and as he turned his attention to his cuffs, Alice urgently counted her breath. *One . . . two . . . elephant . . . seventy-four . . .*

The shirt came off, revealing his tanned torso, lean, deadly arms, and a certain other anatomical feature that, had it been included thusly on Michelangelo's *David*, would have tripled museum profits due to the crowds of visitors. Daniel gave the shirt a crisp shake and began to fold—

"Um . . ." he said, blinking with surprise, as Alice snatched the shirt from him and threw it to the floor.

"I'm just streamlining the schedule," she explained, and he laughed.

The lovely, rare sound glimmered through her. Her fingers fluttered in response against her bare arms.

"Hm," Daniel said, taking one hand in his. Alice immediately made a fist, but he pried the fingers apart with ease. "These remind me of a poem I once read in an old American newspaper. I enjoy seeing them 'leaping like leopards in the sky.'"

As she watched him kiss each fingertip, emotions broke through the haze of physical pleasure and threatened to overwhelm her. "I'm going to stab you," she whispered.

"Uh huh." He stroked his tongue across her wrist.

She shivered. "I'm going to break your legs."

Unperturbed, he began kissing up her arm. "Behold, thou art fair, O my love," he murmured against her skin. "Behold, thou art fair; thy eyes are as those of doves."

Trust a Catholic to quote the ultimate book in a moment like this.

"Behold, thou art fair, my beloved," she answered. "Also, our bed is green."

Daniel frowned at her with mock solemnity. "If I didn't know you were quoting, I'd suspect you of breaking the rule about jokes. This mattress is indeed disturbingly mildewed."

Now Alice was the one to laugh. Daniel bent to kiss it greedily into his own mouth. She could taste his desire and wanted to serve it—with all her heart, wanted to please him. So she reached down rather awkwardly to make his intimate acquaintance—

"*Alice,*" he growled, pressing his brow against hers. But it did not sound like an order for her to cease operations, so she continued. A few salient questions occurred to her, such as *Do you like it when I employ my thumb in this way?* but Daniel's breathing became so erratic, conversation would be impossible.

"Wait," he said finally, wincing as he struggled to control something within himself.

Alice moved her hand away. "Are you ready to be finished?" she asked cautiously, giving one thought to the unfinished schedule and one to the strained look on his face, and not knowing whether to be disappointed or apologetic.

He smiled at her then, that beautiful, melting smile which always made her want to sigh a little, hug him a little, marry him a little, and take him away to live in the peaceful countryside. "Most definitely not, which is why I need you to stop. Or else I will be finished far too soon." His smile faded slightly, and she recognized in him the same shyness she felt. "Are you saying you want to be finished?"

"No." She looked away. "If I asked for more, please, would you forgive me for referencing Dickens at such an inappropriate moment?"

Daniel laughed. "God, I love you."

Idiom! her brain declared at once. But her heart swelled with helpless wishing. She began trembling, frightened she might murder him in that moment out of sheer joy. He must have seen it—naked against her nakedness, he must have felt it—for he gathered her in his arms and held her close.

"Tighter," she growled, "in case I break free and strangle you."

He laughed softly into her hair. "I'm not scared of that."

"Then why are you restraining me?"

"I'm *hugging* you."

"But you've already done that."

"Alice, sweetheart, you deserve all the hugs I can give."

Sweetheart. Was that an idiom too? And was she a fool for glowing inside at the sound of it?

Daniel kissed her throat, her jaw, kissed words against her mouth. "You deserve to be cared for, Alice. You deserve everything."

He would not let her argue or explain the logical fallacies in his statement. And she would not let herself weep with desperate yearning for it to be true. Instead, they kissed, hard and deep, with a languid, heavy passion. And while he kept her occupied with that, Daniel quietly spread her legs, pushed up her knees, and advanced the schedule.

Pain shot through her. Alice closed her eyes, silently counting one cycle of breath and then another, willing her countenance to remain undisturbed. According to her scientific reading, women did not enjoy sexual intercourse, but if they waited patiently until the man was finished, they'd feel a sense of achievement that would be satisfying indeed. Alice rather doubted this, considering the discomfort she was in, but she was prepared to endure.

"Sorry," Daniel whispered, withdrawing.

She caught at him with something akin to panic. "Don't leave."

He smiled. "I'm not going to leave you, sweetheart." Shifting his angle, he moved closer, deeper, again. "I just don't want to hurt you."

"You can hurt me," she answered promptly. "I don't mind."

"I do." And shifting his angle again, slow, patient, he watched her face until its disguise faded and she was helpless to pretend. Her breath became an unmeasurable mess of gasping and broken sound. Then he moved more firmly. Things began to feel ~~nice delightful~~ *oh my good God she wanted to do this and nothing else for the rest of her life.*

"Alice?" he asked gently.

"Umhunmghm," she replied—which was about as effective a rebuttal to science as it was possible to get. She glanced at him, and their eyes accidentally met.

He stilled.

She stopped breathing altogether.

The whole universe tilted on its axis, pouring starlit silence into the small, shy distance between their eyes.

And when Alice exhaled again, it felt like her soul emerged with it to embrace Daniel, drawing him close for a kiss that was only soft, brief, yet somehow more profound than any they had shared before.

He smiled, making her shiver right through. "You know when you open a new book and realize it's going to be perfect?" he whispered.

"Yes," Alice said.

"That's how I feel when I look at you."

He gave her no chance to respond as he lifted himself to a steeper angle and, discarding rule after rule, made her climax even more emphatically than before.

"Oh, valiant dust!" she cried out, overmastered.

Daniel's movements grew almost desperate then. The bed shuddered and wailed. Alice lay rocking beneath him, feeling boneless, defenseless, peaceful at the eye of a storm. He lowered himself once more, fingers twining with her hair, mouth so near hers they breathed the shivering fragments of each other's breath. He said something she could not quite hear but it sounded a great deal like the inarticulate love and grief that lay at her own core.

"Daniel," she whispered.

He went suddenly taut, as if she'd stopped everything in him—as if speaking his name had broken a curse. Then he collapsed. For a sweaty, overwrought moment they clung to each other, still connected in deep and wishful ways, while the bed sagged as if it was equally exhausted. At last, Daniel rolled away.

Alice felt the sharp flash of the world against her body. Immediately, she moved to press herself against him again. He had one arm up, his hand clutching his damp hair, and he laid the other around her shoulders. She relaxed then, safe in his steadiness.

"Are you well?" she asked tentatively.

"Should I escape cardiac exhaustion in the next few minutes, I am well indeed," he said. "Are you?"

She wriggled up a little so she could kiss the inexplicable tears on his face. "I am. Yes, I am, now."

He smiled at her.

And the bed broke apart.

✤ 22 ✤

Alice's imagination was by habit ridiculously inactive; when the door was not open it didn't even try the window, but sat morose in the room until a need for lateral thinking let it out.

Daniel's imagination was a stone.

And yet, after dragging the bed's mattress safely to the floor, they managed between them to invent several creative variations upon the theme of lovemaking, thus occupying the long hours of the night. This was, as Alice pointed out, *professional behavior*, since sleeping must surely be ill-advised when the Wisteria Society might at any point re-engage the hunt. They needed something to keep them alert. As it transpired, they were rendered so alert, so many times, that when dawn arrived, it found them lying naked and stunned on the mattress, barely able to move.

"I must say," Alice mused as she watched the darkness fade to gold, "my neck doesn't hurt as much as I feared it would."

Daniel turned his head to look at her. His eyes, bright with new sunlight, unguarded by glass, held an expression she could not decipher, and yet it made her pulse flutter.

"You are . . ."

"Yes?" she asked. And when he didn't answer, his eyes darkening, she repeated it more warily. "Yes?"

"I feel I should apologize," he said.

"Oh?" Her pulse went from fluttering to threshing. Her heart shredded. But all she did was blink. "Do you have regrets about last night?"

"Yes."

"I see." Her brain marched in, swept up the remains of her heart, and shoved them into a trash can along with certain idioms.

"We ought not to have done what we did," Daniel said.

"Uh huh."

"I ought to have controlled myself until I had access to candles, soft blankets, or at the very least a clean bed, to give you the romantic experience you deserve." He smiled shyly. "I'm so ruinously in love with you, Alice."

Ta-dah!! Her heart burst from the trash can in a sparkling confetti shower of happiness.

"Oh," she said primly, even while her nerves donned red dresses and began to do a tap dance. "I understand," she added through the fizz of champagne being poured by her ego. Snatching a glass of it, her brain stood on a chair, pink feather boa about its neck and champagne raised for a sentimental toast she could not quite hear through the thumping of her heart. *Love!* it beat. *Love!*

"This is certainly an interesting development," she said. "As it happens, I am in love with you also."

She clenched everything inside herself nervously, but the world did not end. Academy staff did not come bursting through the window with birch switches at the ready to chastise her. Nor did Daniel assassinate her. In fact, he almost looked *soft*.

"That is welcome news," he said. "Most convenient."

He held out his hand, and Alice shook it. They gave each other a brisk nod.

"How are we going to inform Human Resources of this unforeseen consequence to the mission?" she asked.

His eyes went still. Her heart went still. For one silent moment, the truth lay between them.

There would be no informing Human Resources. Were their relationship to be discovered, they'd be separated—quite possibly from themselves, and certainly from each other. Years ago, Alice had befriended a stray cat outside the Academy dormitories. She still bore scars from when her tutors found out—one across the back of each thigh, and one through her brain, the ragged memory of what they did to the cat.

She smiled tightly at Daniel.

He gave her the exact smile in response. A barricade. If there were dead cats and desperate, hopeless dreams in his heart, she could not see them.

"We'll think of something," he lied.

She nodded. "It's fine, either way. After all, we have only known each other a week."

"Have we?" He moved suddenly, rising to straddle her hips, setting his hands on the mattress at either side of her head. "Alice Dearlove, you have dwelt in my heart since the moment I first saw you in Clacton-on-Sea, a year ago."

Alice gazed up at his mouth and the calm line of his cheekbone— for looking too long into his eyes overwhelmed her even more now than it had before. He thrilled every nerve in her. He engulfed every thought.

And yet he was so familiar, she could have sworn she'd seen him every day of her life.

"I loved you even back in the Academy, years before we met," she said, reaching up to trail fingers down his rose-and-thorn tattoo. "I was so alone as a child, so different from everyone except Student B, who had gone through ahead of me, and who had left a trail of psychological reports and broken brooms for me to follow. Each time I hid under the table because shooting practice or laundry class got too loud, the instructors reminded themselves of how they'd managed when B did that same thing. When I threw a knife into the chalkboard after Professor Hambly touched my arm without warning, it widened the crack B had made throwing a textbook—"

"Actually, a volume of Shakespeare's complete works," Daniel said. "I was reading *Coriolanus* when Professor Hambly walked behind me without warning. I'd just got to the line 'action is eloquence,' and it seemed instructive. Considering I only attacked the chalkboard, not the man, I still don't understand why they were so furious with me."

"Did they beat you?"

"No, they took me to the range and showed me how to get a better angle on—" He stopped, his expression tightening. "Did they beat you, Alice?"

"It does not matter," she said. Turning her head to the window, she squinted against the light, determined to see neither the mingled look of love and lethality in Daniel's eye nor the wan, sad ghost of a girl who had been caned repeatedly over the years until she learned to mask her oddness behind a thousand faces.

"It does matter," Daniel argued. "You matter."

But she knew that she did not. Not the woman she was deep within, nor the girl she had been. Neither did the love she shared with this beautiful, dangerous, gentle man matter. The mission might be finished, but A.U.N.T. owned her soul.

"Day is coming on," she said, her voice as faint as the misty autumnal horizon. "We must escape before the pirates wake and rem—"

Daniel caught her jaw tightly between his thumb and forefinger. Turning her face back to him, he bent and kissed her hard. She clutched at his hair, kissing him back harder, waging a desperate battle with his tongue. Passion lit a fire under emotion, and only when all that remained was smoke and coals did they pull away, breathing heavily, safe again from the dangers of feeling.

"I can't believe you're alive!" Veronica exclaimed for the third time as they stood in her tiny bedroom, faces pale with weariness in the morning shadows.

Daniel frowned. "We won't be alive for much longer if you don't keep your voice down. Now, listen, we are going to collect Snodgrass and depart at once. Your mission—"

"Whatever it is, I accept it!" Veronica said, bouncing excitedly on her heels.

Daniel's frown darkened. "I am not giving you a choice, V-2. There are two suitcases in our bedroom. Secure them, and ensure they are sent with all haste and security to A.U.N.T. headquarters. This is vital."

Veronica gasped. "Do they contain weapons?"

"In a manner of speaking."

"Guns? Knives? Explosive devices?"

"Books."

"Oh." The girl sagged a little. Then her eyes narrowed as she looked from Daniel to Alice and back again. "You seem different, somehow."

"What makes you say that?" Daniel asked stiffly. After all, Veronica was not long out of the Academy—how astute could her discernment really be?

"Agent A, your complexion is pinker than usual," the girl noted.

Alice shrugged. "It's a warm morning."

"Agent B, your cufflinks are crooked."

"Hm," Daniel replied irritably.

"And you're holding hands."

Realizing this was true, they immediately snatched their hands apart.

"We're staying in character," Daniel said. "Now, this conversation will end in thirty seconds. Do you know what you're doing, V-2?"

"Suitcases. Headquarters." Veronica saluted. "It's an honor to serve!"

"Yes." Daniel reached for the door handle.

"One day I hope to be as reputable an agent as yourselves!"

"Uh huh." He turned the handle.

"Really, I cannot believe I got to meet the greatest—"

"*Goodbye*, V-2." Opening the door, Daniel stepped aside to let Alice precede him, then closed it on the sound of Veronica's voice extolling their virtues. Glancing in each direction to ensure the corridor was unoccupied, he led Alice toward the back stairs.

"I'll collect Snodgrass. You prepare the cottage for takeoff."

"Shouldn't you do that instead?" Alice asked. "You know I'm not capable of the flight enchantment."

"No," Daniel said. He wanted her out of this building, away from the pirates. A night spent in her arms, discovering all that she was, had roused every protective instinct in him, and he was determined she not be caught by the Wisteria Society. Just thinking of the damage she would inflict upon them with her terrifying combat skills sent a chill up his spine.

Besides, the pirates would certainly demand a ransom for her from the Home Office, and that would raise awkward questions—i.e., *When you say you work for the government, which one exactly do you mean?* In that case, Daniel would probably be assigned to assassinate her, so as to protect the secret of A.U.N.T.'s downstairs existence. He was reluctant to do that, especially since he intended to find some way to spend the rest of his life with her.

"Pick us up some food for breakfast," Alice told him, entering the stairwell. "I'll see you in ten minutes."

"See you," Daniel answered, turning away.

Alas, if only he had read a penny-dreadful novel or two, he would have been alerted to danger by this casual farewell. But it was with an overly erudite innocence that he headed for Snodgrass's bedroom, not even glancing back.

Alice left the castle through a ground-floor window (a perfectly reasonable door stood unlocked nearby, but old habits are hard to break), and running across the frosty grass, she reached the A.U.N.T. cottage without being noticed. Upon arrival, however, she recollected Daniel had the key.

"Bother," she muttered, leaning wearily against the door.

It swung open with a creak.

Alice's instincts immediately leaped into action. Pressing her back against the wall beside the door, she listened carefully through the slight opening.

A muttering sounded from inside. Then something went *twang*, and the voice rose briefly with a curse. Alice nudged the door open wider and slipped through.

The hinges creaked, and a figure at the wheel turned with an alarmed cry. Alice did not pause to enter into conversation with them. Rolling head over heels to present a confusing target, she aimed for the sofa at the center of the room. Then crouching behind it, she reached to where an emergency gun was taped to its underside. As the weapon came free, tape still adhering to it, she shifted her stance and took aim over the sofa's arm at the intruder.

"Don't move! Put your hands up!"

"I say!" came the tremulous, high-pitched reply. "Which one?!"

Sighing, Alice pulled back the gun. "Dr. Snodgrass," she said with exasperation, rising to her feet. "What are you doing here?"

"I-I-I came to check on—on things," he explained, his marshy eyes widening as he watched her peel the tape from the gun's barrel. "What are you doing here?"

"The mission has been aborted," Alice informed him. The tape was now sticking to her fingers, and she shook her hand in an effort to dislodge it. "Agent B is searching the castle for you."

"Jolly good!" Snodgrass said—then, when Alice cast him a confused frown: "I mean awful! Terrible! You should return at once to let him know I'm here."

Alice smacked her hand against the sofa's arm, causing Snodgrass to jolt, but the piece of tape clung stubbornly to her fingers. Snodgrass murmured something beneath his breath. Glancing at him, Alice took in his blanched countenance and the fervent manner in which he clutched the wheel. She smiled reassuringly, which only made him grow more pale.

"Do not worry, Doctor," she said. "No doubt Agent B will realize you are missing and should arrive here any moment."

Snodgrass's high-pitched laugh in response jangled her nerves, which had been coiling themselves tight again after Daniel had so assiduously loosened them. Alice ignored them, for she had far more important matters to contend with than her dislike of the scientist. With an irritable sigh, she tossed the gun onto the sofa cushion and applied herself fully to getting the dratted tape off her fingers.

Suddenly Snodgrass lurched forward, taking Alice so much by surprise she could only stare at him, wondering if he was experiencing some kind of seizure. Seconds later, she understood her peril, but by then it was too late: Snodgrass had snatched the gun from the sofa and was aiming it at her.

"Don't move, what! And—and—put your hands up!"

Alice gave him a long, cool look. He shook the gun, and slowly she obeyed. Her nerves advanced from jangled to outright jittering, for although she'd managed to remove the tape, her fingers were now sticky, and with Snodgrass holding her at gunpoint she could not immediately wash her hands.

Unmoving, barely blinking, she calculated the distance between herself and the kitchen bench with its kettle of water, including the necessary steps—two to the left, seven forward, one leap, a hard step (horizontal) against Snodgrass's solar plexus, a karate chop to his throat rendering him unconscious, then several more steps to locate a razor so as to shave off his abominable mustache—before arriving at the kettle.

"Don't try it," Snodgrass warned with unexpected perspicacity. "I will shoot you. I will."

"You won't," Alice scoffed.

He pulled the trigger.

Horsehair and fabric exploded as the bullet slammed into the sofa. Alice noticed a flash before her eyes—not her life, but sparks produced by a coiled spring within the sofa cushion. She raised one disapproving eyebrow at Snodgrass, who appeared far more startled than her by what he'd just done.

"Deliberately damaging A.U.N.T. property is cause for a fine, perhaps even suspension," she told him.

He laughed rather hysterically. "I shall soon destroy more than a sofa, Miss Dearlove! Before I am through with my plans, the name Cornelius Snodgrass will become synonymous with Terror (and Quality Devices for the Discerning Villain)! What!"

"What?" Alice asked.

He opened his mouth, then closed it again, clearly blindsided by the question. Then a renewed fervor arose in him. "If I cannot inspire love, I will cause fear!"

"That's monstrous," Alice responded coolly. "And also unethical. If you quote Mary Shelley, you ought to provide an attribution."

His expression swayed wildly as he tried to process this advice. Alice took the opportunity to re-examine the various clues he had presented over the past week, from his determination to prove himself authorized for the mission to his trying to shoot her just now. "The trap Jane set in the library," she said, amazed she hadn't realized earlier. "It was your work. The ribbon in the library ceiling was written over with the incantation, wasn't it?"

Snodgrass nodded with such excitement, his mustache struggled to keep up. "And the tie around Wordsworth's bust. Er, that is, the neck of his bust. It was a brilliantly devised deadfall trap."

"Except it failed."

"Only because you interfered! I tried for days to assassinate you, but you kept—"

"Wait. Miss Darlington said the pirates hadn't tried to kill us. I assumed she was lying. But you were responsible for the washroom door explosion after all."

He jutted out his chin. "It was an excellent piece of magical engineering. Just a little more sensitive to vibrations than I anticipated."

"So a case of premature explosion? Interesting."

Snodgrass flushed and shook the gun at her, but Alice was too involved in her deductions to even notice. "You crushed the cake—no doubt testing your plan. And I see now you have a scab on your hand from where you must have cut yourself with the cake knife. And you were the one who shot at Agent B with a crossbow, weren't you?"

"And I put the snake in your bed!" Snodgrass burst out, as if he could not help himself.

Alice frowned. "What snake?"

"I have all along been a force to be reckoned with, Agent A! You should have feared me! Fear me now!"

"There was a snake?"

Snodgrass made a strangled cry and shook the gun yet again. Alice tried not to roll her eyes at these overwrought dramatics. Her mind was humming with a low, aggravating white noise that she supposed meant an encroaching headache. The stickiness on her fingers would incite her to murder if she could not wash it off soon. And she really wanted some breakfast.

"Look," she said briskly. "Why don't we discuss this over a cup of tea? I'm sure Mrs. Kew will release you from your A.U.N.T. contract so you can pursue a career change to Nefarious Criminal. I'd be happy to write you a reference. I can certainly vouch for your expertise in aggravating people."

"It's too late for that!" Snodgrass shouted. "If only you and the other A.U.N.T. agents had taken me seriously, I'd not have been *forced* to the recourse of maniacal vengeance! I won't turn back now. Triumph shall be mine! *Aereo!*"

Abruptly the house lurched up from the ground, rocking perilously as it ascended without control. As Alice gripped the sofa for support, she realized her mental hum had in fact been magic loitering in the air, waiting for Snodgrass to finish speaking the flight incantation.

"What are you doing, Doctor?" she demanded as the house groaned and rattled around them.

"Flying back to London!" he said. "The Mayor's Parade is today! The streets will be filled with city officials and hundreds of innocent bystanders! Ha ha!!"

Alice paused, but he did not continue. Finally, she prompted him: "And?"

He frowned. "And what?"

"And what is your plan? Really, Doctor, if you want to be a professional villain, you need to fully reveal your plan."

"I say!" He rubbed his mustache gleefully, then pointed across the room. "That crate is an atrocity!"

"It certainly is," Alice said, eyeing the crate set before the sofa in lieu of a table, its wooden sides gritty and stained.

"I mean, *literally*, Miss Dearlove! Inside is a special device incantated to detonate upon contact with the ground!"

"Huh," Alice said. She thought back to her first day in the cottage, opening the crate and seeing what she had supposed to be a fire extinguisher. She'd fiddled with one of its switches and, at the resulting internal clatter, had assumed it broken.

"Well, I do concede that is fiendish indeed," she said.

"Yes! Jolly fiendish! And it was under A.U.N.T.'s noses for weeks, in my lab. No one appreciated my genius enough to suspect me."

"But Jane said there was no weapon."

"None that *she* knew about," Snodgrass scoffed. "It's true that, when she approached me with her nefarious commission, I was inspired to create The Big Banger™. But, I say, why would I waste it on merely assassinating one person? Jane Fairweather's silly little plot gave me practice with villainy, but ultimately I have bigger fish to fry!"

Alice frowned in confusion. "You want to take up cooking?"

"What? No! I'm going to drop my bomb on the Mayor's Parade,

killing *hundreds*. Then no one will ignore me! I shall be instantly inducted into the Hall of Infamy! What!"

Alice shrugged with professional nonchalance. "I will stop you."

"I'm afraid I can't take that chance." He yanked the black tie from around his neck and dropped it to the ground. *"Descendeo rapido!"*

Alice had just enough time to think fiddlest—

And the ceiling fell on her.

⚛ 23 ⚛

If Daniel had a flower for every time he thought of Alice as he searched Starkthorn Castle for Dr Snodgrass, he would not have been able to walk at all, due to being completely overladen with roses. He did not consider it in such terms, of course; rather, he calculated his thought-to-step ratio as being so high it overwhelmed decent mathematics.

He could not regret making love to her last night. To have had just that small part of her—that physical pleasure, between one mission and the next—even knowing he could never have the whole. To have told her a mere whisper of the truth about how he felt for her. These had seemed like impossibilities even a day ago. Like a dream, a year ago. And now they would live forever in his heart, behind barricades, barbed wire, machine guns, where not even A.U.N.T. could get at them. Strictly speaking, he should not have done any of it. But he found he could not disapprove of himself.

That was all he found, however. Ten minutes' effort did not uncover Dr. Snodgrass (although he did come across the Earl of Sandwich, trussed up in the laundry room, impatiently awaiting a ransom). Frustrated, bemused, and hearing the pirates begin to arise, cries of *tally hoooo!* resounding through the castle, he decided to join Alice in the cottage to discuss their next move.

So focused was he on seeing her again, touching her hand, inhaling the serene freshness of her scent, watching the slow, lush sweep of her eyelashes as she—

"Hello there," said a cheerful male voice.

Daniel reacted instinctively, as a consequence of which he discovered, when next he blinked, that he was pushing a man against the frame of Starkthorn Castle's open front door, one knee shoved into the fellow's back while a carotid restraint around his neck wordlessly promised unconsciousness or death at any moment Daniel wished to advance it.

"Nice reflexes," the man remarked, and Daniel realized he'd just attacked Ned Lightbourne. He would have apologized and stepped back at once, but a gun barrel pressing against his spine recommended against this.

"Good morning, Bixby," Cecilia Bassingthwaite said behind him. Her tone was cool, pleasant, but the metal of her gun was also cool, significantly less pleasant, and Daniel knew she'd shoot under the least provocation. "If you would like to die some other day than this one, I suggest you release my husband."

Daniel removed his arms from around Ned's throat and held them up in surrender. "I do beg your pardon," he said. "I wasn't looking where I was going."

The gun was lifted away, and Ned turned with a smile. "Don't worry, old chap. Who amongst us hasn't almost murdered an acquaintance while lost in thought?"

Cecilia shrugged her mouth in agreement while she holstered the gun. From inside the cloth sling draped over her shoulder, baby Evangeline gave Daniel a drippy grin as she chewed on a small wooden sword.

"Will you join us for breakfast?" Ned asked, brushing back his hair with the kind of nonchalance that suggests one more wrong move and Daniel would never move again. "I'd love to hear all the gossip, such as why you no longer work for Alex, why you are wearing a piratic earring, and why you appear to be some kind of government spy infiltrating the society of my friends and family."

The charming smile gleamed, and Daniel warned himself to be very careful indeed. He was reluctant to die just as he'd secured Alice Dearlove's affections.

"Breakfast sounds good," he said. "However, I must rendezvous with Miss Dearlove in our—"

He turned to point, and his arm froze halfway through the gesture.

"—cottage," he finished blankly as said domicile jerked and shuddered away from the ground.

"Oh dear," Cecilia murmured. "It seems Miss Dearlove is departing without you."

"She would never do that."

"Loves you too much?" Ned said.

"It would break Regulation 11," Daniel answered. "There must be trouble."

He was about to begin a futile ground pursuit when suddenly Ned caught his arm, twisted it up around his back, and set a dagger to his throat.

"Sorry," the pirate said with a blithe lack of sincerity. "No offense. I just need you to listen to what I have to say, and I suspect this is the only way you'll do that without trying to kill me again."

Daniel considered protesting but had to admit it was true. Even now, watching the cottage lurch higher, a homicidal terror seared through his nerves. Alice moving through the skies haunted him, phantom-wise. One stiff breeze and that building was going to fall apart. And if he lost Alice, *he* would fall apart.

"You can't catch her by running," Ned said, his tone so aggravatingly calm it was just as well he had Daniel restrained. "We'll take you in our house."

Daniel's pulse bashed hard against the dagger blade. "You'd do that?"

Cecilia smiled at him. "Just imagine what Charlotte would say if we failed to help you."

All three of them shuddered.

"But we must hurry," Cecilia continued, "before the other guests see us."

Ned released Daniel and they set off at a run across the grass to where the rose-swathed brick cottage known as Puck House awaited, smoke drifting from its chimney. Evangeline chortled piratically with every step, and Cecilia told her, "We're going on a lovely escapade, yes that's right, coochy—uh, I mean *tally ho!* It's going to be such fun!"

Daniel frowned. Watching the A.U.N.T. cottage swoop and jolt on an ungainly course eastward did not feel like fun to him. It felt like the Great Library of Alexandria was aflame in his stomach.

The red front door of Puck House opened before they reached it, and a young woman dressed in black, with dark ringlets tumbling from her mobcap, saluted jauntily.

"I didn't expect you back so soon," she said as they rushed into the small, warmly lit entrance chamber. "Please excuse the mess of ecto-plasm and pitiful moaning. I'm still in the middle of exorcising today's ghosts."

"It's fine, Pleasance dear," Cecilia answered, even as Ned closed the door behind them and began dashing in and out of rooms, shutting windows. "Would you please take Evangeline for a little while? We are just going to help Mr. Bixby here with a spot of hot pursuit."

"Of course, miss," Pleasance said, reaching for the baby. "Shall I bring a tea tray up to the cockpit?"

"That would be excellent. Come with me, Mr. Bixby."

She began speaking the flight incantation as she led the way up a series of carpeted stairs. Books were stacked at the side of each tread, and on shelves in the landing above, and lining the walls of a bedroom Daniel glimpsed as they took a short corridor to a staircase rising into the cockpit: a cozy attic furnished with plump sofas, cushions, and baskets of toys. Lush golden lamplight illuminated an array of bucolic artwork; furniture polish scented the air. The large oak wheel overlooked a gable window, and next to it stood a child's high chair with a play set of sextant, telescope, and lockpick cluttering the tray.

Having spent years in the shambles of Alex O'Riley's battlehouse—and then months in the pristine environment it had become after Charlotte moved in, bringing with her a squad of cleaners and decorators—Daniel felt strangely wobbly at the experience of this homey battlehouse with all its books and family comforts. So wobbly, indeed, that he actually used a word like *wobbly* to describe his feeling.

Cecilia strode to the wheel, still incanting. As she set her hands upon it, the house glided up with an ease that spoke of her skill. "Pardon me, but are you certain Miss Dearlove did not just leave?" she asked as she held the cottage to a smooth, rapid incline. "After all, no pirate would have stolen your house. We might shoot it down, but it would go against our code of ethics to *steal* it."

"I know that," he assured her. "But I also know Miss Dearlove would not depart without me. For one thing, she cannot manage the flight incantation. I suspect we've been double-crossed, perhaps by someone with a grudge . . ." He paused as his thoughts began lining up

neatly toward a conclusion . . . "Someone with a ladder, who knows
how to use the incantation to make a ceiling collapse, and who happens
to have disappeared. *Snodgrass.*"

"Well, have no fear, Mr. Bixby. We shall catch them."

"Hm." Gazing out the flight window, he was forced to squint
against a painfully bright glare of sunlight. "I do not see the house."

"It has disappeared beyond those hills," Cecilia said. She smiled at
him, but Daniel did not smile back. He had served this woman dinner
in Alex and Charlotte's house, watched her rock her baby to sleep with
a pirate lullaby (*"Mama's going to steal you a diamond ring . . ."*), and
listened to her chat with Charlotte for hours about shoes and swords.
But in this moment all he could think was that even the most dreadful
Wisteria Society member feared Cecilia Bassingthwaite for what she
might be capable of doing, due to her grim heritage.

It eased his mind somewhat.

"Trust me," she said. "The world is not large enough for them to
hide from me."

Once Puck House cleared those same hills, however, the A.U.N.T.
cottage was nowhere to be seen.

"Hm," said Cecilia with mild surprise.

"Hm," said Daniel in a considerably dark tone. He crossed his arms
tightly, as if doing so would prevent his heart from beating right out of
his chest.

"Could they have landed?" Ned suggested. He had brought up the
tea tray and, having just served Cecilia a cup of tea, was now pouring
whiskey into another for Daniel. He moved with such languid calm,
Daniel wanted to bash the tray over his head. The gurgling of the
whiskey as it poured from bottle into cup sounded like quicksand
sucking time into its airless depths, and Daniel had to force a four-
count breath upon himself just so he knew he wasn't suffocating.

"They might have gone to ground," he agreed. "But if we circle to search, and they have in fact flown ahead, we'll never catch up." He heard a tapping noise and looked around in aggravation for what was causing it—only to realize his own foot was responsible, knocking fretfully against the floor. He gave it such an intense scowl, it went still.

"Why would this Snodgrass kidnap Miss Dearlove?" Cecilia asked. "Has he lost his heart to her?"

"Not yet," Daniel muttered, and sent a memo to himself: *Obtain a spoon for the extraction of Snodgrass's cardiac organ.* Then a memory rose: Mrs. Kew handing Alice and him their fake wedding rings and intoning, "What the mission requirements have joined together, let no one put asunder . . . but if they do, these rings will reunite you. Snodgrass designed them specially."

Yanking the band from his finger, he peered at the words inscribed on its interior. *"Coniungo cum socium meo,"* he read aloud.

Immediately the ring began to tug against the prevailing gravity.

"'I connect with my partner,'" Ned translated. "What a charming inscription for a wedding ring."

"Actually, it's a tracking device," Daniel told him. His hand followed the magic, and he smiled grimly. "Starboard, if you please, Miss Bassingthwaite. One hundred and twenty degrees from the front door."

Murmuring Latin, Cecilia turned the wheel as directed. The house veered, tilting against the flow of the wind, and increased its speed even more.

Tap-tap-tap. Daniel forced his foot into stillness once more and almost sighed, thinking of Alice's beautiful, restless fingers. Emotions were pitching wildly through him, sharp as knives and equally dangerous. Thoughts began stuffing gunpowder into every instinct they could get hold of.

"Have a drink," Ned urged, holding forth a cup. Daniel glared at him, and Ned immediately stepped back. "Then again, alcohol might not be wise at the moment. Cecilia, darling, if I should be killed by Mr. Bixby's look, I give you permission to remarry."

Cecilia huffed a derisive laugh.

"One hundred and thirty degrees," Daniel snapped.

Puck House slipped into the new course. So competent was Cecilia's piloting, and so well articulated the stabilization phrase of the incantation, that it almost seemed as if they sat on the ground, despite that ground blurring past, far below. Although Daniel rationally knew they were moving at speed, he wanted to pick up the house and throw it at the horizon. But all he could do was stare out the window, foot tapping again with an unfamiliar sense of helplessness, fingers gripping the wedding ring as tightly as fear gripped his heart.

Snodgrass had better enjoy his flight, because when Daniel caught up with him he was going to take the villain apart, piece by piece—by spoon or by hand, or perhaps by a damn incantated toothbrush—then transport him to a hospital like an ethical man should do, ensuring that quality medical care put him back together—just so he could take him apart all over again.

Alice opened her eyes slowly, afraid of what she might see. So much sensation throbbed inside her, it felt as if she made at least seven respectable persons. Every limb and bone ached, and every thought shouted at every other thought in such a clamor, she wished someone would take off her head. But checking herself with bleary-eyed trepidation, she saw just (1) woman seated on the floor with her (2) legs stretched before her and (3) hairy caterpillars grinning at her in the most hideous way.

She blinked wildly, and as her vision came into focus, she realized what she'd seen was Dr. Snodgrass's mustache stirring as he grimaced with the effort of tying a final knot in the ropes that bound her to the cottage's steering wheel.

"I say, you're awake!" he exclaimed, sitting back on his haunches. His hair was in disarray, his eyes bright with what Alice suspected to be LSD (Lunatic Scientist Disorder). "How remarkable," he said, "considering my ingenious device sent the ceiling falling to pieces on top of you!"

Alice peered achingly beyond him to where a narrow length of timber leaned against the dust-covered sofa. "That is only one plank, Doctor. And I do believe it's just plywood. Yet again you have failed."

Snodgrass's face flushed scarlet. "I have not failed, what! You're the one tied up! And when this cottage crashes in London with you inside it—I having first made my exit using my emergency escape hat the bomb will detonate upon impact with the ground. *Boom!* Then who will be the failure?! Go ahead and scream with despair while you still can, before I gag you! Ha ha!"

"May I point out one small flaw in your plan, Doctor?" Alice asked calmly.

"Flaw?! There is no flaw!" His eyes narrowed. "What flaw?"

"The fact that I am not tied up."

He had only the briefest moment to frown in confusion before she extracted herself from the inadequately knotted rope. With two quick, efficient strikes against his neck and jaw, she rendered him neatly unconscious. He toppled back with a thump, his mustache reverberating.

Shucking off the rope, Alice got to her feet. "I'd utter a pithy witticism," she said, "but I have a city to save." (Besides, she could not think of one.) Brushing ceiling dust from her shoulders and skirt, she turned to evaluate the situation.

"Bother."

It took only one glance to ascertain that matters were dire indeed. Dust and cobwebs had fallen everywhere. The sofa was ruined. Coils of rope, gunpowder packets, and other accoutrements of maniacal vengeance lay scattered about the floor. Worse, the tea supplies had tumbled from their bench during the cottage's unstable takeoff. It was going to take hours to get the place tidy again.

Not to mention that her fingers *burned* with stickiness from the lingering tape residue.

Oh yes, there was also the fact of a whopping great bomb in the middle of the room.

"Someone was overcompensating, I think," Alice muttered, casting a grim look at Snodgrass's sprawled figure before turning to consider the view from the flight window.

Farmland stretched beneath her, dotted with houses. The horizon offered nothing more than a luminous haze—but Alice knew London lay beyond, and she frowned.

There existed now no danger to the city's population. She would ultimately do whatever necessary to save civilian lives, even if that meant crashing the cottage into an empty field. But she was reluctant to die just as she'd secured Daniel Bixby's affections.

At the thought, her wedding ring seemed to tighten around her finger. She adjusted it abstractedly. Where was he? Did he fear her kidnapped? Or was he even now sending a telegram to A.U.N.T. headquarters, reporting her as delinquent?

No. She shook her head in denial of that possibility. She knew that he'd know she'd never leave him, and also knew he'd know that she knew it. (She paused, checked back through that sentence, then nodded to herself in agreement.) Daniel would absolutely come for her!

After all, Regulation 23 required it of him.

However, there was no time to wait for rescue. Rolling up the sleeves of her bodice, she marched across to the wooden crate and tried pushing it toward the front door.

She met with immediate success!

But only if her goal had been to strain several muscles in her back, get a splinter in one finger, and not move the crate even half an inch.

"Confound it," she muttered. Then taking a determined breath, she applied her posterior to the edge, set her legs at an angle, and pushed with greater force.

This time she got further!

Insofar as she strained all the muscles in her legs as well as her back.

Opening the crate's lid, she scowled down at the bomb. She saw clearly now what she'd not noticed before: incantation phrases scratched into the metal casing. She smelled the dynamite. Peering closer, she even read *The Big Banger*™ along its length. Several buttons, switches, and red and black wires offered false hope—for she understood the explosive was bound in the magic of the incantation, and no amount of button pressing or wire cutting would disarm it.

She turned back to the scientist, resolved to rouse him and make whatever threats necessary for him to reveal the defusing process. Her view of him, however, was blocked by his fist propelling toward her at speed.

Even as Alice's brain strove to process what it was seeing, her body reacted. She ducked, and as Snodgrass punched the empty air, she slipped around behind and shoved him hard. He tipped forward into the open crate, and Alice slammed the lid on his back.

"What!" he screamed.

Alice lifted the lid once more, intending to heave the man's entire body in with his bomb, but he took her by surprise, kicking at her legs. As she stumbled, he hauled himself up and came at her, fingers hooked like claws, face contorted with rage. He began attacking her in such an undisciplined manner, Alice could not respond sensibly. They wrestled across the room. Alice twisted his arm, Snodgrass ripped her bodice, Alice punched him in the midriff, Snodgrass shouted an old Latin word.

The cottage door flung open in response. Cold wind screamed into the room, snatching at Alice's hair, chilling her blood. The building rocked wildly as its stability magic was overcome. Snodgrass's emergency parachute hat tumbled out. Snodgrass himself, bug-eyed, cackling with what must surely now be described as professional lunacy, shoved Alice in the same direction.

Glancing over her shoulder, she saw a vast, bright emptiness, and realized she had only moments left to live. A "privacy of glorious light" would soon be hers. The irony of her brain quoting Wordsworth at this juncture invigorated her. Bending at the waist, she shoved her shoulders against Snodgrass's torso and rose with as much force as she could summon. The scientist flipped over her head and—uttering a high, squealing cry of *I say!*—fell right out the door. Alice slammed it shut behind him.

And tossing back her hair, she said pithily, "It seems your fancy has taken flight, Doctor."

The cottage shuddered as if in laughter at her excellent wit. Alice felt rather smug for a moment. Then she recollected she was still in mortal peril, and ran to the wheel. It spun back and forth in magical defiance of gravity, and Alice grabbed the spokes, dragging it with teeth-clenching effort back to a centered course. But the wood trembled in her grip, and she knew she would not be able to hold it for long. The magic was too awry, the threads of stabilization loosened by wind. She tried desperately to recall the incantation, but all she could think was *willows whiten*, in a habit of self-defense that would kill her if she did not break it in the next few minutes.

Then a shadow filled the flight window. Looking up, Alice stared uncomprehending as Dr. Snodgrass came into view, grinning at her like a madman.

ONE SMALL STEP—SKY HIGH—DANIEL LOSES CONTROL—
CHARMS AND FOREARMS—THE SUFFERING OF WOMEN—
ALICE COMMITS A HEINOUS CRIME—
OUR HEROES ARE THREATENED WITH TORTURE

There was something at work in Alice's soul that she did not understand, but she suspected pretty strongly was horror. At the sight of Snodgrass's grinning face, she lost all grip on rationale, since what else could be happening but that his dreadful ghost had arisen to seek vengeance against her?

The only flaw in this conclusion was that Snodgrass was not rising but descending—and, as Alice stared, he continued to do so, slowly but surely, until she realized he was clinging to a rope net. And this net originated from the window of a brick cottage that was gradually filling her view through the window, replacing the sight of Snodgrass. She glimpsed Cecilia Bassingthwaite through a gable window and blinked dazedly as the pirate woman nodded a greeting to her, before the cottage lowered further—

And then her soul sighed. *This* feeling now, she understood.

Daniel stood on the roof of Puck House, one shoulder leaning against its chimney, ankles crossed, hands in his trouser pockets as he looked calmly across at her.

"Fiddlesticks," Alice whispered with love.

Daniel waited until Alice had opened the flight window, then he smiled. "Sorry I'm late."

Alice gave him a pale, sober look. "Did you remember the bread and milk?"

"No. I can go back for them—?"

"That's fine," she said. "I should probably save the world before having breakfast. Snodgrass left a bomb here, inside the crate. It's set to detonate as soon as the cottage touches down. I plan to fly south and ditch the building in the sea. I'm ready to dutifully sacrifice my life for the sake of England's safety, and ask only for a small mention in the next intra-agency gazette as my reward."

"Hm," Daniel said. "Or—just brainstorming, you understand— you could jump over here and we'll shoot the building down into an empty field."

Alice shook her head. "What if some girl is lying unseen in the long grass, thinking of her wedding day and wishing it was going to be with the butcher's son rather than the wealthy but heartless viscount?"

Daniel stared at her. "What?"

"What?" she echoed defensively.

He gave it up. "Very well. Instead of crashing the house, I'll come over and dismantle the bomb. If I fail to do so, we'll revert to Plan A, and just hope gentlewomen in Hampshire are still a-bed."

She considered this for a moment, then shrugged her mouth and nodded.

"Good." He smiled at her, warming himself with the feeling of love in it. "Say '*circumroto sinistram*.'"

"Circumroto sinistram," she echoed.

The cottage spun port-wise in response to the line of incantation, groaning with the effort and shedding a few roof tiles. As the door aligned with Daniel's view, Alice opened it. With her disheveled hair and red petticoat, she seemed almost piratic.

"That Latin gave me a headache," she complained.

"I'm sorry. Come over here and I'll make it better."

She disappeared inside the cottage, and a few seconds later re-emerged, running across its threshold. She seemed to soar between the buildings, her petticoat billowing, her face serene. Landing midway up the roof of Puck House, she climbed easily to the ridgepole.

"Nicely done," Daniel said as she arrived beside him. She shrugged mildly, and in response he pushed her back against the chimney, grabbed her face, and kissed her.

Puck House jolted like a horrified chaperone, but Daniel barely noticed. Alice clutched his shoulders, trying to pull him even closer. Her petticoat swirled around them in the cool, gold-lit wind, and Daniel felt his heart's blood swirl too. He could not restrain his anger that she'd been in danger, and his relief that she was safe now, and his vast, bright love; he almost thought he might step off the roof with her and the force of the emotions would hold them up, defying gravity. Every nerve and muscle in his body began to prickle. It was what he'd always feared, this loss of emotional control.

Damn. If only he'd known how glorious it would feel, he'd not have wasted so many years being frightened.

Breaking the kiss at last, he gave Alice a fierce look. She gave him one right back. Her skin was flushed, her eyes vivid, and if she had said *Kill the world*, he would have done it for her in that moment, he would have done anything; she had become his new and forever obsession.

"Headache gone?" he asked.

"I have a head?" she said dazedly in response.

He laughed. "Go downstairs and let them know our plan. But be warned, they're friendly pirates, which is a great deal worse than fiery ones. I'm afraid nothing is going to stop Ned Lightbourne from giving you a warm welcome."

She frowned. Daniel wanted to kiss her again, to taste that wonderfully prim disapprobation and take it with him across the sky, but the A.U.N.T. cottage rocked and groaned in a manner that suggested it was going to fall at any minute.

"Right," he said. "See you soon."

Running down the roof of Puck House, he flung himself without hesitation into empty air. The A.U.N.T. cottage lurched away from him, and only by extending his arm to the maximum degree was he able to catch hold of the doorstep. He hung painfully in a one-handed grip as his body re-established an internal balance. Pain ripped through his body. Gravity tried to introduce him to its friend, the solid ground several hundred feet below.

Swinging wildly, he pushed a finger against the bridge of his spectacles to straighten them. Then he hauled himself up over the doorstep, into the cottage. Glancing over his shoulder, he saw Alice's unimpressed face and discovered in himself a depth of impatience he'd never experienced before. Even five minutes was going to be too long away from this woman.

The cottage shuddered, reminding him that it would be an eternity if he did not dismantle the bomb and get the building landed safely.

"*Stabilis sicut vadit,*" he chanted as he shut the door and strode over to the crate. The cottage immediately began to settle. Incantating a holding pattern, he lifted the crate's lid and stood quietly with his arms crossed, contemplating the device therein.

The triggering incantation seemed straightforward enough, but this being a Snodgrass creation, Daniel knew he needed to be even more cautious than usual. One touch in the wrong place—or perhaps even in the right place—and he'd go up in flames faster than an erotic novel in a Puritan community.

"Hm," he said eventually. Unbuttoning his cuffs and folding up his sleeves, he obtained a paring knife from the kitchen supplies and, leaning one hand on the edge of the crate (which had an interesting effect on the muscles of his naked forearm, not that he was aware of this), he used the knife's pointed tip to alter the engraved incantation. He changed an *i* to a *t*, an *n* to an *m*, then paused, trying to recollect Latin declensions. A ticking began inside the device, which was both alarming and helpful—for it suggested he'd tripped a timer, but also sounded so much like Professor Michaels tapping a fingernail against a chalkboard that anxiety instantly tossed up the word he needed. He returned to etching—

Suddenly, the cottage rattled, sending a shower of dust down over him. Daniel caught his breath, not wanting to accidentally turn the *i* into a *j* and blow the whole place up. After a moment, it calmed, and he was able to etch one final serif. Rapping a knuckle against the metal cylinder, he heard only silence within. Satisfied, he closed the crate lid.

And the cottage plunged.

Thrown off-balance, Daniel staggered against the crate. *"Subsisto!"* he shouted over the thundering of his pulse.

The cottage jolted to an uncertain halt. Splashing sounded in the water closet; noxious soot billowed from the fireplace. Daniel sighed at the thought of all the cleaning that would be necessary for the place to be habitable again.

But this was no time for indulging in fun. *"Descendeo lente,"* he commanded with the authority invested in him by several pages of insurance contracts. To his relief, the cottage began a more gentle descent. It landed near Puck House in a field of grass, and Daniel began incantating the anchor phrase.

He managed two syllables before the entire building fell apart.

For a moment it felt as if the world had become a ball of thunder. Walls toppled; the roof clattered down; the wheel broke free from its stand and rolled out of the wreckage. At last, quiet settled, and Daniel rose from where he had crouched beside the crate, pushing aside fallen roof beams and what appeared to be an ossified opossum. He brushed dust from his hair and shoulders. Bringing forth a handkerchief from a trouser pocket, he employed it to clean his spectacles. His shoes needed an urgent polish and he'd murder someone for a jacket, but there was nothing to be done about it at this moment. Stepping over shattered bricks and plaster, he departed what was now only nominally the cottage, and went in search of Alice.

"I really must go in search of Mr. Bixby," Alice said, frowning at her reflection in Cecilia's looking glass. Dressed in yellow frills and blue lace, she wouldn't have recognized herself were it not for her fingers tapping with a desire to assassinate the pirate's housemaid.

She'd barely arrived inside Puck House when Pleasance had taken one shocked glance at her stained petticoat and torn bodice and declared a makeover necessary. Cecilia happily offered her wardrobe. Pleasance impressed as an insightful woman. And so Alice agreed, for she seemed to be in sensible hands.

Ten minutes later, she was prepared to surrender her Expert Intelligence Officer card in disgrace.

"All done!" Pleasance said cheerfully—then held yet another dress against Alice's body and contemplated its effect. This was the seventh, or possibly the seventieth. Its combination of green and pink made

Alice's brain ache. Its high collar was an itch waiting to happen, its waist sash derided any foolish notion of breathing, and its floral print just begged to be obsessively examined for any tiny flaw. This was, in short, not so much a dress as a torture device.

"Beautiful!" Pleasance declared. "You could be proud to wear this in your coffin! And with a few ribbons in your hair, and face powder, and perhaps we could pluck your eyebrows just the slightest bit, your husband will be *all adoration!*"

"You are too kind," Alice said in a tone that suggested a whole lot less kindness would be appreciated. These people were so friendly, and so concerned with her happiness, she wondered if she'd entered an upside down world. Her heart kept growing and shrinking, and altogether she felt not quite herself. "However, duty calls. I am sure Mr. Bixby will not care what I'm wearing."

"Oh, he'll just *love* to see you in a pretty dress," Pleasance enthused. "Take it from me and the Blood Countess."

"The who?" Alice asked, perplexed.

Cecilia, sitting nearby, touched her temple discreetly. Pleasance, however, would not have recognized discretion even had someone pointed to it in a dictionary.

"A ghost what possesses me," she explained. "She says the flowers go perfectly with your eyes."

Alice looked at the sprigs of pink and wondered if she should feel offended.

"To be fair," Cecilia said, "Miss Dearlove should dress for herself, not for her husband."

"Precisely!" Pleasance agreed. "It *will be* for herself when he kisses her because the dress is so pretty."

"Kisses me," Alice scoffed, pretending to inspect a satin bow so as to hide her blush.

"I should hope Miss Dearlove's husband wants to kiss her no matter what she is wearing," Cecilia argued. "It is her soul that matters, not her attire."

"Don't mind the mistress," Pleasance whispered loudly to Alice. "She's one of them feminininists. While I agree that women suffer and we *should* rage about it—"

"Suffrage," Cecilia corrected her gently.

Pleasance shrugged with all the carelessness of a woman who has to tidy away her employer's voting rights pamphlets at the end of the day. "—that's all the more reason we should have fun looking pretty. And I declare, if Mr. Bixby does not miss a step upon first seeing you in this dress, I will eat my hat."

"Good heavens!" Alice exclaimed, staring at the woman. "Don't do that, it would be dreadful for your digestive system! The straw—let alone the ribbons—!"

Pleasance blinked. "Er . . ."

Sighing, Alice considered the dress. Hideous thing, absolutely hideous.

"Miss a step, you say?" she murmured, stroking a swathe of lace across the bodice. Its texture was much like Daniel's unshaven jaw had felt that morning against her cheek . . .

"Absolutely," Pleasance said, sensing weakness. "He might even stumble. In fact, it ain't impossible he could outright *trip*, and end on his knees before you."

Three minutes later, Alice was encased in itchy, cumbersome layers of taffeta, with her waist cinched as tight as an antiquarian's grip on Shakespeare's First Folio, and with no possibility of undressing unless someone else released the dozen buttons down her back. Never in all her years of undercover work had she looked so . . . so . . .

Ridiculous, she thought.

"Adorable," Pleasance said with a happy sigh.

"Hm," Cecilia added, frowning. "Tell me, Miss Dearlove, why Mr. Bixby married you."

Alice stared at her blankly. *Because Mrs. Kew ordered him to* did not seem an appropriate response.

"Because he loves you," Cecilia replied on her behalf. "*You.* Is this ensemble representative of you?"

"Uh . . ." Alice said. A childhood in institutions, followed by a career as a spy, left her unequipped to answer the question. The fact that someone was asking it at all threatened to short-circuit her mental processing system.

"Never mind." Cecilia's eyes glinted with piratic determination. "Based on my understanding of you, gained over the twenty minutes I've spent in your company—and furthermore my knowledge of Mr. Bixby, which comes from having glimpsed him now and again in Captain O'Riley's kitchen—I consider myself eminently qualified to make this decision on your behalf. Take off the dress. I have a better idea."

Daniel had survived a house crash. He had survived several days in company with the Wisteria Society. For that matter, he'd spent ten years as an elite agent, undertaking missions so dangerous they made his debriefers cry, and had survived that with ease.

But making small talk with Ned Lightbourne might just be the final straw.

The pirate bounced his daughter on his hip as he chatted away merrily, undaunted by Daniel's lackluster replies. At their feet, Dr. Snodgrass lay bound and gagged. Behind them, the red door of Puck House remained closed. Daniel frowned at it. He'd been waiting ~~bloody forever~~ ten minutes for Alice and could not understand the delay. By now, they should be on their way to London. Instead, he was being forced to smile and nod to a man who seemed to think that amiable conversation was perfectly reasonable behavior.

"Such nice weather," Ned remarked, and Daniel wondered if stabbing him just a little would shut him up. But at that moment the red door of Puck House finally swung open.

And every thought in his brain spontaneously combusted.

Alice appeared in the doorway. She paused, fingers flickering and eyes scanning for danger, before stepping out. Daniel's eyes, heart, groin, ached as he beheld the vision drifting toward him. Her head bore a nimbus of golden sunlight, her feet seemed to barely touch the grass, and she had been clothèd—not just clothed, insisted his reverent brain, but *clothèd*—in a plain white dress. Altogether, she looked like one of the angels on the prayer cards Daniel had collected when a child. Her brown hair was smoothed from a central parting to a chignon at the nape of her neck, and it provided the calmest, simplest, most perfect frame for her face—a face such as Byron must have envisioned when he wrote of beauty, a pure and dear dwelling place for her serenely sweet thoughts . . .

"What an appalling mess!"

Daniel blinked, his reverie shattering. Alice jammed her hands on her hips and frowned at the tumbled remains of the A.U.N.T. cottage. "Could you not have managed things more tidily?" she demanded.

"Um," he said.

"Is that all you offer in your defense, Mr. Bixby? While you dallied, I have been wrangled into various states of fashion and ruthlessly interrogated as to my opinions on jewelry. My fingers remain sticky even though I washed them, I had a splinter in one, and this dress smells of lavender."

"Oh dear." Taking her hand in his, he kissed its fingers softly, brushing his tongue against a tiny scratch he found.

Alice's frown deepened. "Wrong hand."

He looked up at her from beneath an arched eyebrow. "Really?"

She shrugged, her expression irreproachable. "Perhaps."

So he took her other hand and kissed that too, and she rolled her eyes, *tsk*ing through a barely repressed smile.

"There," he said at last, keeping hold of the hand, pressing it tightly within his grip. "All better, I hope. And the bomb is disarmed, and the day saved. I believe a degree of relaxation would not be inappropriate."

"You speak too soon." She pointed skyward, and Daniel looked up, squinting against the sunlight. A sudden chill went through him.

A swarm of pirate battlehouses was descending upon the scene like seagulls at a picnic, albeit enormous seagulls, wooden, architecturally designed, and —

Just give up, his brain advised wearily.

"How did they know where to find us?" Alice asked.

"Pirates have an unerring internal compass for drama," Ned told her, and both Daniel and Alice jolted, belatedly recollecting his presence. Daniel released Alice's hand and she stepped back.

Ned did not smirk, but his whole demeanor exuded such a smirkful attitude, Daniel felt tempted to punch him. The pirate shifted his daughter from one hip to the other, and Evangeline reached toward Alice, grasping for something to steal.

"Hello," Alice said with mild reproof . . . then withdrew from her sleeve a lace-trimmed handkerchief embroidered with Latin and roses. This she handed to Evangeline, who scrunched it in her tiny fist.

Beeeeep! Beeeeep! Beeeeep!

Now Ned was the one to jolt as the handkerchief began screeching. But Evangeline giggled and flapped the cloth. *Beeeeep! Beeeeep! Beeeeep!* Ned whipped a deadly look at Alice, who gazed back with the placid ignorance of everyone who gives a noisy present to a small child.

"Atrocious!" someone shouted over the clamor. They turned to see

Mrs. Rotunder striding across the field, her enormous pink bustle swinging from side to side and her skull-and-crossbones earrings a-clatter. She jabbed the tip of a furled lace parasol into the grass ahead of every step, testing for cow pats. "Why did you not wait for us before blowing up your cottage?!"

"Actually—" Daniel began.

"And what do you think you are doing, Mr. Lightbourne, exposing The Baby in such careless fashion to the Great Peril?!"

"Captain," Ned said automatically, but Mrs. Rotunder ignored him. She flicked her wrist, and the parasol opened with a *thwomp* that sounded like disdainful commentary on Ned's parenting ability. Reaching out with her free arm, she removed Evangeline from him.

"There now," she murmured to the child. "No risk of freckles under Aunty Gertrude's shade." Casting a black look at Ned, she marched away.

Ned blinked rather stupidly. Daniel and Alice exchanged a glance that didn't know whether to be amused or anxious, but that mostly wished it could go sit in a corner somewhere and read a book.

"Dear," came Cecilia's cool voice. Everyone turned to see her exit Puck House. "Did you just allow Mrs. Rotunder to kidnap my child?"

"I—" Ned began.

Beeeeep! Beeeeep! Beeeeep!

"Good God!" Mrs. Rotunder could be heard exclaiming. "Give me that at once, Evangeline."

"*Waaaaahhh!*"

"No, don't cry . . ."

Beeeeep! Beeeeep! Beeeeep!

Five seconds later, Ned had Evangeline back in his arms and Mrs. Rotunder was hastening away, muttering something about going for a nice quiet cup of tea (splashed with rum).

Glancing again at Alice, Daniel noticed her eyes glazing over in a way that alerted him to her overwhelmed state. He was not feeling particularly calm himself under the barrage of noise. "Shall we leave?" he asked.

"Oh, you cannot go yet," Cecilia interjected. "Not when there is tea on offer."

Daniel looked around in bewilderment, uncertain when anyone had offered him tea.

"May I mention the Wisteria Society's efforts last night to capture us?" Alice said.

"Oh, that was yesterday," Cecilia told her blithely. "Today you have provided new entertainment, and so all will be forgiven. The Wisteria Society are—"

"Volatile," Ned said.

"Mad," Alice and Daniel chorused.

"Whimsical," Cecilia told them with a delicate frown. She turned to where Pleasance stood in the doorway. "Dear, would you put on the kettle? Mr. Bixby and Miss Dearlove are joining us for morning tea."

Morning tea? Alice mouthed behind her hand to Daniel. He shook his head, nonplussed.

Elsewhere in the field, pirates began drifting from their houses, servants laden with tea tables and parasols behind them. Cows watched in fascination; at a nearby farmhouse, someone was frantically barricading windows.

"Just a cup or two," Cecilia said with a smile, "and then we will fly you back to London. After all, we have you to thank for saving my life, and—"

Beeeeep! Beeeeep! Beeeeep!

Cecilia's smile tightened. "Evangeline dearest, can Mummy see your new toy? In return, you may play with my pearl-handled dagger."

As a scuffle ensued between child and parents, Daniel took Alice by the elbow and led her aside. "Tea," he said in a low voice.

"Conversation," she added direly.

"Badminton!" Mrs. Ogden shouted from a short distance away, holding up a racket and a basket of grenades.

Daniel and Alice shared a panicked look.

And then, just in the nick of time, the cavalry arrived.

❧ 25 ❧

It had been the last dream of Alice's soul that she escape from the Wisteria Society without further infliction of tea and entertainment. But when she saw the brick shed speeding low above the field toward her, unnoticed as yet by the rest of the company, with Agent M's face visible at the flight window and salvation close at hand, she contemplated for one brief, vivid moment throwing away a lifetime's duty and taking up the teapot of villainy instead.

Pirates were dreadful! raucous! endearing! They had shown her what it meant to be truly amiable. Over the past week, she'd been welcomed into company, asked her opinion, fussed over, and acknowledged as an individual more times than she had in her entire life.

(She'd also been threatened with torture and kidnapping, but that was beside the point.)

Having always believed herself contented alone, Alice was surprised now to realize the prospect of returning to the sober, isolating life of service did not seem as appealing as it had even one minute beforehand. But that was nonsense! If asked to repeat a mission like this one, she'd never say "again"—never!

And yet . . .

As the little shed raced closer, churning up grass and dirt, Alice glanced at Cecilia Bassingthwaite. The red-haired young pirate was reciting a Byron verse to her daughter and making amusing faces to accompany it while Ned stole the handkerchief from Evangeline's tiny hand.

"Anytime you wish, you are welcome to visit me and borrow a book from my library," Cecilia had told her. Alice's heart gave a little flinch of wondering shyness at the memory. She quickly looked away—and caught sight of Miss Darlington picking Mrs. Rotunder's pocket while the latter argued with Mrs. Ogden about the proper length of time to steep tea.

"You certainly display moxie," the grand old pirate had told her, what seemed like weeks ago, as Alice sat wet and shivering in her ~~lair~~ elegant sitting room. *I can't leave,* Alice thought suddenly. *I still don't know what moxie is!*

But the shed was upon them, skidding as it swiveled on one corner of its foundation before coming to rest. The pirates all looked up with an astonished gasp. "Well I never!" someone cried, and Alice came very close to laughing.

The shed door flew open and Mia Thalassi appeared, dressed in servant black, dark eyes flashing. She held out her hand. "Come with me if you want to give—!"

Suddenly she coughed, having breathed too fast, and pressed a hand against her throat.

"—your mission report today, back at headquarters!" she concluded weakly.

Alice found herself moving without thought—primarily because Daniel was pushing her toward the shed. She stumbled, and Mia caught her arm, pulling her inside. Seconds later, Daniel was behind her, hauling Snodgrass with him. The doctor complained incoherently through his gag, but Daniel shoved him to the floor. Slamming shut the door, Mia dashed for the wheel. Chanting Latin, she guided the shed into a soaring ascent.

Alice and Daniel staggered. The building was only ten feet square, containing nothing more than a munitions box, two small windows, and, painted on the wall, the A.U.N.T. rose entwining a set of kitchen scales, below which was written "Fealty, Dignity, Laundry." Alice and Daniel had no recourse to stability other than gripping the walls the best they could. Snodgrass wailed as he rolled into a corner.

"Hold on!" Mia advised, spinning the wheel. The shed veered steeply, and Alice set her feet farther apart, her fingers digging into the clay seams between bricks. Wind was howling through invisible gaps in the walls. The door rattled.

"How did you find us?" Alice shouted over the noise.

"I was heading for Starkthorn Castle when I noticed the gathering of pirate houses," Mia shouted in reply. "Using my deductive powers, not to mention my telescope, I—"

Bang!

The shed lurched. Bricks exploded within clouds of thick, gritty dust, causing Snodgrass to scream.

"Cannonball," Daniel reported calmly, looking out the back window. "It's Rotunder in her glass conservatory again."

"How narratively appropriate," Alice said as she stumbled across to the munitions box.

Opening it, she discovered inside several rifles, flamethrowers, and a rather nifty portable rocket launcher. Taking out a machine gun, she tossed it to Daniel. "Load this."

Then, with a decidedly piratic smile, she reached for the rocket launcher.

"We won't outrun them," Mia reported almost cheerfully, as if she had nothing better to do that day than be shot at by pirates.

"We won't have to," Alice said. Pulling on a string that hung from the ceiling, she drew down a ladder, which automatically opened the trapdoor above. As she climbed one-handed, the rocket launcher propped on her hip, boots catching on her skirts with every step, she thought fondly of the Turkish trousers Mrs. Rotunder had loaned her. Lovely lady, really; shame about the unrepentant criminality. And the cannonballs, she added as the shed rattled from another blow.

Rising through the trapdoor into the high, cold sky, she narrowed her eyes as wind rushed against her face. Now *this* was more like it. This quiet, this wild peace high above the grim and exhausting toil of spying, shopping, and making pleasant conversation. Here, a woman could be comfortable—pirates certainly had the right of it as far as that was concerned. Turning on the ladder's upper rung, she wedged her skirt bustle against the rim of the trapdoor, propped one booted heel against the other edge, and lifted the rocket launcher to her shoulder.

"Ahoy there!" Mrs. Rotunder called jovially from the open flight window of her battle-conservatory, some thirty feet away. "You left without saying goodbye!"

"Goodbye," Alice called back, and launched the rocket.

Boom! Flames and black smoke burst from one corner of the conservatory.

Crash! Glass shattered.

"Well done!" Mrs. Rotunder cheered, grinning. Beside her, Mr. Rotunder waved a greeting before lifting a rifle.

Alice ducked. Bullets ricocheted off the trapdoor roof. The A.U.N.T. shed rose abruptly, flew over the conservatory, then spun ninety degrees horizontally to face its rear. Pulling a rocket from her waistband, Alice reloaded the launcher, braced herself, and shot.

She only winged the conservatory this time, but it teetered wildly, the magic destabilized. Cool-faced, Alice dropped the launcher back into the shed and bent to take the machine gun Daniel handed up to her. The shed circled around once more to the conservatory's front door, moving at a speed that sent wind rushing through Alice's bones until she felt as though she was a bird cutting the airy way. Raising the machine gun, she took aim.

Mrs. Rotunder looked up from a dainty teacup to consider this new development. Her mouth shrugged. "Nice weapon," she called out.

"Special issue," Alice told her.

"Ooh!" Mr. Rotunder said eagerly.

"You must come to dinner one night and tell us all about it," Mrs. Rotunder said. "I'll send you an invitation."

"You won't know how to find me."

The Rotunders glanced at each other and laughed. "Oh, I think I have a fair idea where you'll be," Mrs. Rotunder said. And as Alice fired the gun across her glass roof, shattering panels, the pirate saluted her with the teacup, cried *tally ho!*, and swooped away in a trail of flaming smoke and flaring magic.

Alice lowered the gun with a sigh.

That was that, then. The pirates were gone. The mission and its subsidiary perils were over. And the Alice she had been, leaping on furniture, dancing, eating mysterious stews, loving Daniel . . . that Alice needed now to shrink back down to size.

"All right up there?" Daniel called.

"Fine," she told him, although her voice was too low for him to hear. "Time to go home."

Everything was the same as it had always been. Alice felt oddly surprised by this, like one who wakes from lucid dreaming to discover the real world seems less vivid, feels less profound, than the one she'd visited in her sleep. The corridors in A.U.N.T. headquarters were still shadowy and quiet—not rich with sunlight from an unbounded sky. The plain black uniform of the staff was still orderly—but in a way that now struck her as rather dour. And not dour in the usual good way. Depressing. As she followed a senior valet toward Mrs. Kew's office, she could not resist reaching up to one of the portraits displayed in a precise line along the corridor, tipping it ever so slightly.

"Hooligan," came a whispered voice that she might have mistaken as her own inner monologue were it not for the presence behind her. She did not have to turn around to know that Daniel was giving her a sternly disapproving look—but that his gun-gray eyes were smiling. She stood a little taller, swayed a little more fluidly, just for him.

And perhaps for herself too. I am a ~~professional~~ woman, she thought. That at least was something she could carry forward with her, a secret in her inner dark.

Upon arriving at Mrs. Kew's door, the senior valet turned to them with an expression like a clipboard. "Agent A, enter here," he said, pointing at the office door. "Agent B, continue following me."

"Why?" Alice asked without thinking, and the man's eyes widened. Alice imagined him writing a large red cross on his checklist of her character.

"I appreciate you have just spent time undercover, Agent A," he said, "but I will remind you we are not ribald criminals here. We do not ask questions. Understood?"

She bit her lip, trying not to laugh. Behind her, a tight silence suggested Daniel struggled with the same impulse. Alice's heart rose at the thought of it. She wanted to hug him (and kiss him, and perhaps bite him a little), but the valet was waiting, his eyes growing even larger, so she curtsied and said, "Understood."

The valet huffed, then, without a further word, turned and marched away in the full expectation that Daniel would follow. Alice's pulse began to shake inexplicably.

"We'll talk later," Daniel whispered as he passed her.

"Later," she whispered in reply, extending a hand, her fingers glancing his in the lightest of touches before he moved out of reach.

Goodbye, she thought, watching part of her soul go with him.

"Alice?" Mrs. Kew called from inside the office. "Is that you? Come in, dear."

Alice startled as she entered the room, although only someone with a microscope would have noted it on her countenance. Beside the Chief Servant on the plump, lacy sofa sat Hazel Coombley, the agency's clinician. Pale-haired, dressed in flowing robes, and bedecked with such a plethora of jewelry she must live her life in dread of magnets, she did not look up from her teacup at Alice—but the sense of absolutely having her attention made Alice want to turn around and run screaming from the room.

"Welcome back, my dear!" Mrs. Kew trilled, gesturing with a lace-gloved hand for Alice to occupy the armchair opposite. "Sit down, sit down, come tell us all about it!"

"Thank you, ma'am," Alice said as she crossed the room. "Please excuse my appearance."

"Your appearance?" Hazel asked in the soft, stroking voice she employed to lull her patients while dissecting their psyches. Every nerve in Alice's body immediately donned armor and helmet. In a state of perfect tranquility, she lowered herself into the chair, busily straightening her skirts and aligning her sleeve cuffs so as to have an excuse for not looking up. Meeting Hazel's lush gray eyes would be like willingly diving into quicksand.

"My hair is rather windblown," she explained, "and this dress was not quite so covered in brick dust when I began my journey home. We encountered some lively pursuers who needed dissuading from shooting us out of the sky."

Hazel leaned forward, long earrings clattering as she regarded Alice intently. "And how did that make you feel?"

Alice reached into her mind for an appropriate response but found only silence. She twisted the wedding ring on her finger, then became engrossed in getting it to an exact ninety-degree angle. Mrs. Kew chuckled.

"Really, Hazel dear, I don't know why you bother. You know they don't talk about their feelings. I'm not even sure they're capable of it. Tea, dear?"

Alice glanced up for long enough to ascertain Mrs. Kew was asking her, not Hazel. "No, thank you, ma'am."

Mrs. Kew poured a cupful anyway. "We have received a report of the week's events from Agent V-2, who called us up on her hairbrush."

That made Alice raise her head again. "V-2 had a communications device?"

"Indeed," Mrs. Kew confirmed. "And luckily so, considering the urgency of her report. Remind me, dear, do you take one sugar or two?"

"None," Alice said. "I fail to understand the urgency."

"Failure is uncomfortable for you, isn't it?" Hazel asked, and Alice glanced at her fleetingly in confusion.

"V-2 was concerned by some aspects of how the mission played out," Mrs. Kew explained, handing Alice a cup. She took it numbly. Something was wrong here—very wrong. Trying to calm herself, she sipped the tea.

And almost spat it out.

"There is no sugar in this tea," she said in a stark voice, staring into the black liquid. A faint, wavering reflection of her face stared back.

"That's right, dear," Mrs. Kew said with a bewilderment so delicate, so gentle, it was patently false. "You just told me you don't take sugar."

"Interesting," Hazel murmured. "Can you share with me your thoughts on sugar, Agent A? Does it remind you of something from your childhood, perhaps?"

"I didn't have a childhood," Alice answered before she could stop herself—and then thought, *Damn*.

"Uh huh," Hazel said slowly, significantly. "Tell me more."

Fiddlesticks. Alice inhaled with deliberate calm, lowering the tea cup and its saucer to her knee. "V-2 needn't have been so concerned. The mission went exact—mostly as planned. Not only was Jane Fairweather's trap thwarted and the safety of the Queen assured, but we uncovered Snodgrass as the true villain, disarmed his bomb, and have delivered him to the cells downstairs."

"Yes, the cell keeper just now rang up on my sugar canister to inform me of that," Mrs. Kew said. "Shocking business! A perfectly good fire extinguisher, ruined! I had Snodgrass investigated when he signed himself onto your mission without authorization, but I'd never have guessed he held such extreme intentions. Luckily our crack team of intelligence analysts managed to locate his diary."

"Hm, hm," Hazel Coombley said, nodding sagely.

"Where was it?" Alice asked.

"Lying open on his desk," Mrs. Kew said, "containing a note scribbled in red pen: 'I shall blow them all up on the ninth of November in London!' Our analysts decoded this moments before the diary self-destructed! (Or had tea spilled all over it, I'm still not sure of the exact story there.)"

"Amazing detective work," Hazel murmured, her voice breathy.

"It's unfortunate that my efforts to advise you over the shoe-telephone did not work," Mrs. Kew continued. "Obviously someone in the lab was a loafer on the day they set that incantation—once we find out who, we'll give them the boot—but you saved the day nonetheless. And you may also be sure Snodgrass will get what he deserves."

"Several years in prison," Alice suggested, remembering Daniel leaping for the cottage and almost missing. She struggled not to tap a finger against the teacup.

"Several years!" Mrs. Kew exclaimed. "No, such genius as his cannot go to waste! He will be receiving a promotion—perhaps even a medal!"

"Hm," Alice said without inflection.

"You are holding that cup very stiffly," Hazel noted. "What is happening for you right now? This is a safe space for you to express your feelings."

Alice repressed a laugh at that. Hazel's concern for her was as well-polished as a pirate's sword and just as deadly. She lifted the cup to her lips, then set it back into its saucer with an entirely reasonable, not-worth-analyzing *clink*. But Hazel smirked, no doubt interpreting her entire psyche from that one small sound.

"The job has been concluded in a very tidy fashion, as always," Mrs. Kew said. "Well done, Agent A dear! You continue to be my star! I am certain there will be a bonus in your next pay packet! Having said that . . ." She shrugged apologetically, but her eyes were sharply focused, and Alice did not dare move for fear of being impaled by a direct question. "V-2 did feel you and Agent B might be struggling somewhat with the, uh, *interesting particulars* of the mission."

"I assure you we were not," Alice replied. "V-2 is a junior and not as perceptive as she believes."

"Well . . . I would not describe V-2 as a *junior*, per se."

"Oh?" Alice inquired with a tranquility that belied the sudden shuddering of her pulse as instincts, secrets, and wishes began urgently packing suitcases and consulting maps for getting the hell out of her brain.

Mrs. Kew winced. "She may be—just a little bit—our best assessor. Watches agents, checks they are obeying the rules, runs secret tests to reveal any flaws that may become an impediment to them doing their job properly."

"I see," Alice said, thinking of Veronica encouraging her and Daniel to share the bed, trying to make them waltz, talking about his golden gun . . .

Her stomach lurched. Hazel leaned forward slightly as if she could sense it.

"V-2 reports that you and Agent B clung to each other quite a bit?" Mrs. Kew winced for having to even mention it.

"Our disguise was a married couple," Alice said. "It naturally required some clinging."

"And last night you disappeared—"

"Hid from the pirates threatening to ransom us."

"—and returned in the morning *slightly disheveled.*"

"Hmmm," Hazel said, fascination tugging at her lips, and Alice almost threw the teacup at her.

"Of course, it is nothing," Mrs. Kew said with a loose shrug, even as her gaze tightened. "I am fully confident you and Agent B didn't contravene any regulations. After all, you are no silly, emotional fool, following her heart at the risk of serious consequences. You are a professional."

"Yes, ma'am," Alice said.

"You would never behave in a manner contrary to the agency's Code of Conduct."

"No, ma'am."

"Because this is a thriller, not a romance, isn't that so, Agent A?"

"Yes, ma'am."

"Drink your tea."

Alice lifted the cup to her lips.

Mrs. Kew turned to Hazel. "What do you think, dear?"

Hazel continued to regard Alice steadily. "I think Agent A is a good servant. She needs no reminder that, after all the resources poured into creating her, she belongs to A.U.N.T. and no one else. Her feet are firmly on the ground and her head nowhere near the clouds. I am certain A.U.N.T. can rely on her from here on."

Alice listened to this praise and understood it for the warning it was. She half expected Hazel to bring out a birch switch for reinforcement.

At that thought, her back and thighs tingled, reminding her unnecessarily, but vividly, what it would feel like. She blinked, and tea trembled in the cup.

"Good, good," Mrs. Kew murmured. "So we can confidently reassign her?"

"I believe so," Hazel said. Alice swallowed dryly, for, in all her years as an agent, she'd never heard a death threat so clearly stated.

She imagined Daniel sitting in some other room in this building, getting the same message. She remembered his fingers hard on her jaw as he kissed her into peace. Just the two of them ensconced in a tiny, safe bubble of love, pretending it could last for longer than a bubble ever did.

"We care about you, A dearest," Mrs. Kew was saying, her voice like a cuddle from someone wearing a cardigan—the soft, fluffy wool kind that itches your skin and leaves you with a rash. "We are doing this for your own good. You'll leave straightaway. Agent O is waiting to accompany you to Bath, where he will introduce you to your new mission subject. First, though, you'll need to be outfitted in servant garb. We'll have that dusty dress burned."

Alice nodded, not even glancing at the dress Cecilia had gifted her, not touching its soft material or inhaling the delicate scent of it. She set her teacup on the table and went to rise—

And then paused.

"My books?" she inquired. "I left them in V-2's care."

Mrs. Kew's laugh fluttered through the lace-fretted lamplight. "Oh goodness, don't worry about them!"

Alice exhaled in relief.

"They will be discarded once V-2 returns to London. Can't have my star agent distracted on the job, can I? No, dear, better just to read the A.U.N.T. operations manual from now on." She produced a smile as sharp and pitiless as the thorns along Daniel's spine.

Alice curtsied to her.

"Yes, ma'am," she said.

✵ 26 ✵

DANIEL IS TRANQUIL—REFLUX—ALICE IS TRANQUIL—
REDUX—BUTLERAMA—DANIEL TAKES A HOT BATH—
ALL'S WELL THAT ENDS WELL

No words. He had no words.

He stood outside A.U.N.T. headquarters in the waning light and absolutely could not think of one single word. They had taken away his books—that didn't help.

They had taken away his heart.

"It's not safe to see her again," they'd said, pouring him another cup of tea, not even disguising their movements as they tipped tranquilizer into it—because they were not idiots, giving unpleasant information to a man who could reach over the table and kill them in seconds then sit back down without even wrinkling his suit. Of course they would tranquilize him. Everyone understood this; there had been no need for obfuscation.

"She's already gone," they'd said, watching him drink the tea.

Not long after, the medical officers had inspected the empty cup, frowning in bemusement. "Exactly how much tranquilizer did you give him?" they'd asked the debriefers.

"Clearly not enough," the debriefers had answered from where they lay, bleeding and bruised, on the floor, amongst the shards of furniture. Then, catching sight of Daniel sitting quietly against one wall, waiting for the mess to be cleaned up, they'd whimpered and wailed and had to be carried to the sick bay.

He'd gone on sitting there alone for a while longer. Maybe hours. Maybe days, for all he knew. He'd stared at the white walls, overwhelmed by their vividness, and by the roaring volume of the silence, and worst of all by the snarling, weeping tangle of his own thoughts. Finally, a squad had entered, dressed in black combat attire, guns aimed at him. He'd been handed a book, and the squad had backed out again.

It was a paperback edition of *Anna Karenina*, and it got him up off the floor, out of the room, and all the way out of headquarters. No one stopped him—no one was in sight at all, but he could sense them behind locked doors, waiting for him to go.

Mrs. Kew met him on the street outside. "Cupcake?" she asked, trying to hand him something pink-iced and so sweet-smelling his olfactory senses nearly imploded.

Daniel just looked at her.

She shrugged. "I'm letting you live because I expect you back here tomorrow morning. New day, new assignment. Understood?"

"Where is she?" he asked.

Mrs. Kew sighed. "It's my fault. I decided you ought to be assessed after working so long undercover with O'Riley, but I failed to appreciate the depths of your emotional vulnerability. I've seen the reports of how you reacted when you thought Agent A was in danger. We simply cannot risk a weapon like yourself misfiring in such ways. It will be desk work for you for a while, young man! Just until we have you back in proper condition."

"Is she safe?" he persisted, although he dreaded the possible answer. A.U.N.T. was not above pruning anyone who grew the wrong way.

"*Tsk,*" Mrs. Kew said. "The mission is over. Agent A is gone. To-morrow I want your heart where it belongs—on the Scottish rumors file I'll be giving you."

He said nothing, staring unblinkingly past her shoulder at the untidy shapes of the city.

Mrs. Kew beamed. "There, I was sure you'd be reasonable after all. You're my star! Get some rest, then back here nice and early! We have a laird to save from blackmail."

Daniel took a step to leave—

"Wait!" Mrs. Kew cried.

He stopped.

"Dear boy. Please." She held out a soft, beckoning hand, and Daniel looked at it sidelong.

"Give the ring back."

She spoke like a sniper with a gun aimed at him—unflinching, and entirely capable of wiping him out. Without a word, he yanked the fake wedding ring from his finger and dropped it into her palm.

"Excellent!" she chirped, bouncing a little on her heels. "Now, what is your plan for the rest of the day?"

"Ma'am," he said, "I'm going home."

And before she could smile at him again, he turned and walked away.

It was almost night by the time he stopped. Rain was beginning to shiver through the afterlight, dampening his shirt, chilling him. He did not notice. Standing before a familiar mahogany door, he stared at the gold crucifix bolted to its center panel. His heart sighed, hugging itself, whispering prayers as if they were old, wild poetry. But his brain remained grim and silent.

He ought to knock. Just knock, and it would be done. *For everyone who asks receives, and he who seeks finds, and to him who knocks it will be opened.* But he was too exhausted to be brave.

Knock. On. The. Bloody. Door.

He lifted a hand, lowered it again. Perhaps he should just leave, go somewhere else, pretend—

The door opened.

Daniel stared at the woman on the other side of the threshold. She was radiant, and not only due to the light from a nearby streetlamp slanting over her rich, bright hair. Holy love seemed to illuminate her from within. Daniel's pulse beat so hard in his wrists, it hurt.

And then a sudden wash of greenish pallor crossed her face. She held up a finger, and Daniel stopped breathing—waiting, although for what, he did not know. Her throat heaved, and she clamped a hand over her mouth, eyes growing wide. With an urgent, muted sound, she rushed back inside.

"Huh," Daniel said blankly. "I was not sure of the reception I'd receive, but I did not expect to sicken anyone."

Alex O'Riley appeared; leaning against the doorframe, he grinned. "Don't mind Lottie, she's suffering from what she calls 'a temporary indisposition.'"

"But she looks well," Daniel said. "Indeed, I have never seen her so—"

"Frightening?" Alex suggested.

Daniel gave him a reproachful look. "Glowing."

Alex shrugged carelessly, but his eyes bore an unusual sheen of emotion. "That happens, apparently. The problem is, so does nausea, increased sensitivity to everything—and I mean *everything*—and an unprecedented desire for foot massages. Not to mention the foul temper. Thank God Jane tried to assassinate Cecilia when she did, or else Lottie might just have tried assassinating the entire Wisteria Society. She refused to give up on finding that bloody weapon, but secret passageways and stolen bedrooms are *not* ideal places for a woman in her condition."

"Cholera?" Daniel asked anxiously.

Alex rolled his eyes. "No, Bixby, not cholera. You look rather un-well yourself. Why are you here at my door, coatless, in the rain?" He paused, his eyes narrowing, his expression becoming deadly serious—which was not something one generally liked to experience with a no-torious pirate, but Daniel felt his breath ease at the sight. Alex took in his wet shirt, dirty shoes, the green stain around his ringless finger. The deadly expression softened into concern.

Damn it, Daniel thought. *Don't look concerned. I have no desire to stand on your doorstep weeping.*

"Can I help you?" Alex asked, gruff and tender, frowning and worried.

Daniel straightened his shoulders even more than they already were. "It is possible I may . . . require . . . need . . ." He stopped hard against the limit of his vulnerability. Swords and bombs rattled inside him, demanding stoicism. Insisting on isolation. He clenched his jaw, blinked to focus his vision . . . and a tear slipped down his face.

"Bixby," Alex said in a tone Daniel did not recognize, never having heard it used with him before. The pirate stepped aside. "Come in. Come in. We'll figure this out, whatever it is, together. Come in, my friend."

"I—" Daniel said, overwhelmed. He'd not been surprised by what A.U.N.T. had done. All his life, they'd said he could have no heart and he'd agreed—all of them sure it would be like Snodgrass's bomb, set to explode at the first grounding. But he'd found that heart, and they'd taken it from him. They'd taken Alice. He'd been surprised every sec-ond since by the grief and fear and desperate wishing.

But nothing surprised him more than Alex O'Riley putting a hand on his shoulder, holding him steady while he faced the threshold be-tween service and love.

"Tell him to hurry up!" Charlotte called out grumpily from the interior. "These pickled onions aren't going to fry themselves!"

It was the season of Light, it was the season of Darkness. Miss Agapantha Ketlew moved between white shirtwaists and deep plum dresses, yellow scarves and black stockings, overwhelmed by choice. She had everything before her! It was a feast of fashion, and her heart sprang with hope! She had nothing before her! It was a wasteland, and she despaired.

"If I don't find the perfect ensemble for attending Lady Mellard's soiree, my life will be *utterly* ruined!" she declared.

"Yes, miss," Alice said tonelessly from behind a stacked load of shoeboxes.

"I'm sure you don't understand!" Agapantha gave a loud, prolonged sigh. "You probably don't even *know* the difference between cerise and pink!"

"No, miss," Alice replied.

Agapantha turned to share a smirk with her other servant, Mr. Olliver, but he just stared into the middle distance with all the blank professionalism of a ~~secret agent for an underground government~~ valet. His hands were occupied with various shopping bags, but Alice imagined the speed with which he might produce a gun from a concealed holster in the event that she threw the shoeboxes at him and ran for her life.

Which of course would not happen. She was a good, obedient servant. No reasonable person could point to her and say she looked like she was planning an escape (by distracting Mr. Olliver, dashing out the door, jamming it shut with her hair slide, scaling the front wall of the boutique with the help of the grips she had hidden in a secret pocket, then making her getaway across the rooftops. For example).

Certainly no one could produce a map drawn in her hand, detailing how to leave Bath without being caught by any of the agents who shadowed her (heading south to the train station, then doubling back and stealing a horse from the public mews—hypothetically speaking).

Indeed, so tranquil was she, Mrs. Kew must be getting rather bored with the daily reports about Agent A's dedication to A.U.N.T. duty.

Which is exactly what Alice was counting on.

Nobody stole her books (and her Mr. Bixby) and got away with it.

"Dearlove!" Agapantha snapped, reclaiming her attention. "What do you think?"

Alice blinked at the orange dress held up before her. "Ma'am," she said without inflection.

"Uuughh!" Agapantha sighed explosively. "This is *impossible!* I need proper advice from someone who understands fashion!"

Tinkle tinkle.

Alice glanced around at the opening door. She caught her breath. Ned Lightbourne walked in.

"I do love Bath," he was saying to someone behind him.

"I am rather fond of the place myself," came an elegant voice in reply.

Agapantha stared wide-eyed as Cecilia Bassingthwaite entered. Beautiful, refined, the pirate woman moved with the quiet grace of someone who knew that all she beheld could be hers at the merest flick of a finger (which is to say, a finger set against a gun's trigger). She was outfitted in a gown of deep amber stolen from the very best haute couture provider, and it made the dress Agapantha held up look like a sunburned squirrel in comparison. Her hat was a work of sculptural art.

"One meets the most interesting people in Bath," she said, smiling sweetly at Ned. He grinned in response.

Alice's nervous system began to smolder.

"For example," Cecilia said, trailing her fingertips across a rack of blouses, "there is an interesting gentleman standing outside. Handsome and well-groomed, wearing a very dapper suit."

"Ah, nothing beats a dapper suit," Ned replied, picking up a decorative metal glove stand. The shop attendant gave him a wary stare, and Ned nodded amicably to the man.

Alice's nervous system began sparking.

"I suspect nothing beats this gentleman," Cecilia mused. "If they tried to, they might not live to regret it." She removed a blouse from the rack and, stripping it from its wooden coat hanger, let it fall to the floor. The shop attendant gasped.

"Just standing outside the door, you say?" Ned tossed up the glove stand and caught it again.

"Yes, waiting in case any ladies need help crossing the street to the other side, where a cottage happens to be parked." Cecilia spun the coat hanger around her hand effortlessly. "Charming little house, exactly the sort one would use if one wanted to get themselves a holiday away from town."

"So, a getaway house?" Ned suggested.

"*Dearlove!*" Agapantha snapped, shaking the dress so its beaded trim clattered. "Are you listening to me?"

Alice turned back to the girl. "No, ma'am."

"What? What?" Agapantha gaped at her. "That is *complete*—"

"The dress is hideous," Alice interjected dispassionately. "It wearies the eye and suffocates the brain. Therefore I urge you to buy it, as it will suit you perfectly. Now, if you'll please excuse me." Swiveling on her heel, she threw the shoeboxes at Mr. Olliver.

"Ahh!" he shouted, arms flinging up in defense. Even before the shoes could tumble from their boxes to the floor, Alice introduced the heel of her own boot to Olliver's midriff. He bent double just as she lifted her knee, causing a collision between it and his nose, immediately whereafter she elbowed him in the back of the neck. He collapsed atop the shoes, and for a pièce de résistance Cecilia whacked him with the wooden coat hanger.

"Thank—" Alice began, but was interrupted by the shop assistant vaulting the counter in a manner that suggested he'd trained less in ironing blouses and more in secret agenting. Unfortunately, however, he must have skipped class on the day "Dealing with Pirates" had been taught. He was still in midair when the metal glove stand, whizzing at speed across the room, smacked into his face. He joined Mr. Olliver in unconsciousness upon the floor.

"That's what you get for selling such hideous orange dresses," Ned said.

"Oh no!" Agapantha cried in horror. Everyone looked at her, fearing she'd been harmed. "It really *is* hideous, isn't it? What am I to *do*? Lady Mellard's soiree is *tomorrow!*"

Before an answer might be provided, two shopgirls appeared from the stock room, flicking tape measures like whips. "Goodness," Cecilia murmured to Alice. "Your organization really does want to keep you."

"Or kill me," Alice answered with a shrug.

"Go on outside, dear. Ned and I will handle this."

"It'll be fun," Ned added cheerfully. He snatched the orange dress from Agapantha, threw it at the shopgirls, then pointed to a peach-colored gown displayed on the other side of the room. "That one," he told Agapantha, pushing her toward it.

"Thank—" Alice tried again to say, but Cecilia was already shooing her away. So she hurried to the door, reached for its handle—

And it opened from the outside.

"Ma'am."

Alice glanced at the gentleman holding the door ajar for her. "Here at last, I see, Mr. Bixby," she remarked, surveying his well-dressed form as she walked through the doorway. "*I* would have got here days earlier."

He gave her a polite bow. "That is because you are far superior to me in every conceivable way." Closing the door behind them, he moved to her side, placing his hand against the small of her back as they both scanned the street. At his firm touch, her nervous system ignited in white-hot flames.

"I do not need rescuing," she informed him. "I was just on the verge of self-rescue when you arrived."

"Of course."

"I am leaving A.U.N.T."

"Oh?"

"Yes," she replied calmly, as if she was talking about sampling a new breakfast cereal rather than discarding the entire purpose of her life thus far. "They're planning to destroy my books."

"Indeed? By happy chance, I myself have left A.U.N.T.'s employment—"

Alice raised an eyebrow.

He shrugged, as if the relinquishment of his complete identity thus far was of no consequence. "I haven't finished reading *Madame Bovary*. I wish to get it back. Consequently, I'm free to join you on the recovery mission—if you want, that is."

"I want," she said at once, grasping his hand in a sudden fit of reckless passion. A lady passing by noticed and *tsk*ed loudly in horrified disapproval. They ignored her.

"I'm sorry it took me a few days to track you down," Daniel whispered.

Alice squeezed his hand. "I'm sorry I couldn't escape sooner to find you."

"Alex and Charlotte took me in. They made me tea—then waited while I remade it properly—then offered to bomb headquarters for me. They . . . listened." He winced slightly, and Alice guessed all he was not describing—the fear of being left without orders, structure, discipline; the confusion about how exactly to be from now on. She'd experienced it herself. If it hadn't been for her determination to escape and reunite with Daniel, she might have fallen into a terrifying insouciance. Knowing he'd gone through the same thing made her feel a strange, shadowy pain. Could this be the "empathy" she'd read so often about in novels? Or did she need to visit a doctor?

"After I talked," Daniel was saying, "they kindly let me scrub their floors and wash their dishes, which helped most of all. By the time I had the laundry folded, I no longer wanted quite so much to slaughter Mrs. Kew and the Academy tutors. I just wanted you."

Crash!

Something slammed against a wall inside the boutique, causing the door to shudder. Alice did not even notice. All she knew was Daniel.

"We made a plan, Alex, Charlotte, and I," he said, touching a button on her dress in a way that reminded her of a moonlit room, a list of rules they had broken kiss by kiss. "Alex called in some favors. And here we are."

"Here you are," Alice whispered tremulously. She touched his hair, his jaw, as if to assure herself of the reality.

"Of course I am. It would be illogical for me to stay away from the woman I value above all things in the world. You are my prime number, Alice. My eyes are for you only."

"My heart is yours," she countered.

He grinned. "You win."

"Get used to it," she warned with a crooked smile.

From inside the boutique came another crash; farther along the street, several pedestrians in black coats began to walk toward them. The air grew charged with anticipation.

"Is that Captain O'Riley's house across the road?" Alice asked.

"Yes." Daniel rubbed her button between two fingers, and she swallowed heavily. Anyone getting between her and the moment Daniel did the same thing with those fingers elsewhere on her body was going to be very, *very* sorry.

"It looks like we have a clear path ahead," she said.

"Look again." He pointed upward, and Alice noticed then a black shed hovering above them. Suddenly its several doors opened and a squad of butlers rappelled out, bowler hats strapped to their heads and rifles to their backs.

Alice and Daniel began to run.

They reached halfway across the wide street before the butlers landed. Turning, they found several valets converging on them from both west and east.

"Trapped," Daniel noted dispassionately.

"Oh dear," Alice said, scratching at a mark on her thumbnail.

And then—

Whack! Thwomp! Smash! They punched, pummeled, spun, and leaped into the air with legs extended horizontally. Noses shattered, knees cracked, heads were smashed together. Several hats were completely destroyed.

"Who is in charge of combat training these days?" Alice asked with exasperation as she tossed a mustachioed butler to the ground.

"I don't know," Daniel replied, slamming the heel of his hand into the windpipe of a valet. "But I'm not impressed with their work."

"They should bring in a consultant," Alice said while kicking another valet in the groin. "Perhaps a freelance company run by experienced, retired agents."

"Hm," Daniel said, intrigued, as he smacked a butler in the face with the man's own umbrella. "A company also available to civilians? Offering combat training, information analysis, housekeeping advice?"

"Exactly." Alice absent-mindedly punched a valet. She still could not quite look away from Daniel, so unruffled in his black suit, polished shoes—and with a silver ring in his ear. Her heart gave a hot little shiver at that.

"This service," he said, straightening his cuffs, and the shiver became a veritable earthquake. "Would it have a base?"

"Perhaps it might be mobile?" Alice said, striving not to march over to him and rip off his cufflinks just so he had to arrange them again. "A townhouse or villa, equipped with a wheel and the latest in flight instrumentation. Something tidy, of course, with plenty of space for bookshelves. Behind you."

Daniel rammed the butler's umbrella backward. A valet who had been lunging at him gave a brief cry and collapsed. "It would need to have a catchy name," he said. "For example, The Bixby Battle Consultancy."

"Hm," Alice mused. One of the bleeding men lying around her stirred, and she set her foot upon his chest. "We wouldn't want it to be another Auntie: dull, conservative."

"True," Daniel said. "It should have a name that serves as a bond between concept and action."

"And I'm not sure why it should have your name when we would own it in equal partnership."

Daniel stepped toward her. ("Ow!" cried out one of the butlers, whose hand he trod on.) Angling his head to one side, he smiled rather shyly at her. "I was rather hoping the name might belong to us both."

Stopping a few inches away, he stared at her—not one part of him touching her, and yet his energy pressing against every inch of her body. Alice stared back. Her fingers tapped her thigh and Daniel skipped a breath, as if she'd drummed them directly on his soul.

"Are you proposing I change my name by deed poll?" she asked.

His smile deepened. "Actually, I was proposing marriage. A real marriage, this time."

"Oh!" She tried to compose a perfect response, but all her inner dictionaries had turned to flowers. "Well, that seems like a reasonable idea," she managed to say. She held out her hand. "I accept."

Daniel took her hand, but he did not shake it as she expected. Instead, he held it against his heart. "I love you, Alice," he said.

"I love you more," she answered.

The butlers and valets moaned.

Suddenly, O'Riley's cottage door slammed open. "Are you two coming or not?" Alex called out testily.

"Be patient!" Cecilia admonished from the other side of the road, where she and Ned were leaning back against the boutique wall, arms crossed, watching the fight as if it were marvelous entertainment. "Let them have their romantic moment!"

"They'll kiss soon and it will all be worth it," Ned added, grinning. Cecilia smacked him.

"Kissing on the street in daylight is scandalous behavior," Charlotte said.

"They just beat up more than a dozen men, darling," Alex pointed out, "I think they're beyond scandal now."

Daniel lifted his eyes heavenward. "People," he murmured disapprovingly.

"Friends," Alice whispered.

The space between them grew warm and heavy with amazement, hope, love.

Or possibly with the shadow of the A.U.N.T. shed hovering lower. Suddenly, Agent M opened the flight window and leaned out. "Hello down there," she shouted conversationally.

"Hello, Mia," Alice called back, not looking away from Daniel.

"So are you going to surrender or not?" the agent asked.

"Not," Daniel told her, keeping his gaze on Alice. "We're going home."

"I've got orders to take you dead or alive."

"And—?" Daniel asked.

There was a moment of silence, then Mia shrugged. "And I don't get paid enough to kill awesome people. Oh dear, look at you running too fast for me to catch you. And now you've disappeared into a maze of alleyways where you'll never be found. What a terrible shame."

They lifted their heads then to regard her with surprise, and she grinned in return. The flight window snapped shut.

"Home," Alice said dreamily, looking at Daniel again. "Where is that?"

"I don't know yet," he said. "Shall we find out?"

She nodded. Daniel lifted her hand, kissed it, and her tranquil layers dissolved in a great, possessing rush of joy.

Thank God she'd never before known it was possible to be so happy, or she would have been miserable wanting it.

"Alice, my wonder," he said against her hand.

"Daniel, my love," she answered, smiling.

And she put her arm around him, bringing him close to her side, roses and thorns and all. Together they left the shadow of the A.U.N.T. house and went into the pirate's cottage, and from there flew away to get their books.

EPILOGUE

- Sixteen Months Later -

A wuthering breeze swept through the dreaming midsummer's night, but not even its chill offered persuasion enough to send the three women down from the roof. They sat in a row along the ridgepole: the pirate, the witch, and the spy. And staring out at the limitless horizon, they sighed.

"Forever is so beautiful," Alice said.

"Yes," Cecilia and Charlotte agreed in unison.

A star to the north was flinging off shoots of light as if it could not contain itself. Alice wanted to reach out, pretend to touch it, but decided that doing so would be too strange while in company. She tapped her fingers discreetly on the roof instead. *Her* roof, with its brown tiles sloping above white walls and linen-curtained windows. Her house. She patted it with a fondness that was secretly an adoring, almost obsessive love she never admitted to anyone, not even Daniel—although of course he would know, just by looking at her.

This little bungalow had taken them all over the British Isles in the past year and a half since they left A.U.N.T. Evading the agency's lawyers and assassins, teaching countesses how to fight off jewel thieves, selling bank managers security against the threat of pirates (and then going to dinner with those same pirates, because it was, after all, just business). Trying again and again to find peace.

They even had employees. Agent Mia Thalassi defected to them in exchange for a fast cottage and the secret of Daniel's special choke hold, and two of Frederick Bassingthwaite's chambermaids were on the payroll as inside informants, feeding them secrets from both the piratic society and A.U.N.T. (and doing their laundry every Monday).

They had ghosts too: the children they once were, still haunting them faintly in the background of their selves. Sad-eyed little Alice, held together by alphabets and poetry fragments. And young Daniel, who had learned so thoroughly not to flinch that, even now, he never noticed when he accidentally burned a finger, and was confused when Alice cared about it. But she did care, and he knew the right poems to whisper when she needed them, and every day the ghosts grew a little fainter.

Alice still had not learned how to fly the house. She swore that the magic persisted in overwhelming her—but really, secretly, she just liked to watch Daniel at the wheel. He was so masterful, more than once she'd made him land the building so he could express that mastery in a more horizontal fashion than flying generally allowed.

(Although there had been that one time, half a mile above the Shetland Islands, when she'd stood leaning forward against the open flight window, the wind caressing her face, and Daniel had . . .)

"*Ahem,*" she said, shifting uncomfortably on the roof. Cecilia and Charlotte glanced at her, but luckily the darkness hid her blush.

That particular day had been, according to Alice's calculations, *when* William was conceived. Or perhaps that evening. Or later that night. After discovering her pregnancy, they'd given up any lingering notion of peace. They lived now with their hearts forever exposed in the shape of a small, squirmy, brown-haired baby with eyes like tarnished silver and a seemingly endless capacity for emotions. They lived frightened—enchanted—in love.

But oh, how they lived.

"It scares me sometimes," she said, gazing out at the darkness, "when I think how long I spent alone, trapped in a life other people made for me to suit themselves. The fear I might go back there still grips me every now and again, you know?"

"I know." Charlotte tucked her knees up closer against her heart. "Me too."

"I took all the clocks out of my house when I first married," Cecilia said. "I couldn't bear the tick, reminding me of the long, peaceful afternoons and quiet nights in my aunt's house. But Ned was always running late for burglaries, and then I needed to keep track of Evangeline's routine, and there's the fact our housemaid, who took over when Pleasance got her own battlehouse, suffers from recurrent bouts of amnesia (we suspect she's a lost princess, although she does make an excellent lamb stew). So I brought the clocks back again. Besides, quite frankly, I could do with a peaceful afternoon every once in a while."

Charlotte chuckled. "Yesterday Alex took the twins to visit with my mother so I could have time to do some reading. I just sat and stared into the middle distance and *luxuriated*."

Cecilia smiled sympathetically, but Alice had to look away, hiding the sudden pallor of her face.

"What is it?" Charlotte asked, nudging her with a shoulder. Alice laughed silently, because *of course* the witch had noticed. She rather thought she could lock herself at the back of a closet, covered entirely by a blanket, and whisper that she had a headache—and within the hour Charlotte would arrive at her doorstep with a willowbark remedy.

"I'm sorry, I'm an anxious fool," she said. "Even the thought of Daniel taking William anywhere without me makes my heart shake."

"Are you still getting menacing visits from your A.U.N.T.?" Cecilia asked.

"No. After Daniel taught the last person who tried to assassinate him how to do a carotid restraint properly, Mrs. Kew acquiesced and signed the consultancy contract. The invitation to William's christening probably helped too."

"I get nervous when I leave Alex alone with the children," Charlotte confessed. "I'm sure one of these days he'll decide letting them play with his sword is a grand idea. The only reason I was able to luxuriate while they were visiting with my mother was because I had the house parked across the road and a telescope aimed at Mama's sitting room. So you're not an anxious fool, Lissy. Or, if you are, I am too."

"What do you think they're doing right now?" Cecilia asked, stretching her legs out over the tiles. Moonlight flowed into the white muslin billows of her dress, illuminating her like a love interest in a romantic poem.

"I dread to think," Charlotte muttered.

"I can't hear any crying," Alice said, tilting her head toward the roof hatch. "Should we go down and check on them?" Her heart yearned as always for her boys—but then again, the stars were so lovely, and, as a bonus, no one was clutching at her bosom. So long as she knew they were safe nearby, she was quite content to remain up here a while longer with her friends.

Her friends. Fiddlesticks. Even after more than a year, she still got tingles when she thought of it. In fact, they were more than friends, these women, their husbands—they were an extended chosen family, at least according to Ned, who alone of the group was not afraid to say it. They were honorary aunties and uncles to each other's children.

Alice wished she could reach back to little Alice, hunched alone and hurting on a dormitory bed in the Academy, and assure the girl that time would see her happy and loved just the way she was.

And that the Academy tutors would wake some thirteen years later to find all their birch switches burning atop a pile of their shredded training manuals. Alice smiled. That had been a fun night.

Crash!

The women flinched at the sudden loud sound from downstairs.

"Everything's fine!" Ned called out.

Cecilia glanced wryly at the other two. "I apologize, Lissy. Almost certainly, something is not fine."

Alice grinned at her. "Don't worry. I don't mind a little mess."

"Hm," Charlotte said with a disapproval that sounded almost as stern as Daniel's. She pushed herself to her feet, managing easily in her trousers. "I had better go and check."

"I'll come too," Alice said, standing. On Charlotte's other side, Cecilia also rose, brushing wrinkles from her skirts. The three began to step sidelong toward the trapdoor.

"This reminds me of the time Alex and I danced in Clacton-on-Sea," Charlotte said, swaying a little to keep her balance on the ridgepole. She happened to catch Alice's glance, and a glimmer of humor passed between them.

"What is it?" Cecilia asked. "You've stopped. Is something the matter?"

"I was just thinking," Charlotte said, the humor tugging now at her mouth, drawing it into a crooked, piratic smile. "Perhaps we need not go down just yet."

"Oh?" Cecilia inquired.

"Perhaps we might go up instead."

She held out her hand to Alice, who took it without hesitation. Her other, she presented to Cecilia.

"Lottie Pettifer," Cecilia chided. "Are you suggesting witchcraft?"

Charlotte shrugged and nodded. "Yes."

"Excellent." Cecilia took her hand.

And as Charlotte whispered the magic word, they rose from the roof. Three wicked women who had run away from who they were supposed to be and found themselves, found each other; three wild women holding hands, sharing laughter, as they danced together in the midnight sky, beneath a yellow moon.

The men stood looking at the broken vase. Alex and Ned, holding their swords down, grimaced guiltily. Daniel just smiled and rocked the baby in his arms.

"Don't worry," he said. "I hated that vase and am glad to be rid of it, but never could tell Alice. Mrs. Rotunder gave it to her."

"I clean up!" Evangeline called out happily, running to kneel down in front of the broken pieces. Ned quickly crouched beside her, taking her little hand before she could touch anything sharp. He passed her the bottom half of the vase, which now looked more like a bowl.

"You hold this," he said, "and I'll put the pieces inside it for you."

"Yes!" she authorized, nodding briskly, making her golden curls bounce. Ned lifted a sour look to the other two men.

"So exactly who corrupted my child to this degree? It's bad enough that Aunt Darlington has her testing everyone's temperature, but this new mania for *tidying* is simply not at all appropriate for a pirate."

"Don't blame me," Alex said, raising his hands palm out. "I might have taught her how to use a screwdriver to jimmy open a cake tin—"

"What?!" Ned said.

"—but I still don't know where our housemaid keeps the carpet sweeper, let alone how to use it."

Daniel huffed a laugh. In his arms, William huffed too, mimicking him in a way that reached up, took his heart, and squeezed with a pain he'd come to love, perhaps even hunger for. He smiled gently at his son, entranced by the perfect measurements of his tiny face and the uncanny depths of his eyes, which defied any scientific explanation. *Damn*, he thought. *Don't cry.*

Looking up resolutely, he found Alex grinning at him. Embarrassed, he clenched his jaw but got only sympathy in return, the pirate's dark blue eyes filling with a sentiment that drew him away from the other men suddenly and across the room to gloat over the baby girls cuddled together in a fleece-lined basket near the hearth.

"Would you ever have guessed he'd become so soppy?" Ned whispered.

"When has he ever *not* been soppy?" Daniel answered, and Ned choked on a laugh.

They hastily settled their expressions as Alex returned. "Thank bloody God," he said, dragging a hand through his dark hair. "Still asleep."

"Pirate children learn to sleep through just about anything," Ned said, then fell into discussing vase pieces with his daughter, whose suggestions as to their potential criminal purposes made him smile proudly—and grimace a little with trepidation at the same time.

"What did you break?" came a dry voice, and they looked up to see Charlotte enter the sitting room. With her high, spiky boots and Alex's voluminous, long black coat, she looked more piratic than all of them put together. Hands on her hips, she directed the question to Alex like a knife to his throat.

"Excuse me," he said, affronted. "Why do you think *I* broke something? It could have been anyone."

Charlotte huffed a laugh. "Because I just know you've been showing Ned that clever new move of yours that yesterday broke the crystal swan we acquired from Lady Espiner."

She and Alex began to quarrel contentedly. Daniel did not listen, his attention caught by Alice walking into the room. *She's here*, his heart sang, hugging itself.

She lives here, replied his brain with exasperation for such mawkishness—then sent a smile out along every nerve.

"This is in disarray again," Daniel said to her quietly, touching her unraveling coiffure as she came up beside him.

"We have been dancing," she said.

He leaned closer. "That explains why you look like starlight and dark horizons."

"All tidy!" Evangeline announced, toddling over to Alice with the remnants. Alice smiled, bending down to take them from her.

"Sorry," Alex said. "My fault. I'll get you a new one."

"Thank you, Evangeline," Alice said. "And please don't worry, Alex. I confess I hated that vase, but I know Daniel liked it. Mrs. Rotunder gave it to him."

"Charlotte and I can take you shopping for a new one," Cecilia suggested, and behind her back Ned rolled his eyes.

"You mean stealing," Alice said disapprovingly.

Cecilia waved this interpretation away. "Not at all. We'll sneak into Starkthorn Castle and select one of their vases. It's not stealing when it's family. Thursday, perhaps? We'll take Evangeline along for the fun."

"Fun!" Evangeline sang out, and pointed two fingers like a gun. "Bang! Bang!" Her parents smiled at her dotingly.

"Thursday," Charlotte agreed. "And now, time to go home." She wrapped her arms around herself, and Daniel recognized that her senses had abruptly reached the end of their endurance for the evening. "Alex, will you bring Elizabeth and Anne?"

"Sure," he agreed, touching her shoulder gently as he crossed again to the basket.

"We must be on our way too," Cecilia said. "Ned, remember we have that burglary at Twinkers' jewelry store tomorrow morning."

"Good luck with that," Daniel told her. "We helped them install several new security measures only last week."

"Excellent," Ned said, lifting Evangeline onto his hip and bouncing her a little, sharing a grin with her as she giggled. "I love a challenge, don't I, Evie Angel?"

"You love Evie," she answered, patting his face, and Daniel tried not to smirk at the sight of the pirate's smile melting as his daughter outcharmed him.

Everyone departed, and Alice slipped away to prepare for bed. Daniel stood by the sitting room window for a long, quiet while, rocking William to sleep and watching first Alex's old Irish cottage and then Puck House lift into the sky and fly off. The sky settled, full of stories made of stars. The world softened around him. Finally, Alice reappeared, all clean and fresh in a nightgown, smelling like roses from St. Therese. She put her arm around him, resting her head against his shoulder as she smiled down at their child.

"All right?" she asked.

"Perfect," he said, looking at their reflection in the dark window, falling in love with the whole of them. And then falling in love again. And again. Counting his breath now not by numbers but by each beautiful moment he got to exist with his family. "Do you have any plans for tomorrow?" he asked, just for something to say.

"None," she said. "You?"

"None. What shall we do?"

She smiled, setting her hand to his heart.

"Anything we want."

ACKNOWLEDGMENTS

The moment Bixby and Miss Dearlove appeared in *The League of Gentlewomen Witches*, it was intrigue at first sight for me, and I could hardly wait to write their story. I've since come to love them with my whole heart, and hope I've done justice to the perspectives they brought with them.

There are so many people I want to offer my warmest, heartfelt gratitude for their input and support in the creation of this series, including Kristine Swartz, Taylor Haggerty, Jasmine Brown, Mary Baker, Christine Legon, Stacy Edwards, Daniel Brount, Stephanie Felty, Bridget O'Toole, Eileen Chetti, Katie Anderson, Dawn Cooper, Alice Lawson, Jerome Buckleigh, Tawanna Sullivan, Rebecca Hilsdon, and Jorgie Bain. Thank you all so very much! May you always be blessed with fair winds and fabulous adventures!

This book is even more full of literary quotes and misquotes than its predecessors, simply because both Daniel and Alice set their internal compass to books. Therefore, I want to gratefully acknowledge . . . *deep breath* . . . Lewis Carroll, George Elliot, William Shakespeare, Jane Austen, Charles Dickens, Lord Byron, Elizabeth Gaskell, Emily Brontë, Mary Shelley, William Blake, Johann Gottfried Herde, Alfred Tennyson, Thomas Osbert Mordaunt, Henry James, Miguel de

ACKNOWLEDGMENTS

Cervantes, Gustave Flaubert, Leo Tolstoy, Emily Dickinson, Ben Jonson, William Wordsworth, and Anonymous.

Virtual hugs to the authors and readers who have created such a great community online. I wish I could meet you all in person and give you those hugs for real. And to my family, love as always, forever.

Finally, I want to thank myself. There was a particular moment in my life when the future offered two divergent paths, and along one route the wild witch spirit of comedy beckoned, grinning. With uncharacteristic impulsivity, I dropped all my maps, all my plans, and started running toward her without looking back. The witch slipped into shadows, her job done. A flying house swooped down to pick me up. I went with it.

And apologies to Robert Frost, but that really has made all the difference.

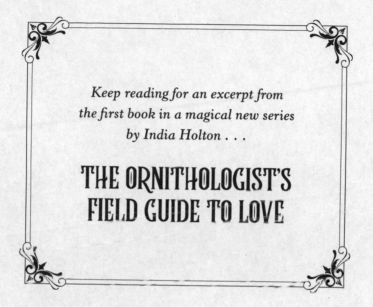

Keep reading for an excerpt from
the first book in a magical new series
by India Holton . . .

THE ORNITHOLOGIST'S FIELD GUIDE TO LOVE

- Spain, 1890 -

It was a fine day for birding. Almost too fine. Sunlight glazed the sky of northern Spain, unrelieved by cloud or breeze. Heat pressed down on the forest path.

Mrs. Quirm and Miss Pickering strolled beneath the shade of hats and lace parasols, employing their white-gloved hands in the manner of fans to cool themselves. Every now and again they lifted delicate silver binoculars to search the surrounding trees. Several birds flitted between branches, singing, courting, and generally participating in occupations typical to the avian species. But the ladies' quarry was one bird in particular, far shyer than the common breeds. They had seen glimpses of it throughout the morning and were intent on pursuit, despite the overbearing weather.

"By Jove, I could use a glass of lemonade right now!" Mrs. Quirm declared.

"Indeed, it is atrociously warm," Miss Pickering agreed.

"Rupert!" Mrs. Quirm snapped her gloved fingers. "Lemonade, if you please."

Rupert, walking behind her, turned to the contingent of porters, guides, and servants walking behind him. He gestured, and a man hurried forth with bottle and glass. Lemonade was poured, the glass was set on a silver tray, and Rupert presented it.

Mrs. Quirm took the drink, but, before she could bring it to her robust lips, she sighted something that caused her to gasp.

"A bastard, here in the forest!"

Miss Pickering stared at her with astonishment. One simply did not speak of people born out of wedlock if one was a lady, and in all her twenty-four years, Miss Pickering had met none more ladylike than Hippolyta Quirm, despite the vigorous galumphing of her vocal chords.

"You do well to be surprised, Elizabeth!" the woman said in what would have been termed a shout had it come from a less reputable person. "The Great Bustard has no business being in a forest! It is a bird of the fields."

"Oh, a *bustard*," Beth said with relief. No doubt the heat had suffocated her ear canal as it was attempting to do with her lungs.

She blew restively at a chestnut-brown strand of hair that had slipped over her damp brow. If only it was decent behavior to remove one's hat in company, or loosen one's collar, or leap naked into a nearby river! Ornithology tended to be a mucky venture—scuffed shoes, snagged stockings, guano splattering one's parasol— but the worst of it was the perspiration.

When Hippolyta had announced they were going to Spain in search of the elusive pileated deathwhistler, Beth had considered feigning illness so as to remain behind. She was British right through to her tea-flavored, rain-colored core, and the thought of a summer without fog and storms horrified her. But in the end she had been unable to resist the opportunity such an expedition offered. To capture the deathwhistler would result in universal accolades. And if anyone could pull it off, it was Hippolyta Quirm, field ornithologist, wildly famous authoress of *Birds Through a Sherry Glass,* and at only thirty-one a five-time recipient of England's prestigious Best Birder award.

Beth was pleased to be the woman's associate. The moment they met in Epping Forest, accidentally smacking each other over the head with their nets while their mutual quarry, a fine specimen of rain-singing robin, flew away in a teeny-tiny storm, they knew they'd work well together. For one thing, Beth was prepared to take all the blame for the mishap, and Hippolyta was glad to give it.

"You can extend your post-doctoral research into the psychic habitats of thaumaturgical birds," the woman had offered as they walked back to town together afterward, "and I can get your help in the field."

"Yes," Beth had said without pausing for thought. Then again, even if she had taken time to consider it, she'd have answered the same way. And now, thanks to their partnership, her career was going places—literally as well as metaphorically. Three continents in two years, and who knows, perhaps one day even New Zealand, land of the giant carnivorous moa.

First, however, she had to not drown in her own sweat.

Buck up, she chastised herself. At least it was not as bad as chasing the fire-breathing sand curlew in Cairo. Granted, she'd been dressed in black at the time, to honor the anniversary of her parents' death, but heatstroke almost saw her following them into the grave. More than once, the only thing that saved her from feverishly tumbling off a camel's back had been the ballast of her petticoats. If Hippolyta hadn't discovered that the curlew liked arrowroot biscuits, and was thus able to lure it into a cage for the voyage back to London, Beth's career would have burned out before it properly began. Again, literally as well as metaphorically—which seemed to be the usual state of affairs when one was involved in magical bird chasing.

"The Great Bustard can be taken as a good sign," Hippolyta was saying, and Beth pulled herself out of the Egyptian frying pan back into the Spanish fire. "No doubt it was attracted to our deathwhistler's thaumaturgic vibrations. We're getting close, mark my words. Oberhufter tried to convince me to search farther south, but I knew he was talking nonsense. He always does. I am a far superior ornithologist to him." She tossed her head, blonde curls fluttering.

"Absolutely," Beth murmured loyally.

"I still cannot believe that man was voted High Flyer of the Year. What rot! He is an idiot, and I know for a fact he bribed the awards committee with spotted nightspinner feathers."

"Mm-hm," Beth said, in lieu of pointing out Hippolyta had bribed them with strix claws, despite having no hope of succeeding— since, in addition to the spotted nightspinner, Herr Oberhufter had bagged a scarlet thrush, a fire tit, and even a breeding pair of horned frogeaters, which he donated to the Natural History Museum (and then had to come take away again, as they made such a noise they drove several curators to the brink of madness)—all in the second half of 1889.

Granted, in the course of getting these birds, he had also broken the leg of one rival ornithologist and tricked another into catching a train to Siberia, from whence they sent an excited telegram reporting they'd found the mythical yeti owl, and thereafter were never seen again. The awards committee, however, cast a blind eye to such nefarious behavior. A bird in the hand was worth more than two birders in the bush, any day.

"Oberhufter will go down in history as a knave and cheat," Hippolyta persisted. "And once we return to London with the pileated deathwhistler, I shall campaign to have his Ornithological Society membership revoked."

"Good idea," Beth said, blowing at the wayward strand of hair again.

"A little blackmail should do the trick. But if that fails, you can always seduce the committee chairman."

"Um," Beth said.

"He won't be able to escape your feminine wiles, not in those ridiculous sandals he wears over his socks."

Beth, having been unaware until this moment that she possessed feminine wiles, and not entirely sure what they involved, could make no sensible reply. It did not matter however, for Hippolyta's attention had returned to the trees.

"The deathwhistler is near, I can feel it in my water! And my water is never wrong! Keep your eyes peeled, Elizabeth. We're looking in particular for charred leaves or swarms of insects." She turned her head to shout at the servants. "Insects, gentlemen!"

The servants looked back with expressions suggesting they would like to take her advisement and shove it somewhere with significantly less sun than the Spanish forest.

Suddenly, the trees rustled. Hippolyta and Beth paused, their faces lifted and their senses straining for a sight, sound, or magical vibration of the pileated deathwhistler. Behind them, the servants took this opportunity to lay down their burdens (literal: toolbags, bird cage, heavy boxes, picnic hamper, picnic table, and chairs; and metaphorical: weariness for the drudgery of their job). They wiped their brows and pushed up their sleeves in a manner Beth would have envied had she not been so intent upon the trees.

"There!" Hippolyta tossed aside her glass of lemonade without looking (braining a red tufted mousetwitter that happened to be pecking about in the undergrowth, thereby bringing an end to its species on the Continent and losing herself, had she but known it, several thousand pounds). Her attention focused instead on a flutter of gold amongst the leaves. "Quick, the net!"

But even before Rupert could order a servant to obtain the net from a porter and bring it to him, whereupon he could present it to Hippolyta, the deathwhistler was off. With a swoop of wings, it lifted its coin-colored, peacock-size body from a branch and began to fly away along the forest path.

"After it!" Mrs Quirm shouted.

Beth lifted the hem of her long white skirt and hastened after the deathwhistler, Hippolyta hot on her heels with a rustle of yellow taffeta. They ran along the path, parasols bobbing, dust billowing as their boots struck the dry earth. The servants watched them blankly.

"Faster!" Hippolyta urged.

But suddenly, Beth staggered to a halt. The bird glided on a short distance then descended to the path, its wings folding, its bronze crest glinting in the sunlight.

"Why do you stop?" Hippolyta demanded—and at Beth's urgent reply, staggered to a halt herself before she ran headlong into a chasm. Dropping her binoculars in surprise, she watched them plummet several hundred feet to break against jagged rocks below.

"By Jove!" she shouted.

"The deathwhistler seems aware of our predicament," Beth said dryly as the bird flicked its long-feathered tail at them.

"The chase is not over yet!" Hippolyta averred. "I am determined to protect that bird from unscrupulous hunters"—i.e., her rivals—"and see it safe in the Duke of Wimbledon's aviary. No deathly chasm shall stop me! Propellers!"

Beth tugged on a cord attached to her parasol handle. Hippolyta did the same with hers. Long metal shafts arose from atop the parasols' caps and, with a whirring buzz, began to spin. The two ladies proceeded to arise from the path.

Behind them, the servants sagged down onto boxes, hamper, and chairs. Before them, the pileated deathwhistler pecked the ground as if entirely undisturbed by the introduction of this boisterous new avian species. A glint in its small dark eyes suggested, however, that it was amused and intended to wait for the most aggravating moment possible before taking off again.

Hippolyta and Beth angled their parasols in such a manner as to traverse the deep but narrow cleft in the earth, then alighted on the other side. As they drew the parasols shut, Hippolyta held out a hand toward Beth, palm up, without removing her steely gaze from the bird.

"Net," she commanded.

"Er . . ." Beth said.

Hippolyta snapped her fingers impatiently, but to no avail. They had forgotten to bring the net with them.

"Bother!" Hippolyta said. "Well, never mind." After all, she had not become the preeminent ornithologist of the British Empire, and the slightly-less-eminent but still famous ornithologist of the Continent, without being able to bounce back from such calamities. She began divesting herself of her puff-sleeved jacket. "We shall sneak up on it and toss my jacket over its head."

"Good plan," Beth said. She was about to wish her luck for such a risky venture when the woman handed over the jacket.

"Now remember, Elizabeth! When frightened, the deathwhistler makes a dreadful, fatal noise, like—"

"*Oi! Look out below!*"

At this holler, Hippolyta and Beth did exactly the opposite of what it commanded: they looked up, into the canopy of the forest. A man came leaping down from a tree, his long brown coat soaring behind him wing-like.

Birds startled and took to the air. For one awful moment, Beth heard the first perilous notes of the deathwhistler's cry. But even as her heart began to shudder, the man snatched the bird and tucked its head beneath his arm, rendering it silent. Tawny feathers ruffled wildly, briefly, then settled into calm.

The interloper bowed as much as was possible with a sizable bird in his arms. He was slightly unshaven, and a lock of black hair fell over one dark eye roguishly. "Good afternoon, ladies," he said, grinning.

"Mr. Lockley!" Beth's shocked exclamation only just hung on by its fingertips to decorum. "What do you think you are doing?"

His grin deepened. "I think I'm stealing your bird, Miss Pickering."

"Who is this rogue?" Hippolyta demanded.

"Devon Lockley," Beth explained, frowning at the man as he shook back his hair. "He's a professor at Cambridge's ornithology department." She had been introduced to him during the annual Berkshire Birders meeting last month. He'd not made much of an impression—shabby coat, nice smile, more interested in the sausage rolls on offer than in talking to her. A typical male professor. He certainly impacted more today, jumping down before them in a style that evoked derring-do, bravado, and no cumbersome petticoats. It was provocative behavior, to say the least, and his unstarched trousers, clinging to strong thighs, only made matters worse. Beth absolutely would not blush, for she was an Englishwoman, but inside, her heart was fanning itself urgently with a handkerchief.

"Cambridge," Hippolyta said in the same manner with which one might open their steak pie and say *maggot*. "And what sort of name is Devon Lockley?" she added, never mind that her own name, Hippolyta Albertina Spiffington-Quirm, ought to have disqualified her from asking.

"The sort that unimaginative parents living in Devonshire give their child," the man said. "It's an honor to meet you, Mrs. Quirm, especially as you so kindly shepherded the pileated deathwhistler into my trap. Both myself and my associate, Herr Oberhufter, thank you."

"Oberhufter!" Hippolyta immediately withdrew a dainty silver pistol from a pocket of her dress and aimed it at him. But Devon's smile only quirked.

"I sympathize, madam, but there is no need to do that."

"There certainly is! Hand over my bird at once, you rapscallion, or I will shoot you!"

"Perhaps I misspoke," he replied calmly. "What I meant was there is *no point* in doing that. We took the liberty earlier of removing your bullets."

Hippolyta gasped and shook the gun, as if this would inform her of its contents.

"We?" Beth asked.

In response, Devon glanced over her shoulder. The ladies turned to see half their servants tied and gagged, and the other half absconding back along the path with tools and food hamper. Seated at the wrought-iron picnic table was a large gentleman in a tan suit; he lifted his derby hat to the ladies in cheerful greeting.

"Oberhufter!" Hippolyta exclaimed again. "By Jove, this is outrageous!"

"No madam," Devon said. "It is ornithology."

Devon knew he ought to have immediately hotfooted it out of there. Mrs. Quirm was the wiliest, most unscrupulous birder on the circuit, and she'd just proved the lengths to which she'd go in order to obtain possession of the deathwhistler. But he couldn't resist sparing a moment to smile at Miss Pickering. He remembered her from a recent meeting in Berkshire, where he'd been so bored he'd asked for an introduction to the pretty Oxford professor, intending to flirt a little to pass the time. She'd proved so courteously agreeable, however, that his boredom veered toward stupefaction, and he'd been forced to risk the digestive perils of the buffet just to make himself feel alive.

But dang it, she really was pretty, with eyes as blue as the Alaskan catcatching warbler, a mouth as soft as a morning kiss, and a sweet, heart-shaped face—although it was also a rather sweaty face, and currently scowling at him as if she'd like to stab him with her furled parasol. He wished she would. Pretty was nice; naughty was ever so much better.

He had a job to do, however, and Mrs. Quirm was reaching for her hatpin in a manner that suggested a mastery of naughtiness even he could not handle. So he took an abrupt step forward and snatched Miss Pickering's parasol.

She gasped. "Good heavens! There is no need to be so zealous! I'm sure we can negotiate—"

"*Negotiate?!*" Mrs. Quirm cried out with horror.

"I'm happy to negotiate," Devon said. "Here is my offer: I take the bird, and you wave goodbye nicely."

With that, he flicked open the parasol and engaged its propeller. Miss Pickering's eyes widened, and Devon feared she might cry. Poor girl, so downtrodden, so timid, she was no doubt—

Er, actually, she was beating him with Mrs. Quirm's parasol. Having grabbed it from the other lady, she spared no effort in whacking him about the legs as he began to rise from the path. Delighted, Devon grinned at her. Then, with one kick, he knocked the parasol from her hand, causing it to fling away into the chasm.

"Sorry!" he said without the slightest remorse.

"I do not accept your apology!" she called out in reply. This defiance cast a lively flush upon her face, and Devon considered some flirtatious provocation, perhaps a blown kiss, just to see if he could tip her into truly bad manners. But the mechanized parasol was already carrying him away.

Until next time, he promised silently, and his blood throbbed at the thought of it (or possibly due to the beating she'd given him).

Beth seethed in a most unladylike way as she watched Devon fly across the chasm and land easily on the far side. Beside her, Hippolyta had forsaken "ladylike" and moved directly on to hooliganism, with several muttered profanities escaping from between her clenched teeth. (Beth could not fully hear them, but nevertheless was rendered shocked indeed.)

On the other side of the chasm, Herr Oberhufter rose languidly, fanning himself with his derby hat. He performed an extravagant bow to the ladies.

"Thank you for your assistance in tracking the bird!" he called over.

"Blighter!" Hippolyta shouted, firing her gun several times at him and thus proving its chambers were indeed empty.

Herr Oberhufter did not even do her the courtesy of laughing villainously. He turned to help Devon place the pileated deathwhistler into the large iron birdcage Hippolyta had brought for this very purpose. Devon covered the cage with Hippolyta's picnic tablecloth, thereby creating a calm darkness to appease the bird before it could utter its deadly cries. Then, without further ado, the men walked away, carrying the stolen deathwhistler (which is to say, attended by one of the ladies' servants carrying the stolen deathwhistler), leaving Hippolyta and Beth in the middle of the forest, miles from civilization, several thousand pounds poorer, and almost certainly not in the running for an award at the International Ornithology Conference in July.

"I'll pluck your feathers yet, Oberhufter!" Hippolyta shouted after them.

"Too right," Beth agreed. And, as Devon Lockley turned his head to throw one last crooked smile at her, she wiped the back of her hand across her heated face in the most scandalous manner indeed.

INDIA HOLTON lives in New Zealand, where she has enjoyed the typical Kiwi lifestyle of wandering around forests, living barefoot on islands, and messing about in boats. Now she lives in a cottage near the sea, writing books about unconventional women and charming rogues, and drinking far too much tea.

Ready to find
your next great read?

Let us help.

Visit prh.com/nextread